Respectable Horror

Respectable Horror

Respectable Horror edited by K. A. Laity

First Edition

conversion by TJ Everley

ISBN: 978-1-910462-02-7

Published by:
Fox Spirit Books
www.foxspirit.co.uk
adele@foxspirit.co.uk

Contents

Introduction

K. A. Laity

I have been a horror fan since I could remember. As a child I devoured ghost stories. I grew up watching programs like *Night Gallery*, *The Twilight Zone* and *Kolchak the Night Stalker* which were staples of network television in the early 70s. The devil took over in the wake of the murders of Sharon Tate and the La Biancas, so we got films like *The Devil's Rain*, *Race with the Devil*, *The Initiation of Sarah*—mostly made-for-TV movies if I recall correctly—as well as the bigger budget efforts like *Rosemary's Baby*, *The Omen*, *The Exorcist* and of course Ken Russell's *The Devils*, which still awaits an official release for the home market in the US. Like the post-apocalyptic trend in narratives now, it seemed to speak to a chthonic fear rife in the west.

My tastes have always run the gamut. I think maybe the finest writer the US has ever produced is Shirley Jackson: it's just a bonus that many of her stories creep deeply into horror (and humor—two sides of the same coin, all about the timing). Her prose is perfection. Likewise Toni Morrison's Beloved, which brings to vivid life a ghost that the US still hasn't dealt with (as the last election demonstrates). But I glory too in the Gothic excesses of Ann Radcliffe, so lovingly spoofed in Jane Austen's *Northanger Abbey*—so much so that I wrote my own Gothic spoof novel (*The Mangrove Legacy*) just for fun as a serial during a low point in my life.

I love the baroque excesses too, from the splatterpunk glories of Poppy Z. Brite's *Lost Souls* to Clive Barker's poetic evocations of monstrous awe. No one who's dived into *The Books of Blood* can emerge unchanged: we are opened and red. From the knife thrust of 'Dread' to the shock of 'In the Hills the Cities' he took every tired trope of the genre and turned it inside out, sometimes literally. Then he went on to the Faustian tale of *Damnation Game*, to epic (galactic?)

fantasy in *Imajica* (still chock full of horror), and on to the Books of the Art because magic and its misapplication has provided horrors aplenty throughout known history.

I could go on and on: I've been a member of the Horror in Film and Literature online discussion group for more than twenty years. We've discussed everything. I mean, everything.

In recent years, technology has allowed horror films to accurately portray just about any horrible thing that can happen to a body in glorious Technicolor. That can be effective: I'm a huge fan of Dario Argento's wild gruesome artistry. He literally paints with blood at times. But overuse of anything becomes banal. All the worst clichés about horror films that you try to defend them against become real: interchangeable bland actors dispatched endlessly in bloody set pieces that make no sense as far as plot.

The film world moves faster than publishing so it's easier to see the changes happening; the move away from phantasmagoric gore toward suspense and shivers is evident. Fans have embraced spooky tales like *The Babadook*, *It Follows*, *The Witch*, and *A Girl Walks Home Alone at Night*. These films focus more on atmosphere than simply punch-in-the-face violence and gore. It's a nice change of pace. Change is good.

MR James is another writer I used to give writers a sense of the mood of this collection. I am fond of the man because I evoked his name to explain to my dissertation director why, in the midst of writing a study of medieval saints, I wrote fiction. James was also a medieval scholar, something his ghost story fans might not know. People ask me how I can separate fiction and non-fiction: why would I? They inform each other. Inspired by James I wrote a Lovecraftian tale that relied upon deciphering runes ('Wordgeryne') that used my knowledge of Anglo-Saxon poetry.

But what I really learned from him—and from so many others—is a love for the story that takes a turn from something entirely innocuous and steps into increasingly dark territory with an inevitability that suggests there is no turning back now. The imp is on your shoulder and there is nowhere to run or hide to avoid the fate it gibbers into your ear.

I have gathered writers from around the world to lead you down dark corridors into strange places that will change you forever. There is some blood here and there, but mostly you will shiver from the uncanny currents in the air and gulp for breath when the floor disappears beneath your steps. Beware, strange things lurk in the damp corners.

Take my hand…

The Estate Of Edward Moorehouse

Ian Burdon

Cousin Edward's estate would have been a lot easier to settle had he the decency to leave his corpse behind, although I don't suppose he had much choice in the matter.

Edward disappeared in the pellucid light of a warm summer's day. There was no-one else: we were both only children and our respective parents are dead. Neither of us had girlfriends, or 'partners' as it seems we must now call them. I obtained power of attorney to manage his affairs.

In the end my only option was to have him declared as presumed dead. He left no will—who would at his age? Everything came to me by the rules of intestate succession. The estate was substantial, and very welcome: I was working to complete my doctoral thesis and flat broke, spending most of my time in the stacks of the university library or in the National Archives.

I found Edward's journals when I first tidied his flat. His rooms surprised me by being full of framed family photographs. He had never seemed to be a family man, always buried in his research, but there we all were, the generations frozen and preserved behind glass. I even recognised some of them, and was pleased to see the redoubtable Great-Aunt Megan, whose regular grace at Sunday lunch—*bless us and bind us, and hide us in a hole where the Devil can't find us*—rang clear in my memory, though she's been dead for twenty years.

The journals were a series of A4 Moleskines filled with neat, somewhat old-fashioned handwriting in blue-black registrar's ink. Cuttings and photographs were pressed between the pages. I still hoped that he was alive so I didn't read them. Although we weren't particularly close, we were cordial enough with each other and I didn't want to invade his privacy. Even once he was declared dead and the journals came to me as part of his estate, I didn't hurry to open them, feeling I would be intruding somehow. I only looked at them properly a couple of months ago.

In the beginning the entries were routine: reflections on his day, notes for future purchases of books and music, and sporadic attempts at writing fiction and verse. Over time a new theme emerged and became dominant. Inspired by archaeology programmes on television, and especially re-runs of Time Team; Edward became something of an archaeology buff. His Facebook photographs at the time show he was probably the only person ever to take fashion tips from Phil Harding. He volunteered with local digs, and soon signed up for a part-time degree course at Edinburgh University. He wrote a lot about Orkney, Caithness and Sutherland. Drawn at first by the excavations at Ness of Brodgar, he became fascinated by Skara Brae and its emergence from the dunes that both hid and preserved it. He wrote:

It is remarkable how such a thing could be hidden simply by sand, to be uncovered, eventually, by a storm. Recent discoveries around our coast show quite clearly that there is more to be found. Perhaps I should have a look for myself.

Which is what he did. Shortly afterwards he bought his first metal detector and was soon making and recording finds.

His initial discoveries were small: a coin here and there, the occasional brooch, but they came steadily, and he catalogued them and notified the appropriate authorities with the pedantic rigour of the amateur enthusiast. He researched in libraries and archives as well as online, outside of his course requirements, looking for accounts by eighteenth and nineteenth century diarists, hoping for hints of local legends of buried settlements. As a student he could access all the university libraries, and it was in the lower stacks of the School of Divinity that he stumbled upon *The Householde Booke of Ane Highlande Gentleman* in an uncatalogued bequest from a deceased minister's collection.

The Householde Booke covered the period 1745 to 1770. The ink was relatively unfaded, and the hand quite legible, albeit with wayward spelling and stylistic flourishes. The text comprised household accounts, records of yields from crofts and cots, basic meteorological information and notes of family occasions.

Edward spotted an entry of 13 June 1766 recording *curious eventes* in a coastal township, where stones collected from the beach for building showed signs of mason's working and bore strange markings. The minister, Mr. Colquhoun, attended the beach to perform a blessing. The diarist accompanied the minister because the locals refused *in feare and trembling engendered by their primitive superstitiones.* The stones were put back where they were found and the book makes no further mention of the events.

The Householde Booke was part of Edward's estate too. As the university had not asked for it back, I guessed he hadn't told them that he had 'borrowed' it. I couldn't find any references to it online and I believe it was not previously known to exist. I daresay it was of considerable historical importance, so I regretted burning it, even as I dowsed it in paraffin and tossed it into the heart of a garden bonfire last night.

Edward became obsessed with identifying the township: its name was given in the book in Gaelic (I omit all identifying place names from this account). Aside from the generality of the location, no other specific features were described. No place of that name is on modern Ordnance Survey maps of the parish and district, nor is it found in Groome's Ordnance Gazetteer of Scotland of 1882, or any surviving almanac.

I need not recount the many dead ends and false trails Edward encountered. It's enough to say that three months of meticulous cross-referencing of Ordnance Survey maps, online satellite imagery, and records of derelict townships, suggested three candidate sites.

And there Edward's journals, which also went into the flames, ended. I didn't think they had made much impression on me, but over the following weeks the story crept uninvited into my mind like the riff that becomes an earworm.

My own research interests are post-Reformation Scots criminal law, and I flicked through the *Householde Booke* for any interesting snippets (additional footnotes are always welcome in a PhD thesis). I found one oddity that Edward missed, or perhaps disregarded. On 29 July 1766 the minister quit the Parish without warning, leaving everything behind. He wrote to the Presbytery complaining of harassment by local children and persistent visitations by *the Devil's minions*. He is not mentioned again, and a new minister was called some months later. Curious, I traced the Presbytery records and found a notice from 31 August 1766 of the sudden death, in Brechin, of the Reverend Mr. Colquhoun. His body was found in the chair in his study surrounded by smashed mirrors, his face *grotesquely distorted, presumed to be the result of ingesting poison at his own hand, though none was found nearby, which was the cause of much perplexitie*.

It crossed my mind that I should go up to Sutherland, and this notion soon turned into a strong conviction that I must. I can't put my finger on why. Perhaps I made some connection through reading the journals; perhaps there was a residual sense of family business to be concluded by paying final respects; or perhaps it was both of those things or neither. I fear it was another voice calling, though that might just be imagination masquerading as hindsight.

I knew where to go. Edward's journals were precise. So two (or is it three?) days ago, on Wednesday morning, seven and a half years almost to the day from when he was last seen, I set off. The drive north was uneventful except for the usual dance of death with camper vans and motorcyclists on the single tracked roads beyond Lairg, and I reached my B&B in good time.

The next morning, I made small talk over breakfast, and praised the excellent locally smoked kipper. The landlady, whom I'll call Mrs. MacKay, is an efficient, bustling woman in her late fifties. I liked her instantly, though I couldn't imagine her having a Christian name or, if she had, that I would ever feel able to use it. No mention was made of any Mr. MacKay.

The property was a typical mix of modern bungalow and original croft house, built, and extensively renovated, with European grant money. The guest areas were carefully designed, but furnished with the chintzy sensibilities of Granny's Hielan' Hame, careening along the boundary of taste. A framed sampler above my bed read *The cottage sweet, the hills of home, are mem'ries dear, where 'ere I roam.* Bookshelves were stocked with discarded Robert Ludlum and Dan Brown paperbacks, spines heavily creased and broken, and my room had the comforting smell of fresh sheets, beeswax and damp. Perhaps it was a residual Calvinist aversion to vanity that explained the absence of mirrors.

The view from my window was over machair and marginal ground, patrolled by indolent sheep and bored collies, with the sea beyond. In the field behind the house ancient tractors and other relics of farming machinery were in advanced stages of decay, littering the tufted grass and bog like the fossilised ribcages of stegosaurs. A thrush sang its heart out from the chimney pot, its fluting voice beautiful to hear except, I discovered, at four-thirty in the morning.

'Another pot of tea?'

'No, no; that was perfect, thanks. It looks like it might be a fine day too.'

'Och, well. We'll see. You can never be sure here. What brings you this far?'

'I'm here for my cousin.'

'Will that be someone I know?'

'My cousin Edward. He went missing seven years ago.'

'Oh! I'm so sorry. I remember it well; terrible it was, everybody searching, and him never found. I heard the Court declared him dead.'

'Yes, that's all done.'

'So have you anywhere in mind to go?'

'I do. He came here to do some research. He was training to be an archaeologist. He wanted to visit some beaches so I thought I'd look at them too and pay my last respects.'

'Really, an archaeologist? I never heard that; and what would he be wanting with beaches?'

'He thought there might be something buried in the sand, an old place like Skara Brae.'

'Well, my family have lived here for generations. He could have asked and saved a lot of bother. Oh! Sorry! I didn't mean to... Which beaches?'

I pointed to them on my OS Map. There was a long pause.

'It's not often anyone goes to any of them. Wasn't his car found here?' She indicated a spot at the end of a croft road.

'Yes, I'm saving that for last. I thought I'd start with this one.'

'Och, there is nothing there at all, and it's so far out of the way. There's always sheep getting stuck there – the rocks are treacherous. And it has a bad name, there are old stories about it.'

'Really? It sounds like just the place Edward would go.'

'Aye, well; don't laugh, but when I was just wee the old folks used to talk about mermaids there, deceiving sailors. No one takes it seriously, but old tales have a way of sticking and people stay away just in case, you know?'

'Well, maybe just a short stop there, then.'

'Don't say I didn't warn you.' She cleared away my dishes. 'I'll make you some sandwiches if you want and a nice flask of tea. You'll need them, you'll have to walk a while.'

I spent five minutes at the first site before moving on. There were no signs of human habitation at all, and I was conscious of the sheep watching me closely, curious about this interloper. Also, it was raining.

The second beach was about four miles from an impromptu car park, reached by a moorland track. The 'track' was barely worthy of the name and, though visible, didn't show any of the significant erosion that has damaged so many such ways in Scotland. The track wasn't marked on the OS map and I only knew where it began because Mrs. MacKay gave me directions. The rain stopped so I pulled on my walking boots, hoisted my day sack onto my back and set off.

Other paths are managed by conservation bodies, but not that one. Possibly it was the lack of management that protected it: it had not become a highway like the trail to Sandwood Bay, diminished by its own popularity. The marginal nature of the track meant the walk through untouched wilderness was lovely. Sunlight drifted through scattered clouds and dappled the rough terrain, catching on highlights of hare's tail cotton grass amongst the sphagnum moss and peat bogs. Scrubby heathers clung to peat in which ancient lateral cuts lingered, a way of life preserved in the topography. There, men and boys sliced the land with their *tairsgeirs*; there, their mothers and grandmothers carried creels laden with *fàds* to stack against the gables of long-lost black houses.

Forty minutes later I crested a ridge and the beach lay before me, shocking in its beauty. The filtered shafts of sunlight now stippled the seashell sands sandwiched between breakers and dunes. Kittiwakes and fulmars wheeled about a stac to the north, while gannets and terns dived into the grey-blue water. Common seals lounged on offshore rocks while, on an inland loch, I spotted a pair of black-throated divers. There wasn't another human being to be seen.

I left my boots and socks in the lee of rocks above the tide line. Is there anything to compare with the pleasure of walking barefoot in soft sand with the breeze in your hair and a salt spray sun on your face? If so I have never found it. To my right the dunes rose, bound with marram grass, speckled with bird's-foot-trefoil. It took fifteen minutes of contented meandering to reach the northern end of the beach, watching the tide line for any oddities swept ashore, finding only the punctured remains of crabs and weathered skeins of blue and orange rope. Black-backed gulls and skuas patrolled overhead, watching for an easy lunch.

I sat against a dune to eat my sandwiches, letting the place envelop me as the keening peeps of oystercatchers punctuated the rhythmic rushing of the waves.

The tide was on the turn when I set off back to find my boots. I stayed closer to the slip-faces of the dunes looking for hints of human activity, but, aside from heavily corroded lager tins and a discarded condom, I found only a deep wash of contentment with an undertow of yearning. The moment I left I wanted to go back.

The final beach could wait until the next day (that is to say today, or I suppose, that's now yesterday). A bright red hatchback was parked in the shade of the rowan tree by the gate of the B&B when I got back. The car belonged to Janet, a freelance journalist, fresh-faced and inquisitive in branded hillwalking gear which she wore as casual attire. She was tall and slim, with hair of a redness that left no doubt about her genetic ancestry. She already knew who I was and why I was there, as, I realised, would most of the surrounding community by now. Over a shared pot of tea she looked at me with open friendliness tinged, I thought, with a degree of pity.

'So how was it, then? Did you get any closure?'

I was never popular with the girls at school and had few friends, let alone female friends, and felt uncomfortable with the question. I wasn't sure whether her directness was refreshing or intrusive or both. And I thought the question was silly.

'I was out at ___. It was lovely, I could have stayed all day. Maybe I'll come back with a tent some time and spend the night by the dunes.'

'Did you find anything? Anything archaeological?'

'No, just the beach and the waves and the breeze through the grass. No mermaids, either.'

'Mermaids?'

'Mrs. MacKay suggested I might be spirited away by mermaids.'

'Did she? Are you sure your cousin went there?'

'It was on his list.'

'List? I don't remember the police saying anything about a list.'

I unwrapped a chocolate biscuit, wondering how to respond.

'Were you there?'

'Aye, I covered the search for the regionals – they pooled my reports. There was nothing said about archaeology or lists, I'd remember something like that.'

'Well, he had one.'

'So what was he looking for? Mrs. MacKay said something about Skara Brae.'

I fiddled with my empty cup, feeling as though I were under interrogation, though her manner was personable.

'Edward was fixated on finding another Skara Brae, buried under the sand. He came across an old story about things found on a beach somewhere up here in the seventeen hundreds and narrowed it down to three possible sites.'

'Wow, this is a new angle.'

I could see the story already dancing in her green eyes.

'Well, it was a while ago. I'm just here to say my farewell, wherever he is, and then be on my way.'

'But you must be curious too; about what happened to him I mean.'

'I was, when he first disappeared. Now I'm resigned to not knowing. And maybe it's better that way.'

'Don't you want closure?' That was the second time she'd asked that.

'Closure? No, that's for pop psychologists and journalists. He's gone, and that's an end to it.'

'So you're heading home tomorrow?'

'Not quite. I have one more beach to visit and then I'll be away on Saturday.'

'Can I come with you?'

'Well, I don't know. I don't want to be rude, but, you know, this is a personal thing.'

The evening passed in amiable silence in the lounge, though I found myself looking at her frequently. It was a fine sunset that I went outside photograph, trying to waft away midges that swarmed in the gloaming. She watched from the door. After a late snack of local goats' cheese on biscuits and a couple of drams of good malt whisky I took an early night. I was surprised by a swift kiss on the cheek from Janet as I retired, her petite breasts brushing my chest as she leant in.

I hadn't thought of her in an overtly sexual way while we were talking but the unexpected touch of a breast can do strange things to you: it's a man thing. I went to sleep thinking of her face, her full lips, the lines of her body, her oversized spectacles; and I imagined her lying close beside me, as inadvertent lovers do—not that I'd know about that.

I don't know what time I woke up, but I knew I was not alone in the darkness. For a brief moment I thought—hoped—it was Janet, but it wasn't.

The air was close and humid; I struggled to breathe and a cloying stench, sickly and bilious, made me gag. Coarse wheezing from the foot of my bed filled me with paralysing dread.

And the voice.

'Hello James. It was nice of you to come to say goodbye.' I reached for the light. 'No, don't. I'm not at my best, not since I died.'

'What?'

'You know, dead; to all intents and purposes anyway. So thank you, but now go home; you must not stay here.'

Bless us and bind us, bless us and bind us…

I rubbed my eyes and pushed my hands back through my

hair and tried to control my panic. Part of me insisted I was dreaming, while the other, the ancient part, knew this was real.

'But I haven't finished looking on the beaches.'

'Go home.'

'But...'

'Go. You won't be warned again.'

Then nothing except the lingering smell in the thick air.

Acute dread gave way to simple terror. I needed to go to the toilet but my body refused to get out of bed. Every noise in the house stirred primal fears, the duvet, damp with sweat, clung to my legs like a winding sheet, and I swear that something watched me from the dark corners, the recesses that the forty watt bulb refused to illuminate.

Bless us and bind us…

I almost packed and left there and then, but woke with a start to find the early morning sun filtering in through thin curtains, greeted by trilling bursts from that damned thrush.

I wanted to convince myself that it was just a nightmare brought on by goats' cheese and whisky, but I did not believe it even as I refused to accept the truth.

I finally gathered the courage to swing my legs over the edge of the mattress, but my bare feet stepped on a pile of damp sand at the foot of the bed. It smelled foul and louped with biting sand flies.

The smell of cooking bacon made me nauseous. The crackle and splutter of frying eggs and the squeaks and slides of cutlery on Janet's plate were a physical assault. Every shift of light and shadow in the room squirmed in my peripheral vision. In my discomfiture I was self-conscious about the frequency with which my eyes strayed to Janet's fitted T-shirt; I was paranoid she would notice and think me gauche. We had only just met, but I wanted her to think well of me, or at least not take me for a complete idiot. The memory of the brush of her breasts lingered and I was embarrassed to make such a thing out of an accidental touch. That women have breasts was a big deal when I was fourteen but I had hoped to grow out of it by now.

Perhaps Mrs. MacKay and Janet picked up on my strange mood and made a tacit compact not to enquire; in any event they bided their time before pouncing.

'Have you a plan for today then?'

I looked up from my mug of tea.

'I've decided to go home. I don't think there is much to be gained by staying.'

I thought I saw relief in Mrs. MacKay's face.

'Oh, that would be a shame. But maybe it is for the best; the forecast is a bit grim.'

Then up spoke Janet, now the tension was broken.

'What about the third beach? Where was it anyway?'

'___, where Edward's car was found.'

'Are you sure?' She looked puzzled. 'I thought it was found by ____.'

There was a clang from the kitchen as a pan dropped onto the counter. Mrs. MacKay came back through, dish cloth in hand.

'Och no, it wasn't there: who ever goes there?'

'No, I'm quite sure,' said Janet. 'I remember because I was there in the pouring rain when the police identified it, trying to write shorthand in a damp notebook.'

'It doesn't matter now; like I said, I'm going home.'

'It's a long way to come back if you change your mind.'

'I think Mr. Moorehouse has made the right decision,' said Mrs. MacKay. 'Would you like another packed lunch?'

Janet left soon afterwards. We shared a chaste shaking of hands, which I found somewhat inadequate. To be fair, she had never given the slightest sign of any emotional engagement with me beyond friendliness and a dash of professional curiosity, but I wished she had at least managed another peck on the cheek.

I couldn't think of any plausible explanation for the sand on the carpet, so I'd swept most of it into a plastic supermarket bag, which I sealed by tying the top. I'd discard it in a roadside bin later. It was already in my car along with my bag; I did not want to go into that bedroom again for any reason.

For all that, I had mixed feelings about leaving. I struggled to believe I was woken by a visit from my dead cousin and that was acting on his warning. My rational mind insisted that if Edward were dead—and I wondered what he'd meant by to all intents and purposes—then he could not have given the warning. Although I try to stay open minded, I didn't accept the idea of a supernatural visitation. Yet the alternative was that somebody crept into my room, pretended to be Edward, and left rancid sand on the carpet as an unpleasant practical joke.

I pulled round a blind corner on a single track road and had to brake hard. Janet's red hatchback was pulled over to the side, steam rising from the engine.

'Oh, hello you! You can be my saviour. I need a lift down to the next place I can get a mobile signal to call my editor and the road rescue company.'

I made a show of looking at the steaming engine in a suitably masculine manner but, as a mechanical ignoramus, saw nothing that meant anything to me. I drove her to the first place we could get a phone signal, then back to her car until the rescue company arrived from their depot twenty-five miles away. With pathetic enthusiasm, I agreed to stay until the repaired car could be picked up, some five hours hence.

'So,' she said, 'What would you like to do?'

Adolescent images flashed through my mind, instantly suppressed. Since childhood I've held a sneaking suspicion that, in the absence of an all-knowing God, other people have telepathic powers and can read my every unworthy thought.

'You tell me. What's there to do here for five hours that doesn't involve a craft centre or a Highland folk museum?'

'Now, now. They make a valuable contribution to the tourist experience.' The corners of her mouth dimpled as she smiled and brushed her hair away from her face. We both looked out over the sea loch and the mountains beyond. '___ is on the way to the garage. If you want to a look before you head south?'

'I don't know if that's such a good idea. I'd quite like to get further down the road when I can.'

'The beach is in the same direction so you wouldn't go out of your way and we can go while we're waiting for my car to be fixed. I'll go with you. No angle, I won't write about it if that's what's worrying you.'

What I was worried about was my to-all-intents-and-purposes-dead cousin who visited in the darkest time of night and left noisome, infested wet sand on the floor, but I wasn't about to tell her that.

'Can we walk somewhere else?'

'No problem: I know just the place,' she said. 'Go down this way and I'll tell you when to stop.'

She chatted away as I drove, inconsequentialities and local gossip, telling stories. As she talked she touched my arm often: friendly, familiar, sexy. Then, pointing:

'That's where your cousin's car was found, by the way.'

It wasn't a place I recognised. I reached across her to the glove compartment, where my OS map was stashed, uncomfortably aware of how close to her body that brought me. I could feel her warmth; smell her scent behind her perfume.

It was a quiet place, remote and far, far from the chocolate-box beauty of much of the west coast. The austerity of this landscape always attracts me, its assertive boldness; but this place went beyond austerity to an astringent brutalism that both fascinated and repelled. We walked up a low rising slope and from the top were rewarded with an outstanding view down the coast, to the distant massifs of Stac Pollaidh and Suilven and an impression, through a haze, of An-Teallach far beyond. Clouds whipped overhead in the onshore breeze and shadowed squalls flicked over the bay. A fine white-gold beach divided sea from land with an easy path down. Janet moved to my side and slipped her arm through mine, leaning against me. Her body felt alert, expectant.

'Shall we?'

And, so help me, I did, holding her hand as we made our way step by step over the machair and through the dunes. As I write this, those lines attributed to Rochester clog-dance through my thoughts, mocking my naivety, for Janet was indeed a frail and slender string, baited and barbed, though I am no king, except of fools.

Thursday's beach was carved from Torridonian sandstone, but this was bounded by outcrops of Lewisian gneiss, pitted and worn in the abrasive spray of countless winter breakers. Faults in the outcrops had split and eroded, leaving a tumbled confusion of ochre and black rocks and sudden dark tunnels. On the inland side, tall dunes stood, three times my height, woven together by coarse grasses. Janet looked off into the distance with unfocused eyes, absorbed in her heritage.

'This is where the stories of mermaids come from. Mermaids and selkies; old stories, the ones grandmothers tell little children in the dark of winter.'

'What do the stories say?'

'They say love is not possession and it is folly to deny your true nature. They warn that trying to capture the transient, the unconstrained, rarely has a happy ending. They are full of strangeness and the unknown.'

'Did your grandmother tell you them?'

'She did; she told them with the same conviction as when she spread village gossip or made us memorise our family tree or her own grandmother's recipes. And there were the other stories.'

'What were they?'

'Things passed down the family through generations, and songs and ballads in the Gaelic, sometimes in English. Stories of the old times, the stories behind the ballads; the deep truths. I've read a lot of books about the ballads and stories but none of them have the depth of Granny's kitchen tales and songs.'

'Why don't you write them down?'

'Because some things are not meant for writing down, James Moorehouse, some things have to be known in other ways. Older ways, if you will.'

The sun came out from behind a cloud as Janet shook out the long red hair that fluttered around her face in the breeze, a breeze to stir up dust devils in the fine sand. She looked very beautiful.

'You reminded me of something just then.'

'Oh? And what would I be reminding you of?'

'Of a feeling I had yesterday: contentment and yearning with a tug of melancholy.'

'That's Sutherland for you.'

We walked further until the sand gave way to stones and rocks. The air was chillier in the shadows and the stiller air held onto the smell of decaying wracks. Janet still held my hand and drew me a little closer. I looked at her face, level with mine, and we kissed. It was simple and natural and eternal and right, and I wanted more.

I broke away and excused myself. My timing was appalling, but I had an urgent need to pee away the two mugs of tea from breakfast before anything else could happen.

'Back in a moment.' I walked to an outcrop and found a gap in the rocks to slip behind. I reconsidered the wisdom of heading back to Edinburgh when there was a sudden, unexpected benefit to staying. That was when I noticed the bag stuffed in the depths of a crack in the stone, just above my head and out of the normal eye line. It was one of those bags that you get to take liquids through security at an airport. It held three things: a stone with inscribed markings, an SD card from a digital camera, and a slip of paper bearing Edward's name and address. I knew his handwriting straight away.

'Aren't you done yet?'

I slipped the bag into my pocket, zipped up my flies and walked back out. She was about twenty metres away in the sun, stripped down to all but her panties and looking at me with eyes that held no coyness or pretence. I knew that I wanted her then and forever. She ran towards the sea, limbs in free motion, hair streaming behind her. My imagination turned to urgent desire.

'See you in there.'

I sat on a rock with my back to the dunes to take off my shoes and socks. Around me, other stones were scattered around the foot of the dune with the same markings as that in the bag, reminiscent of Ogham but with other shapes and sigils suggestive of the enigmatic motifs of the Picts.

A movement at the edge of my sight made me look into the gneissian shadows where darkness seemed to twist in on itself in confusing ways. The paralysing dread came on me again, and I sat, enthralled. The darkness formed itself into Edward, moving towards me out of his own blackness.

'You were warned.'

Bless us and bind us…

Behind me the sand trickled down the face of the dune, slow rivulets at first, building until it was like a burn in spring spate; things struggled to clamber out from beneath. My throat caught the foul stench that slunk out with them.

I stood, somehow, but could not walk as sand whipped

around my ankles, silicate fingers clutching at my trouser hems, seeking purchase to drag me under. There was no birdsong; I realised there hadn't been any since we descended to the beach. There was only the slither and slide of the shifting sand.

Squally clouds blackened the sky as the threatened bad weather came in and the temperature seemed to drop ten degrees in moments. I had an abrupt fear for Janet, whom I could see through the gloom, waving and beckoning from the surf, her body taut in the cold water. But her voice was lost in the wind and the deepening darkness. Beyond her, grey-black heads, perhaps seals, perhaps not, bobbed and ducked in the swell.

And then voices called from below me, as bones emerged: tibulae and fibulae with trailing scraps of ligament. And mandibles, separated from their skulls, biting on nothing as one hand claps, disarticulate, searching for a wholeness to consume. They were children's voices: children singing in different meters and keys, in a language long forgotten—if ever known.

I shook my feet free and ran for damp sand which was firmer. For better or worse I didn't think of Janet, only of myself, running, running, running, lungs burning as the voices clustered behind me in atonal pursuit. The entire face of the dunes writhed, like lovers in a bad porn movie, limbs intertwining and slipping, penetrating and enfolding, lubricious and sensuous, stinking like an open sewer or a week-old plague pit.

Bless us and bind us, bless us and bind us, and hide us in a hole where the Devil can't find us.

I saw the sheep on the hillside, now just scraps of wool draped on skeletal forms, eyes dark with an ancient malice, lips pulled back from tombstone teeth, turning their heads in unison to watch my flight. All the while the sparse topsoil of the hillside drew back like diseased gums from incisors, exposing the corruption beneath.

Bless us and bind us, bless us and bind us...

I seized on the car as my sanctuary though I knew it wasn't safe. The engine would not start (of course it wouldn't!) I had the sense to stop trying for a moment, my dad's voice in my head telling me not to flood the engine. I finally got it running on the sixth attempt. I looked round to see Janet flowing over the hill like a sea fog over a dawn mist. Her red hair surrounded her like the corona of an eclipse. She still wore only her panties, wet and transparent from the sea. I knew a single moment of dizzying eroticism and reached through the open window to touch her fingers. But her flesh fell away from them even as her other hand grasped my wrist and held tight. Her hair hung limp from her skull like the frayed remains of nylon cordage discarded at the tide line.

'Do you want me James? Do you want me hot against you, to feel me pulling you in? We can be together James, for ever, just as you wanted, now and forever.'

The remains of her beautiful face barely covered the skull that glared at me from vacant orbits, the mouth which would kiss me empty save for the twisted and petrified remains of her tongue.

'Now and forever, James.'

With my free hand I rammed the car into gear and lurched away, wrenching skeletal fingers and palm free from her wrist, They crept crab-like up my arm towards my throat. I tried to dislodge them, screaming as the bony digits slipped in the blood they drew from my neck, while I batted and batted at them, trying to control the car at the same time.

I only managed to knock the hand into the footwell, where it groped and grasped under the accelerator pedal. A stretch of open road opened up ahead and I put my foot down hard. I didn't dare touch the still twitching bones so I pulled over and flicked the remains out of the door with the end of a walking pole. In my mirror, I saw the bones scuttling across the road and into a drainage ditch as I drove straight for Edinburgh.

I stopped on the way south, once I was well beyond Aviemore, for a mug of tea and to gather myself. I took the sealed bag of foetid sand out of the back of the car. I gave a shout of disgust when sharp teeth nipped and tore at the thin plastic as the contents shifted and squirmed against my hands. I threw the bag into a stream and piled rocks on top. Further south, I stopped once more and hurled the inscribed stone into the Pass of Killicrankie.

The Householde Book, Edward's journals and my marked up OS map went into a bonfire in the back garden when I got home, despite the hour. Only when I was certain they were ash did I allow myself to relax.

I made a coffee and went through to the bedroom where I fell, exhausted, onto the bed. I remembered Edward's SD card so I switched on my laptop and inserted it. I expected to find a series of scenic views from his last days, but the several hundred photographs on it were pornographic and explicit. As I scrolled through, I realised they formed a continuous sequence. I ran them together as a time-lapse series and played it. The model shook out her red hair, just as she'd done in the sunlight on the beach only a few hours before, and beckoned me towards her, her full lips mouthing *now and forever*. As she leant into the screen, her breasts pressed against the thin plastic membrane, the surface distorted and split as her erect nipples punctured the surface.

I slammed the lid shut, but it would not stay closed, slowly prising itself open as Janet tried to crawl through. I stuffed the laptop into my briefcase and locked it, but she was already emerging through the full-length mirror in the hall, the glass pushing out in sensual bas-relief. I smashed it with the heel of a shoe but the movement continued from all of the splinters. There was a tinkling crash from the bathroom. *Now and forever, James*, whispered myriad voices.

There was a rank smell where a moment before there had been none. I felt a touch on my foot. I looked down to see my uneaten packed lunch ooze from its Tupperware container, coalescing into a rugby-ball sized slug, with a slashed mouth below quivering eye stalks. Razor teeth snapped, gouging my shoe leather. I kicked out at it and watched it splash against the wood-chip wallpaper, then form itself again as it slid down the wall.

Bless us and bind us, bless us and bind us…

I fled to the hotel where I write this, my pen scratching on cheap hotel paper. Despite my tiredness I cannot sleep. I am alert to every sound in the corridor, every drip in the cistern, every click and groan of the air-conditioning, every creak of the floorboards in the corridor. I cannot look into any of the mirrors.

I'm leaving for the airport soon, if I can make it through the school-run traffic. I can hear children singing in the street now, though the sun has not yet risen.

The Feet On The Roof

Anjana Basu

Mrs Sinha Roy walked on the softest cushions of feet imaginable. The toes were well formed, the big and first toes of an even height, with the others slanting away, each in perfect proportion to the other. The arch under the foot was as high as a ballet dancer's or, as she preferred to say, as a Maharani's, even though many Maharanis were known to have carried their dignity on the flattest of flat feet. The high arch ended in two cushioned pads of flesh on either side, equally perfectly proportioned. People stopped to admire her footprints in the dust on the stone flags of a thakurdalan, or among a mash of marigold petals and milk left over from the puja. As if the goddess Lakshmi had stepped out of her lotus flower and condescended to bless those mundane steps. No wonder, people said, that she had been so blessed in her life. The possessor of footprints like those was bound to lead a fortunate existence.

Fortune - it had overflowed like the pan of milk that had been set on the fire as she stepped over the threshold in a flare of red and gold brocade . Good fortune had overflowed from the three storeyed roof into the green curve of the garden that held the house in its embrace. Good fortune had covered Mrs Roy's plump white and black bordered person, giving her a creamy gloss well into her widowhood. She had three creamy white daughters and an equally creamy son. The son looked far too like the daughters to be considered perfectly masculine, but when he grew older, a small moustache and crinkled waves of hair put him into the mould of the god Kartik and gave him distinction. Yes, Mrs Roy was fortunate. She inhabited three acres of prime property in the heart of Calcutta and sat idly at her exquisite ivory inlaid desk while the city's promoters vied with themselves in promising her crores of rupees . Everyone agreed that she would need many crores to compensate for the discomfort of moving out of her twenty room house into a flat.

There had been a Mr Roy once, who had inherited the aforementioned three acres from his forefathers and who had husbanded them wisely. But Mr Roy had been removed from his wife's sphere long before he became inconvenient. Widowhood gave her a distinction which she had lacked in her creamy white youth. The promoters who, she sighed, bayed on the fringes of her life like hounds, were reduced to awed whispers in her presence. The Mataji was not to be disturbed with all this talk of filthy lucre. She was the goddess Lakshmi in person. If they could, they would have backed out of her presence like Queen Victoria's courtiers. Of course, the whispers did not inhibit their offers. They walked into the green embrace of the house and breathed green cash - so much for the Mataji just to sign a paper, so much to sweeten the mouths of her children a little. They oozed chocolate and ghee on auspicious occasions and Mataji was too elevated a person to refuse the offers. Mrs Roy never mentioned their constant presence in her life at the little gatherings where she and her contemporary widows came together and arranged the lives of everyone around them. At those gatherings the fate of many a socialite was decided and sealed, alliances were made and family loyalties broken. They were a group of women as soft and as cushioned as Mrs Roy herself and they all understood the power of filthy lucre. 'How many today,' Mrs Chatterjee would ask, while arranging her tatting - she was crocheting a blouse for her youngest granddaughter, a lace straitjacket of ruthless lines, 'Such a sweet little thing, so hopelessly modern!'

'Three,' Mrs Roy would sigh, picking up her nimboo pani as if the weight of all the world were on her shoulders.

'Ayan should really help you a little.'

'Yes, but he's so tied up with his studies. These intellectual boys ! Now, my eldest daughter on the other hand - He spent so much on her education. Remember, Belait, all that problem we had…'

'Ah, yes, your eldest…' There was a universal sigh like

a ripple that disturbed the placid surface of the circle for a second. 'Your eldest.' Noyonika, of course, was fast on her way to becoming a byword in society. It was only the power of the circle that kept her aberrations from becoming more widely known. After all, she was the daughter of one of them, no matter what her shortcomings were. If her mother was creamy white widowhood, placid unruffled milk, Noyonika was jagged green lightning, or at any rate a curdling influence in that hygienic dairy atmosphere.

She had returned braless from London long before it was the fashion, jiggling and wobbling through Customs under an inadequate broiderie anglais blouse. The whole of Dum Dum airport had turned to watch her wheel her luggage out. Her father, alive then, had not known whether to rejoice at his daughter's return or groan at the spectacle she was so obviously making of herself. 'When we get home,' said her mother crisply, cutting through the dilemma. There was nothing legal about Noyonika's silhouette. When she bent to pick up the bag, her blouse gave an extra bounce and the servant wheeling the trolley started involuntarily and cannoned into the trolley in front of him and there was a suitcase crash right outside the International Arrivals Lounge. As an arrival, it was cataclysmic to say the least. It could have been worse, the suitcase could have crashed into a car, the car could have rolled into an old lady and the whole thing could have spun out of control like the House that Jack Built. Of course, it didn't, but as far as her parents were concerned, it was already as bad as it could be. Whatever the Roys did, they didn't do it in public.

Noyonika had been sent so that she could dignify the family's glorious legal past with an equally distinguished present. To date, she had shown no signs of doing that. She plummeted into the conversation about the promoters like a lead weight headed full fathom five. Fat cats, she called them, snapping her fingers in their faces and shattering the atmosphere of incense smoke and reverence that her mother had so carefully created. The old ladies knew all about that. Now if only Ayan would be less studious and a little more worldly wise, they sighed, but then, after all, a son was a son and Ayan was a precious gift after three daughters. 'How much was it today,' Mrs Sinha enquired, orchestrating her maid's movements with the tea.

'Five crores shown and seven unshown.' There was a moment's pause followed by the tinkle of a cup put precisely down into a saucer. 'Of course I told him that was impossible.' There was a little chorus of tinkles, as if of applause.

Shown, unshown, by now those words were familiar to the sandesh circle. All the plump, cushioned ladies were well aware of the distinctions. Shown money went into the bank to be counted by the tax man and the government. Unshown, on the other hand, went in its crisp stapled wads to tin boxes, there to pay for the purchase of new diamonds or gold, for trips to children in America and London, or for parties that demanded more than sandesh and singaras. Unshown was bliss for its sheer practicality. Quite a few of them had conveyed their sprawling houses into two or three adjoining pocket handkerchief flats. 'And they're laughing all the way to the bank,' Noyonika declared because, per force, she handled some of their conveyancing.

It was the way she said things that grated on Mrs Roy more than the way she dressed. The clothes could be handled - she had dragged Noyonika home from the airport and stuffed her into the tightest Maidenform bras she could find - but speech could not be muffled. 'Can't you speak English the way we've always spoken it?' she would demand. 'Or Bengali for that matter? Did I send you all the way to England to forget everything you ever learnt?' Noyonika's sisters were docile, convent bred girls who might dream of swinging down Soho but who never let a hint of their dreams stray into reality. They wore their sister's cast off T-shirts demurely and lisped in Bengali. Mrs Roy had found suitable husbands for them. But Noyonika? She had insisted on finding her own husband! A boy who didn't believe in wedding presents or in dowry! Now, while the latter might have been to the Roys advantage, the former certainly wasn't.

Arun spoke Noyonika's brand of jagged green lightning and wafted around in what seemed to be a perennial haze of incense. He had to be spoken to three times before he would lift his head out of the crow's nest tangle of his beard and answer. 'My *rabindric* son in law,' was the way Mrs Roy referred to him. 'Rabindric' was being kind. The only thing Arun had in common with Rabindranath Tagore was the hooked nose and the beard.

He belonged to a crumbling red brick house in some mofussil that the Roys refused to recognise. When pressed Mrs Roy would admit that Arun's family was decent and his features worth notice, but that was as far as she would commit herself. Coincidentally, a month after the wedding, Mr Roy suffered his fatal heart attack It was all that was needed for Mrs Roy to cast her son in law into Outer Mongolia or the Black Hole of Calcutta society or whichever place she considered blighting enough. That the fact of the widowhood was responsible for her triumphant transformation was tactfully ignored by everyone privileged to hear her confidences.

As everyone predicted, Noyonika found life in the mofussils intolerable and ran back home after a year. Court was the excuse. Noyonika was distinctly frayed at the edges, but she trailed her husband behind her like a slightly bedraggled victory standard, silencing any other comments that Mrs Sinha Roy's friends might possibly have raised. It was widely whispered, that Arun was a drug addict and that titillating fact made up for any disappointment that Noyonika's failure to divorce might have caused.

The house had, according to Mr Roy's whim, been divided vertically, a floor for each child, according to age. Noyonika had the floor just below the roof, Ayan the floor below that and Noyona and Nayantara the last two floors which they shared with their mother. The ground floor, with its public rooms, was Mrs Roy's territory. She had her office there, just off the verandah that curved with the green lawn. Most of the time, the family was to be found sprawled in the ground floor rooms and there was much laughing talk of a lift, especially among Noyonika's friends.

Noyonika's floor, like Noyonika, was a kaleidoscope, a chaos, a mishmash of Op, Pop and mahogany. Mr Roy's maids wandered among the confusion like lost souls, startling at the mannequin supported glass topped tables. '*Emni ghor aamra kothao dekhey ni*,' they would declare with bewildered pride. 'We've never seen a room like this before.' Noyonika had had a collapsible iron gate added to her part of the stairs so that no one could wander up when she was out. A shiny Navtal padlock dangled prominently on its hasp. 'It was the wisest thing my husband ever did, secluding her up there,' Mrs Roy declared, wincing whenever the hard beat of rock shook her meetings with the promoters. Ayan and the others were Beatles fans at their most extreme.

Noyonika was against the sale of the house. She had made her stand clear from the beginning. 'I'm not giving any money to those fat cats. And I'm perfectly comfortable with the house as it is.' She paraded her attitude in front of them, even while she went into the nitty gritties of conveyances and agreements. 'I can't help feeling that my daughter is just a tiny bit unprofessional,' Mrs Roy confessed to her circle. 'Oh, not that she's a bad lawyer - Lily, I must say she handled your probate rather well. Just, well… you know.' The circle did know. It was all part and parcel of her braless return. 'Such a nice child she used to be, so sweet, so friendly.' The inference was that the grown up Noyonika was far from nice. They tinkled and bustled around her wondering how such a deviation was possible in their sedate ranks.

Perhaps it was the precision of her cushioned white mother that irritated Noyonika, she who was so imprecise in her movements. No one would have compared the print of Noyonika's feet to that of a goddess - she had large flat feet, Bata size 8's that refused to be crammed into dainty slippers or elegant stilettos. Her pedestrian chappals would sit uncomfortably next to her mother's Cinderella ones in the rows outside a wedding reception room. As Noyonika scrabbled into her slippers, her mother would seem to look down and sniff. Perhaps Mrs Sinha Roy never did look down. Perhaps Noyonika imagined it, but the imagined sniff was part of the wall that mother and daughter had built between themselves. Did the wall start on that braless day at the airport? Neither of them was really sure. The small toddling Noyonika had never been aware of it, but then, the toddler had taken her placid acceptance for granted. As people, they would never have been friends, would never even have cared to know each other. Arun would observe, dreamily through the clouds of his reefer, 'Whoever said women grew into their mothers couldn't have known you.'

The two women, mother and daughter were ranged on either side of a wall with the other family members as hostages, but no one talked of or even acknowledged the state of war. Hostages were frequently exchanged and peace treaties contemplated under the guise of family dinner conversation. Ayan, the only man apart from Arun, frequently shrugged out of it. 'You and Ma sort it out.' But, with a hasty brown flicker at his mother, 'I'm sure Ma's right. She usually is.'

'How can she be right? She's got no legal background at all.' The fights were normally legal ones - the presence of the complacent promoters with their shiny blue packets of pann masala. Mrs Sinha Roy would sigh heavily, 'You must have got the acumen from somewhere. Now your father always said...' and she would retire into graceful reminiscence. Mrs Sinha Roy always retired gracefully from any field of battle - it was her strongest weapon. Where the enemy looked for confrontation, she would give way, only to resume hostilities from the rear at the most unexpected of moments. 'I don't like the promoters any more than you do, shona, but I don't see the point of antagonizing them.' One of them had just presented her that morning with a moth's wing sweep of crinkled tussore, discreetly black and brown bordered. 'You must admit, for a person like that, the man has exquisite taste.'

'Bribery,' Noyonika mumbled, though not too loudly.

Mrs Sinha Roy raised a finely plucked eyebrows, 'But I didn't promise him anything. He said it was from his mother to the only other woman he called 'mother'. How could I possibly refuse?' Certainly no woman with her heart in the right place could refute the sentiments.

'You had better give up, Nika,' Arun sniggered. 'You'll never get the better of Ma.' He was at the table, quite obviously a little high.

'I thought this was a family matter,' Mrs Sinha Roy observed, with an exquisite emphasis on the word 'family' and a pointed arch of the eyebrow at her son in law. Arun, flying higher than a kite, and impervious to the delicacy of the rebuke, guffawed long and loud, while a dreadful hush fell on everyone else present. The incident should never have occurred at all. It showed how deplorably Noyonika's standards had fallen. 'I mean, to accuse her own mother of accepting bribes!' The ladies' circle cooed in sympathy and Mrs Sinha Roy's daughters had run backwards and forwards with balm all that morning to soothe away her tension headache.

Noyonika had tiptoed on the fringes of her mother's migraine with an anger heightened by guilt. She had never meant to say 'bribery' and she was aware that Arun should never have been at the table after a sustained hour of joints. She consoled herself by flinging herself into his drawers and throwing out all his joints so that he flung out of the house with a bulging Shan bag dangling from his shoulder. Her mother rose slightly rumpled from her migraine to be informed by the servants that Borda had taken a taxi to Howrah Station.

The ladies' circle was perfectly in sympathy with all this. The Sinha Roy house was in some senses a microcosm of their own. If they didn't have recalcitrant sons in law, they definitely had feuding daughters in law who instructed their maids not to remove the rest of the family washing from the clothesline if it rained. 'And you can't get pettier than that.' However, something must have shifted in the balance of the relationship between Mrs Sinha Roy and her daughter - at least everyone said later that something must have shifted, how could one put up with being accused of bribery by one's own daughter! For a while it replaced the shown-unshown discussions among the starched napkins. But what was even more distressing was the fact that Arun and his Shan bag showed no signs of returning.

That state of affairs persisted for over a month until it was no longer possible for Mrs Sinha Roy to hide it from her circle. 'I didn't tell you before,' she said, 'because I thought it would blow over... Kintu Arun to aar pherot aashey ni.' He was not back and Noyonika was defiantly silent on the subject or, what was worse, maintained she had done it because he had upset Mrs Sinha Roy. 'What can you say to these girls? To have a son in law who takes drugs is bad enough...'

'*O kee heroin khai*, or cocaine...'

Mrs Sinha Roy shrugged. 'I don't know what he takes. My poor husband had the strongest objections...'

'It's surprising that it didn't happen before. I mean considering that Nika is your daughter...'

'Yes, but to happen like this...'

Noyonika flung in and out of her apartment. No one knew

when she came or went except for the gatekeeper and even he couldn't be sure in the afternoons because he was sleeping off his spiked tobacco. She was not to be found when the promoters demanded her presence and her behaviour held up the proposed sale of the house even further. 'The rest of us are all agreed on the sale. Now if Noyonika would just draw up the agreement.' Tinkles of cups and a soft scrunching of lemon tarts. 'Two flats each, my dears. It would even take care of the Arun problem.'

'Which promoter was this, Sabita?'

'Oh, Motiram Bhai, the one who gave me the sari. I must confess he has exquisite taste. It quite reassures me about the flat detailing. He's bound to look into things like bathrooms.'

'And your son in law?'

'She refuses to talk about him.'

The ladies ran their soft hands up and down Mrs Sinha Roy's white sleeve. 'It must be hard for you. It must be so hard...' She was like a child under the touch of their fingers, soft, yielding and plaintive. 'Why she had to marry that man. Thanks to him she won't let us sell the house...' All at once she stiffened under their fingers. 'Why, look at the time! Thank you so much for your sympathy. I don't know what I would do without friends like you.' That moment of soft confidence was never to happen again, but the ladies realised that they had been privileged - Sabita was normally so brave, she struggled on despite the odds, Ayan was too young to be a help and as for Noyonika, well, we all have our crosses to bear. Yes, they told each other, we have been good friends to her.

The atmosphere in the house soon became so tense that a hair would break if dropped. The tension centered around Noyonika. She snapped at the maids when they came to dust her rooms, she forgot to leave the key behind when she went out and she squabbled with her brother and sisters if they even said hello to her. Soon they said, she would be reduced to fighting with shadows. The comfortable cushioned world that Mrs Sinha Roy had created began to acquire a jagged edge - as if a spring had worked its way through the foam to attack the unwary. Everyone in the house was aware of the sharpness, but no one knew what to do about it. If it had been a real cushion, an upholsterer could have been called in, but this had nothing to do with Dunlopillo.

Despite the tension, sleep still wrapped the house in its cotton folds, every afternoon swathing it from the topmost floor to the gatehouse at the outer edge of the lawn. Visitors were actively discouraged between one and five and those unfortunate TV repair men and couriers who strayed into the gate found themselves confronted by an unflinching sweep of teak door that was impervious to all their persistent ringings. It was not that Mrs Sinha Roy's house boasted a discreet bell that clucked like a koel. Instead, it had a brass monstrosity handed down from the Raj that bonged up and down the marble walls and staircase. However, the stentorian brass was less insistent than the summons of sleep. Outsiders could not understand the weight that the siesta hour laid on grand zamindari houses: it was like the spell of the Sleeping Beauty. Noyonika herself claimed not to understand it after her return from London but Mrs Sinha Roy indulgently told the world that her Nika was to be found sleeping like a baby at three thirty, despite all her claims to liberation. Later, the other girls maintained that afternoon sleep was a strangler with soft hands, a kind murderer, but people always said that that was imaginative hindsight.

That afternoon, Mrs Sinha Roy rose with a slight headache and rang indignantly for her tea. The maid was clumsy with the tray and one of the old bone china cups splintered on the dark red stone of the floor. 'I should have seen it as an omen,' Mrs Sinha Roy declared impressively to her ladies, her reflection distorting on the side of the fat silver teapot. It was only the pot that was disturbed because the tranquil pool of Mrs Sinha Roy's outward life never seemed to be so. She sent the maid for a mop and newspaper and while the wiping was in progress, the girls appeared in their dressing gowns yawning and rubbing their eyes.

They sat and compared sleep notes: the youngest had been reading by shutter light again, her sister complained, the stripes of sunlight hurt her eyes. Ayan knocked and walked in, saying he had slept like a log for four hours and the servant hadn't woken him even when an important phone call came. It was the whining of a normal family afternoon before their muscles tautened into evening. Noyonika wasn't there, but Nika had never been part of it ever since her return from London.

It was only when the mellow sunlight had bled away into darkness that the maid came to complain that she couldn't get upstairs to sweep the baro didi's room. No one was opening the padlock. 'It will soon be late and I won't have finished. *Aami rattirey joley haath ditey chai na.* I don't want to wipe the floors after dark.' She was prone to coughs and colds and had a doctor's certificate excusing her from contact with water at night, even on the hottest of summer nights.

'She must have gone out,' was the general opinion. Mrs Sinha Roy told the maid to do the rest of her work and go home. No one was alarmed or even moved to call the gatekeeper up to ask him if Noyonika had indeed gone out. In any case his testimony to anyone's whereabouts in the afternoon was suspect.

Night proceeded without Noyonika - her place setting was removed from the dining table and carried away in a gleam of ominous ceremony. Mrs Sinha Roy sat at the head of the table rubbing her aching temples and grumbling about the inconsiderateness of people who vanished without letting the rest of the house know where they were going. It was an angry grumbling evening like a hundred others before it, remarkable more for Mrs Sinha Roy's headache than Noyonika's non-appearance.

The next morning, the brass padlock was still on the gate and the maid whining again about her work. 'So let it get dirty,' Mrs Sinha Roy said. 'If she goes off without telling us, that's all she can expect. *Aamar meyeh jey emni*… my other daughters aren't like this.' Ayan claimed that he suggested phoning Arun, but everyone was full of claims afterwards and no one knew who to believe. Mrs Sinha Roy had a meeting with her promoter and had no time to spare on her son in law. 'Half the time Arun doesn't know where he is. I'm certain he won't know where Nika is. I have a bad feeling about this meeting. With my mood the way it is…' But she was all smiles when she walked in and all smiles when she walked out. 'As soon as Nika comes back we'll draw out the agreement. Motiram Bhai is ready to sign. I knew that sari meant he was softening.'

'I thought Nika was against selling the house?' one of her friends pointed out.

Mrs Sinha Roy shrugged. 'She'll do what's good for her. I can't see her sitting on the top floor of this building without the money to maintain it. Sometimes I think I should have been the lawyer instead of her.' Everyone at that tea agreed, though not one of them knew about Noyonika's disappearance from the house. 'Why should I say anything to anyone? My daughter has humiliated me quite enough.' Mrs Sinha Roy told the police, and no one could dispute that with her.

No one was sure when the first footprint materialised. Three days after Noyonika walked out in the afternoon? Or as much as a week? It appeared on the wall of Ayan's room and was found by the maid brandishing her jhuljharu at incipient cobwebs. The stain looked like paan smears and she sent angrily for the bearer and accused him of spitting paan juice on the babu's wall. The squabble brought Ayan erupting out of his bath demanding to know what the matter was. 'It certainly looks like paan, ' he agreed, staring dubiously at the wall, but he didn't believe that the bearer was responsible. He also thought that it looked like the splotch of a bare foot. Not that it alarmed him- he mentioned the matter idly at lunch, only to have his mother laugh at him and tell him to concentrate on his studies.

The second footprint appeared the next morning, in the dust outside the thakurdalan, defined this time in an ominous shade of rusty brown that looked more like blood than paan. This time Mrs Sinha Roy found it. She saw it as she was about to step onto the first of the treads leading up to her puja room and she stood there frozen for a moment in mid air before recovering her equilibrium again. The servants and the priest gathered at the steps, all thoughts of puja forgotten. Mrs Sinha Roy was as white as a leper and there was no way that the blotch in the dust could be transformed into a shubh symbol. And because it was the second time it had happened in the house, the word spread like wildfire.

Soon there was a muttering, murmuring crowd outside the gates straining to look inside. Half of them were convinced it was a miracle. The other half were in favour of a murder. Shortly afterwards, the police arrived, alerted more by the murder than by the miracle. Mrs Sinha Roy had been borne by her faithful retainers to the verandah and had collapsed there in her reclining chair. Ayan was raising a teaspoon of brandy to her lips when the Inspector walked in.

He asked if anyone was missing and, when told about Noyonika, wanted to know if anyone had spoken to her since her disappearance. Mrs Sinha Roy feebly complained about undutiful daughters and their inconsiderateness. The policeman agreed politely but suggested a call to Arun was imperative. 'Just to allay this suspicion of a murder, you understand. And is there another key to the upstairs quarters?'

So, after all, Mrs Sinha Roy was forced to make the call. Arun was not at home, but his servant said that boudi had not been seen at the house. There was a duplicate key, oiled and wrapped in cloth. Mrs Sinha Roy produced it from a bundle in her Godrej. 'I don't know if this will fit,' she said. It did and it seemed stupid to say that no, she had not wanted to set foot in Noyonika's apartments because she and her daughter had not seen eye to eye. 'The police won't sympathise with that, Sabita,' the sandesh circle reminded her with equanimity.

Noyonika's rooms were coated with week old dust. Mrs Sinha Roy ran her finger disdainfully over the glass of the kneeling girl table and was about to say something by way of condescending apology to the Inspector - he was a Communist, after all - when a reflection in the glass top choked her words off. She looked up and the warm ivory of her cheeks drained to chalk white. The others looked up with her. The footprints were splashed across the ceiling of Noyonika's drawing room as if they had bled through the whitewash.

'What was I to say to that man? A policeman in my house? And those on my ceiling!' Mrs Sinha Roy said in her shame she instinctively bent down and found one of Noyonika's slippers under the table. 'Nika toh leaves her slippers all over the place. You can imagine the state - one week of dust, little cockroaches breeding!' The Inspector claimed he found it. Whoever found the slipper, there was little doubt once the proof was in their hands that the footprints were Noyonika's. No one wanted to speculate on how they got wherever they were: her presence was blowing like a cold wind through everyone's bones. She was there on the stairs, she was stamped indelibly on the foundations of the house.

'The house should be searched,' the Inspector said.

The gatekeeper maintained that no one had passed him on that fateful afternoon. 'I sleep stretched out across the threshold. Even a shadow would wake me.'

'She has to be in the house,' Ayan muttered reluctantly, not looking at his mother. 'Those footprints...'

Soon the house echoed with slamming doors. The noise rolled down the marble staircase and out to the gatekeeper's lodge where the crowd still waited debating the miracle or murder. 'There must be a body under one of those marble statues.' '*Hanh, zamindari baritey* these things happen all the time. I remember once in Barisha...' and the speaker launched into a long complicated tale of adultery and ground glass in a sandesh. 'We are so vulnerable,' Mrs Sinha Roy told her friends. 'Thanks to what the state has become, a bhadrolok has no standing anymore.' Not that anyone noticed because most people were overawed by her stately presence. The Police Inspector was not a Communist, but he didn't come from the landed classes that Mrs Sinha Roy recognized. '*Kee bari*, ' he told his colleagues at the thana. 'It was exactly like a museum. And then those footprints. I thought *ekkhuni dracula tacula bariyeh aashbey*.' But he held his stand. The house had to be searched from top to bottom, from the cabin trunks to the Godrej almirahs.

They found what they were looking for on the roof. A black sludge with a fur of flies. The roof buzzed and whined and the wings caught the light sprouting like so much fungus. Crows dotted the TV aerial and added their own wing flapping accusation. 'It's a wonder no one noticed the crows,' The Inspector said, 'but then, there is a rubbish dump in the vicinity.' Fresh garbage was dumped every morning and every day the crows and the flies assembled in their wing flapping hordes. It had been one of Mrs Sinha Roy's greatest afflictions - 'the neighbourhood is getting so bad. I don't know where all these people come from.' The garbage of three restaurants added their richness to Mrs Sinha Roy's normally perfumed atmosphere when the wind blew fresh from the east in the morning. At the end of the black sludge was a pair of feet.

She had to identify the feet - the maids turned up the whites of their eyes and Ayan was obviously in no shape. Large flat size eight feet that embarrassed her at biyeh baris. 'Could any daughter of mine have such indelicate feet? Once you could tell a bhadromahila by her high arches.' Arched cushioned feet rouged softly pink with alta. Milk and roses feet treading goddess prints - Noyonika's feet had embarrassed her since the day she was born. Ayan was sick in the tomato plants that the mali insisted on secreting in their feathery profusion all along the terrace.

Murder? Suicide? Everyone recollected that they had felt a strange atmosphere about the house when, in reality, no one had felt anything at all. 'It was obvious to me that the mother had done it,' the Inspector wrote in his diary at the thana. 'She was as cool as milk, as cool as a wet cat.' She was also well connected - half the politicians and judges in Calcutta ran along her bloodlines. She didn't even have to make a court appearance - and everyone could vouch that she had awoken with a headache that fatal afternoon - if the death had occurred that fatal afternoon. The sludge was so old and so evil that Forensics could make nothing of it beyond identifying the feet. Mrs Sinha Roy wrapped herself in the sanctity of her white tussore and seemed as unruffled as ever. She gave sympathetic audience in her cane chair with attendant maids bearing trays of cold drinks. No one noticed that the maids changed far more frequently than they used to and that the new ones were so uncertain with the trays that they occasionally dropped them. But then, the ladies were far too shaken in their loyalty to make such distinctions - in fact, for three months they had quite ignored Mrs Sinha Roy.

The footprints? Motiram Bhai came to hold his 'mother's' hand and enquire delicately as to the truth of the footprints. 'Paan stains,' she tinkled and showed him one on the wall. He left not as convinced as anyone would like, with a five crore cash deposit hanging in the balance. 'Two flats each,' he had said, 'five crores unshown and may the Income Tax Department bury themselves in their mounds of paper chasing it. I promise you clean money, Mataji, for your pleasure.' And they had multiplied it into diamonds, trips to New York and all the other things their kind of people didn't normally do. All except Noyonika. 'I won't be bribed by a dinner at Taj Bengal,' she had sniffed.

Mrs Sinha Roy did not believe in ghosts. 'I believe that we are punished for our sins here.' To the end of her days - and there were many of them - she would repeat that statement. She even ordered down an expert from the Horticultural Gardens who inspected the stains and diagnosed them as a rare form of fungus. As an explanation, it sounded more scientific than paan stains.

But the house was never sold. It hung about their ears with a taint of something evil about it - whether ghosts or garbage was left to the imagination of the person concerned - the maids insisted the footprints on Noyonika's walls bled through six coats of the most expensive lacquer wall finish. Mrs Sinha Roy padlocked the flat permanently, but the promoters did not return. 'Garbage,' she averred, when the wind was blowing high and ripe from the east. 'Nothing but garbage - people have delicate noses these days.' And she stretched her white arched feet out in front of her on the marble tiled floor and took comfort from the green embrace of the lawn.

Spooky Girl

Maura McHugh

The first moment of video: Lindsay pushes open the hulking front door of Heath House, strands of purple and black hair seeping from the knitted cap on her head. The massive door scrapes open reluctantly so she pivots to shove her shoulder into its weight. She turns her face to glance at the camera, her forehead creased in frustration.

'Jesus Jas, put down the phone and lend a hand.'

Bright laughter and a shake of perspective to indicate no.

'Tania, will you help the weakling?'

Tania, taller, slighter, in a leather biker jacket and ripped skinny black jeans, steps into the shot, and touches the door. It slips open and Lindsay stumbles into the shadowed interior. A heavy, ornate staircase is suggested in the gloom beyond the rectangle of light impressed on the slate floor.

'You weren't kidding about this place, Tania,' whispers disembodied Jas. 'It's Gothic central.'

Tania, her body in light and her face in shadow, turns to the camera. 'It's revival, but you wanted a Hammer film vibe...'

From the darkness, Lindsay's tetchy voice. 'Where's the shagging light switch?'

The image judders as Jas steps forward. The camera scales badly to adjust from the daylight to the shuttered dusk inside.

'It's perfect,' she says quietly, her tone conveying awe and respect. The picture resolves into a dirty image of a large atrium, with the indistinct form of Lindsay patting down the wall under a huge framed landscape, and Tania standing at the bottom of the staircase, looking up.

'Pause it Iris!' Matthew Wolsey barked at me, and stabbed his thick finger into my laptop screen. I wanted to slap his paw off my precious machine, but it's not considered polite to hit a client.

I checked out where he pointed. A grainy blur suggested a third figure standing at the top of the first flight of stairs. Perhaps a woman in a long skirt, or a person standing still with legs tight together. A gleam indicated polished, pointed shoes.

'And your expert couldn't clean this up further? That could be a suit of armour, or a piece of furniture covered in cloth.'

I glanced up at Wolsey, who was leaning over my desk. His intense grey eyes under heavy brows glared at me. 'You'll see when you get there. That landing is clear. It must be a person.'

I leaned back in my chair, the tableau frozen on my screen. I'd read the police report, and all the newspaper stories over the past three years.

The girls had vanished. All that remained was this one piece of footage that had been uploaded to Jasmine Healy's cloud service a few minutes after it was taken.

They had hiked to the house from the nearby village of Lanslei that March afternoon, but not a scrap of evidence had remained of their visit: no clothes, no phones, no back-packs. A few scattered prints and footprints in dust. No signs of struggle, nothing to indicate that they had stayed there beyond a short tour around the house.

Wolsey was an obsessed cousin of Jasmine's. They were a year apart, and close. They'd gone to the same uni, and talked regularly. She didn't have much family other than him: her parents were separated and differently broken.

Lindsay came from a large, uncommunicative clan. They had hunched together, clamped-mouthed in grief, and waited for the police to solve the problem.

Tania was more elusive. She'd never been a registered student, even though the girls had lived together in a small flat near the university. Her name wasn't on the bills - they had all been in Lindsay's name, the designated responsible girl, from what I could tell.

I only discovered what was probably her name, Titania Molyneux, through my obsessive digital diligence: combing through texts, forums, and web sites that Jas and Lindsay frequented. I'd discovered they were all users of an occult forum called Dark Pathz, and with a little bit of cracking I'd gained access to Tania's profile, and from that to her email account. Surprisingly sparse. It had the hallmarks of an account opened solely to link to that forum.

After the initial rush of stories about the disappearances the mystery lost oxygen after a terrorist attack a few days later suffocated the news agencies with pictures of actual dead bodies. Only the occasional local rag ran the obligatory 'What happened?' piece on them afterwards.

Three women vanished, and the world seemed indifferent.

Except Wolsey.

And me, I guess. They were a funny little band of girls, the kind that coalesce in their late teens when true personalities emerge once the weight of adolescent expectation eases. I examined their pictures frequently - Jas had the most selfies - imagining them going about their daily lives, and figuring out their dreams and goals; Lindsay had the most drive. Perhaps if they had been given another five years they would have drifted apart as jobs and partners pulled them into different directions.

But on that March afternoon they were united in a mission. And something had intervened.

'Tell me again what Jas said the day before they left.'

Wolsey let out a long exasperated sigh. It's a familiar sound to me, made by someone who has said something so many times that it has become rote information he resents retelling.

'She said she was taking off with Tania and Lindsay to some grand old pile to take pictures. Jas was studying production design, and had landed a gig with an amateur production of *Dracula*. Her and the other girls liked that whole *emo*, *goth* business.' He shook his head, but I spotted the fond remembrance that lightened his usual sombre puss.

'Jas was in it for the *style*, she wasn't into that black magic shite really. She did it to stir people. Lindsay seemed serious about it, but that was her thing you know, if you do something then all in. And Tania...'

He paused. 'She was quiet. Like stillness gathered around her. People tended to lean in to hear her speak. She had this way of making you... take stock.'

'Of what?'

He shrugged, and the perpetual annoyance settled on him

again. 'What do I know? It's been a long time. I forget what they were like, what Jas was like.'

He paced away to the lone window in my cramped office to watch the rain slide down the filthy pane. 'Is this what happens? You just forget those who die? Act like they never lived?' His tone was belligerent.

I placed my palms down on the table and slid them across the smooth polished walnut surface; my father's desk. Where he had read and written books.

'We continue after they have stopped,' I said. 'They're no longer part of our every day. It's a natural process of letting go so we can continue.'

He turned, his fists clenched. 'Well *fuck that*! Jas was like my sister. And I'm going to find out what happened to her.'

His anger sputtered at my raised eyebrow. 'Well, with your help Ms Khouri.'

I picked up an invoice from my printer tray. 'First, my expenses so far. And once we've settled up we can discuss the trip to Heath House.'

He smiled. It looked unnatural on him.

***

After he left I stood up from my desk, grabbed my battered white plastic kettle, and stuck it under the tap over the tiny sink in the corner of the room. The only space that wasn't bookshelves or a window.

I brewed jasmine oolong tea in my black dragon Yixing clay teapot. As always I rubbed the tips of my fingers over his arching tail that formed the handle. For luck, as my mother always said. The routine, the light floral fragrance, and the hot tea settled me. Wolsey tended to disrupt my space, like several of my clients.

I had to cast an oracle of some kind before this trip to Heath House. I'd read its history, and knew the girls had picked it for more than its vibe. They had planned to do a ritual there. Something the police dismissed as youthful delusion, and thankfully the press never had time to exploit. If the story had broken during a more humdrum period that might not have remained the case.

I stood in the centre of my office and closed my eyes, noticing the presence of my charms, and my more active artefacts. Inhaling, I centred myself and exhaled doubt and distraction. At once I knew to use my oldest tool: Aunt Frieda's tarot deck.

I opened the ancient biscuit tin decorated in skull stickers where I kept it, and unwrapped the silk scarf in which it lay.

I sat back at my desk and closed my eyes, feeling the rasp of the cards against my hands as I shuffled them, the bumps and small tears in the fading paper. Clearly, I gave my intention: what to expect from my journey.

Five cards slipped out easily, and I opened my eyes to a dangerous vista.

In the centre, the seven of swords, flanked on either side by the nine of swords, and the Queen of Swords. And alongside them The Moon and the High Priestess.

'Damn,' I whispered, taking in the gleaming weapons at the heart of the spread.

I better suit up, I thought.

***

We set off early in Wolsey's car, a sporty blue Honda Civic, with gleaming surfaces and shiny instruments. He handled the car with the distracted finesse of a pro once we broke free from the congested roads around York and hit the clearer roads that swept over rolling hills stabbed with skeletal trees. The previous day's deluge had tempered the clouds into a dull, flat grey. It wasn't even ten and it could have been five o'clock in that perpetual twilight.

I'd taken precautions. A defensive amulet I'd created based off an ancient Talmudic design hung around my neck on a plaited white, red, and black cord. Sheathed on my belt, and covered by my denim jacket, was a small athame I'd fashioned years ago from the broken tip of an Anglo-Saxon sword Dad had kept in his office. My jacket bristled with a hodgepodge of plastic badges and decorative pins from favourite TV shows and films, which made me seem like a nerdy shut-in;

always a good way to be under-estimated. They were blessed and bespelled in a variety of ways. Anything weird and wishing me harm would feel like it was grabbing slivers of glass if it made a go for me.

Plus stretchy jeans, and good old Doc Martens: 9 holes and cherry red. It made me nimble and able to get a good kick in if the trouble was more corporeal. Of course, I did have a 5 Yen coin embedded in each sole... just for luck. I'd also tucked away a couple of crystals and a bag of salt about my person, and had some extra supplies in my lightweight backpack.

I'd started the day with a lavender bath and scrubbed myself with Dead Sea salt - a great way to clean off the psychic muck, and keep your skin in good condition.

I felt strong, but not cocky. I'd seen enough weird situations go wonky as a result of big egos obscuring the potential danger of mischief by incorporeal rascals. And Heath House had a reputation.

It wasn't one of those loud and in-your-face thug mansions. Nope, it was the sly, persuasive kind that stole your soul while fooling you into thinking it was really on your side.

So, no splashy multiple murders and debauched parties. Unfortunate accidents was more its speed. The rotten branch that snaps as the toddler is on the swing, the pond that's deceptively cold and deep, which attracts the late night drunk or the bragging teen. The badly wired socket. A leaking gas stove. The crippling fall down the stairs because of that loose step.

Occasionally, the bald-faced move: a single death. Like Silas, the grand-nephew of Horatio Heath, who built the house. Silas committed suicide in 1916 while on leave from The Great War. He hanged himself from the banister of the first floor landing, using barbed wire. He was discovered when the family returned from chapel on Sunday morning. His neck was almost severed.

His sister, Eloise, was committed to an asylum a year later, and never returned to the house. A fact that might have given her some respite in her final years.

The house allowed some people to thrive under its roof,

while like a huge, mean, territorial cat it singled out the sensitive and the troubled for its laconic, malicious mauling.

I knew to enter this house would be the equivalent of a priest kicking down the door of a brothel. The best I would get was the silent treatment, and the worst could be a violent attack. There was little I could do to affect such a systemic malaise. I could perhaps force a few secrets loose, or nail close its doors in a metaphorical sense.

I guessed that Lindsay and Jas were long gone. Tania, maybe not. She had led the others there. Perhaps sensing its nature and misidentifying it as a cool locale for spell casting, or she was bringing along snacks for her tame, monstrous building.

All I knew for sure was that the other trails were cold, except this dark path. I snorted sardonically at my ironic observation.

'You're not one for chit chat,' Wolsey commented. He kept his attention on the road, his hands gripping the wheel firmly. 'I like that. For a girl with a spooky occupation you seem pretty *real*.'

'You'd be surprised how many people knock on my door positive they've got a poltergeist and are pretty peeved when I discover it's a case of subsidence or a bored dog.'

He nodded, and I could sense the gears turning in his mind. 'So how many cases turn out to be... unusual?'

'More often than not there's nothing strange going on, and it's family troubles manifesting. I know a few good therapists to recommend. Although I've had at least one business card thrown in my face with the accusation I was a psychic dullard.'

He flashed a grin. 'They called you a *dullard*.'

'Maybe they didn't use that word...'

'So, what about the genuine cases?'

'Yeah, they're often messy and not my idea of a fun time. But you know, someone's got to clean up the spills on the dance floor.' I shifted in my seat. He wanted juicy details of an exorcism or a spectacular astral battle so he could feel better about being forced to turn up at my door, and ammunition if he wanted to dismiss me later.

'I saw a ghost once,' he said, matter-of-factly.

Now he had my attention. I watched his expression, and gave him a small psychic prod. His eyes squinted and he glanced about as if a fly had just bumped his forehead.

'Did it scare you?'

'It was my gran, and I was five. She sat on my bed, and I smelled the soap she always used. She smiled and I felt *safe*. I found out later she'd died that night in the nursing home.'

I looked away to stare out the window of the car and the occasional thump of the wipers brushing away the scattershot rain. 'That's a nice memory,' I said.

He bobbed his head.

'Did you ever tell Jasmine?'

'No. That wasn't *our* grandmother... *thank Christ*. She was a cow. I never told anyone that story. Jas was imaginative. And once she got into all that hippie crap I knew it would be chum in the water. She *claimed* she saw some things, but it sounded like bollocks to me.'

We crested a hill and a sign proclaimed that Lanslei was five miles away.

'I rang old man Heath and said we were popping by. As far as I know he hasn't let anyone but me into the house since the girls... went away.'

'Not that you know,' I said.

He threw me a quizzical look. 'What, you think he's holding out?'

'I think if that house hasn't been fed in three years it's starving.'

***

'Psychic defence is like driving a car,' my mum, the agnostic Jew who had been dealing with weird shit all her life, taught me. 'Repeat the basics until they're muscle memory, and keep refining your techniques. Once day you'll be driving a Jaguar doing handbrake turns while talking to Ganesha in the front seat and fending off a ghoul in the back.'

I looked up from reading the prophecies of Mother Shipton, and gave my mum a dead-eyed stare. I was sixteen and a know-it-all.

'Now you're being stupid. Who'd want to drive a Jag? Give me a Dodge Viper any day.'

She dipped her head to return my glare over the tops of her red plastic glasses.

'Style, class, and grace my dear, they never go out of fashion.'

'Tell that to the ghoul that's messing up the leather seats in the back!'

She laughed, and returned to reupholstering an Art Deco chair she'd picked up cheap in a flea market. My mother did not like waste, and loved the lived history of old objects. Some of them became the best wards in our house.

I frowned suddenly. 'And what's that ghoul doing outside of a cemetery anyway?'

'I don't know, why don't you tell me? You're the one with the ghoul problem...'

And so we would go, back and forth, in our cluttered living room/library/workshop until Dad called us for dinner.

***

Arthur Heath looked as I imagined: a white-haired old man in a cardigan, tweed trousers, and brogues. He lived in a two-up two-down on the edge of the village, with a well-tended front garden.

He ushered us into his compact front room, which was decorated in a minimalist style, with a big flatscreen TV on one wall. He shuffled into the room with a tray bearing a cafetiere of coffee and a teapot, along with cups on saucers, a bowl of brown sugar lumps, and an astonishingly ugly china milk jug in the shape of a cow.

As he poured me a cup of tea I pointed at the creamer. 'That's a striking object,' I said.

'Oh Bessie!' He laughed. 'She's quite hideous to anyone with taste, but when I was a child I loved her. I refused to eat porridge unless she was used to deliver milk on top. She's the only thing from the old house that I wanted.'

I tipped Bessie over to pour the milk into my tea, and though she displayed a rather annoyed countenance there were no harmful energies attached to her.

'When's the last time you were in Heath House?' I asked.

Arthur settled himself into his black leather easy chair, with a cup of coffee in his frail hand.

'Gracious, let me think. I prefer not to go into the dreadful place of course. Three months ago.' He nodded to himself. 'Yes, when they were filming for that television show. The one that celebrates the old class system with queasy nostalgic romanticism.' He made a disgusted noise.

Mum's parents were Hungarian refugees, and Dad was from Lebanon originally. They considered themselves resolutely British, but their calling as historians did not allow them to gloss over the more unhelpful vestiges of Empire.

I darted Wolsey a quick look to see what he made of this wrinkle, but he was focused on Mr Heath.

'I thought that would be right up your street Arthur old boy,' Wolsey said. He stuck his little finger up and winked at him.

'Don't mind his teasing Miss Khouri,' Arthur replied calmly. 'He knows I've been a socialist all my life, much to my parents' horror. I wasn't supposed to inherit. But, the duty has fallen to me now.' The lines of his face set in a stoic acceptance. 'The money from the production company has been a Godsend. It's allowed me some comforts, and to keep up the basic maintenance of the house.'

I took a sip of tea to consider the implications of this information. 'How long have they been using Heath House as a location?'

'For two years. Last year it was only exteriors, but this year they filmed in several of the rooms - they had to bring in the National Trust to oversee their work, but it all passed muster.'

Wolsey placed his cup and saucer on the coffee table. 'There's an opportunity there Arthur. Plenty of people love to ramble around old houses, especially if they've been on the telly. You could organise excursions, parties. Breathe some life into the old place.'

Arthur said nothing for a moment but gave Wolsey and me a penetrating look. I got a gleam off the old man. He was a sharp one.

'Thank you for the suggestion, Matthew, and a member

of the production staff has already come to me with such a proposal. I declined.'

I glanced between the two men. Clearly they had struck up a friendship over the years, and there was some unstated understanding hanging between them.

I always prefer the direct approach. 'Is this because you feel that something untoward might happen if Heath House became active again?'

Arthur met my gaze. 'To be the custodian of such a legacy and remain as I am has been difficult Miss Khouri. It has been the result of distinct boundaries and a careful, guarded exposure to the house. I'm vigilant about who I allow onto its grounds.'

He glanced over at Wolsey, who was contemplating the floor. 'I truly regret that Jasmine, Lindsay, and Tania crossed its threshold. Tania had asked me for permission by letter, but I had refused. Unfortunately, for some reason I cannot understand, the house was unlocked the day they arrived. I have wracked my memory repeatedly, but I'm an old man. I cannot confidently state I remembered to lock it up prior to their visit.'

I noticed a tremble in his hand, and without any special intuition I knew this burden lay heavily upon him.

'Tania was somehow familiar with the house. I got the impression she had been inside before. Do you know any of the Molyneux family?'

He started. 'Why that's not a name I've heard in some time. Yes, my cousin who owned the house before me had a partner, Lilly Molyneux. They had not been married, so when he died she had no claim on the place.' Arthur's face darkened. 'I'd told Bertie to do the right thing, but the man was an idiot. And because of his obstinacy Lilly had to leave, cap in hand, and I was crippled by the family burden.'

'There were no children?'

'No. I never saw Lilly again after the funeral.'

Wolsey stood up and put his hand on Arthur's shoulder. 'We better jog on. I want to be in and out before dark.'

Arthur nodded. He rose slowly and patted Wolsey's arm. 'I'll get the keys.'

***

I waited in the car doing swift research on my Smartphone.

Wolsey opened the door and settled into the driver's seat, a large ring of keys jangling.

'What did you find?'

I looked up from my screen. 'Lilly Molyneux had two children later in life, a girl and a boy with a Simon Foster. The girl's middle name was Titania. Her first name was the rather more nondescript Mary.'

'So any news on Mary Foster?'

'I'm searching right now. There are millions of them.'

He turned on the engine of the car. 'Let's get to the house while you're Googling.'

***

I seethed with frustration at the slowness of my search with an erratic signal while Wolsey wrestled with the heavy chain and lock on the iron gates at the entrance to the estate.

He drove us into the driveway, and got out to lock the gates behind us again.

I imagined what information I could dig up with half an hour at my laptop and a fast broadband connection.

'*Lófasz!*' I muttered as I slammed the door shut on the car.

Wolsey looked puzzled. 'Come again?'

'My mum never cursed in English, but had some choice Hungarian phrases she used when I was a kid. My grandparents nearly had a fit when they heard me use them.'

My distraction meant I hadn't paid attention to the house as we had driven up the long yew tree-lined driveway.

Now, standing before its bulk, I stepped back to take it in. Grey stone covered in swathes of green ivy, with battlements along the top of the walls, a round tower visible on one side, and a rectangular clock tower spiking from the middle. Dragon gargoyles jutted out at the corners. The Heath coat of arms and motto were carved above the enormous double doors.

'*Espere mieux.*' I said. Noticing Wolsey's puzzled expression

I pointed up. ' "Hope for better", the family motto.'

He grimaced. 'Glum bastards. But, they must have impressed the neighbours.'

I nodded because the unnatural chill seeping from the house captured my attention. It was aware of my arrival and it was giving me the first rebuff. I checked my phone again - only one bar and no data available.

Wolsey noticed and said, 'I can never get a signal up here.'

Sighing, I put it away.

While Wolsey attended to the lock on the door I grounded and guarded in moments. It was reflex now, like hitting the start button.

The house did not have a single point of malice, but functioned more like a hive-mind: linking numerous active spots in the building to each other, all of which fed off the residual imprints of the pains and hurts experienced in the space over the centuries. It was composed of many tortured personality fragments working together.

Snapshots of people's face appeared in my mind. I did not engage with the emotions attached to them, but allowed the images to scroll past like a carousel.

I realised the door was open and Wolsey was staring at me. His shoulders were tight, and his expression was of resolute determination. Clearly he had some sensitivity, which was why he'd searched for someone like me to investigate this problem after so many other dead ends.

'Imagine you are wearing a suit of armour,' I said to him, locking his gaze to mine, and adding a bit of *oomph* to my direction. It was a simple image, but one that worked well for most people. I noticed his stance shift slightly as if he was slightly encumbered.

'And remember. There's no guarantee I can discover anything from this trip that will give you peace.'

Peace, I thought, *must be blissful.*

I crossed the threshold and felt a pulse of glee. I was on its territory now, and subject to its rules. I inhaled a steadying breath: I was going to teach this outdated bully what happened when you tangled with a spiritual specialist.

Wolsey released the deadbolt on the other door and heaved it open so more of the grey afternoon light penetrated the large atrium.

I scanned the room, remembering the film, and the young, happy women who had entered here.

'Let's not pussy-foot about,' I said out loud, moving further in. 'I'm here to find out what happened to these girls, and then I'm out.'

I clearly projected the faces of Lindsay, Jasmine, and Tania, like handing out snapshots of victims to witnesses of a crime scene. 'If I have to start dismantling some of your vortices to get answers I will.'

Then I broadcast my credentials. A mental burst like a resume so it knew I could carry out my intentions.

The first wave of hatred came fast. A body blow expected to stun, and no doubt to be followed by an uppercut to knock me down.

I stood my ground and it passed over my shields. I glanced behind at Wolsey's pale face. He was just inside the doorway.

'Stay there. You are not to follow me. If you feel ill then walk outside.'

A curt nod in response. No doubt his macho notions were being short-circuited by that older part of his brain which was sounding klaxons. It was unlikely the house had ever shown him the full force of its ability.

I started towards the staircase. My stomach roiled at the emotional miasma I moved through. The suicide and its discovery was an old scream stuck on repeat. I dialled down the input as much as I could but I couldn't block it all out.

I called upon an ally for help, and at once the ghostly image of a magpie sailed in wide circles above my head.

Dive, I instructed.

It shot like a bullet to the first floor landing piercing through a figure coalescing as if it was a badly pixelated image.

I heard a muffled *mumph*, like a denotation, and the cackle of Magpie's laughter as it swept back up to perch on the cloth-covered chandelier.

The house recoiled in shock. The atmosphere in the atrium immediately lessened, and it seemed as if more light streamed in through the doorway.

'The girls,' I said throwing their images at it again. 'What happened?'

There was a sense of regrouping and conferring. This place was not used to direct challenges or outright attack. The cost of energy was substantial, even though its metaphysical batteries were well charged from its contact with humans over the past two years.

It was now aware it could be harmed.

I sensed the approach of an envoy - it looked like a scullery maid, dressed all in white, but with scarlet eyes in her pallid face, and her hands coated in red gore up to her wrists.

Her mouth never moved while she spoke to me, but she restlessly wiped her hands up her forearms, spreading streaks of red.

'They were an offering, so we did not decline, *Albi*.'

I refused to rise to the bait of my father's affectionate name for me, but I deadened any sympathy.

'Did all three die here?'

It smiled, displaying pink teeth, and a pulse of triumph escaped it.

'We supped upon them well.'

I frowned, there was a deceit hidden in truth.

'There must be remains.'

'Our agents disposed of them.'

Magpie screamed a warning, and I dodged to one side. Wolsey thundered past me, but snapped out an arm and snagged my backpack.

I staggered but slipped it off immediately - this was a move I had practised many times.

Around me the house gathered for a full assault while it tugged Wolsey's puppet strings.

I scooped dust from the floor and dashed it into his face. He yelled and dug at this eyes.

The maid extended her fingers, now hooked with wicked talons, and rushed at me.

I drew my athame and lunged. My hand sank into her chest and it was like plunging it into icy water.

A shock wave exploded in my face and I was knocked back. Magpie screeched and I sensed it diving at Wolsey, as he stumbled drunkenly at me.

My head pounded with a sudden, vindictive headache.

But I gripped the shaft of the athame tight to ground myself again, and transferred it into my left hand.

Wolsey seemed to be fighting off the effects of the house's influence, but I couldn't have him getting in the way again. I bent my legs slightly to brace myself, swerved out of his clumsy grab, and punched him hard in the solar plexus.

I heard a gratifying *whoosh* as the air left his lungs, and he toppled to the floor. The pain should have been enough to break the connection, but I wasn't going to bet on that. I slipped the pouch of salt out of my jacket and inscribed a quick circle around the man. Then I buzzed through a shorthand of a banishing ritual I use for stopgap situations.

Magpie flew above my head adding its force as I intoned the words of cleansing.

At the final phrase the atrium fell silent, and all sense of presence withdrew.

Wolsey moaned. I backed away a few arms lengths toward the door in case he came up swinging.

'Stay in the circle,' I snapped at him.

My knife was back in my right hand, held up. Threatening, sure, but I don't take chances.

He got up on one knee, his hand over his stomach, wheezing.

'Did you hurt those girls?' I asked, watching him carefully on all levels. Magpie circled above his head.

He raised his head and devastation was written all over his crumpled features. 'Jas was the only one who ever stood up for me when were kids. I would never have hurt her on purpose.'

'But you know something.'

He looked past me, lowered his face, shameful. 'Tania.'

I spun around, and there she was: older, better dressed, her hair cut professionally. Radiating power and assurance.

'Let me guess, Mary Foster, you now work in television?' I sent Magpie to circle above her and also sent out a careful probe to take stock of her abilities.

The dead wall I encountered indicated a person with considerable skills. I offered up a prayer to my Guardian spirits. It had been some time since I'd had to battle an adept in person.

She smiled with the smug satisfaction of a queen. 'Tell your little birdie to fly away or I will fry its feathers.'

Magpie drifted back but chattered curses at the woman.

Tania's gaze flickered to Wolsey. 'Get up Matt and beat her to a pulp.'

I scooted to one side so I could keep both them in my view as much as possible.

Wolsey stood up straight, his hands protective of his stomach, and shook his head. 'No.'

She narrowed her eyes slightly and I sensed a whip of influence cracking between the two of them. She must have him under thrall in some fashion, but the circle in which he stood also protected him from her.

'Don't move Wolsey,' I said. 'She can't sway you while you're in that circle.'

Tania's pretty crown slipped and I spotted the malevolent, greedy, darkness at her core.

'You!' she spat, 'Think you can take *me*?'

Half a dozen bolts of pure energy zipped at me. I went down on one knee, placed my knuckles on the ground, and bolstered my defences. They hammered at my shields but did not penetrate. I knew it was a test. After this, she would have a better sense of my capabilities.

But of course, that worked both ways.

'My turn,' I said, as I slipped my black tourmaline crystal out of my pocket. As I stood up I used the momentum to whip the stone at her head along with a piercing spell.

There was a satisfying *crack* as the stone smacked off the side of her forehead. I was already running at her as she staggered and I tackled her to the ground. I quickly rolled her into a hold, with her neck in my elbow. Carefully, I watched her eyes flutter as she fell unconscious.

Once I was sure she was out cold I dashed to my backpack and got out the plastic ties I kept there. As I cinched up her wrists behind her back I glanced over at Wolsey. He looked relieved, and anxious.

'What hold does she have over you?'

'She had some charm. I can't resist any of her orders for very long.'

I quickly searched her, removing all objects - she was wearing an extremely potent necklace of lapis lazuli beads with a jewelled scarab pendent, and a cantripped ornate silver ring.

'Let me guess,' I said as I continued frisking her, 'you slept with her when you first met. And you've been doing her bidding since.'

He nodded.

'Hate to tell you bud, but semen is very effective if you want to bespell someone.' Deep in her coat pocket I found it: a glass vial with a stopper sealed in wax. Inside I saw hair, nail clippings, and a few herbs. The thing radiated cruelty and lust.

'Yuck,' I said, and fished a blessed white linen cloth out of my backpack. I rolled the item up in it, and stamped on it with my Docs.

As it shattered Tania woke up. Good job she didn't have lasers for eyes or I'd have been a smoking ruin.

'What was the plan, Tania, bringing me here for your house to get a supercharged morsel? So confident your hold over Wolsey was impregnable?'

She sat up, her wrists behind her back, and glared at Wolsey.

'If you set me free now I will forgive you. Otherwise I will tell the police that you killed your cousin and Lindsay, and have been threatening me so I would remain silent ever since.'

I laughed. 'How about I tell them that you have been working to get control of the legacy that your mother felt she was cheated out of all those years ago? They'll also wonder why you inveigled your way into the girls' lives under a false name.'

I looked at Wolsey. 'You'll have to come clean for your part in this. You owe Jasmine and Lindsay that.'

Tania pushed herself up on her feet, and her face was twisted into a furious visage.

'Even if I'm in jail I can curse you both. I will twist all who love you against you. Instead of comfort you will only ever know hatred.'

I walked over to Wolsey, who seem both looser and smaller, and kicked the circle of salt so it scattered wildly.

The house had been watching, I could sense it coiled up and waiting to strike at the weakest.

I indicated to the door. 'Close up one of the doors.'

He hesitated, and looked between Tania and me. I locked my gaze with his. 'If you want to be free, then do as I say.'

He moved quickly to the doorway and slowly pushed closed one of the big doors. The shadows increased in the room.

I backed out of the remaining open door, and crossed the threshold to the other side.

Tania tottered toward us. 'You can't leave me in here.'

I thought of Jas and Lindsay, and hardened my heart.

'You wanted to be Lady of the Manor,' I said. 'Enjoy your time together.'

She attempted to rush out but we swung the door closed on her frightened face. Wolsey locked it on the faint thumps as Tania threw her body against the door.

I could feel the house seeking her out.

'What now?' asked Wolsey.

'You're going to the local police station to explain, and in a few hours they will come back here to collect Tania. What's left of her.'

As we left I could hear her imperious commands through the thick doors.

I fancied they turned to screams before we departed the grounds.

The Recovery

H. V. Chao

In the Gers, there are towns so small they could fit into the palm of your hand. Sauveterre, in which I had taken a room that summer, had a charm both wayward and homely: Time with its rasp has rounded every surface. The shops — there is one of each kind in a row, as in a picture book — post no opening hours. At night, cats scatter trash from the empty square to the old gate with its single lantern. In the market hall, the gutted ducks lie Sunday-ready, necks drooping from the trestles.

My room was in a pension with weathered green ogival doors. The dulled brass doorknocker took the form of a lady's hand — lace cuff and wedding ring — as if proffered for a kiss.

I was the only guest until the last week of August. The proprietress claimed her new guest was a producer of films: late one night, several days before, the old woman continued, he had fetched up in his expensive shoes, ruined by the rain — like the leaf, monsieur, that receding floods bequeath to one's doorstep. She straightened from serving me tea and glanced over her shoulder. The back door was open, the hallway dark, the house still shuttered against the morning.

Town houses keep secrets from those who walk the streets and never enter their parlours. The pension's meagre façade belied the extent of its back garden, which sprawled between swaybacked walls down to the overgrown bank of a fast-running stream. There stood a disused mill, part of a former priory annexed during the Revolution.

I derived a certain pleasure from my breakfasts at the white cast-iron table, next to the trellis with its cloying roses. Never once had the new guest joined us. I made small-talk with my hostess. Floods, storms — surely these were rare this time of year? We resumed discussing the weather.

I am unskilled at eliciting gossip, a talent whose lack I have often mourned. A fondness for surfaces — their continued seemliness — keeps me from prying. Or perhaps it is my native reticence: my desire to remain unremarked. Somerset Maugham complained that admissions of his profession prompted wild confidences, in the hope he would use them in his stories. The South of France looks much the same as it did in his day. These country routes and the sudden, triumphant processions of plane trees in the towns; slanted light minced by moving shadow.

Imagine my delight when my unseen neighbour began making nightly assignations in the garden. I had doused my bedroom light and closed the shutters, but the windows were open to garner in the night air. I was in a haze of half-consciousness when I first heard the unmistakable murmur — plaintive, vehement, aggrieved — spurned in his love

He had been unlucky, suffered setbacks, unwisely tied his finances and flirtations. But now the heaving rehearsal of injustices had found a sympathetic ear. Night after night, he unburdened himself freely of the grossest banalities as if they were the most fantastical occurrences. I learned to sift his voice from the verdure's rustle, the flow of the hidden brook, just as Midas' servants learned to hear the barber's secret filtered through the whisper of the reeds. What else could I do? I listened.

***

I am a writer, and require seclusion. I came to Sauveterre to be unknown: to have no conversations, no community, to eschew so much as the single bar-tabac where the départementale, rounding a bend toward the Pyrenees, rushes right past the road into town. The owner, all bones and gristle, like a stripped chicken, does the crossword on the terrace, pen in one hand and cigarette in the other, her princely Alsatian bored to stupor beneath the table.

Of course, no sooner had I sequestered myself than inspiration failed me. The notes I had brought from home seemed a stranger's reminders. And so, to hide my shame, I made an act of idleness. I strolled the empty streets at sunset.

By then, the day's dust has settled on the cobblestones. That still hour... The trick is to hold the town intact while taking possession of it. These façades, these alleys — I pocket their descriptions. And then... an imperceptible pushing forward, beckoned by suggestion, past the slit of a gate ajar, a gap in a fence, a fallen span of wall disclosing a courtyard where weeds grown taller than a man have rumpled the flag-stones. Crumbs of mortar dribble from between brick teeth bared over a window's gape — black, until twilight picks a rafter from the gloom. The slightest violation, the infiltration of surmise. A havoc of swallows bursts forth, fleeing south past the loggias. On a drawn-out after note, a shutter drifts open, the Pierrot-head meant to hold it shut has nodded off.

If I could not be the person I had meant to be in coming here, I might at least play the role of the visitor. What was I waiting for? For the town to reveal itself?

And so I received the nightly confessions of my fellow-guest with glee. If I became their amanuensis — how willingly they lent themselves. The mystery of what went on outside my window seemed somehow irrelevant. Moreover, my neighbour's vomitous shudders had taken a new direction.

What tender shoulder pillowed his complaints? I pictured a girl from the local peasantry, a slip of a thing, arrogant with youth. Lavished on her, it left her sullen. With a downturned mouth, she bore beer on trays to loud boys crowded round a table in a bar the next town over. Boys in soccer jerseys their fathers wear in photographs on the wall.

Of course, he was a film producer. He had been put-upon, a father all his life, nagged to pieces by creative egos, long-suffering before they met. What exits, what escapes had he promised? Her whole history, had it led to this moment? Or had it abandoned her here, on the damp grass, staring at her hands in her lap? She was silent, quelled by the steady stream of words. Or else she murmured quietly, so I could not hear. He spoke of her flesh, praising its rose and pearl, caressing it. He narrated his ministrations, every nibble and bite, detailed the accomplishments of his fingertips.

Those limbs, each despite their slenderness drowsily leaden. Torpor of a sort that excites, incites. The waste of

youth upon her like a sentence.
How exactly I know her.

***

I am an inveterate eavesdropper — an aureur, if you will. I obtain, from overhearing, pleasures I should blush to mention. Shall I tell you of my sexual awakening? It was late — I was twenty-three — oh, late — half-past midnight. It happened in one of those pitiful, calamitous flea traps that prey on the young and poor. The room was a trundle bed jammed into a bay window. When unfolded, it blocked the front door. I lay bathed in the pallor of lighted signage through the listless curtains. I had thought myself alone upstairs. So did the couple in the next room.

Her cries were neither loud nor long, but startling and unearthly. And over, before I quite knew what they were. (It had this in common with the only earthquake I have ever experienced.) But of course the body quickens while the mind trails behind. To think such sounds could be wrung from pleasure, from someone adored. When it was over, I rose to clean myself but thought better of it. The only bathroom was down the hall, and I would have had to fold the bed. I wished to do nothing that might announce myself, embarrass the couple, revoke their trust in the delicious night. Their utter unabashedness had made a ghost of me, and I was surprised to learn that that was how I preferred it.

I had heard (and seen) such acts before in films. And I went looking for that feeling again: to no avail. Neither her ecstasy nor her cries gratified me, but the surprise of them did, reaching through a wall to rivet the viscera and hasten the heart. I, the painlessly ravished and effortlessly ravishing, in this theft whose victim was unaware, in which the mere idea of theft remained unsuspected. Listening is a perfect crime.

Had the serpent only sampled the fruit of that private frolic, he would never have urged another on the Edenic duo. And even today, when I hear love through the walls, I stiffen.

***

The landlady was wrong about the weather. A spate of squalls has suspended all garden trysts. My days had shaped themselves about these incursions. I am left privy to nothing.

I go out squinting at noon, the driest hour, stepping over puddles. Viridian lichen bakes on red roof tiles. A brow of gable pierced by an occulted oxeye, rheumy with piled belongings. The black, compacted wood of half-timbered houses, all the more stalwart for its warp. Plaster like a scab torn from a wall, brick pink as a wound beneath.

The bridge is low to the lazy olive river, gorged on rains. Blowsy branches trail in the current. Thronged by green, a single Calla lily with its furled spathe seems to mark a virgin spring, or the spot where a saint pricked his finger. The moss along the low stone walls sends up brown tendrils like hair raised along an arm by the breeze.

And I, having completed my submission to distraction, wait alone in my quarters for a single fly to age and slow, so I can swat it.

***

When the nightly trysts resume, my fellow guest returns bearing gifts: a pair of costly earrings he asked her permission to affix. And all the while he prattles on (forgive my condescension): she is a blessing he cannot comprehend, but does not question. What miracle created and imprisoned her here for him to find? He cannot but imagine her unique in all the world.

I too admit to curiosity. Why does she never say a word? Sometimes on the route des Pyrenees, empty by nine on a Saturday night, a motorcycle pulls up at the blinking red light beside the old men playing petanque. A bare thigh pressed to the seat and curled into a boyfriend's. Long hair spilling from under a helmet. Or summer cashiers, five to a car, laughing their way to a roadhouse with a buvette outside, the light from its counter spilling over the gravel lot. I wonder. Perhaps if I only saw her, I would understand. I might confirm my intuitions, or shred and discard them.

Tonight, I hiked to the chapel of the town's patron saint. On the way, you pass something like a chimney sprouting from the ground. Topped by a Madonna, it marks the spot where the saint is said to have sauvé la terre, vanquishing a dragon by throwing his ring in its mouth. The chapel is flanked by pines and had been locked against vandals. On a nearby rise are the remains of a long, low barn: the fractured roof timbers, a wall of wattle and daub still whole but reeling as if from a mighty blow. The decrepitude bespoke neither neglect nor the cheap residue of expedience, but the weight of centuries withstood. From atop the hill, I could see the cemetery.

The whole town was there, gathered by a grave. Their backs were turned to me, and a tremor passed through the group: shoulders swayed, weight shifted to the other foot. I saw the butcheress draw closer to my landlady and further from the cheesemonger. I watched until the group slowly scattered, then I skittered down the hill to the graveyard. Wrought-iron masts and crosses, plaques, shattered flowerpots. On the tomb were a shovel and a bottle of wine, but the grave was empty. I was still standing there when it began to rain.

A village is a murder mystery. The conversation of townsfolk is rich in allusion; red herrings in shared histories you don't understand. The air of conspiracy inspires you to imagine a crime. Everyone has something to hide, but you cannot tell if it pertains to the case at hand, or if it will merely prove a false lead: another skeleton in another closet, a private and irrelevant embarrassment. Yet surely this suspicion of wrongdoing is only a hallucination of exclusion. After all these months, I was still a stranger to the town, while my neighbour had found not only love, but he would abscond with it.

My landlady was already back when I returned to the pension. I must have looked a sight. Tumbledown, bedraggled and bereft, from my chin tucked in my collar to my sopping shoes, every inch the visitor none wishes to receive. Yet I was not turned away. Indoors threw its warm arms around me.

A hallway two steps down, and immediately the low, solid beams oppressed with the weight they shouldered. If wood could groan! Ushering me into the dim kitchen, my landlady sat me down for soup beside the massive brick hearth which anchored the house. Perhaps there are two towns: a town of sidewalks and exteriors, where visitors stroll, and another of hidden courtyards and garden doors under armfuls of bougainvillea. Locals, if they wish, can go from their kitchen to the baker's without ever setting foot out of their front door.

I stayed late in the guests' library that night. Lying in wait, or in hope of companionship? These swaybacked houses shouldered upright by their neighbours, these towns time has brought to one knee, idyllic and sinister. How much they have seen. Leafing through a gilded history, I perused the account of a woman from the region, murdered and dismembered collectively at some ritual banquet of the town's, the various parts buried each in different places. The stump of a foot filled the exact centre of a cornerstone. An elbow folded in a corbel, a hand weighting the mantel of a hearth, fingers distributed to individual bricks. The eye that watched from a keystone, and another blindly immured, untraceable but for a green weeping stain down the creamy stucco. A tibia, entrusted to the reliquary of a doorsill that Time has scooped out like a shallow basin.

That night I had a dream. The mayor, while his wife is asleep with her eye mask and her rejuvenating creams, wakes beside his white phone on the tulle-trimmed nightstand. He finds his glasses without turning on the rose-shaded lamp. He slips quietly from bed and pads across the thick carpet. Downstairs, taking the steps one by one in the blue dark. In the kitchen, he opens a cupboard, and behind the sugar, the flour, the baking powder, is another, smaller cupboard, in every way identical to the first. He opens it. There is nothing inside but a pair of lips, fixed to the back. Carefully, he applies his wife's lipstick. A faint, enticing smile plays across them, and they begin to speak. They tell him who has been sleeping with whom, who has cheated on his taxes, who is buying up property along the river, who, based on dinner chatter, will rise to oppose his motion at the next town meeting. They tell him everything my neighbour has told his young lover, about the women who've hurt him, and the places he'll take her. The mayor stands on a chair, eyes closed, his slippered feet beside the flour and sugar in decanters, an expression of utter beatitude on his face.

***

Shortly before I was to leave Sauveterre, I treated myself to dinner in the neighbouring town, at a restaurant that was part of an old inn. The courtyard, where the passenger-and-mail coach had once changed horse teams, was now decked with verdure. A lighted pool of opaline modernity completed the oasis.

The terrace was full when I arrived: two couples, a family of five, four friends, and in one back corner, an older man. He sat there, grey hair boiling over a shirt open halfway down his chest in the summer heat. I watched as he smoked a brown cigarette down to the butt — tapping it, from time to time, into the only ashtray on any of the tables. I had never seen the man before, but I knew, even before I heard him order, that he was my fellow guest from the pension.

The edges of umbrellas fluttered in the breeze. Their shadows seem to float when stirred, as if on some clear river above the bed of the ground.

'Monsieur a l'air de savoir bien se régaler,' I said, nodding at my neighbour. I closed the menu. 'I'll have what he's having.'

The only waiter was young and scrawny; partway through the sitting, his shirt tail came untucked. He brought me a perfectly ordinary rump steak and a thin local rosé.

I don't know what I had expected — a business traveller? A cosmopolite? Not the heavyset troglodyte with his crassly unbuttoned shirt, eyes pouched with weariness. From where I sat, the pool's chlorine masked the smell of his cigarette. Half a globe of pistachio ice cream skidded in his dish. Between finger and thumb, he toyed with what seemed a single pearl earring. It was all beginning to take shape in my mind... How little it takes to fire the imagination!

It was entirely predictable, of course, this parochial romance. He was waiting at the restaurant for her. They were to leave together, and never come back. His disappointment was exquisite. What would he try to do now? I did but taste a little honey with the end of the rod that was in mine hand, and, lo, I must die...

The waiter had just brought me my middling mousse au chocolat when my fellow guest got up and left. An assortment of glass vessels were voided on the table, as in an abandoned laboratory. I lingered, savouring my Sauternes. The inn at dusk had the slightly monstrous aspect of being eaten by ivy, the flyspecked white shutters intruders in the green scheme. In the bathroom, cream-white washcloths lay folded and stacked beside the sink.

That night, I worked late, trying to give shape to this summer affair, these pages of scribbled transcriptions. My useless old notes lay shucked in a corner, husks of what another self had once thought sufficiently interesting to say. If that world was shrivelled and gone, so be it. It felt cheap, predatory, melodramatic, messily torn from life, but I was grateful for a sense of renewed urgency, the need to tell and make known. And so I was surprised when I heard the sound of footsteps in the yard.

I waited. I strained to hear, and heard nothing. I saw a sliver of myself, lit by the desk lamp, in the casements to either side. Then, with the vengefulness of one teased with and denied for all these weeks his impending, almost promised release, I flung the shutters open.

I had not mistaken his voice earlier. The man I had seen at dinner was naked in the yard, with his back to me and his buttocks clenched. Was he urinating in the flowerbed along the wall? There was no girl anywhere to be seen. Had she fled?

He half-turned then, though I doubt he ever knew I was there. He seemed blind to the world, to himself. With one hand he held the curtain of green away from what seemed a pale pink patch of wall, and with the other, furiously stroked his erect member. Then in the light from my open window — raging, lunging, wrung and racked, led and funneled by this spurting appurtenance into the world, he splattered himself in arcing gouts and jets over the wisteria, the wall, the night.

The next morning he was gone. Not long after, I too left Sauveterre.

The bed was made, the shutters closed. I had brought scant

belongings, but once they were packed, the room looked barer than before I had come: the wooden chairs and tables unaltered, yet somehow diminished.

When we had finished with breakfast, I stayed in the yard while my landlady took the tray of dishes back inside. I did not know what I was looking for, exactly. Something to substantiate the preceding night. Something to justify or dispel what I had thought to see — a gap in the hedge where lovers whispered; some sordid hole, as in a sheet or a bathroom stall; a tear in a partition — to explain that glimpse of pink wreathed in his glistening expulsion. And there, under the wisteria, I found it, or something. An ear, or the sculpture of an ear, in stone.

The wall around it seemed utterly normal. I could find no evidence it had ever been a part of anything else (a bust, a toppled statue), nor any to suggest it had been added as an afterthought. Time might have removed it from the centre of the stone, as if surfaced from something interred; the wall might just as easily have put forth this growth, or blurred the seam between itself and an addition until both were of the same mottled grey. In the lobe was a single pearl earring. Beside the stone, it had an air of freshness — not the least of which was due to the maroon stain, just beneath it, as of dried blood. I let the curtain of wisteria fall. As the taxi took me from the pension, the town seemed to close behind me, the scalloped shadow of a tiled roof scaling a building, houses crowding an alley till it narrowed from sight.

I have never returned to Sauveterre. The town, like that man, have vanished from my life. And left me with a story to tell, but where, where is that believing ear in all the night?

The Holy Hour

C. A. Yates

Elise closed her eyes and waited. Waited for her atoms to catch up and band together, waited for them to do their job so she could be whole again, so this could be over. The feeling did not come. Yet again. Time after time she had let herself believe it would be different but here she was, still stuck with her grief, still alone. All people ever seemed to say was that she should try. Try, try, try, try, try. Well, she had tried so hard and so often, but every time she was left with the same conclusion – it would never happen, things would never be right again. Sighing, she opened her eyes and stared at the mantelpiece, still covered in condolence cards, thick with dusty regret and thankful grief – thankful that it had happened to her, not them. She knew what friends she had left sympathised well enough, empathised even, but it was a long time since she'd seen any of them and, besides, they were old, with troubles of their own. Anyway, none of them could know what was happening to her because none of them had loved him as she had. None of them knew this particular flavour of wound. They knew their own, but not hers. Anyone that said otherwise was a fool.

The room was cold, the house empty. Every movement she made thundered, but dully, an echo of the emptiness inside her. Greying light added to the sombre mood, night falling again, another day done, another day lived without him. Elise knew all the advice about not wallowing, about remembering the good times, but all she could recall at times like this was his pale drawn face as he had lost the battle, as he had finally slipped away from her, gone beyond her reach. The memory played over and over in her head. What she wouldn't give for one more moment with him, for one more glimpse of those sweet hazel eyes.

The bark snapped her out of her reverie and almost into a

heart attack. Elise jumped up from her place on the sofa, one hand to her chest as she cried out. The bark came again.

Wait. Florence?

But it couldn't be. Could it?

As the sitting room door swung open slowly, Elise's heart froze in her chest, her entire system ringing with alarm bells, but somehow she waited. For a moment there was nothing, the door swung to a halt, and the whole room seemed to wait on her shaky exhalation.

Dog claws tippy tapped across the wooden floor in the hallway, scuttling their owner's way to the sitting room. A white nose appeared around the door, then that face, so achingly familiar, so loved.

'Flo!' Elise's breath rushed from her lungs and she couldn't stop the grin from spreading across her face. Before she knew it, she was across the room and hauling her beloved dog into her arms. Dog smell filled her nose, the warm body in her arms the surest sign of love fulfilled. She buried her face in the white fur, inhaling frantically, deeply, hardly believing she had forgotten about Florence in her grief.

'Oh, Flo. It's so good to see you. You have no idea. I wish you knew.' Not wanting to, but knowing she should, Elise bent to put the odd little white dog back on the floor. As she did, she saw something achingly familiar in her dark brown eyes. Grief. Sorrow. Sadness. That hateful melange. Of course she would know, of course. Had it been so long that she'd forgotten how much Florence had loved him too? Dogs felt loss, didn't they? Felt it just like she did. If there were anyone who had an inkling of what it was to lose him, it would be her.

Florence trotted away from her and over to the French doors that looked out into their garden. She whimpered softly, pressing her wet nose against the glass and staring into the fields that backed onto the house. It was an old familiar habit, one she had not seen in far too long. Flo wanted to go for a walk. Elise smiled, the muscles in her face aching with the unaccustomed usage; it felt as though it had been forever ago since she'd had anything at all to smile about, it had seemed impossible she ever would again.

'Hold on a sec, Flo, let's go find your lead.' She crossed the room and headed for the kitchen, the sound of Florence's pursuit echoing through the otherwise empty house. It made her feel warm for the first time in ages and Elise could feel those atoms of hers beginning to swirl into place at last.

Finding the lead was not as easy as she'd thought. Where had she put it last? Rummaging through drawers and boxes, Elise was reminded of the life she had shared with him. They'd had no children, had very little other family who concerned themselves with them, but they'd had each other, not to mention Florence and her predecessors. Unconventional, but happy, they'd grown more in love with every passing year. People wondered at it, had said as much to her, to him, but the only thing that could explain it was that she was her and he was him and together they were them. What else was needed? As she searched for Florence's lead, Elise found her breath catching at every forgotten photograph, newspaper clipping, and ridiculous memento – there were rocks, feathers, tiny plastic children's toys - from a thousand different adventures, a million moments encapsulated. The smile on her face did not fade. How lucky she had been. How lucky to have loved and been loved so well in return.

In her grief she had forgotten, had seen only her loss, but now with fate forcing her hand, she remembered. Tears spilled over her lashes and down her cheeks, but she paid them no mind. The memories kept coming fast and hard as she sat on the floor sorting through them. It was the sort of thing that should have been a release, that's what all the bumf she'd been given on grief and grieving had said, but she found it had the opposite effect. The more she saw, the less she could contemplate finally saying goodbye. Catharsis be damned, she thought.

Then, *that* photo. How she had always loved it, remembered so clearly the day they'd taken it, standing together at the cliff's edge, daring each other to get closer and laughing like children, and they had been a long way past that by then. She had kept it in her handbag for years. How had she lost it to the wastelands of the kitchen drawers? His face, smiling, happy, carefree, looking at the camera, at her, and every ounce of love he had for her shining through the old forgotten lens into her present day soul.

Catharsis be damned indeed.

Oh, how she wanted him back, wanted him now, in her arms, in her kitchen, in her life. She wanted him where he belonged. His loss was not fair, it wasn't right. How dare he be taken from her? How dare he leave? Elise felt her old friend anger burn through her, felt it take hold, making her muscles shake with the force of it. This was all too much; she felt the balance shift, felt despair waiting for her. She had lost everything, why should she be reminded of that so brutally? It wasn't enough to remember and smile. God damn all of it. God. Damn. It. She'd tried grieving, she'd tried it, but it wasn't working. She didn't want to say goodbye, she didn't see why she should. Who was to say what they'd had was enough? She'd said forever and she had meant it.

The balance tipped, finally, and she threw the drawer she'd taken from the dresser hard, the contents spilling from it mid-air, photos, half burned birthday candles, balls of string, and ancient takeaway menus scattering to all four corners of the room and then, finally, the crash of wood smashing against the wall. The sound should have been shocking in the quiet house, but all Elise could hear was the wailing that was coming from her own mouth. She couldn't stop, couldn't make it stop. Clapping her hands across her face, she tried to quell it, but the sound kept coming, cranking up to a high pitched keening noise that should have shattered glass.

The bark shocked her out of it.

Florence.

How could she have forgotten?

That damned lead, where was... There. On the table, as though she'd placed it there on purpose, was Florence's lead. Bright red against the pine, it waited. She felt it waiting, felt Flo behind her waiting too. Walkies, that was it, it was time for a walk.

Elise grabbed the lead and shoved it in the pocket of her jeans. She found her wellies, still encrusted with mud from that last walk together a thousand years ago, in the bottom of the cupboard by the sink, and wedged them on her feet. Her old wax jacket, a bottle green cliché, was still hanging by the back door and putting it on after all that time was like coming home; ironic considering she was leaving. The rush of fresh air as she threw open the back door was invigorating, solidifying her resolve. It pinked her skin and made her nose tingle. The scent of spring was in the air – odd because it was December – and it was intoxicating. Suddenly, Elise couldn't wait to get out there, to stretch her legs and run, run far from this empty place and the memories that taunted her.

'Come on, Flo,' she said, patting her leg as she called to her, just like she always had. The dog came running, just as she always had.

They flew down the steps together, Elise laughing, Florence barking. They ran across the grass, away from the festering frustration of memory, and through the gate that led to the fields beyond. Euphoria had taken hold and they were both embracing every moment of it. The grey evening light was much darker now, but somehow she could see her way, only losing sight of the white dog in the gloom every now and then. She always came back though. That's a dog for you. They always come back and they always bring you home.

They walked and ran for what felt like hours. Elise threw sticks and Flo chased them, almost bringing them back. Almost, just like always. They walked farther than Elise had for a good while, but she felt almost as though she was young again, energy seeming to pour through and out of her, warming her against the chill night air as it came on.

Dark woods bordered the fields about three miles from the house. Elise was surprised to see them. Had they really come that far? It was hard to believe, but then the day just seemed to be that way. For the first time, she felt trepidation. She'd never walked through the woods without him, had always been a little afraid of doing so. Did she dare? Flo barked, as though to remind her she was not alone. She would be okay; Elise smiled to herself, of course she would. Taking a deep breath – she'd always been good at saying the words she wanted to hear, less so at believing them – she followed Florence as the dog charged into the thickets ahead, displaying a typical lack of canine concern. She didn't want to tear her trousers in the thick undergrowth, but carried on after her anyway. In for a penny and all that.

Soon, she saw there was a path, could thankfully see it as soon as she stepped into the gloom. Small white pebbles had been laid either side to show the way. She'd never noticed them before. Maybe it had been so long ago since she'd seen them, she'd simply forgotten. Or maybe not. As her foot came down on the track, she felt a little better, as though the pebbles somehow formed a barrier against what lurked in the darkness beyond. Lord, she hoped they were something of the sort, because as soon as she could no longer see the fields behind her, when her passage had been all but subsumed by the gloom, Elise began to hear noises. The soft cracking of twigs at first, the rustle of dead leaves half-mulched into the floor. Then came the wind through the winter-stripped branches, creaking and groaning like a woodland banshee. The sound sent a shiver down Elise's spine, the portent of death ringing in her ears. She remembered the stories her mother had told her when she was a child, stories from the old country, how those women of the barrows keened when someone was about to die. She remembered how, as a teenager, she'd researched the mythology and found that a possible explanation for the phenomena was the screech of the barn owl and how, despite the enlightenment, it hadn't seemed any less frightening for that. She'd been scared by an owl in these very woods, years ago, a ghostly apparition that had sent her scuttling home. There was no turning back now, however; she could feel it in her bones. Her atoms were settling, fixing fast and at long last on her course, and she was committed. To what she did not yet know, but her feet kept carrying her forward, following the small white dog as she ran ahead of her, weaving in and out of trees away from the path, digging holes and sniffing everything in sight. It was as though she was saying there was nothing to be afraid of and Elise felt better for it.

Despite the forward impetus, every step was hard. Her feet weighed a thousand pounds one step, the next they were feather-light, keeping her equilibrium reeling. She felt light-headed, like the time she'd given blood and, just after the needle had gone in, she'd passed out, slipping from the chair and hitting the floor as she'd lost consciousness, the moment before impact bright with giddy wonder. Everything had seemed so clear in that moment, so perfectly lit and full of sensation, then nothing. Passing out was not an option now, however. She had a destination, she felt it in the air around her, felt it in the impatient glances Flo shot her way every time she paused to check her mistress's progress, as though egging her on, ever on.

The wind was stronger now, having gathered pace without her registering it before. Elise pulled the edge of her jacket around her, her fingers suddenly too numb to contemplate tackling the zip. The banshees keened louder, the branches snapping and swaying angrily in the rising breeze. The dark night was making itself felt and the unease that had trickled through her earlier now etched its way down into her flesh, chilling her to the bone. She kept watch around her as best she could, head snapping to and fro in a neck jerking spasm. She felt like she was closer, to what she did not know, but she knew she was nearly there and she wouldn't, indeed couldn't, stop walking. There was a place, she knew it, a somewhere to discover. It was a journey worth taking, worth the fear and uncertainty, worth the cold and, now, rain. It fell in sheets, as though the sky had split like overripe fruit and could no longer contain its slick contents.

And still she walked. Still, she followed the white dog.

Then, suddenly, there was an opening in the trees. Elise couldn't see the clearing properly until she had stepped out into it, a surprise considering there was a faint glow of light emanating from the small building set at its heart. It was barely there, but it should have been enough to pierce the dark night beyond the vague boundaries of the clearing. Perhaps the incessant fat drops of rain had obscured it but, as Elise surveyed the small structure, she instinctively understood that the light was only for those who entered it, not for those who stayed outside. To access its comfort you had to make a choice.

Florence was standing a few feet from her, tail wagging and tongue lolling as she panted happily from her exertions. She seemed content with their progress and was now waiting while her mistress decided on her next move. It was tiny, a church perhaps, old, white and wooden. It didn't belong to the architecture of the area, she could tell that much even in the gloom. It wasn't unfriendly but it didn't seem as though you were being encouraged to enter either, unusual for a church. Frowning, she scanned the building, trying to work out what was making her uncertain. Suddenly, she laughed at herself. She'd walked for miles through the deep dark woods and now a building worried her just because it wasn't sounding bells and blowing whistles at her coming? The wind had picked up, that was all; there were no banshees heralding death, no oogie boogies or serial killers waiting for her inside. Why not go in and light a candle for him? She wasn't a devout woman, but she believed in something, that there was another place beyond this one. Maybe she was here to say goodbye… no, she wouldn't say that yet. She would never say it. She had set her course and she would stick to it.

The church bell rang out suddenly as though heralding her decision, but it was not cacophonous in the gloom. It was as though it supported her choice, as though this was indeed the holy hour and she had come to the right place.

Resolved, and more than a little comforted, Elise started towards the church. She would go in, sit a while, light a candle, ask for guidance maybe – who knew, maybe she would even get a miracle. A second coming. Smiling to herself, she reached out to grasp the brass handles of the doors, noting how surprisingly shiny they were in the dark, and hauled them open. The wind whistled past her, streaming into the church as though some giant had bent to inhale on the other side of the building. Elise felt as though she was sucked through the threshold, rather than pushed, and fell to her knees on the floor, her palms coming down hard on the stone beneath her. The sting and shock of it robbed her of breath and it took a long moment for her to gather her wits. She was not young, had not been for a very long time, and she wasn't used to this sort of exertion. It all came flooding back to her, the grief, the walk, the darkness, the fall… In the sudden silence that followed her entrance, a surge of everything she had and should have felt shot through her – shock, denial, bargaining, guilt, anger, depression, hope. All seven stages. All at once. It was the last, however, that stayed with her, that buoyed her back to her feet. Hope. That old scoundrel, the number one tease. With one hand on the pew to her right, she swung around to look into the body of the church proper. The nave.

Quiet bodies were scattered amongst the pews, bowed

heads in prayer. As each raised their head, having finished their particular invocations, they rose and slipped away into the night, not through the door, but into the air, their bodies evaporating like mist into the ether. Elise blinked as one supplicant faded and another took their place. Once they had appeared, they would sink to their knees and kiss the ground before settling themselves onto the wooden pews to pray. She did not understand at first what she was seeing, but somehow she found herself sitting amongst them, towards the back of the nave.

That was when she saw him. At last. He was sitting alone in the middle of a pew a few rows in front of her. She would recognise the back of his head anywhere. Tears smarted at her eyes, but she blinked them away, not wanting to ruin this impossible sighting. Hope. Again. It was irresistible and she couldn't stop herself, could not hold back. Standing, she ignored the sudden shaking in her legs and walked out of her row into the aisle, heading forwards, making her way to him.

The air was soft around her, the candlelight, which could not have been candlelight because there were no candles, guiding her on her way. A few small steps and she would be there with him, beside him.

At last.

The sound of children laughing behind her, of them playing long forgotten games with nothing but their imaginations rather than the technology that ruled the younger generations these days, did not deter her from her path. She knew they were there, knew they were the souls of those lost too soon. They were no threat to her. They were merely waiting for their people, for when the time came for them to say their prayers and be together again. Her heart ached for them, for those waiting to be with them, but still she walked on. Those few small steps seemed to last forever.

And then…

He turned to look up at her as she approached him, the warmth of recognition lighting up his familiar face. How she loved that face, how lost she had been without it and, now, it was there in front of her, he was there in front of her and coming home had never felt so wonderful. He did not speak; just smiled that beautiful smile of his. Her heart swelled to bursting and she went to him, her hand outstretched to grasp his as soon as she could manage it. His touch was thrilling, like the first time he had touched her when they had read Shakespeare together for her college course an eternity ago. The frisson of excitement she felt was more real than anything she had experienced since well before his funeral, since she had watched them all say goodbye to him as the curtains had closed and he had gone into the furnace beyond. She had slept with his ashes ever since, not telling anyone lest they thought her crazy. It had been months. Nothing in the house had been touched since that day; the cards still sat on the mantelpiece, the teacups in the dishwasher doubtlessly consumed by mould. Her friends' patience had been the only thing to change. She wasn't sorry to lose touch with them. So utterly lost in her grief, why would she have been? She had longed only for him and now here he was in front of her, his hand in hers, his eyes on her face, his smile only for her. She had promised him a thousand times or more that she would never leave him. She kept her promises.

'Hello sunshine.' She whispered the familiar endearment, not wanting to raise her voice and break whatever spell this was. His smile deepened and he pulled her towards him. As she sat next to him, their hands still clasped, Florence joined them, nestling between her feet, her muzzle resting on her knee. Elise reached out with her free hand to touch the wiry white fur. Florence belonged there as much as they did, she knew. It shouldn't have been a surprise. The urn containing her ashes had sat on the mantelpiece long before the condolence cards had joined it. It had sat there for five years, four longer than the cards. Such a long year, but now she was here it didn't matter. She had waited long enough. They were all together at last. Resting her head on his shoulder, she closed her eyes and smiled.

***

The rumours concerning the discovery of Elise Harper's body spread like wildfire through the town. How could it not? It wasn't a place much accustomed to anything happening let alone a suicide. It was the next best thing to a murder. Not many people had known the old woman well, although many knew her by sight. She'd kept to herself for the most part, even more so since her husband had died the previous year. Few of their friends were left now and those that remained had not spoken to her for some time. Isolated herself, they said, couldn't come to terms with his death, they said. Marie Travis at the Post Office reckoned she must have been planning it for a while, saving the painkillers for her arthritis to go with the expensive bottle of brandy she'd bought from Wilmington Wines, the one Bob Wilmington had thought he'd never shift. She couldn't, however, explain why Elise had left the back door to the house wide open so any Tom, Dick or Harry could just stroll in and take their pick. Mind you, it was anyone's guess as to who stood to inherit it all. No one could decide why she had chosen that day to end it. She'd lost her husband less than a year ago and they'd been married in May not December, so it wasn't an anniversary as far as anyone knew. Of course, no one could say for sure if it had special meaning for her or her husband – they'd had virtually no family, just each other, and their secrets died with them.

Most of all, however, no one could explain the red dog lead she'd been holding in one hand.

Malefactor

Alan C. Moore

The explosion hurled me into the dark and frigid ocean waters.

The journey towards my landing was surreal and painful. I feel the burns on my scarred body just before hitting the choppy surface. I float, unable to move because of my injuries. Strength leaves me like a deserting lover. Waves rock back and forth as I witness the *Untraveled Destination* split in half from the flames and sink. The boat had been my home for the last two months at sea, and in a passing moment the deep gray and blue aqua claimed it as a victim.

Fire from the *Untraveled Destination* extinguished as the ship sank. The clouds blotted out the moon and stars, leaving blackness as cold as the water. As the flames dissipated, the final bit of light in my world died. The horrible sound of destruction quieted in a moment. It seems I must have been the lucky one. I can spot no other survivors.

Just yesterday we performed an extensive inspection of the ship. Everything from the engine room to the bridge was in tip-top shape. The boatswain made sure of that with a tongue like the crack of a whip. When on duty we worked our hands to nubs cleaning, fixing, and drilling. We had prepared for all scenarios, or so we believed.

Yet, I know the explosion must have begun in the lower decks for which I was responsible. As assistant master mechanic; I knew every inch of the engine room. My job was to make sure everything worked efficiently and safely. Twice a day we inspected every major piece of equipment. In my last inspection there was no oil or other liquid underneath the engine. Each hose was new and without visible cracks. I could find no salt trails, oil film, or rust on any parts. No chemical odor permeated the air. All the seals were tight and gearbox secure. The fluids were at appropriate levels and the fuel flowed into the engine without problems.

Negligence was not the cause of this calamity. In fact, I doubt it was any accident. This fire was sparked by malice. There is no other explanation. Yet for what purpose? I see no other survivors. There are no boats in the area to pick up their confederate. We are not at war and pirates plunder ships, not destroy them. If this was intentional I know no motive.

I suppose it matters not given my current situation.

The aching in my body exceeds rationality and I reconsider just how lucky I am. With no means to prevent the fall, my body slips further under the salty blanket. The weight above me increases with each foot of descent. Water fills my ears and nose. I drop like a waterlogged piece of wood.

My mind wanders towards many things. I think of my new wife. We married a week before my sea journey. A man in my position does not dictate when and how he takes work. I take what I can when I can. I would have loved nothing more than a long honeymoon with my beautiful bride. Instead, I only had a few short days of passion.

Every night we lay under the covers of our measly bed with her head pressed against my chest. Her flowing brown hair rested from under my chin to my belly button. No such blankets exist that are more soothing. Her fingers moved with gentle rhythm on my side as we drifted into slumber. I lived for that moment. In all of space and time nothing existed more pleasurable or meaningful.

Would my bride recognize her Jonas now? The pain touches every molecule of my being. My body must resemble a charred tree branch more than a man.

I am sinking faster. The swelling in my lungs aches. I can sense the panic begin on my brow. There is not much time before my breath releases.

Damn the deformed man. He lied. Death is close. His promise was nothing more than a fool's errand. I should have known not to fall for such superstition and lunacy. He had no power or influence over the universe. I wanted to believe but desire cannot prevent fatality.

I blame my upbringing. That shaped me into such a cod, willing to accept falsities as gospel. My mother believed in gypsy curses, herbal remedies for serious illness, and even carried silver to ward of werewolf attacks. I was required to say prayers at specific parts of the day lest we invite evil spirits into our house. I often would cross my fingers in secret out of spite of my mother's ridiculous rituals. Yet apparently I inherited her propensity for belief in the merits of snake oil.

The air supply in my lungs expires. There isn't much time now.

A few more seconds.

My arms and legs still refuse to cooperate. I cannot push myself to the surface. My strength has deserted.

Here it comes.

Goodbye my love. Mother, do not greet me with anything but open arms.

My breath releases in an instant. The life support is gone.

The agony of anticipation is unparalleled.

I breathe, knowing the end has arrived.

. . .

The water fills my lungs. Then something extraordinary happens.

I breathe out.

The water expels. I breathe in again. More water enters and exits.

I am no fish. The sensation is excruciating. I want to cough with every fiber of my existence but cannot. I gasp for air but there is none. Death has not taken me, of this I am sure. My sinking intensifies. I am falling faster as the weight of the liquid increases. What has happened? Where is the afterlife?

Then an image of the deformed man enters my consciousness. Was he telling the truth? My God, he was.

The final words he spoke ring in my head as if he swam next to me: 'With all the benefits and horrors, I bestow upon you your wish.'

I hear a noise through the surrounding waters. It penetrates my soul. What is that?

***

I have been a sailor my whole life. As a youth I spent my first voyage as a cabin boy en route to London. The merchant ship brought goods for trade to the people of the King's land. I performed as menial tasks as are available. From washing the deck to polishing the boots of the captain; if there was a lowly task to carry out I was your man.

After months at sea I realized two things: First, I loved the ocean as my sea legs came quickly and; two, the janitorial duties were not beneath me as long as I was on a ship. Put me in a stuffy bank or factory and I would walk out over such deplorable conditions. With the salty wind blowing through my hair and the view of never settled blue waters, I could do anything.

I learned everything there was to know about boats and how they operated. Within five years I could explain the intricacies of the ship's bowsprit, the components of a good hawser, latitude, longitude, and how to navigate using the stars.

I found my true love in the bowels of the ship in the engine room. I looked upon the turbines and pistons as most kids gaze through candy shop windows. Everything connected for me. I could look at a part and see where it went and how it worked in an instant. At an early age I spent most of my time talking with the master mechanic, taking notes, and wandering through the engine room. Soon, I became a mechanic myself. I had found my calling.

I have been on several voyages. Although still young I am considered a grizzled veteran by my peers. I gained a reputation for facing fear. I once jumped over the side of the ship to save a passenger's poodle. Another time I led an effort to put out a raging fire in the hull. While others ran away, I sprinted towards the flames. Nothing would ruin my life at sea.

Things changed when I met Gertrude. We were on leave at the port of Baltimore. Sailors rarely spend their shore leave in the more respectable parts of cities and I was no different. Always up for cheap drinks and thrills, the slums of local bars did me right. Though I never thought I would meet my future wife in the doldrums.

I walked into a seedy waterhole by the name of the Rusted Rudder. It was a lively joint with drunkards and call girls roaming as free as grazing cattle. Slurred speech, quarrels, and drunken laughter filled the air. My type of place! There was something else though. A beautiful sound filled my ears. Although faint, I could hear it well enough and it soon drowned out the tomfoolery in the background.

In a few moments I placed the sound. It was Pachelbel's Canon in D major - my favorite melody. Never has an equivalent to such a lovely piano piece been written. It fills my soul with warmth and takes me to a place of total relaxation. When things run out of control, I think of Canon and am calmed. That is another reason I possess no fear. Pachelbel removes my strife and fills me with confidence and reassurance.

In my years of frequenting dives, I have never heard old Pachelbel singing his tune. Usually the best you can hope for is some brigand on a squeeze box belting out drinking songs. I searched the room for the source. In a dimly lit corner away from the noise was the piano, and sitting upright with a posture unknown to sailors, she sat and played. No one but me seemed to take notice. She performed as if for me alone, cutting through the merrymaking like a sword.

When she finished Canon I found myself next to her. I know not how I slid over to that position, it just happened. She glided her slender fingers over the keys as if stroking an obedient pet. Then she looked at me with eyes that shifted from green to blue depending on the light. Her long brown hair was up in an elaborate bun, held together by a yellow silk bow. She wore a velvet dress, modest but fashionable and elegant. Her skin was soft and unblemished aside from a few brown freckles on her upper cheek. Those beauty marks were the last thing I noticed before falling in love.

'Any requests, good sir?' She said with the voice of the angels.

I responded with, 'uhh.' Then I stared.

She laughed. So did I.

'Forgive me, madam. I was awestruck by your playing. You left me without words.'

'You're too kind, good sir,' she blushed. 'I'm glad you appreciate Pachelbel.'

'I appreciate you and your talent, it's magnificent.'

Her neck turned splotchy with red marks.

'You embarrass me.'

'Forgive me twice m'lady. I meant no malice. I'm taken aback by your presence. This doesn't seem like the place a woman of your grace and skill should frequent.'

She laughed again and squeezed my arm.

'Well, you are a gentleman, aren't you? I suppose saying 'what is a girl like you doing in a place like this' is too low-brow of a pickup line for you?' She leaned back and crossed her arms.

'I, uhh.'

'I tease, don't worry.' Her lip curled. 'Buy me a drink. My name is Gertrude.'

I bought her that beverage and joined her with a beer. I did not have a drop of it though. Her beverage remained as undisturbed as mine. For the next few hours we unraveled each other's history and personality.

She was a music teacher who supplemented her income by playing charity balls, parties, and other events. Tonight though she performed for free. The word passed to her that a piano lay more as a decoration than an instrument in this particular watering hole. To Gertrude, this was a travesty of terrible proportions. She had a piano at home but playing in front of others was too much of a draw. Whenever she was free she came to the *Rusted Rudder* and played until her fingers ached.

Until that moment I had never met someone who had the same passion for anything as I did for the sea. Her love of music matched the intensity of mine for sailing. We both recognized this similarity in an instant.

In six months we married. On our wedding night I promised to spend eternity with her. There is no one I want to live my life with other than Gertrude.

It was her I thought of when I accepted the gift from the deformed man. If it worked I could ask for the same for Gertrude. We could live together on our terms forever. I fear now that my greed was prelude to insanity.

***

My ship left Baltimore Harbors for Papua New Guinea

by way of the Panama Canal, Hawaii, and the Northern Mariana Islands. We carried goods for trade and a few passengers aboard for private business. There was nothing out of the ordinary until we spotted the deformed man.

The crew stopped their tasks when he arrived. The man, at least seven feet tall, wore a black suit, long charcoal gray cape jacket, top hat, and a matching black tie on his white silk shirt. His complexion was splotchy with bits of hair and warts covering his hands, face and neck. He looked more like a potato than a man. The deformity was in his skull, which sloped downward in the middle top of his head like a V. The cleft pushed his left yellowish eye to the far side of his face. He tried to hide his deformity with long hair and a scraggly gray beard, but it did not help.

After he boarded rumors swirled through the crew. Some said he resembled a long extinct race of demons that travelled the world with evil intentions. Others took it as an omen for disaster, arguing a man with such a horrific appearance would naturally project those deficiencies. Superstitious sailors can convince you of anything even as ridiculous as their theories on the deformed man.

'Have you ever seen such a person?' The master mechanic asked me one day.

'Can'ts say I have.'

'Be glad for that. You thank whatever God ye pray to such a curse hasn't walked yer path before and ask such a thing to never cross ye again.'

'Oh come now, because of his deformity you're afraid?'

'Nah mate, it's what's I know of such things. Listen and ye listen well. An old sailor friend of mine was hauling machine parts to Calcutta twenty years ago. A maelstrom knocked them off course and blew a hole in their fuel tank. For two weeks they floated around the Bay of Bengal without power or hope.

'One day they came across another ship just wandering about as astray as them. When they got close they boarded and looked for the crew. Not a single person could be found. The engines worked fine, they did, but were turned off. The ship's log had no mention of the maelstrom or any problems. There were no bodies, blood, or signs of foul play. It was as if the sea came in and sucked them to the bottom of the watery depths it did. And it happened quick like too. Meals were sat out half eaten in the mess. A cold cup of coffee sat next to the captain's chair. Jobs were stopped in the middles of doing them. They searched every inch of that ship for two days but found nothing.

'They used parts and materials from the ship to fix their fuel tank and siphon off enough diesels to get things moving. The marked the ship's position and vowed to send a tugger to take it to the nearest port once they was safe.'

'Well so what,' I interjected.

'Calm your young soul down, I haven't finished me story yet. Just prior to shipping off my friend walks into the captain's quarters of the vacant ship for one last looksee for clues. On a whim he looks under his bed and finds a sketchbook. Apparently the captain was an artist. Inside he found hundreds of pictures, all the same thing. I'll be the king of the faeries if he didn't describe what he saw as the spitting image of that there deformed man who now haunts our passageways. Page after page of the man with the caved in head and dark yellow-like eyes.'

'So what does that prove?'

'It proves the captain was obsessed or driven mad by the same man a few decks above us walking about plotting our demise. The sketches got darker. The final pages were nothing more than splotches of red over dark images of the man. In the end there was one inscription that haunted my sailor friend the rest of his natural life. Scratched with obvious duress it said 'do I condemn myself to hell if I accept his offer?'

'That man is no good I tell's ya. You'd be best to stay away from him. Whatever he wants he might not be looking fer on this here ship. Perhaps his business lies in our destination. Let him be and not give any excuse to incur his wrath upon us humble crew.'

I could not tell if the master mechanic was happier just to tell an anecdote than he was afraid of the deformed man. Me though, I did not care of such things. His story had no effect on me. Sailors are famous for their yarns. I was no different and had made up a few tales myself. When you are stuck at sea for months you have to find ways to pass the time.

One blustery night I found myself on deck. I gazed at the sky lost in thoughts of my beloved. A rustling sound on the other side of the ship disrupted my meditation. I turned to see the deformed man with a similar gaze as he sat in a foldout chair with his legs on the railing before the waters. He watched like he waited for Neptune himself to jump out of the ocean and greet him with the pleasantries of a close friend.

He moved little. I was not sure if he was asleep or awake until I gathered the nerve to approach. Unfazed as I was by the master mechanics story, the anticipation of meeting this strange individual proved heavier a burden than I expected. Until this chance sighting he had mainly remained in his cabin away from fearful looks. I walked with soft feet and gazed over the railing onto the sea a few feet from him. I turned as natural as I could force myself and locked eyes with the deformed man.

'Oh beg your pardon sir; I didn't see you sitting there.'

He frowned, and then curled a sneer into a hint of a smile.

'No matter,' he replied with a creaking old voice.

I couldn't place his accent. It sounded similar to an ancient African dialect from a world long since passed away.

'I'll take my leave sir and leave you be,' I said.

I paused. Hearing no reply I walked in the opposite way.

'It's Jonas, is it not?' The man stopped me with his words like a spell.

'You flatter me sir. I didn't expect a passenger to know the name of a lowly mechanic like me.'

'I find it useful to be aware of my surroundings and the people who inhabit those spaces. Can I ask you something?'

'If it pleases you.'

'It does,' he said matter-of-factly. 'Are you not afraid of me and my hideous appearance?' He motioned over his face with his hand.

'We're all God's children sir. I place no judgment on the looks of anyone.'

'God, you say? Is God in the habit of abusing his so-called children for sport?'

'I know little of such matters. I believe free will determines causality more than any of us would probably like to admit though.'

The man drove a stake in my heart with a devilish look. Then he emitted a faint laugh that cannot be described better than like a weasel on helium. 'On that we agree,' he said.

I mustered a fake smile. There were no doubts in my mind that nothing could be put over this man.

'I'll beg your pardon now sir and leave you to your thoughts. I must tend to the engine.'

'Yes, of course. I spend my nights on deck in this spot if you feel the need to exercise your free will to a conversation.' He turned his attentions back to the waters.

My eyes followed his out to the ocean. 'If it pleases the master, take care.'

I performed my duties then went straight to my bunk in the crew's quarters. Sleep failed to take me that night. There was something so different about talking with the deformed man. As I lay staring at the hammock of my master mechanic above me it occurred to me that I did not even know the deformed man's name. Despite my failure at common courtesy there was a level of understanding I had not experienced with any such stranger. That laugh of his stuck with me. Do evil creatures laugh in such a preposterous way? And what did he know of free will that was so intriguing? Probably nothing there aside from my wild imagination. His gentle offer was a nicety. Regardless, I was drawn into seeing him again. That decision had been made in my mind after taking leave.

The next night I returned. The deformed man sat on his folding chair as if he had never left. I approached. Within ten feet the man said, 'Hello Jonas,' without looking my way. 'Forgive me sir,' I eked out as I came closer. 'I could not remember if we had exchanged greetings. I must've introduced myself but failed to ask you your name. I'd rectify that if you'll permit me.'

'Jonas, you are just too polite for words. But, my name isn't a simple thing.'

'I don't understand.'

'My mother was a rather odd woman. Well, odd by the standards of the modern world. Though, her behavior was as commonplace as you experienced in your upbringing I'd wager.

'Where I come from fathers leave before their children are born. It is a custom which trains us for the harsh realities of life.'

'That can be a tough pill to swallow if you don't mind me saying so. Where do you hail from?'

'Understandable. I grew up in a small village of a large empire scattered throughout the unknown world.'

'The unknown world? What is that?'

'A place you have no experience in, nor will you. Be thankful for that.'

I didn't know what he was referring, but I found it fascinating. His words hooked me.

'Go on, if it pleases you sir,' I said.

'Yes, my mother never gave me a permanent name. She objected to the so-called 'Christian nomenclature' associated with formal names. She didn't resist any particular name mind you, just the societal need of such. She insisted others call me as they saw fit and to adopt whatever name suited me in a given situation.'

'That seems rather peculiar.'

'I assure you it is the custom in my village. I thought we were all God's children, didn't you say that? Doesn't that mean our differences are baseless in the eyes of your deity?'

I hesitated. No one enjoys witnessing their hypocrisy exposed.

'I meant no harm sir. So what have people called you through the years?'

'Many things. I've been called Josiah, Cain, Titan, Tomatohead, Azazel, and others.'

'What do ye prefer these days?'

'There is one name that always comes back.'

'And what might that be?'

'Malefactor.'

I blinked and cocked my head to the side like an intrigued hound. His potato face lit up and I could see his beady brown teeth which I could almost swear were sharp fangs. He closed his mouth and spoke with his lips drawn over his teeth before I could confirm.

'I'm but a simple sailor sir, what is the meaning of

'Malefactor'?'

'Someone who accepts the true nature of humanity.'

'I don't understand.'

'No need, you will. Now I've given more details than I usually volunteer. You must tell me of yourself. What of your wife? Gertrude, isn't it?'

'Uhh yes, Mr. Malefactor. I forgot mentioning her to you.'

'Well how else would I have known her name?'

'You're right, of course,' I agreed. 'She's the love of my life.'

'Yet you spend half the year at sea? Maybe longer?'

I hesitated. Was this an insult or an observation? I let it go. 'The sea was my first love. But it's different.'

'You are divided against yourself. There isn't enough time in the world to devote your life to two great passions.'

'I never thought of it in such a way. It as a matter of priorities, not time. I have struggled though. We recently married, so I figured I'd be able to make a decision soon enough. I suppose I've avoided deciding between my wife and the sea. The truth is I love them both.'

'Wouldn't it be wondrous if you didn't have to choose?'

'What do you mean sir, make Gertrude a sailor? She's a piano teacher. The ocean is no place for her.'

'Time is another of God's curses. There is but a finite amount before death. Mortals must decide where to spend it. Most people discover their attentions should have been elsewhere: with loved ones, doing what they love, charity, and etcetera. Regret is the blanket of your death bed.'

'You speak of 'mortals' sir. Are you not mortal yourself?' I released a nervous chuckle. The deformed man stared at me without expression for a full minute. Then he smiled again, revealing those sharp teeth for just another moment.

'What does mortal mean anyway?' he said. 'I'd argue it's more of a state of mind than anything biological. There are many definitions of what it means to be human.'

'As I alluded to before, I'm a simple sailor, sir. I know not of such things.'

'If you'd like, come back tomorrow and we can discuss.'

I said goodbye and headed for my bunk for another sleepless night. The deformed man had a way about him unlike anyone I had ever met. His words were captivating. His voice was creaky and low yet intoxicating. I suppose the gift of the silver tongue is a necessity for someone with such an appearance. The lack of communication skills would have been a further handicap. My shipmates had dismissed and labeled him cursed. I knew if they had just talked to him they might find him as fascinating as I did.

His comments about my divided passions hit me hard. I knew spending so much time away from Gertrude would not be good for her or me. But in my heart I couldn't stop being a sailor. I am alive on a ship. It was my home and my calling. I needed more time to share my love. It may sound callous but I could not decide between Gertrude and my life at sea. I loved them both.

The next night I determined to seek the counsel of the deformed man. There was something mystical about him. His tone portrayed him as someone with an answer just waiting for the question. I could not place what he was getting at but had to discover it for myself.

He greeted me before I could. We exchanged awkward pleasantries. I did a poor job of hiding my angst. I had not slept a wink in two days and my mind shot around like a tennis ball. He could sense my discomfort as soon as I came into contact with those yellow eyes.

'You know, Jonas, I might not have the answers you're looking for,' he said rather poignantly.

'You can tell I'm troubled. How?'

'Let's say I have heightened awareness. I struck a nerve last night did I not?'

I shuffled my feet and looked down with a sheepish look. 'You cut me to the bone sir. I can't bear leaving my wife for my work, yet the thought of giving up the sailor's life sickens me. Is there an answer?'

'There's always an answer. It depends on how you wish to proceed.'

'I beg, tell me.' My voice trembled.

'Suppose you could live forever, shed your mortality and become something more - immortal.' He tapped his fingers on his chair.

'That's the talk of folksy legend, it is.'

'Perhaps,' he said with a raised eyebrow. 'You remember

me speaking of my village? Well, we have many customs, rituals, and potions.'

'And a recipe for living forever? Come on now,' I scoffed. 'You will not offer me eternal life for my soul or something ridiculous like that are ye?'

The deformed man leered at me. 'You're a smart boy, Jonas. I wouldn't expect you to be taken up by charlatans. In fact I sympathize, I really do. What fool would I have to take you for to convince you I have the power to grant eternal life simply by my word?'

I could not look him in the eye. 'I didn't mean to insult you sir.' I took a seat on the ship's railing. He watched me move to my new position every step. 'But we are just telling stories are we not?'

'Are we?' His frigid demeanor did not change.

'Man is mortal, we die, and that has always been true. You must be pulling my leg, sir.'

Malefactor opened his coat pocket, reached in, and pulled out a long skinny case about a foot in length. It was made of solid red mahogany and had but a simple latch.

'And what do we have here?' I asked.

'Look inside, do not be afraid.'

He opened the case then turned it towards me. I stood and moved closer. Inside I saw something long, pointy and speckled. Whatever it was it gyrated ever so slightly. Then one side opened like a yawn.

'It's a snake!' I almost screamed.

'Harmless, I assure you.' The man petted the creature.

'How did that thing stay alive in a box with no air holes in your pocket?'

'There is a magic in this world, Jonas. A select few have found inroads into its mysteries. My people have made many a discovery into this power. My friend here has tasted from the *Elixir of Athanasia*. He has been with me way past his lifespan.'

'Not to be rude,' I cut in. 'But how do I know this isn't a parlor trick meant to make me look foolish?'

'Test the veracity of my claim,' he said, almost expecting my question. 'Find a morsel of food and douse it with poison. I wager you a dollar my snake will live through whatever you offer.'

'Hmm,' I pondered. 'I'm not much for killing defenseless animals, but if you insist I'll oblige.'

I ran to the galley and pilfered a crouton. Then I made my way to the janitorial room and spotted a box of rat poison. I covered the crouton with as much poison as I could dust on and ran back up to the deck. The deformed man sat with the snake twirled around his fingers. Seeing me arrive he laid his hand flat and placed the beast curled around in a circle.

'Did you find your poison?'

'Aye.'

'Then feed him.'

I dropped that poisoned crouton just in front of the snake. Without hesitation it gobbled it up then continued to lick the air with its forked tongue.

I watched as the snake continued to slither around the man's hand. It showed no sign of fatigue, let alone death. Such a small creature should have been dead by the amount of ingested poison.

'Satisfied?' Malefactor said with another of his smarmy smirks.

I didn't respond for another minute. Truth is I was not sure what to say. Never had I seen such a trick. But was it a trick? Could this strange man be telling the truth? And if he was, to what end?

'So let's say I believe ye,' I said. 'What then? If your potion gives eternal life, or at least immunity to poison, what is in it for you to give it to me? What do you want?'

Malefactor closed up his snake back in its box and returned it to his pocket. He leaned back in his chair, propped his feet, and interlocked his fingers with the pointers rested against his chin. He looked me up and down then said, 'I ask that you and your lovely wife live a long life, because that's what you want.'

'And what have I done to deserve such a reward?' My voice strained. I hoped he did not notice.

'You are my type of man. I believe you would do the same as I do given the situation. But I must warn you to think it through. Living forever can have its drawbacks.'

I looked out at the still waters of the ocean to calm my

nerves. 'What of my wife? I couldn't stand to see her die someday.'

'If you wish, I will administer the *Athanasia Elixir* to her. I will speak with Gertrude next time I am in Baltimore, which will be soon enough.'

My fear turned to excitement. What if the deformed man was telling the truth? I still had my doubts but what harm could there be? He asked for nothing in return and would gain nothing from giving me this gift. How could this be a mistake?

'All right sir, I think I'd like to have a taste of yer potion,' I said with crossed arms.

'I'm glad to hear that. I always like to give young people what they want.'

'And you're sure there's nothing you desire in return? I will not see you show up at my door someday looking for my first born will ye?'

His laugh echoed over the deck. 'I have no desire for such things. You don't understand. My reward is seeing you in the position you're about to be in. It fuels me to find another person for whom I can give this gift.'

I forced myself to think through this decision once again.

'Is there anything I'm not considering?' I questioned. 'This seems too good to be true.'

'I can't tell you what to consider or not consider. This is your choice.'

I paced back and forth. The pervading thought was of Gertrude and my life as a sailor. If there was more time to love each then there was not a choice at all, just a formality. 'Ok, sir. I'll take your elixir.'

He handed me a bottle of a purple liquid. He wore a bizarre look on his face, like a proud parent looking upon his newborn for the first time. The potion tasted earthy and dry on the lips. Going down though, it burned. The initial feeling was painful but as it hit my belly warmth caressed all over my body. Then I felt as normal as I did prior to drinking the strange substance.

I opened my eyes to see the man standing in front of me. He rested his hand on my shoulder and said, 'With all the benefits and horrors, I bestow upon you your wish.' He nodded and walked past me towards the lower cabins.

'Thank you, sir, thank you so much,' I offered as he walked away. He did not respond or turn back.

What did he mean by 'horrors?'

Before I could consider it further a loud screeching noise filled the night. Then an explosion rocked the ship. With no time to react the deck turned to fire, engulfing my body like an oil soaked rag.

Total chaos.

The fire burned as smaller explosions went off throughout the ship. A final blast blew me into the sea.

***

So here I fall into the deepest part of the ocean and I can hear nothing but a strange swooshing sound. I breathe the water in and out, gasping for air with every breath. I yearn to have the sweet satisfaction of tasting air. Madness takes me with this torture. The panic is the worst part though. I sink and I know the pressure will increase. There is no chance for rescue or relief.

But what is that sound? It gets louder.

The clouds above the surface dissipate just enough for light from the moon to illuminate the water. I must be a mile down and am moving faster.

Then I spot the source of the noise. A dark silhouette is heading straight for me. As it comes within view I can see a man. Another sinking body? No, it is a swimmer. Their arms move with the grace of a bird gliding through the air.

I am falling faster now. The pressure makes me feel like it will explode from the weight of the water. The burns are excruciating and breathing water with no relief is pure hell.

I open my eyes just enough to see the swimmer approach and grab my shoulders.

It is the deformed man, Malefactor.

He will save me! Oh thank God, this man is my savior.

But we continue to fall. I look him over. His hair floats back and forth and I can see two pointy lumps on his head I never before noticed. He gives me a full smile and I can see his teeth are indeed sharp. His yellow eyes irradiate as he smiles at me.

I want to scream out, 'save me!' but the ocean or my strength will not allow it. I am stuck.

In my head I can hear his voice clear as day. His lips do not move but I hear that weasel-like laughter. That shrill voice rings loud. His deceitful demeanor is on full display as he mocks me. That is when I realize he is not here to save me. He came to watch me fall to a watery prison.

'We won't meet ever again,' I hear in my mind. 'In fact no one will ever see you again. But I will keep my promise to you.'

'You bastard, what are you talking about?' I reply through whatever telepathic means in which we are communicating.

'Your wife, Gertrude. You condemned her too. I leave to bestow all the benefits and horrors of your wish upon her. Remember that as you spend eternity on the bottom of the ocean.'

I want to cry, scream, and destroy the deformed man. But I can do nothing. I am stuck, falling faster.

The weight on my body is unbearable.

Water passing through my lungs is agony.

The coldness of the ocean is numbing.

This is lunacy, pure insanity. How can such a thing be so cruel?

'What are you?' I think in a panic.

The deformed man has not broken that evil smile since he grabbed me by the shoulders. It mocks every decision I have ever made.

In a voice sounding like a host of monsters speaking together it says, 'We are Malefactor.'

It releases me. I sink faster. My last sight before the darkness is that of the deformed man shooting to the surface like a dolphin.

Then, nothing but cold and heavy shadow.

A Splash of Crimson

Catherine Lundoff

Blood-red in the gaslight, a butchered beast, her dress catches my eye before she fades back into shadow, like smoke from an ill-stoked hearth. When I force myself to look at the spot where she stood a heartbeat before, there is nothing, nothing but smoke and shadow and the sense that I am being watched. I close my eyes and turn away, resisting. I will myself to see nothing, to feel nothing.

No one will give a mad governess a post. No one will give a mad governess a post. No one...

The thought trails round and round in my head until I clap my hands over my ears to try and shut it out. I can almost hear her laughing at me from the shadows and I run back down the stairs to Miss Violet's room, seeking refuge.

But I catch myself at the door, my hand poised to knock. Miss Violet is a young lady now, ready to be launched into society. She has no real need of a governess and I am now assuming the less visible, less authoritative role of chaperon and lady's companion with each fortnight that passes. My dismissal cannot be far behind. I must not hasten that day, must not let doubts arise as to my fitness for duty.

Sir Charles says that he has already given my references to several good families of his acquaintance. He must not doubt me. She must not question me.

No one will give a mad governess a post.

I flee for the stairs and the scant safety of my small room. A poker in the barely smoldering fire, the gas turned up, and the shadows are banished. She cannot come to me now and my heart stills, comforted by that hope. It was not always so with us. When she was alive, she was my mistress, almost, but never quite, my friend. Now, she is... she was... I close my eyes.

I drink my cold tea. I shall forget her. I shall look away

when I see that flash of crimson that tells me that she is near, that she is watching. I shall use my Sunday leave to go to church. And there will be never again be any séance that includes me as an attendee. Perhaps I will ask the vicar what he thinks of spirits that linger on after death. Perhaps he has a way to banish them.

Or else, he will think me mad, overexcited, prone to hysteria. So there must be no vicar, not here. Not one who knew her when this house was hers. No one must ever know that I have seen her. No one else sees her. Only me.

I will insist that she stop appearing to me. I was nothing to her in life. She was... nothing to me. Nothing that I can speak of, now. I will banish her with the force of my will, once I summon it to do so.

If I were a Papist, I might confess, might find absolution in their rites. One of their priests might be persuaded to come to the house while the family is out and put her spirit to rest. But what, then, of the servants? One can never forget the servants. Those watching eyes and listening ears, such tales they would bear to Sir Charles! And what, then, of my references?

I fall asleep in my chair as I watch the fire die and the room grow dim. She walks through my dreams but I remember nothing but a flash of red and her face when I start awake at the distant sound of a jangling bell. Yawning maids are tumbling from their rooms to roam the house and scrape the grates, start the fires and fetch the tea. And today, I resolve that I will join them. I will gather myself together, determined to be as I was before, to deny her that last bit of myself that she seems to want to possess.

My dress is changed and my face is washed, all trace of night terrors wiped away when I present myself at the schoolroom for Miss Violet's final series of lessons in deportment. By then, I have drunk my tea and eaten my crust and my hair is in place. I catch a glimpse of myself in the hall mirror as I enter the room, noting with approval the simple tidiness of my dress. I carefully avoid meeting my own eyes, knowing that they must be wild and red from broken sleep.

Miss Violet is a younger version of her mother, beautiful but light and mockingly cruel one moment, deceptively sweet and manipulative the next. I wonder if I might not be in a better light if I asked Sir Charles to dismiss me now, to set me free from this house of dust and shadows and half-glimpsed crimson gowns. But I know that he would never agree, not until her daughter is safely affianced. There are so many dangers that can beset a young lady's reputation; I must endure and linger, abiding by my fate.

The realization that I will see her again makes me tremble, makes my heart race. But I conceal my agitation from Miss Violet. She might use it against me, coaxing favors and sweets as she did when she was younger and saw my weaknesses. Looking at her now, I can see only that she will become her mother one day, perhaps destined to haunt her children's governess in a crimson gown.

But I must not say 'haunt.' It is not a proper word for children, especially well-bred children. What if Miss Violet were to hear me say it and were to repeat it when in company? She might be mocked. My former mistress merely lingers in my imagination. She does not haunt me. I do not see her on the stairs, I do not see her in my room at night, I do not...

Miss Violet's voice cuts through my thoughts. She wants to take the carriage and go visiting. I plead the headache, but am obliged to attend her when she disregards my feeble words. I yield to her wishes and change my dress. Then I fade into the wallpaper of each drawing room we visit, becoming more like a shadow myself with each passing hour. Miss Violet ignores me, all smiles and extravagant gestures while I perch on uncomfortable side chairs and listen to an endless flood of chatter about balls and dances and picnics.

Miss Violet is at the end of her mourning for her mother and all these delights are now once more open to her. I wonder if I shall ever be permitted to end my mourning for her Ladyship or if she will come with me wherever I go, dogging my steps in her crimson gown. Resentment boils through me that her daughter can leave her behind so easily, but I am seemingly doomed to keep her by me forever.

Then, a very young lady tugs on my skirt, interrupts my thoughts with offers of tea and secrets, and I forget Miss Violet and her mother in my charmed enthusiasm, at least for a time. In the next drawing room, a lady's companion sits near me and we engage in commonplace conversation. In the house after that, I converse with the governess. Biscuits, tea, gossip, the weather: it is all so very ordinary that I know that I must have imagined these last few fortnights. I have simply allowed my fancies to run wild, like another governess's charges.

I know that there will be no shadowy red figure waiting for me when we return because I have dismissed her from my mind. I am once more in command of myself. That was all that was required.

Miss Violet notes as much as we enter the carriage to return home. 'You seem quite over your headache, Hill. You look much more the thing now.' She smiles pleasantly at me and I thank her for her trouble and soon we are home and under the eagle eye of her father. Sir Charles seems pleased as well, however, and there are guests and supper and tea to be got through. The guests have brought a handsome young man with them and Miss Violet is immensely diverted. And I, I am happy to be distracted.

When at last I tumble into exhausted slumber, I do not light a candle or turn up the gas in my room. I do not dread. I do not dream. I have nothing to fear.

Yet, when I awake some hours later, I know that I am not alone. I can see nothing. Something cold touches my cheek and I bite back a scream. Something whispers to me, or I think that something whispers to me. The difference is not material.

I do not know what you have to say to me. Are you entrusting Miss Violet to my care? Are you begging me to conceal some past indiscretion of yours from Sir Charles? Or have you come with some message concerning my own fate, my own past indiscretions of thought, if not deed?

These are my thoughts after she is gone, after I twist away from her touch and light a candle with trembling fingers. Perhaps she said nothing and merely came to disturb my slumber. In any case, I cannot recall anything with certainty, not once I am able to stop gasping from swallowing my screams. *No one will give a governess with nightmares a post.* Though of that last, I wonder a bit. Perhaps my drawing room companions have nightmares of their own, things too terrible to speak of over tea and biscuits.

When my terrors abate a bit and the room is bright with gaslight, I allow myself to contemplate all of the things that my mistress might have returned or lingered to say to me. None of them seem sufficient enough to explain why she would come to me, rather than her husband or her daughter. I wish she would not. And yet... some part of me is flattered, drawn to the notion that someone sees me at all, let alone defies Death itself to haunt me.

You see, I am dispensing with any attempts at displaying good breeding. Even as an example to the children. I rise and contemplate my reflection in the tiny mirror that she gave me as a gift when Miss Violet was still a little girl, and a face not my own meets my gaze. I stagger away, trying to close my eyes but to no avail.

I am looking at her, as she was, before she... left me. Her eyes meet mine and I fall into their dark abyss, waking only to the sound of breaking glass and a swath of red on the white wall next to my bed. I imagine that I am still dreaming, still abed. Then I realize that a maid is kneeling next to me and calling for assistance. The room, the mirror, the maid and the red, red blood all turn to gray, then disappear.

***

When I awake, Cook has bandaged my arm and placed a wet rag on my forehead. She is one of a string of motherly, nameless women who have managed the kitchen in Sir Charles' house since my arrival. Each is known as 'Cook' and none stay long.

I am lying in my own bed and there is nothing strange to be seen in my room. Nothing but Cook's calm presence, so rarely seen above stairs, and I am deeply grateful for it. She asks if I still feel unwell and I deny it, because what truth can I utter that will be enough to convince the household of what I have seen?

Thus, my former mistress makes a liar of me after her death, as she did in life. Miss Violet enters, all solicitude and kindliness, but her eyes are her mother's and I close my own against their assault. I cannot bear to look at them again so soon. She mistakes this for illness and is soon gone, fearful that any contagion I may have will interrupt her pleasures. Cook tends to me until I fall into a deep sleep.

Sir Charles comes to see me when I am awake and dressed. He asks such questions as tell me that he fears that I may becoming too old, too unsuitable even to serve as compan ion to Miss Violet. He leaves discomforted, despite my best efforts. My mistress told me once that I would have been dismissed long ago if she had not persuaded Sir Charles that I should stay, and now I thought that she might have told me the truth.

Is this, then, what she has returned to tell me? I cannot make myself believe that, this last bit of foolish longing that she might care for me more in death than in life. Instead, I try to remember the face of my mother, long dead, and try to imagine that it is she who will come to comfort me tonight. But it isn't her face that I see when I close my eyes and try to rest, and I rail at myself for my weakness.

But that is of no avail and her face hovers behind my closed lids, clad in red. I surrender to my terrors. Why is her dress always red? But then I, of all people, know the answer to that puzzle better than anyone else. A memory of broken glass, splashes of red, her gown turning red under frantic hands.

I wonder whose hands they are. Then I remember.

I scream, unable to hold it back any longer, but no one comes to see to me, to pull me back from this nightmare. I must still be dreaming, I must...

I am overwrought. I remember nothing. I am a governess and I am not mad. I cannot be mad. There was never any broken glass, no silk gown turning from blue to red before me. No mistress staring back at me from black eyes growing dim and sightless, despite all that I can do. I am feverish, I am imagining it all. It cannot be true. The servants would have known, would have come at my call.

There was no quarrel, no accident. My mistress comes only to leave her beloved daughter in my charge. I must guide Miss Violet, must help her behave with the utmost propriety until she is married to a gentleman. A gentleman like Sir

Charles. He is depending upon me to assist her because her mother is gone.

Sir Charles would never allow a mad woman near Miss Violet, so I must not be mad. I am her companion, her governess, her mother's trusted confidant. The keeper of her mother's secrets. A man's face, eyes blue, with a dark beard intrudes upon my thoughts. Sir Charles has gray eyes and no beard. I must be mistaken. Perhaps he is just a tradesman, a stranger glimpsed in passing. He was no friend of my mistress's or of Sir Charles'. I would remember him, as I do everyone who visits here.

And yet... and yet... *the sound of shattering glass, the blue turning to crimson, her eyes, dimming, a man's face, my hands, my hands, red, like her dress.* I tell myself I am wrong. I tell myself I remember nothing. I must regain control, must be a proper companion to Miss Violet, must stop imagining crimson, carmine, scarlet, splashes of red. So much red.

It coats my bed, my nightdress, the walls. Everything is red, even Cook's face as she stands over me. And Sir Charles, Sir Charles is the brightest red of all. And she, she is standing behind him in her crimson gown and she is watching him. He is speaking to Cook, but I cannot hear him. I try to speak, but I cannot.

She is watching him and she is watching me. And there is broken glass on the floor now. I heard it crunch under Sir Charles' feet. I hear him come closer and I cringe away. I want to tell him that I remember nothing, no young man, no blue turning red under my hands. No broken glass on the rug.

But he is suspicious. I can see that he thinks that I remember, that I remember what cannot be remembered. He thinks that I will speak, that I will reveal my mistress's secrets. That I will reveal his secrets. But I do not know his thoughts and I would never betray my mistress. That is why she comes to me now, because she trusts me as she did in life.

And I could not have told Sir Charles anything. I would never dream, would never dare. Perhaps it was the servants, with their watching eyes and gossiping mouths. One can never trust the servants, as my mistress always told me. But she trusted me and I loved her. I would not have betrayed her, exposing her secrets to breaking glass and quarrels and blues that slowly turned to reds. I could not.

Because she loved me, just as I loved her. We were like sisters and she confided everything to me. And I would have confided in her, had I any secrets that I might share. But I had only one and she already knew it without my speaking. The young man, with his handsome face and sharp blue eyes, he was nothing to her, still less to me.

He had nothing to do with my foolish fancies, my memories that are not memories. She is in the room now and walking toward me. For an instant, I think I see her pass through Sir Charles and he shudders away, blinking at the empty air. Can he not see her? She is so beautiful and red suits her, far more than the blue ever did. I lose myself in her eyes, just as I did before. Before there was any broken glass or quarrels.

I throw my arms open to her. I was only ever happy when she spoke and I listened. We will be like that again. Like sisters in a tale, one beautiful as twilight sharing her secrets, the other plain and dull but able to listen and to love. We will be like that once more and forget all these foolish fancies and terrors!

But her face grows haggard, her eyes fierce and I realize that she is angry with me. My hands fall away and I wonder if I am to be dismissed. I wonder who will accompany Miss Violet on her visits, who will fade into the wallpaper of a dozen different drawing rooms. I wonder what will become of me and I weep, begging her to forgive me.

There is a strange man in the room now, and he walks through my mistress as if she were made of dust and shadow. He has something in his hand and Cook takes it from him and places it at my lips. I swallow and all the red turns to gray, and then to black.

***

When I awake, the maid tells me that the doctor has come and given me a draught to help me sleep and drive my fever away. Of course, I am ill! Sir Charles is too much of a gentleman to have broken glass and red rugs in his drawing room. My mistress died of a sudden illness, leaving the household bereft. I remember no blue-eyed man, no quarrels.

I see no red, apart from that in a pattern in a shawl on my chair. A gift from Miss Violet, who hopes I am feeling better, so the maid tells me. I am charmed, as what governess would not be when remembered by her charge? Miss Violet will be a fine lady, like her mother.

I do not shudder when my eyes fall on that red again. It means nothing, reminds me of nothing. The mirror, broken, lies on my dresser and I am disgusted at my carelessness in breaking it. But then, I am ill and it was an accident. Broken glass reminds me of nothing except how dear it will be to employ a tradesman to replace it.

Sir Charles brings the doctor again and this time, there is no scarlet-gowned figure for anyone to walk through. I drink my draughts and my broth and my weak tea and try to recover. I must be fit to chaperone Miss Violet to her first ball. It is what her mother would have wanted, if she could not do so herself.

I will be at her side as I was at her mother's. Soon, she will tell me her secrets, as her mother did, and we will grow to love each other like sisters. She is so very like her mother that I see my mistress now each time she looks at me. Perhaps I will tell her my secrets too, since she does not know me as well as her mother did, and cannot know them already.

And there will be no quarrels, no gentlemen, no red stains on blue silk. No broken glass will come between us. I will be governess to her children and I will rock before a warm fire, wrapped in my red shawl. And I will remember nothing.

In these Rooms, these Houses

Jonathan Oliver

He didn't feel like reading. The press of bodies surrounding him, the muggy warmth of the bus, made it difficult to concentrate on the words, and, so, having read the same sentence eight times, he closed the book and looked out of the window.

They were out of the city and into the suburbs. Rows of near identical houses scrolled past; the occasional pedestrian pushing their way through the weather, battling with flapping coats or battered umbrellas. The child in the pushchair a few rows in front of him began to grizzle, accompanied by the sighs and tuts of his fellow commuters, as though one so young should have a better handle on their emotions. He sympathised with the boy; he was tired and fed-up too.

The bus slowed as the traffic bunched up, and he turned back to the window, the procession of houses. Some rooms had lit windows, the curtains not drawn, and through these he could see snapshots of life.

The back of a head rising above a sofa, a television playing something bright and fast; a woman reaching into a kitchen cupboard; a man gesturing emphatically, his glare directed at someone out of sight; a man standing at a kitchen counter, chopping vegetables.

The bus stopped as a traffic light turned red, and the man looked up and caught his eye.

He looked away immediately, his face flushed with embarrassment. There was something shameful in these voyeuristic glances, these domestic peepshows. But even so, as the bus pulled away, he turned from his book back to the window.

The next time they stopped, the doors opened, passengers alighting as a blast of freezing air entered, whipping a stray newspaper along the aisle. It slapped against his leg and when he peeled it away, he saw that it was the property section – prices beyond the reach of most, conveniently situated, robust character; houses that would never be a home, at least not for him.

He scrunched the newspaper into a ball and dropped it at his feet.

The mother with the crying child alighted next and he was glad of the peace, though he felt for the woman now battling through the squalls with the pushchair. He remembered days like that with his own children.

As the bus pulled away he looked back out of the window. Across the way, a man was chopping vegetables in his kitchen. It was the same room he had seen earlier, it even looked like the same house, the same man – he urged him not to look up, though he couldn't stop watching; had no desire, or will, to look away.

The bus took the house from sight, and replaced it with another that looked just like it, and another.

Slightly breathless and feeling dizzy, he returned to his book, hopeful that the words would anchor him, the story sever him from this floating feeling of dread. Again, the same sentence slipped through his mind, and no matter how many times he returned to it, its meaning was lost.

He looked back out of the window and wished he hadn't.

The same man, the same room – but, of course, how could that be? This time the man turned from the kitchen and entered the adjacent living room. (He wished that people would keep their curtains closed. Why display such intimate scenes?) The man kissed a woman seated at a table and ruffled the hair of a child sat beside her. He just had time to look up and catch his eye again before the bus passed.

The first thing he did when he got home was close all of their curtains. They didn't get much traffic on their narrow private road, but he didn't want to put their lives on show.

There was the sound of a key in a lock. The front door opened.

'Brian?'

'In here,' he called.

'God! The traffic was murderous,' his wife said, entering the kitchen. 'How was your day?'

'Yeah, you know...'

'Uh-huh. Darling, would you be a love and chop some vegetables for dinner, seeing as you're here? I just have a quick call to make.'

Most evenings were like this; just the two of them. The boys rarely joined them for dinner; he wasn't even sure where they were.

He went through the vegetable drawer in the fridge and found two carrots that looked almost identical. He sliced the first one into eight approximately equal pieces before applying the knife to the second.

He remembered the man looking at him through the kitchen window – the illicit glance that made the connection. He pressed down with the knife until a sudden sharp pain in his thumb made him look at the chopping board.

There was a fat scarlet disc next to the orange coin of the sliced carrot. He looked at the blood trickling down into his palm as he held up his hand, and a voice at his shoulder said, 'Oh Brian love, you need to be more careful.'

'Sorry,' he said. 'I was miles away.'

It didn't matter how long he left it. Each time he stepped from the door, his neighbour would be stepping from his own home, briefcase in hand, his greeting always a jovial, 'Off to work are we?' which he smiled and silently nodded at; he had no desire to engage him further.

The bus was overcrowded as usual that morning, and as usual he found something comforting in being part of the mass, losing his identity in the crush of swaying bodies. He couldn't see the windows from where he stood in the centre of the aisle, and so could not observe the houses that swept by.

The phone in his jacket pocket vibrated.

DAD. AM AT JASES TONIGHT. OKAY? He texted back FINE before realising that he didn't know which of his teenage sons he was responding to.

When he got to work, he'd barely sat down before his colleague at the adjacent desk leaned over and said, 'You'll never guess what's happened.' How on earth was he supposed to respond to that? Regardless, it didn't seem to matter as Charles ploughed straight on. 'Charlotte is preggers, and I think we all know who the father is, don't we, Brian?'

But he didn't know who Charlotte was let alone the father of her unborn child.

'Honestly, Charles. I have to get on.'

He turned on his computer and glanced around the office as it booted up. All the way down at the other end of the large open-plan room he could see his manager moving behind the window of his private domain. Was he dancing?

After he had entered his password and logged onto the server, he opened the task list for the week only for an explosion of windows to erupt onto his screen. They kept multiplying, layer upon layer of nonsensical data, broken web-links and blank rectangles. No matter what he did, he couldn't shut them down; they appeared far more quickly than he could get to them.

'Ah, it's happened on your machine too,' Charles said, leaning over his shoulder. He shrank away, aware of the warmth of his colleague's bulk so close to his back; the slightly stale odour of his deodorant. 'Yeah, it's the whole office. One of the temps working late last night thought he'd try and download a naughty movie. Bye bye firewall. Anyway, IT are on it but it could take a while. It's sort of hypnotic isn't it?' Charles gestured at the endlessly spawning windows. 'I dunno, what would you call it... An infinity of windows?'

His stomach lurched as he gazed into the screen, and he had to turn away. When he opened his eyes, the room was still spinning, swaying in time with his manager in his room, turning, his arms outstretched.

Like the computers in the office, the traffic was jammed. It took over an hour for the bus to turn up, and it then crawled sluggishly through the city. The bad tempers of his fellow commuters were barely contained by their dark muttering as they jostled against him. It was well past seven o' clock when they reached the outskirts of the town where he lived. One man standing towards the front of the bus had lost his patience, and was berating the driver for being lazy and blaming the bus company for running a shitty service.

The driver responded by stopping the bus and opening the doors.

'I'm going to have to ask you to remove yourself from the vehicle, please, sir.'

'Is this a joke?'

'No. And unless you want to delay your fellow travellers further, and want me to call the police, then I suggest you step down.'

'Are you kidding me?'

One woman sighed deeply and shouted, 'Look, just get off the bus. We're all going to be even later because of you.'

'Yeah!' Another passenger called out. 'Sod off out of it so we can all get home.'

He swallowed, dry-mouthed, feeling the tension rapidly rising. Squeezed as he was between many other bodies, he was acutely aware of his own vulnerability should things get worse.

The driver was barely managing to contain himself now, as he shouted, 'Get off the bus, or I will call the police. Get off the bus, or I will call the police.'

'I ain't moving, mate.'

But he was, thankful for his slim build as he made his way through the press of bodies – not caring about the muttered profanities his egress elicited as he forced his way into the night.

He quickly outpaced the flow of traffic. Had he stayed on the bus it would have taken an hour or more to get home, but on foot he could make the journey in half the time.

Out on the pavement, the houses he passed sat mostly in darkness, as though their inhabitants were stuck in the sluggish stream of vehicles that flowed beside him. The few lit windows he did pass, he couldn't help but glace into. Most of the rooms were uninhabited – television sets playing to themselves, kitchens where pans bubbled with no one to attend them. A lot of the houses were larger than his, and he felt a pang of jealousy as he wondered how much they were worth.

He came to a house fronted by a glass porch, looking out onto a broad, newly-paved drive. He slowed his pace as he gazed into the enormous living room—warmly lit and tastefully furnished. He could imagine himself there, sitting on the plush sofa, reading a book as he sipped a glass of excellent red, waiting for his sons to join them for dinner, perhaps bringing along their girlfriends, introducing them to the family for the first time with shy smiles and coy hand holding. Yes, this looked like a place a family could live and be happy.

He'd taken two steps up the driveway before he realised what he'd done. He backed away, shame and embarrassment making him hurry towards the pavement, the sound of the front door opening and a voice calling out behind him quickening his pace.

It was only when his name was called a second time that he turned.

'Brian, I thought that it must be you. Really, you should have parked the car on the drive. After all, we have more than enough space.'

'I-I don't have a car.'

'Written off the beemer, eh? Don't tell me that you took public transport. Not on a day like this.'

'Well—'

'Tell you what, let's get a G and T in you and then you can tell me all about it.'

As he stepped into the warmth of their home, not even the sound of the door closing behind him gave him pause for thought. Once over the threshold, he knew that he belonged.

The man left him in the lounge as he hurried away to prepare his drink, and as he sat on the sofa, the cushions settled to his form — not too soft, not too hard.

'Just right,' he sighed with pleasure.

A woman entered, her face lighting up at the sight of him. 'Darling,' she said, opening her arms. 'Brian. So good to see you. I didn't notice your car in the drive.'

'Yes, well, managed to write off the beemer, unfortunately.'

She appeared to be a little older than his wife, though she was taller and more shapely. He could feel the push of her considerable bosom as they embraced.

'So sorry to hear that,' she said. 'How on earth did you manage to get here? Not public transport, I hope. Not on a day like this.'

The woman gestured towards the window, but there was not a whisper of traffic on the road.

'There you go, old chap,' the man said returning and putting a drink into his hand.

He wasn't accustomed to drinking at home. He wife took the odd glass of wine with a meal, but he had never really developed the taste himself.

As he took his first tentative sip, the man and woman watched him expectantly. The tonic did little to disguise the burn of the gin and he had to suppress a cough as he swallowed.

'Nice and strong, eh?' The man said. 'Just as you like it.'

He noticed that neither the man nor woman had a drink in their hand.

'Now,' the woman said. 'I've promised a certain someone that if he's very good, he can come down and say hello before he goes to bed.' The woman leaned out of the lounge door. 'Sweetie?' she called.

There was the thunder of small footsteps descending the stairs and then a young boy ran into the room, crying, 'Uncle Brian! Uncle Brian!'

Without thinking, he embraced the boy, looking down at the curly strawberry-blond hair as the child threw his arms around his waist.

He pulled away and looked at the child, his breath catching in his throat as he saw the boy's face properly.

It was as though he were looking at his own son, Stephen, at five-years-old. However, where Stephen had been an unusually surly toddler, seemingly full of contempt for his own father, this boy was clearly delighted to see him.

'Can we play, Uncle Brian?'

He looked up at the boy's parents, who were smiling at this familial scene.

'Okay, but five minutes and then bed, young man,' the woman said. 'I should be getting on with dinner. My love, can you give me a hand in the kitchen?'

The man and woman left.

On the thick-pile carpet of the cosy lounge, he and the boy constructed skyscrapers out of colourful bricks, before knocking them down with savage glee. He lost himself in a playful, constructed Eden, adding to the boy's stories, delighting in their invention.

He sat back on his heels as a thought came unbidden, as vicious as a lance: Barbara saying, *But you never play with them, Brian. They miss you terribly when you're not here.*

'I had to work,' he said. 'I did it for you all.'

'Uncle Brian?'

He came back to himself, to the scatter of plastic bricks and the innocent eyes of the child. 'Yes, erm...'

'I need a wee.'

'Oh, well. Do you need my help?'

'No, thank you.'

The boy scampered off, and he looked down at the house they had been building together. It was an elaborate construction, they had even gone so far as to place a family within: a plastic mum and dad with their plastic boys, each identically happy.

He listened for the flush of the toilet. The boy must have been in there for at least ten minutes now. How long did it take to go to the toilet, anyway? There were no sounds from the rest of the house, either. He would have expected a clatter of pans from the kitchen; the smells of cooking.

It was so quiet he could hear the ticking of his wristwatch.

Outside, the soft whisper of traffic built to a steady roar. The phone in his breast pocket vibrated and he took it out to see that he had missed several calls and there was a text from his wife, *I'm not angry, I just want to know where you are. That you're safe.*

He looked down at the plastic house, a feeling of claustrophobia driving him towards panic.

He left the house, his stride just short of a run. He flagged down a cab and then sat frozen as his mind refused to deliver his address. Eventually, it came to him and the car made the short journey to his house.

There were lights on in the upstairs window when he alighted, but when he stepped through the front door and called out no one answered.

In the kitchen he made himself a sandwich and listened to the sounds of footsteps crossing the ceiling. He waited for his wife to descend the stairs, but the footsteps retraced their path and then there was the creak of the bed settling. When he got into it a short time later, it was cold and she wasn't there. There was no light on in the bathroom and both the boys' rooms were silent. He just had the energy to text his wife – *Home now xx* – before sleep took him.

***

There was no one in the house when he awoke, though the lingering smell of toast in the kitchen reassured him that his wife must have set off early for the day.

As he stepped out of his front door, he turned to the right, expecting to be greeted by his neighbour, but the adjacent door was closed.

It wasn't the weekend already, surely? He looked at his watch and saw that it was Wednesday; that felt about right.

Even so, there was a strange atmosphere on the bus into work. His fellow commuters were as blank as ever, the bus driver, as usual, almost aggressively disinterested—he just felt that he was out of place somehow.

In the office the sense of disconnect continued. He spent much of the morning wondering where he had left himself, feeling like a ghost as he sat on the same chair he had inhabited for twenty or so years.

Charles, for the first time since they had been working together, had dispensed with his usual false bonhomie. He swung his chair fractionally to the right. 'Boss wants to see you.'

'About what?'

'Not a clue. Computers are working again, by the way.'

His manager had rarely been pleased to see him; in fact he was lucky if he ever got more than a slightly raised eyebrow in lieu of a greeting, so when he entered the office and was welcomed with a smile, he felt himself to be on the back-foot.

'Brian, good morning. Do have a seat. Scotch?'

'I... Scotch?'

'I don't usually advocate drinking during working hours, but a little pick-me-up, I find, helps to ease one into the day.'

'I...'

'Excellent. On the rocks, isn't it?'

'I must admit, erm... Neil, that I'm not a big drinker.'

But the Scotch was surprisingly smooth and went down a lot easier than last night's gin and tonic.

'Sorry to hear about the beemer, by the way. Stan told me you totalled it and had to get a bus, of all things, to his and Kit's place. Dreadful way to travel. I would have caught a cab myself.'

Stan and Kit? He must have meant the couple from last night. The fact that his boss knew them went some way to easing his creeping sense of dread. It was possible, he supposed, that they had been introduced at some point and he had just forgotten.

Then he remembered the boy and, 'Uncle Brian! Uncle Brian!'

'Anyway, Brian, two bits of good news. First, you'll be getting a company car, so you don't have to worry about that beemer. Secondly, you've been way below your pay grade for a while now, so how do you feel about a ten kay raise and a promotion to regional manager?'

Ten thousand pounds? He realised then that they would finally be able to afford that extension, and they deserved a holiday, the boys too.

'That sounds wonderful. How about we seal the deal over another Scotch?' he said, raising his glass.

He drove home, a small part of him wondering why he hadn't had to sign anything before taking the car, but his worries were soon allayed by the smooth workings of the vehicle, the smell of new leather, the sense of whispering through traffic, rather than pushing against the homeward-bound exodus.

As he drove onto the motorway, he began to overtake his usual bus, and he slowed, wanting to see the faces of the passengers, wanting them to acknowledge, with an envious glance, that he was no longer part of their herd. All he could see through the heavily-misted windows, however, were pale ovals hunched above seatbacks, or swaying below wrist straps.

Usually there would be more traffic at this time of the day, but his journey home was effortless and he listened with pleasure to the crunch of gravel under his tyres as he parked on their drive; a part of their house that hadn't seen a car for a good decade or more.

He was brought up short as his key refused to turn in the lock. He knew things hadn't exactly been amicable between him and his wife, but surely she wouldn't have gone so far as to change the locks? He rang the bell, and was disturbed not to hear the usual electronic tinkle – just two tones, one high, one low.

Ding-dong.

His neighbour answered the door in a stained apron, a knife in his right hand. 'Brian? Can I help you?' He looked past his shoulder. 'Of course, if you need the space you're welcome to park there, but can I ask what is wrong with your drive?'

'Oh, I'm... this isn't...'

'Your house? No. Listen, I can see you've been overdoing it at work again, and really it shouldn't be our place to say this, but shouldn't you be thinking of spending more time at home with the family?'

'Of course, sorry. Sorry again to disturb you.'

He moved the car to the adjacent driveway, and this time his key fitted the door just fine.

The door opened grudgingly, pushing a slew of unread mail before it. The house was cold and dark. He thought he heard footsteps descending the stairs, but when he looked up there was nobody there. He walked from room to room, always with the feeling that each time he entered, somebody had just left.

The house felt wrong, and was this actually their lounge? He couldn't remember the sofa being that colour, and he certainly wouldn't have permitted that wallpaper with the bunches of tropical fruit and the parakeets. However, when he looked at the mantelpiece, the photo that stood there clearly showed him and his wife, and their two smiling boys. He wondered where that had been taken. They looked happy.

He took off his tie and sat for a moment in silence, looking at the blank screen of the television and his dim, distorted reflection.

He wished he could recall having lived in this house, but he didn't have any recollection of the place at all. Clearly they had created a home together; the pencil marks on the wall by the door showed the boys' heights, year by year; the photos on the bookshelves showed beach holidays they had apparently taken together – he supposed he must have been in love, the happy smile on his face in one picture was testament to that.

He and his wife should be celebrating, toasting his promotion with champagne and an excellent meal, but there was nobody here to acknowledge his success

As he sat and waited dawn rose. He couldn't remember sleeping, though he supposed he must have, as he didn't feel tired. He half expected to find the company car gone when he looked out the window – if anything, that really had felt like a dream – but it was still there.

He drove to work. He had his own office now, adjacent to his boss's and almost identical. He opened up a spreadsheet on his computer and stared at it blankly for a few moments before he realised that he actually had no idea what he did. The phone rang and he picked it up to be told that his first meeting of the day was here.

The door opened and a large man blustered into the room, gripping his hand in a handshake that bordered on the aggressive.

'Great to see you finally being given the recognition you deserve, Brian. Long overdue. Long overdue.'

For the whole of the hour that the man was in his office, he had little idea what he was talking about, though the interjections that he were made were greeted with enthusiasm and emphatic agreement. By the end of the meeting he had come to the realisation that he *did* deserve his promotion and, really, what had taken them so long? He clearly was one of the most efficient and incisive members of staff they had.

Buoyed by his new sense of success, that evening it felt as though his car drove him, rather than the other way around. He sat back and relaxed as the streets scrolled past the windows; the glass and metal towers of the business district stepping down to make way for the grimy terraces at the edge of the city, these, mercifully, giving way to the greenbelt that, in turn, was soon threaded with streets of neat semi-detached houses and soulless bungalows. Once he would have stopped here, but such a vehicle as he rode in didn't belong on any of the driveways he passed. Such a man as he would not be at home in any of these houses.

The properties he passed became more widely-spaced and larger; grand gardens given each house the illusion of privacy, the residents the lords and ladies of their own exclusive estates.

The car slowed and indicated, turning into a long, gravelled driveway that led to a three-storey Georgian house. As soon as he saw it, he knew that this was what he had always envisioned for himself. There really was no other place for him, or those he loved.

The porch was lit by the soft glow of a carriage lamp. The door opened onto a large hallway and reception room. Everything was tastefully furnished , beautifully appointed, nothing like the house he had set off from that morning. That, after all, hadn't been his home.

Whatever was cooking in the kitchen smelled delicious. As he sat on the sofa in the vast living room, a drink was put into his hand, a kiss placed gently, and warmly, on his cheek. He smiled as her subtle perfume lingered. The solemn-faced boy that was ushered before him, just before seven o'clock, told him all about his day at school, and then beamed with delight at the praise he received, throwing his arms around him and saying, 'I love you, Daddy,' before scampering off to bed.

There was soft music coming from somewhere. In the fireplace a log popped and the flames wavered. He looked at his glass and realised that it was empty. He waited for a while but no refill was forthcoming. The lazy warmth emanating from the fire was making him soporific and his head fell back against the cushions for a moment before he snapped awake. He looked at his still empty glass and got to his feet.

Beyond the living room, the corridor felt narrower than it had before. A chill breeze blowing under the front door cut across his ankles. The kitchen door was closed and there were no sounds issuing from the other side.

He knocked. 'My love? Hello? Any chance of another drink?'

When no one answered, he opened the door and stepped through.

The woman who was kneeling beside a seated figure at the table looked up at him with accusing eyes. He had never before been looked at with such hatred, and it made him take a step back.

'And where,' she shouted, 'have you been?'

He recognised her, but, for the moment, couldn't place her face.

'Brian? Didn't you hear me? What happened to you?'

This was... Barbara. His wife? He wanted to take another step back, close the kitchen door, return to the well-appointed living room, gaze sleepily into the fireplace. But when he turned to look behind him, he found not a carpeted corridor, but a narrow flight of stairs.

'Brian! I'm talking to you.'

'I'm... I'm sorry, my love.' He took two steps into the shabby kitchen. There was that stain on the ceiling, put there one disastrous pancake day; those sun-faded curtains that they had always intended to replace but had never got round to. With a sinking feeling, a dread that filled the pit of his stomach, he knew for certain that this was his house. No, *their* house.

'Never mind where you've been, Brian,' Barbara said. 'The fact is that you're never here for the boys.'

There was a sob from the young man sitting at the table and he moved round so that he could see him. It was his son... Jase? No, not Jase. That was who he had been going to stay with the... was it the other night? This was Stephen, with this mousy brown hair, his perpetually slumped shoulders. He of the monosyllabic answers, sneers and contempt for his parents. He sat, his head in his hands, blood dripping from his nose, falling to the table; fat ruby coins.

He didn't know where their other son – Paul – was; Barbara probably didn't either.

'What happened?' He managed to say.

'He's been dealing again. I'm surprised he wasn't killed for his troubles this time.'

He remembered playing with a child; their triumph and joy as they constructed plastic castles and houses, peopling them with happy plastic families. He remembered warm arms around him and, 'I love you, Daddy.' He remembered houses that should have been theirs, lives that had been lived, but not by them. He remembered looking into passing rooms with yearning and envy.

He supposed he could tell them about his promotion and the company car, but he didn't think that they would believe him.

He went over to the kitchen door, closed it and opened it, again and again – closed, open, closed, open. Each time, however, the scene beyond stayed the same: the same short hallway, the same narrow flight of stairs.

'We don't have to stay here,' he said, turning back to the kitchen.

'This is our home,' Barbara said.

'Trust, me, I'd rather be anywhere else than this fucking dump,' said Stephen.

He looked at them looking back at him, hurt and confusion in their eyes. It *would* work, he just had to trust in his own instincts, believe in what he wanted for all of them.

He took Barbara's hand, put his other hand on Stephen's shoulder.

'Come outside. I can fix this.'

Barbara looked at him and he thought she might be afraid. 'What do you mean?'

'We deserve better than this.'

Reluctantly, his wife and son followed him outside.

'Come on,' he said, opening car's passenger door, 'in you get.'

'Brian, just tell us where we are going.' Barbara said.

'Just trust me on this. Please.'

Barbara's features softened a little. 'You've got a lot to make up for.'

He got into the driver's seat and turned the ignition key. It took a few tries to get the car started, as though it had sat unused for the best part of a week, but finally, with a sound somewhere between a cough and a groan, the engine spluttered into life.

He looked to either end of their road. He could see nothing beyond the weak glow of the streetlights but the night.

Though there was nobody to see, he indicated left and turned out of their drive.

None of the windows were lit in the houses they passed, and once past the last streetlight, the headlights illuminated only the road before them.

'Dad, where the are we going?' Stephen said.

He shifted into fourth gear and tried to ignore the darkness that surrounded them. He pictured the miles of road before them, the night giving way to broad swathes of countryside – rolling hills, distant mountains, a far lake catching the moonlight. He pictured the road narrowing, trees crowding in on either side, a canopy far overhead through which soft starlight filtered down. He pictured coming to iron gates that swung silently open at their approach, revealing a long, broad driveway, running straight to a large house. He pictured the warm glow coming from the windows, the soft crunch of gravel under their wheels as they came to a stop.

He pictured all of this as he willed the darkness to give way.

'Brian, where on earth are we going?'

'Home,' he said, shifted into fifth gear, and put his foot down.

A Framework

Richard Farren Barber

The first thing Jackie noticed was the noise. Not just one sound but layers. Her heels against the stone floor, reflected around the strange archways of the corridors. Voices, even when there was no one speaking. The clank of water through rusted pipes. The mournful echo of a ringing telephone.

It was just a trick of the architecture, she understood that, and yet she had to resist the urge to hold her hands over her ears to block out the other sounds as Franklin spoke to her.

He walked the corridor at speed, as if in an urgent need to be somewhere else. His own footsteps were light, almost silent, and Jackie wondered whether this was a talent he had acquired over years of working inside the building. When he spoke his voice was low and his words did not echo. 'It takes a while to get used to the place,' he said.

Jackie nodded, not trusting herself to speak.

'Office hours are typically Tuesdays between four and six, but to be honest you can set your own timetable. The Dean likes you to be visible, he isn't a big one for having us hide in our cells on the pretext of research.'

'Cells?' Jackie asked.

'Sorry, force of habit. Call it an office if it makes you feel better.'

She looked down the corridor. The stone floor. The walls decorated with cracked-glaze tiles of cream and brown that looked like they were original features. The ceiling curved into an arch above her head and she attributed the strange acoustics of the building to this feature which gathered together all the noises and dispersed them again.

'It used to be a Victorian Asylum. You knew that, didn't you?'

'I read it somewhere,' Jackie said. She tried to shrug it off. It didn't mean anything. She wasn't superstitious and the ping of alarm she felt at the back of her mind, like a sonar beacon, was just first day nerves, nothing more than that. She was sure of it.

'Look down the corridor,' Franklin instructed her. 'The walls narrow. In places it's impossible for two people to pass. It was deliberate, so that in the event of a riot they could better contain the inmates.'

'Thanks, I'll bear that in mind.'

'Of course, there will be times when you'll probably think it would be easier to cope with Victorian mental patients than our students, but at least they're unlikely to riot.'

'Not like the good old days.'

Franklin didn't reply and Jackie wondered if he had been one of those straight-laced A* students who would no more consider arguing with authority then he would come to class unprepared. Pity, there was nothing more appealing than the righteous indignation of a bunch of cosseted eighteen year old kids who hadn't worked out that the world did not revolve around them.

'This is your... office.'

She noted the pause and smiled at his kindness. Maybe she had been too harsh on him. He was trying to help, she had to at least give him that.

The door to her office was closed. A wooden arch; it reminded her of church doors or maybe the entrance to a monk's cell. Her name was already on the plate beside the door: *Dr Jackie Waring*. She probably had Franklin to thank for that. She could sense him standing beside her, waiting for her to notice.

'Thanks,' she told him. 'Thanks for the tour.'

'I'm just next door if you need me,' he said, nodding down the corridor.

Towards the thin end, Jackie thought. She could imagine the inmates clawing at each other to try and get through the narrow corridor. She imagined their screams bouncing off the walls until this small space filled with the sounds of their madness.

The woman in the admin office had given Jackie a set of keys and a scrap of paper with her username and password printed on it before palming her off on Franklin. There were two small, bright Yale keys that looked like they had been cut just an hour earlier, and then a black jailer's key which matched the keyhole in the door.

The handle was an iron ring. After turning the key in the lock Jackie pulled the ring to the left and then the right before hearing the heavy clunk of a latch disengage on the other side of the door.

Her office was sparse. A wooden table sat in the middle of the room with a computer screen in the centre. Compared to the rest of the room the modern furniture looked wonderfully anachronistic; take it away and there would be nothing to anchor this place to the present day.

There was a fur rug on the floor; a dirty brown thing that looked like the creature had simply laid down and died there. The floor was red brick, the ceilings the same glazed tiles that reminded Jackie of municipal swimming pools and London Underground stations.

The door wanted to swing shut behind her and so she took a piece of card from the desk to wedge it open. She didn't want to be trapped inside here, listening to the echo of feet passing by in the corridor outside.

She sat down at the desk, *her* desk, and stroked the wooden surface with her fingertips. She wondered what Franklin was doing next door, if he had already forgotten her and was immersed in marking a pile of first year assignments.

'Better make a start,' she muttered, and then made a pact not to talk to herself because her voice echoed back at her from the curved walls of the cell. 'Start. Start. Start.'

The chair creaked when she sat down. It creaked when she leaned forward to open the first drawer in the desk. *Have to get some WD40 on that before it drives me insane*, she thought.

The drawer was empty; just a curl of pencil shavings and a dust bunny huddled in the corner. The next drawer down was the same. Not even a pen or a piece of paper. She thought about going to the next cell to ask Franklin for a few emergency supplies – she wasn't sure she trusted herself to navigate through the maze of corridors to the admin office yet. She'd probably have to leave a trail of breadcrumbs to find her way back to this room.

Someone passed across the open doorway. The movement

caught Jackie's eye but by the time she responded the doorway was empty once more. She shrugged; nothing special, it was a corridor – what was she expecting? Even though most of the kids were tucked away in lecture rooms listening to their tutors drone on, it didn't mean that there weren't other people moving around the building.

So that wasn't why the motion had unsettled her.

She stared into the corridor. Her view was limited to the thin lozenge of the curved wall opposite her door.

It took her a moment to work out what was wrong. She had seen the movement but there had been no accompanying footsteps.

She got up from the chair – creak – and stepped across the floor. Even on the rug her muffled footsteps still sounded through the room. She peered out into an empty corridor. She heard Franklin's fingers tapping on a computer keyboard and she considered going into him, except what would she say? That the building had spooked her? That she was seeing things that didn't exist? The title beside her door said it clearly: Dr Jackie Waring. She wasn't some schoolgirl who allowed her imagination to run wild. She wasn't prepared to let Franklin think that about her.

The corridor was empty. She checked. Made absolutely certain.

It was possible that whomever had passed had already turned the corner or taken one of the spiral stairwells that joined together the passages of the old building. Of course that was possible.

She placed her hand on the door and considered closing it, shutting out the corridor. But that could hardly make things better; trapped inside her cell with the sound of her own breathing reflected back at her. Her watch said that it was a quarter to three, which meant that in the next ten minutes the corridor outside her room would be filled with students rushing between lessons. Given the stillness of the building the idea of a horde of eighteen and nineteen year olds felt almost impossible.

Back at her desk Jackie was unable to concentrate. She turned on the computer and tried to enter the username and password from her scrap of paper but either her ability to copy type had been compromised or there was something wrong with the system. Three times she tried to enter the combination and each time the machine emitted a high-pitched beep and a message on the screen told her that her username and/or password were not valid. After the third attempt the message informed her that her account had been locked and she needed to contact her network Administrator for help.

'Damn,' she muttered. The word came back to her in layers. She recognised the first few echoes as her own but after that it seemed to grow deeper and harsher until they bore no resemblance to her voice.

It took a long time for the sound to fade, and even when Jackie was sure the echoes had ceased it felt like the word was still present in the room.

She picked up the phone and then realised she had no idea who to call. Tacky blue patches beside the phone looked like they may once have held in place a telephone list, but whoever had occupied the room before her had obviously decided that they needed to take everything – telephone list included.

At least it gave her a valid reason to see Franklin. A reason that didn't involve jittery first-day nerves or the uncomfortable way sound travelled through the room.

She stood up from her desk and the screaming started.

The voice, a woman's – young, painfully vulnerable – ripped through the air. It triggered an alarm bell deep inside Jackie. There was something primal about the sound. It cut through the air; no echo, no distortion, and then stopped.

Jackie's arms trembled. The curved ceiling of the room pressed down upon her until it felt like the brickwork stopped just above her head. Her mind replayed the sound over and over. She looked to the doorway, expecting to find the girl standing there.

The corridor was empty. She checked in both directions.

Franklin's door was closed and Jackie hesitated – caught between knocking and barging straight on in. She compromised on rapping her knuckles against the door even as she pushed it open.

Franklin's room was chaos. There was a bookcase at the back of the room with shelves bowing under the weight of books. His desk was in the centre of the room, just like Jackie's, but it was lost under a sea of paper. He sat with his head bowed to reveal a patch of thinning hair. When he looked up at Jackie he blinked, his eyes magnified behind thick coke-bottle lenses he had not been wearing when he had showed her around.

He whipped off the glasses and pushed them aside. 'Is everything okay?'

'Didn't you hear her?' But as soon as she spoke Jackie felt the doubt begin to creep in.

Franklin shook his head slowly. 'Who?'

'The woman. She was screaming. How could you not hear?'

'These corridors have strange acoustics. It can take some time to get used to them.'

'I heard a woman screaming,' Jackie said. *Did you?* She heard the doubt inside her own head and she wanted to scratch it out. This was not going to happen again.

'Sound carries in this place. It might have come from the canteen. Maybe it was laughter?'

'She was in agony.' But now all she had was the memory of what she had heard. Each passing second eroded the certainty she had felt when she had burst into Franklin's room. Could she be sure it was a woman in pain?

'Some of the labs are above us. They get up to some pretty hairy things in there.'

'Aren't you concerned?' Jackie asked.

'I've heard a plethora of strange sounds around this building. You learn to tune out, or...'

From out in the corridor there came a loud bang and then voices swelled like waves cresting on an ocean. The passage filled with sound; the slap of footsteps upon brick and the crash of a door slammed against the wall.

'Class change,' Franklin said.

The corridor filled with bodies. A thick rush of students passed by the open door.

'Stand back, you don't want to be pulled in. We may never find you again.'

He almost laughed as he spoke and Jackie heard the giddy relief in his voice at the interruption. She wondered what he had been on the verge of saying; you learn to ignore the sounds of the building, or... what?

The torrent of students didn't let up. It was like a fast flowing river. She couldn't imagine stepping out into the corridor. She would be swept along with the pack. She heard fragments of conversations; voices raised to be heard above the cacophony. And did some of that sound like screaming? She couldn't be certain, not any more.

She stood just inside the doorway of Franklin's office. Feeling awkward, like an unwelcome guest unable to leave in the middle of a rainstorm.

'I'll just wait it out,' she said. She noticed that now her voice was soft, muted. It was possible that Franklin might not even hear her, but he nodded as if he did.

The crush of students stopped as quickly as it had arisen. In seconds the corridor was empty once more. The door slammed shut behind the last of them and the sonic boom spiralled down the corridor as it echoed into silence. For a moment the voices lingered like a thousand enraged ghosts trapped within the walls of the old asylum, and then they too faded and it was silent once more.

Jackie returned to her office without saying anything further to Franklin. There was nothing she could think of to say.

It's happening again.

No, she told herself. *No it isn't. This isn't like before. I'm over that now.*

She sat down at her desk and then remembered the initial reason she'd had to speak to Franklin: the useless computer still sitting at the side of her desk with *Your account has been locked. Please contact your Network Administrator* still showing on the screen.

Jackie turned off the screen to stop it glowering at her. She could sort it out later, once she had found the courage to venture around the building without a guide.

She looked around the inside of her cell.

Office.

Cell. She hated the word because of the way it made her feel: trapped inside the room, but there was no denying it was appropriate. She didn't know enough about Victorian medical practices to take a guess at what might have happened within these walls but her imagination was happy enough to fill in the gaps. It had probably been something mundane like a store cupboard and yet her eyes searched for signs of iron rings fastened to the walls from which one of the patients might have been restrained. When there was no evidence she moved on; a simple wire-framed bed in the middle of the room with a paper-thin mattress. The young girl – because it had to be a young girl, didn't it, she had heard her – lying on the narrow bed with her ragged nightshirt sticking to her body, damp from the night terrors.

Jackie pushed away from her chair and stood with her shoulders pressed against the curved wall of the room. For a moment she saw the room from two places at the same time: She was Dr Jackie Waring, looking down on a destitute girl tied to the bed in the middle of the room, and she was a stick-thin girl fastened to a bed and looking up into the face of the woman watching her. Both scenes were equally real.

Jackie pushed her fists into her eyes to rub away the vision. She heard her own voice mewling in repressed agitation. Part of her understood that the door of the cell was open and she could just walk out into the corridor and out of the building and she would be free because there was nothing holding her to this place. And yet she found she could not move. If she left the room she would simply dissolve. Cease to exist.

The image of the girl on the bed faded to be replaced by her desk and her chair. And yet Jackie didn't trust that if she reached out and touched them that they would really be there. She tried to picture the room with books and papers and posters covering the raw brick walls. She would have a vase of flowers that she would change every week and she would bring in a stereo to push out the silence. Something harsh and rough that couldn't be bullied into submission – Nirvana or Megadeth perhaps.

She was starting to take control of the room once more, for it to return to an office rather than a cell, when she heard the sound of footsteps out in the corridor.

A single set of footsteps, running across the bare bricks. Somebody late for their next class, perhaps?

They grew louder. Closer.

Jackie watched the open doorway. Waiting to see the girl

in the dirty white nightshirt flee past her. But that made no sense because the girl would be barefoot and the sound was clearly of hard boots against the stone.

The footsteps passed the open doorway and carried on down the corridor. But no one passed by Jackie's office door.

A child began crying. The sound crept into the room. Slipped inside Jackie's consciousness. There was a loud slap; palm to cheek, and the child stopped.

Jackie approached the doorway with baby steps. Halfway between her desk and the corridor there was a pocket of cold air, but as soon as Jackie noticed it it was gone. A stink of raw meat drifted past and was immediately replaced with a sweet, rich stench that caught the back of Jackie's throat and caused her to gag.

The corridor was dark and Jackie immediate understood that the lights had failed. Then she realised that the darkness wasn't complete; there was enough light for her to see the brickwork under her feet and the curve of the ceiling above her head. Off in the distance the light grew brighter and she realised the source was a ragged row of candles that gave off a thick black smoke and a pale yellow light. Now she could smell the tallow from the candle, greasy and dirty.

The closest candle was at the end of the corridor and Jackie walked past Franklin's room to reach it. The wax column was trapped behind a wire frame and the wall above it was stained with soot.

This makes no sense, Jackie thought. What sort of a place would have candles burning, even behind a metal grille?

But it was real. She could smell the flame and she could feel the heat against her cheek.

A wail, like a wolf's cry, ripped through the silence of the corridor. Jackie whirled around but it was impossible to tell where the sound came from. She peered into the shadows at the other end of the hall. The darkness seemed to shift and move beneath her scrutiny. It was just the way the light from the candle moved the air, she knew that, and yet it was impossible to push away the thought that the darkness was actually alive.

Voices chattered and then the echoing sound of footsteps approached her. 'Who's there?' Jackie asked. Her voice clashed against the other sounds in the corridor but there was no reply. The footsteps grew louder until Jackie was sure that the person had to be standing right beside her and even the gloom of the ill-lit corridor would not be enough to hide them, and yet there was still no one in the passage.

There was a shuttering sound like a flock of pigeons taking to the air and the row of fluorescent lights above her head burst into life. Jackie turned back around. There was no candle. There was a small recess in the wall and the bricks immediately above the recess were stained black, but if there had ever been a candle there then it had been removed decades ago.

Jackie put her hand on the recess. The stone was hard and cold. She wanted to laugh, but she didn't know where the urge came from or what it meant and so she didn't trust it.

'This isn't happening,' she muttered to herself. The curve of the passageway picked up her words but when they returned to her they were too soft to be audible. They came back as nothing more than a hiss. 'They told me I was cured.' The corridor returned the comment.

She stood pressed against the side of the wall, as if afraid a raging horde of students would come charging through at any moment. She looked up at the fluorescent tubes above her head as if they were miracles; as if she had been born in the age of candles and the idea of electric light was alien to her.

The pipes running along the bottom of the wall gurgled. There was a loud thump from somewhere else in the building that rolled through the corridor and passed away. She walked up to Franklin's door and pressed her ear to the wood. There was no sound from inside the room. No tap of fingers on a keyboard.

She held the iron ring of the door but for a moment she was too afraid to open it. When she pressed down she heard the mechanism on the other side of the door clank. She pushed the door open and the lights failed again.

Jackie swallowed down a scream.

A single candle flickered in the far corner of the cell. The flame fluttered, rising and falling, carving bright yellow slashes across the room.

There was a simple bed in the middle of the room. A wire frame. A thin mattress that looked worn and faded and stained with blood. Thick manacles hung from the steel frame.

'Franklin?' Jackie whispered. 'Franklin!'

There was nothing else inside the room. No desk. No computer. No bookcase. Just the simple bed and those manacles.

Jackie turned back into the hall. She felt the terror rising within her. It came like a flood. It stopped her thinking about anything except the empty bed. She heard her voice; strained and strange, reflected back at her from the wall of the corridor. 'No. No. No. No.'

She passed the open door to her own cell and was too terrified to look inside, but didn't have the strength to stop herself from turning her head as she drew level. A simple bed. The girl lying on the mattress had her hands fastened to the frame by heavy manacles. She twitched her head from one side to the other and Jackie could barely make out her words. 'No. No. No.'

There was a figure in the shadows at the side of the bed. He hovered out of view for a moment, observing the girl, and then moved forward.

Franklin.

His hair was thin and he moved with a stoop that suggested he had spent his entire life bent over. He wore a dirty white doctor's coat that flapped open at the front. He reached out to stroke the forehead of the girl lying fastened to the bed and Jackie shuddered in revulsion.

Jackie moved, as if the doctor was trying to touch her. The girl on the bed mirrored her movement. It was like looking into a distorted glass. The girl's face; beneath the haunted looks and the wasted skin and the dirt and the pain. Beneath everything the girl's face was Jackie's.

Jackie pushed back from the door and the scream rose through her throat.

A hand touched her shoulder.

'Come on now, let's get you back.'

Another voice joined the first. 'I told you this couldn't work.'

The hand on her shoulder pressed harder and a second

hand took her elbow and tried to steer her into the room.

'No!' She lashed out her arm and fastened her hand to the side of the door to stop herself being dragged inside. Over her shoulder she felt, rather than saw, the presence of a man a little shorter than she was.

She pulled free of Franklin's grip and ran down the corridor. The overhead lights fluttered into life and harsh white light poured down into the corridor. Jackie looked over her shoulder. She could see the open door to her cell, but there was no sign of the man in the white coat.

She stopped in the corridor. Her heart raced inside her chest and the sound of her rapid breathing bounced back to her from the wall.

'I am not sick,' she said.

Her vision flickered and the corridor plunged into darkness. The doctor stood in candlelight and when the electric lights recovered he was no longer there. As Jackie turned towards the door at the end of the corridor she was sure she felt the faint pressure of his hand on her arm, but it was gone as soon as she noticed it.

She pushed her way through the double doors and out of the corridor into another passage. Halfway along the corridor she saw a gap where one of the spiral staircases twisted upwards to the next floor. Somewhere up there were the new lecture rooms: square corridors with straight walls and carpets on the floors. She ran toward the bottom of the stairs.

And the lights failed again.

Doctor Franklin stood in front of her. The stench rose up from his coat; the iron-heavy stink of blood and the sour taste of chemicals.

'This has been allowed to go on long enough.' When he spoke he was talking over her shoulder. Jackie turned her head to see a second man in a lab coat approaching.

'Who are you?' she asked.

She caught a glimpse of herself and noticed she was wearing the ragged dirty-white nightshirt of the girl on the bed. She wiped her hands across the material to prove that it was real.

Franklin held out his arms. 'Come back to your treatment room, Jacqueline.'

Jackie whipped her head from one side to the other. 'I'm not sick. Not this time.'

'Come back,' he said. His voice was soft. She could imagine him using it to hypnotise people.

He took hold of her wrists and held them together. Jackie struggled but even when she screamed he seemed unmoved. She wondered what horrors he had seen that had inured him to her suffering.

The lights flickered on. She stood at the bottom of the staircase buffeted by students streaming down from one of the lectures. Her hands were held out in front of her and a couple of the teenagers stared at her, but most simply ignored her.

'I'm ill,' Jackie whispered.

The corridor was plunged back into darkness. This time she sensed it a fraction of a second before it happened. The smell of burning candles and the taste of thick smoke warned her.

Doctor Franklin wrapped his arms around her and started to push her back down the corridor towards her cell. Even when she screamed her voice bounced against the walls and returned to her; as ineffectual as her attempts to free herself from his grip. He was only a small man of slight build, and yet his muscles defied her attempts to escape.

The door to her cell was still wide open and inside there was only the wire-frame bed.

'Let's get you settled and then we can try again,' Franklin said.

The lights flickered. For a moment Jackie stood in the doorway bathed in hard electric light and looked in on an office in which she was sitting behind the desk tapping on a keyboard. She tried to scream but the woman did not look up and then the smell of candles returned and the woman and the desk and the office melted away to leave only the thin bed.

Franklin kicked her legs out from underneath her and Jackie crashed onto the bed. The steel frame buckled under her weight. By the time she had recovered Franklin had secured one of her wrists and the doctor on her other side was battling to pull her hand through the other restraint.

'Let me do that,' Franklin said. He walked around the head of the bed, out of Jackie's sight before returning on her other side. He took a rough hold of her wrists and forced it through the open jaw of the manacle before snapping it closed.

'You can't afford to be weak,' Franklin said to his colleague. 'They're stronger than they look.'

Jackie pulled against the metal cuff but all that did was scrape the metal edge against her wrist and slice a thin curl of skin away from the bone.

'Settle down,' Franklin said. 'There's no point in fighting, you'll only hurt yourself.' He turned behind him to the other man. 'Are you still taking notes?' He paused, waiting for a response. Jackie heard nothing, but a moment later Franklin spoke again. 'Then we'll continue.'

Running a Few Errands

Su Haddrell

Mrs Dandy looked out of the window and checked the sky. The clouds were high, covering the atmosphere like a thin cotton sheet. The day was still early and Mrs Dandy judged that the sky would be blue at just around lunchtime, which would be nice if she decided to stop off in the park. She neatened the bed sheets, carefully bending down to tuck them beneath the mattress, her old back giving little complaint today. There were some days where her joints and back decided they were very much going to feel their decades of age and she was not going to be able to smell the fresh air, or pop into the bakery, or indeed do very much else other than sit in her armchair watching reruns of Dad's Army on the television. On those days, the weather always seemed a little darker, the room a little colder and her frail body a little smaller. On those days, when she couldn't even take care of Mr Dandy, or let Betsy out the back, she wondered if she would never move from the confines of her armchair again, or if she would simply fade into its depths until she was as much a part of it as the faded brown fuzz of material, or the creaking springs that held the thing up.

But today the sun would shine and the tightness around her knees and hips and behind her shoulders did not seem so pronounced, and so she would be able to trundle into town for a bit of a wander. She put on her favourite purple cardigan and slipped her softer, more worn pair of shoes onto her feet. She walked out of the little room and turned left, opening the door into the larger bedroom next to her own. Arthur lay unchanged. The air smelt stale and so she moved across the room and parted the curtain to open the top window. The terrier from across the road was barking again. Its owners left it out in the front garden during the day, where it took great pleasure at barking at anything that passed in front of the gate with short high pitched yaps that ricocheted around the houses. Mrs Dandy couldn't stand the thing. She took great pleasure from Betsy, their own little cocker spaniel who was happily docile and quiet. They'd had Betsy since she was a puppy, a round black bundle of fur that liked to wriggle on her back for belly rubs. Letting the curtain fall again, Mrs Dandy went and perched on the side of the bed. She took Arthur's frail hand in her own. His fingers were still cold and the papery skin felt as delicate as cobweb. He had been handsome once, and she still saw his thick dark hair and long jaw, long after it had been displaced by withered sagging flesh and fine white strands against his smooth scalp. They had been married forty five years that year, and she still gazed on him as fondly as the day they had started courting.

Arthur didn't move or react to her presence as she quietly told him of her plans for the day, and when she would be back. His jaw had dropped slightly and she pulled her head back, choosing to believe that she imagined the delicate scent of rot on his unmoving lips. She said she'd leave Betsy to keep him company as the little dog couldn't make the journey into town like she used to and preferred to curl up asleep on the bed. She collected the small pile of books from the bedside table, wiped away the red chalk symbols on the wall above the headboard, kissed his smooth forehead and left the room. She left the door open behind her to let some of the air circulate. Downstairs, Betsy slowly uncurled from her bed and waddled towards her owner, her rear end wiggling enthusiastically. Mrs Dandy sat in her armchair and bent to stroke and fuss the old girl. After a while, she stood up again to refill the dog's water bowl and put a handful of dried food out for her. Betsy sniffed at the food, but turned away and the old lady smiled slightly. Her own appetite was of a similar nature these days. She took a plastic carrier bag from the drawer beneath the worktop and placed the pile of books inside. Then she collected her handbag, checked its contents, and sent the cocker up to her master's bedroom to keep him company. Tying a scarf around her curled grey hair, she left the house, closing the front door quietly behind her with a click.

There was a chill in the air, and Mrs Dandy half regretted the decision to leave with just her cardigan on and not putting on her heavier outdoor coat. She attempted a brisk walk to the bus stop, but by the time she arrived, her hips had already started to hurt and she sat heavily on the plastic bench. She wasn't slender, but her clothes hung across her small bent frame like autumn leaves on a tree. The bus pulled in a few minutes later. She flashed her crumpled card and found a seat by the window at the centre of the vehicle. A young couple got on at the next stop, weaving their way to the back of the bus whilst bickering and swearing at one another. Mrs Dandy wondered at the way young folk spoke these days. She and Arthur had often travelled into town together, exchanging pleasantries and sharing mint humbugs and looking out of the window at anything new in passing. Arthur's illness had been swift and brutal. Something related to his engineering days, something in the factory that had lay dormant in his system for many years, had decided to make itself known. It had been a shock to the pair of them. Mrs Dandy, who had spent their marriage on equal footing with her husband, working and keeping the house as much as he, despite their lack of family, suddenly found herself nursing and caring, lifting, cleaning, medicating and carrying out all other necessities that Arthur required. She had done so with as much love as anyone could show for their life partner, fearing that losing him altogether and leaving her alone in the world would be a far greater burden. When he had taken a turn for the worst, she had done a little reading, done a little shopping, and performed the required rites that the books had suggested.

The bus pulled into the busy village, the doors opened with a hiss. Her hips seemed to have recovered, but she stepped off the bus with care. The young woman who had sat at the back with her boyfriend pushed past her impatiently, either oblivious to her standing there, or not caring that she was. Mrs Dandy pursed her lips and adjusted her handbag on her shoulder. She decided to go to the library first. It was not too much of a walk, and the books she carried - great yellowing hardbacks - were heavy on her arm. She turned right and walked down the street, keeping nearer to the side of the shops and away from the roadside. The town seemed noisy and the air smelled of markets and baking and exhaust fumes.

The streets were busy with families and pushchairs , business-men with their briefcases and groups of young folk gathered in packs for the day. The library building had previously been a church, one of the more modern ones with clean blue walls and neat little windows. Mrs Dandy had a soft spot for the building, despite its modernisation. She had once stood at the entrance to the church wearing a soft veil and clutching daisies, working up the courage to enter the building and take the walk down the aisle. The sky had been blue that day too. As soon as she'd entered the cool shade of the church, heard the chime of the organ playing and then finally seen Arthur waiting for her, looking strikingly handsome in his blue suit, then all nerves had fled. They had shared their vows together, and her eyes had shone when her husband had lifted the veil and touched his soft lips to hers. When they heard that the old church was to be shut down, they worked with the rest of the small community to fight the decision. The pair of them spent the summer selling tray bakes and toffee apples, organising jumble sales and standing in the rain at car boots to help raise money for its continuation. The sad news was that the money wasn't enough – would never have been enough. But it was enough to keep the building instead of knocking it down. It was enough of a community effort to influence the council into changing it to a library and she had found that she was content with this decision. Libraries were becoming rarer in this day and age and a well stocked local one could be a godsend to communities like hers. Mrs Dandy had certainly appreciated it when she'd had a need. A set of concrete steps lined with red berried hedgerows led up to the traditional dark wooden entrance door. Mrs Dandy neatened the scarf around her hair, pushed the door open and went inside. The library was bright and peaceful like an empty classroom. Normally Mrs Dandy would have returned her books and browsed the shelves for more, but she wanted to get back to Arthur this morning and check on his condition. A young lady stood at the reception desk waiting patiently.

'Good Morning, Mrs Dandy,' she said, her voice filled with genuine charm. 'It's going to be lovely out there today!' Mrs Dandy smiled with pleasure, her round face creasing at the eyes and her cheeks becoming two little peaches.

'Morning Lucy,' she replied. 'I think you'll have blue skies for your lunch break later.' She lifted the carrier bag onto the desk and the young girl began to unpack them. She was a doughy little thing, her face podgy and weak at the chin, but she smiled easily and laughed often, which was what endeared her to anyone who visited the local library. The young girl's thick forehead creased into a frown as she noted each book title. She opened up the front cover and scanned the code inside with a little hand-held monitor. She glanced up to find the lady carefully watching her with sharp blue eyes. Lucy jumped slightly at the unexpected eye contact and looked back down at the books uncomfortably.

'This is, uh, some heavy reading!' she said, trying to make light of the situation. 'You been needing something to help you fall asleep at night?'

Mrs Dandy's face darkened, as though the light in the room had suddenly dimmed. An image flashed unbidden into her mind; chanting and smoke and the feel of soft flesh tearing beneath a sharp blade. Mrs Dandy blinked. Lucy was watching her with concern. The older woman rearranged her expression back into a smile.

'Just a little research." she said. "They're not overdue are they?' Lucy scanned the last book and shook her head.

'They're all fine Mrs Dandy. Are you coming in today?' she gestured to the metal gate beside the reception desk. Mrs Dandy smiled again.

'Not today thank you. Enjoy the sunshine later!' she said, turning to leave. Lucy watched her go and bit her lip in silence.

The day had warmed considerably in the last half an hour and Mrs Dandy enjoyed the feeling of the sun on the back of her purple cardigan. She felt brighter for dropping the books off, as though a final task had been completed and she could move on. She looked forward to seeing Arthur later, hoping he'd be up and about a little more. Maybe they could sit out in the garden for the afternoon. The flowers and shrubs would start to die off soon. Arthur had always been a keen gardener and their lawn was always immaculately well kept. Since Mrs Dandy had taken over the duty, it possibly wasn't in as neat a condition as it could be, but at least the shrubs were pruned and the grass was cut. It would be nice to sit among the blooms for a time while they still could. She turned left off of the library steps and headed over to the bakery. Its smell was too enticing to ignore. There was a queue inside, someone was buying a batch of cakes for an office birthday. The poor lad behind the counter appeared to be on his own so there was no one else to serve. Mrs Dandy waited patiently, gazing at the display of pastries and wondering at what to choose. She had a penchant for very fresh doughnuts, and although all the other options looked tantalising she would always end up choosing a lovely sugary jam filled one that was still warm. The man at the front of the queue continued to list his requests, each one being placed into a paper bag or white cardboard box and piled onto the counter. With dismay, Mrs Dandy watched the last six doughnuts disappear from their tray. She knew that they'd have another batch waiting out back, but couldn't help the overwhelming disappointment that the man in the suit had taken her doughnut - the one that she had wanted. She glared up at the back of his head, a dark head of hair shaved down until it tucked into the collar of a pink shirt. Mrs Dandy had never liked pink shirts. Arthur had always favoured blue or plain white and she thought they looked smart. For a brief moment, she remembered a passage in one of the books she had read. It seemed fairly simple in its involvement but would result in considerable health issues upon the requested person. She considered returning to the library and borrowing the book again but dismissed the thought almost as soon as it had formed. She had achieved what she had set out to do. No need to get anyone else involved. With a tut, she excused herself from the queue of people and back out into the low sun.

She decided that her last stop would be to visit the butcher. After being cheated out of her favourite treat, she did not want to visit the park today. She wanted to return to her husband and spend the afternoon in the sunshine with him. She crossed the road, turned left and walked down past a half dozen shops. Some of the stores had been open for at least twenty years, the little newsagents, the bric-a-brac shop and Thomas the butcher. Other shops had been taken over by supermarket chains or franchises, but Thomas the butcher had been there for as long as she could remember. Thomas had passed on some years ago and it was his son, Christopher, who ran the family business now. Chris was in his forties and was as genial a family butcher as one could hope for. His own son had just started college, but Mrs Dandy remembered the times when the little toddler would spend the day helping his daddy in the shop. She'd been able to pick him up and he'd point out all the different meats on the counter. Children had never been on the cards for her and Arthur. They'd never looked too deeply into the reasons. At one point, a family was the one thing that they had both longed for, but as time went on and it became more apparent that it wasn't to be, the more they focused on one another and their own time together. Neither had much in the way of their own kinfolk - her siblings had long since moved abroad after their own parents had passed and Arthur was both an only child and an orphan himself. So they had worked hard and earned themselves a comfortable retirement together and in the end it seemed impossible for one of them to be without the other.

'Morning Mrs D! How are you my lovely lady?' Christopher grinned as she pushed through the colourful hanging plastic strips and into the tiled little shop. The air in the butchers smelled of fresh meat, a metallic clean smell that reminded Mrs Dandy uncomfortably of tearing tendons and the sticky slipperiness of fluid on her hands a night or so before. She banished the thought with a prim nod and shrug of her shoulders. 'Very well thank you.' Mrs Dandy replied politely. The smell was setting her nerves on edge, as though spiders of memory were tickling around the edges of her thoughts. She wondered if coming here was a bad idea. She noticed the sharp knives of varying shape and size attached to a magnetic block on the wall. Behind the counter lay another room, its doorway also partitioned by coloured plastic strips, but darkened beyond them. She wondered what happened in that gloomy room.

'What'll it be today then?' Christopher asked her while she gazed around the shop cautiously. His voice seemed to bring her to the present, and she looked back at him sharply.

'A half dozen eggs and a half pound of bacon please.' she told him. Christopher nodded and moved around the counter to the display at the window where he grabbed a handful of bacon from a tray. He moved back and slapped the meat onto the scales, removing a few slices before deciding he was satisfied. He swiftly wrapped the bacon into a little plastic bag and sealed the top with red tape.

'Anything else?'

'Can I have a pork joint as well please?' She asked, coming to a decision.

'Certainly my love,' Christopher grinned. 'You got friends coming over for a Sunday roast?' Mrs Dandy shook her head.

'Oh no, I thought I'd cook up something nice for Arthur and I tomorrow. He always loves a nice bit of roast pork.' she told him. Christopher moved back around to the window display again, but his eyes watched her tenderly.

'Mr Dandy doing OK is he?' he asked. 'Heard he'd taken a turn for the worst.'

'Oh no, I think he's going to be just fine. He'll be up on his feet this afternoon, we were going to go and sit in the garden for a while.'

Christopher nodded while he weighed and bagged the joint.

'Well... I'm glad to hear it.' He said. 'Way that Joan Branter was talking, she was saying he'd not last the night. If you'll pardon my sayin'.' Mrs Dandy beamed, and her peach shaped cheeks seemed to grow pinker.

'That Joan Branter doesn't know my Arthur like I do. He's going to be just fine.' she replied, taking the white plastic bag from the counter. 'Would you mind adding that to my tab? I'll come and pay it off later in the week.'

Christopher raised his hand and nodded.

'That's just fine Mrs D. You and Mr D take care now!'

Mrs Dandy walked out into the warm sunshine feeling immediately better for being away from the smell of the butchers store. She walked up past the row of shops back to the bus stop and waited by the sign; her hips were beginning to hurt again now. She was looking forward to getting back home and having a cup of tea. She hoped Arthur would be up and about by now. Maybe he'd already have a pot of tea on the go and the french doors open so that the net curtains would be blowing in the breeze. There was no shelter or seat at the village bus stop, just a sign high up on a concrete street light. Mrs Dandy waited uncomfortably in the queue of passengers, shifting from one foot slowly onto the other. A mother and child in a pushchair came and stood behind her. Every now and then the pushchair would move forward and the footrests would bash into the older woman's calves. She felt tired. When the bus pulled up and she was finally aboard, she sank into the solid plastic seat with relief. The trip into town had taken it out of her. She barely registered the passing of houses and pausing at stops on the journey back, finding she had to focus on staying awake long enough to reach her own stop. She thanked the bus driver and stepped down onto the pavement, hearing the bus pull away onto the road behind her. The walk home was not as brisk as the walk had been earlier. Her hips and knees jarred painfully with each step. She hobbled slowly along the row of houses, their gardens alternately neat or unkempt. The terrier was still yapping loudly, the high pitched sound making Mrs Dandy wince with every bark.

She reached her front door with relief and took her key out of her handbag. The green paint on the door was faded and cracked, but the Yale key still turned easily in its bronze lock. Stepping into the hallway she closed the door behind her and placed her handbag and the bag of meat and eggs onto the side table. She untied her scarf from around her hair and folded it neatly. She called Betsy, but didn't hear the dog jump down from the bed upstairs. She picked up the handle of the bag of meat and cradled the base of it in her other hand. The bag felt uncomfortably cold and soft in her palm. She needed to get it into the fridge. Mrs Dandy walked out of the hallway and into the living room. Arthur was sat in the old brown armchair. His shoulders were slumped and his limbs slack, but he looked up at her when she entered the room. A glimmer of recognition flickered in his grey eyes. His mouth opened, and a thick drool of red trailed from its corner down to his chin. Mrs Dandy looked around the room and a pang of sorry jolted through her. The cream rug that she had hand-made some ten years ago would need to be replaced. The entrails and fur could be cleared, but she didn't know if the stains would come out of the carpet. She'd need to buy some new air fresheners. The air was already beginning to stink of decay. Suddenly oblivious to the pain in her joints, she sniffed back the encroaching tears and quickly moved across the room to enter the kitchen. She placed the meat and eggs into the fridge. She then took out a pair of yellow rubber gloves and a black bin liner from the cupboard underneath the sink. She went back into the living room. Arthur still sat in a post feed slump. Mrs Dandy reached around behind the armchair and opened the window up wide. The sound of the terrier barking filtered into the room like a hammer on metal. Arthur watched with dull eyes as she cleaned the room. She knotted the black carrier bag and took it outside the front door, throwing the remains into the tall black wheelie bin. She glanced across the road to the other garden. The terrier yapped loudly.

Mrs Dandy walked back into the house and closed the front door behind her. In the living room, Arthur was coming out of his stupor. He looked up when she entered. He groaned, waving his arms at her uselessly. She walked to his chair and gently kissed him on the forehead.

'Are you hungry dear?' she asked her husband. From the depths of a kitchen drawer she found a meat cleaver, one of the expensive Japanese brands where the blades stayed permanently sharp. She hefted the weight of it in her thin wrinkled hand. Then she walked out to the armchair again and stroked her husband's cool head. Arthur moaned, louder this time.

'Let's get you something nice for dinner shall we?' she said and walked out of the front door and across the street to the neighbours' garden.

Miss Metcalf

Ivan Kershner

Chapter One

It was the day before Halloween.

It was a Friday.

Here is what I think happened…

All of us kids knew something was different when our regular teacher, Mrs. Grant, was not in the hall to greet us. Instead, the classroom door was open, and the only light came through the three tall classroom windows. It was dreary and overcast outside; remaining fall leaves hung listless and disinterested.

The air in the room smelled like dried oranges and cinnamon. With just a hint of long-haired cat mixed in.

Hands behind her back, facing the street, a very tall woman was silhouetted against the late October sky. She was standing in front of the middle window. What little sun there was moved around her body like it was afraid to get too close. Her plain black dress almost touched the floor, and a red, silk scarf coiled loosely around her thin neck.

'Your teacher is ill. I will teach you things today.' She was still looking out the window. Her hands were still behind her back. The sun was still not sure if it liked her.

She stood silently until all twenty-two fifth-graders had rattled, rustled, bumped, and jingled their way into the classroom. We hung our coats over hooks in the hallway and unloaded our backpacks and hung them over our coats. As soon as our books and papers had been shoved into the wire racks under our desks, we were ready for business. Twenty-two boys and girls sitting in a darkened October room.

'My name is Miss Met…calf.' Her pause between the two syllables of her name made me think something else should have been said, but wasn't.

Chapter Two

Miss Metcalf turned on the lights. There were four switches. She didn't just use the side of her hand to sweep the lights on like Mrs. Grant. Instead, she pinched each switch and lifted it until the lights came on. She did this until all the lights were on.

A yellow pencil dropped onto the floor and rolled to a stop against the toe of Miss Metcalf's left shoe. Her right eyebrow rose slightly then returned to its dark horizon. Her thick grey hair hung perfectly still on either side of her face.

'Fifth-graders remind me of rodents,' Miss Metcalf said in a matter-of-fact voice. 'And I'm fascinated by rodents.'

Even Ethan, the gifted boy in our class who usually had a clever come-back to whatever Mrs. Grant said, was silent for a moment. 'Rodent' was one of our vocabulary words and we all knew it meant 'mice' and 'rats.'

'Metaphor,' Ethan whispered.

'Exactly so,' Miss Metcalf whispered right back. Nobody else said anything, and Ethan looked down at the top of his desk.

Finally, Madison raised her hand. Miss Metcalf's head slowly swiveled toward Madison. 'Yes?' Her gray hair looked like armor on a battleship.

'I'm the teacher's helper this week. I can take attendance… and show you where the bathroom is,' said Madison, All the time she was talking, Madison kept her hand waving slowly in the air. Madison's finger nails were painted rose red.

'I have already taken attendance. I know where the bathroom is. I won't require a helper.' Madison's hand wilted onto her desk. Thinking back, I don't remember Miss Metcalf doing anything that looked or sounded like she had taken attendance. In fact, I don't remember Miss Metcalf doing anything that was like any teacher I had ever had. But I'll get to that stuff later…

Chapter Three

Miss Metcalf's hands came from behind her back. She was holding a book. 'Take out your reading book and turn to page eighty-three… please.' Again, the pause before her 'please' made me think that being polite was just an afterthought. Or a warning. Like when your mother says something like, 'It's time for you to go to your room… now.' And you know your mother really does mean NOW. And you go to your room quickly. Well, that must be how all of us felt, because I've never seen so many books open so quickly to the correct page. Just like we were little mice, scurrying to safety through a hole in a wall.

'Each child will read one paragraph,' Miss Metcalf directed, 'Read slowly. Pronounce each word correctly. Read with expression. We'll begin with Logan.' From his desk in the front of the line of desks next to the windows, Logan looked back at the other students. Logan was a skinny boy with ears that stuck out beneath his closely-cut brown hair. If you squinted just a bit, Logan did resemble a large mouse. Logan started to read. He read slowly and pronounced each word very correctly. There wasn't much expression.

When Logan finished, Miss Metcalf said, 'Jennifer.'

And Jennifer read her paragraph. Jennifer read with lots of expression.

And then Stephen.

Erika.

Bryce.

Gracie.

Paragraph by paragraph and child by child, I could tell that my time to read was drawing near, so I counted children and counted paragraphs and figured out that I would be reading paragraph sixteen. I was no longer even listening to what other children were reading. I was busily practicing paragraph sixteen in my head. Over and over.

Chapter Four

'Taylor, read paragraph fourteen... please.' Taylor was better at football than reading and he stumbled on the word 'carried'. He said 'cried', instead. Because he said the wrong word, his sentence came out, 'The man cried the sack on his back.' Jordan snickered. Miss Metcalf walked slowly down the row until she stood right next to Jordan. She turned, looked down at Jordan, and placed her right hand on his head. I really don't know if she squeezed, but I do recall thinking that Jordan's toes turned up just a bit. There were no more snickers.

'Katie, number fifteen.' Paragraph fifteen was long and Katie read slowly. I thought she would never finish.

'Click,' went the clock on the wall.

I had pressed my finger on paragraph sixteen so hard that the words had gotten smudged, and when Katie said the last word, I took a deep breath and opened my mouth to read. 'Nicholas, I think I'll ask you to read later. Trevor, please read paragraph sixteen.'

My mouth stayed open as Trevor began to read. It closed when Sydney started reading paragraph seventeen. What had just happened? Why me? What had I done? Didn't every student count paragraphs and people and then practice?

I began making new plans. If she wanted me to read later, that must mean that I would read when Jessica finished. Jessica sat in the last desk in the row next to the door, right next to the encyclopedias and globe. I tried to do the math. If we had twenty-two students and she skipped one, and I was going to read later, then she must be planning to have me read paragraph twenty-two. I started counting and began practicing.

'Dalton, paragraph twenty.' Dalton began to read. My plan was in place. Jessica would read paragraph twenty-one, and I would read paragraph twenty-two. I was ready!

'Nicholas, paragraph twenty-one.'

'Nicholas, paragraph twenty-one.' This time it sunk in that she had just called my name, not Jessica's. It also sunk in that she wanted me to read a paragraph I had not practiced. Sure, it's easy now to think that all I had to do was move my finger up the page one paragraph and begin reading, but I was so confused by what had just happened that I lost my place in the reading book. I sat, looking down at my book, saying nothing. I could already imagine Miss Metcalf's long, dry fingers sliding down on top of head and squeezing. My toes started to curl.

'Dalton, show Nicholas where to begin.' Dalton turned around and jabbed his finger to a spot on my book. As I raised my eyes, Dalton caught my glance and crossed his eyes and stuck his tongue out of the corner of his mouth like he was ill. Dalton was trying to be funny, but I felt like I had just swallowed sour milk.

Chapter Five

I started to read, 'The... children... were... happy... they... were... going... to... the... breach... *the... beach...* for... a... vacation. They... helped... their father... pick... *pack...* the... car... with... umbrellas... buckets ...shovels...and...'

I really didn't remember much more until I heard Miss Metcalf say, 'Jessica, paragraph twenty-two.' Jessica read her paragraph, and I thought I saw a corner of Miss Metcalf's lip twitch like she had something caught between her teeth and it was trying to scramble out. Instead, her lips parted and she spoke.

'Put your reading books away... please. I'm going to deviate from Mrs. Grant's lesson plans for math just a bit today and work on story problems with you.' I'm not sure there were three kids in the whole class who knew what 'deviate' meant, but we all knew that story problems were harder to do than the practice worksheets we sometimes got to do on days when Mrs. Grant watched the clock closely and then tapped her watch as though one of them wasn't working fast enough. Also, every other time Mrs. Grant had a substitute teacher, we got to do worksheets for math. Not today.

'Take out a piece of paper and a pencil. Look at this story problem I've written on the board.' I didn't remember seeing a problem on the board earlier, but it was there… big as life. 'Follow along… please… as I read it aloud.'

Miss Metcalf's story problem was in crisp, sharp printing, but some of her letters looked different from how Mrs. Grant wrote. Her M's had flowing curls, and her S's leaned against other letters like they were about to pounce on them. I felt sorry for her little 'E's'.

'An old woman lives in a big house. She has ten cats. There are mice in the basement of the woman's house. Many, many mice. If each of the woman's ten cats catches three mice a day for five days, how many mice… total… will be caught by the cats?' She paused. 'Begin working.'

I knew her problem needed addition and multiplication, not subtraction and division. But all I could seem to think about was that great big pile of dead mice in that old house. I think Kimberly also was thinking of dead mice as I saw a shiver run up her back. Dalton glanced across the row at Sarah and crossed his eyes and stuck his tongue out of the corner of his mouth. Miss Metcalf was looking at Dalton when he turned back. The fingers of her left hand opened wide and her eyes narrowed just a bit, and he quickly got to work and never raised his head until it was time to walk to lunch. Miss Metcalf's fingers closed like she had caught something and was holding it tight.

As we students struggled with the story problem, Miss Metcalf walked up and down the rows. Occasionally, she would open and close the fingers of first her right hand, then her left. I don't remember thinking it was strange at the time, but I don't remember even one child asking for help. Not even Jake. And Jake's the kind of boy who was most likely wondering what color the cats in the story problem were – like that was somehow a clue to the right answer.

The only sounds for thirty minutes were the scratch of lead pencils, the irritated slide of worn red erasers, and the occasional 'click' as the minute hand of the big clock mounted above the board led us toward lunch.

Chapter Six

Five minutes before we were to go to lunch, Miss Metcalf said, 'Stop,' and the sounds of pencils and erasers slowly faded to silence.

'Click,' went the clock.

'I'd like to hear your answers. No need to raise your hands. I will point to you when I want you to speak.' Like a thin branch, her arm raised and she pointed at Mattie.

'I got eighteen.'

Again, the finger pointed. This time at Dean.

'I think I got eighteen, too.'

Again, it pointed. Austin.

'Thirty-five?' No response. Taking that as a good sign, Austin said with more enthusiasm, 'Thirty-five!'

'Thirty-five what?'

'Cats?' asked Austin. Miss Metcalf breathed in slowly and then breathed out. I heard a door close somewhere in the school.

The finger moved around the room. Children gave their answers. Miss Metcalf breathed in and out. Another door closed. This time it was louder.

Finally, the finger moved toward me. 'Nicholas.' She said my name as a statement, not a question.

I looked at my paper and then at Miss Metcalf. 'One-hundred-and-fifty.' Miss Metcalf's eyes opened a bit wider, then narrowed like a gust of air had moved a window shade.

'Correct. That's a lot of mice, isn't it, Nicholas?'

'Yes,' I said. 'A lot.' I felt as though I was all alone in a dark house surrounded by cats.

Chapter Seven

The morning moved slowly. Each time the old-fashioned clock in the front of the room moved time ahead by one minute, it announced its efforts with a 'click.'

'Click.'

'Click.' Another minute.

Each time the clock clicked off a minute, students' eyes would raise slightly from their worksheets and library books. Occasionally, a student would check to see where Miss Metcalf was, but it never seemed to fail that when somebody did check, she was staring directly at them. After a while, kids just stopped trying to see where she was. She was everywhere. She saw everything.

'Click.'

'Class, it is time to go to the cafeteria for lunch. Please line up by the door.' Miss Metcalf evaluated our frenzied efforts to get into a line and stood silently by the door until everybody stood single-file. 'Go,' she said, and it seemed as though we were tied together with an invisible rope as we walked down the hall, around the corner, and down the stairwell to the basement. At the cafeteria door, the lunchroom lady with the white hair and black hairnet took our names and made a check mark to show we were really there.

Timmy leaned his head near my ear and whispered, 'I bet we're getting greasy gopher guts over mashed-up Brussels sprouts.' He giggled, and I started to turn around to make a face at him. I stopped mid-turn when I saw Miss Metcalf, arms folded, watching us. The fluorescent lights of the cafeteria made her eyes look almost golden.

I pretended I was just wiggling my nose because it had itched. I twitched my nose four times and then wiped it with my hand to prove the point. Miss Metcalf walked over and placed one hand on my shoulder and her other on Timmy's. 'Greasy… gopher… guts. Charming. Gophers are rodents, you know.' She gave our shoulders a slight squeeze. I shivered. Timmy stumbled as he stepped on his untied shoelace. Miss Metcalf opened her eyes wide and let the lids settle. It reminded me of a cover being placed on a pan simmering on the stove in Mama's kitchen. Just because you put a cover on it, the pan didn't stop simmering. And sometimes the pan's lid rattled when steam escaped.

Of course, we didn't really get greasy gopher guts and Brussels sprouts, but we did get hamburger gravy and mashed potatoes. We also got red Jell-O cubes, green beans, a dried-up roll, and a carton of milk. I usually liked the hamburger gravy, but today I couldn't stop thinking about rodents and how I shivered when Miss Metcalf placed her hand on my shoulder. I shivered again, and when I looked across the table to where Timmy was sitting, he had eaten his Jell-O cubes, green beans, and roll, but he still had a whole bunch of hamburger and mashed potatoes left. Glancing around, I saw that lots of kids in my class had barely touched their hamburger and mashed potatoes either. Emily put her napkin to her mouth, 'I've got a hair in my potatoes.' Usually this kind of announcement would cause a bunch of kids to groan and pretend to gag. Today nobody groaned, and only Emily acted like she was thinking about gagging. But she didn't.

When we finished lunch, we banged our lunch trays into a big, grey trash can until most of the gravy and potatoes fell off and then stacked them in the dishwashing window. Our forks went into a metal pan filled with soap and water. Straggling outside for recess, I really didn't feel much like playing football. Neither did Timmy. We stood with our backs to the cool brick wall of the school and watched as Miss Metcalf walked slowly around the playground to various groups of children. As she would come near to a group, it seemed like the children would move closer to each other, stop their talking, and stand quietly until she moved to another group. After Miss Metcalf left a group, it took several minutes for students to begin playing again. Groups never seemed as active after Miss Metcalf had visited them. It must have been a trick caused by the dust kicked up by a sudden fall breeze, but my classmates appeared to be just a bit smaller, as well. Just dust. Just wind. Just Miss Metcalf in her black dress and red silk scarf.

Chapter Eight

After we had gone to the restroom and had settled back into our desks for the rest of the day, Miss Metcalf stood directly in front of the board, took a deep, slow breath, brushed her grey hair back with a hand on either side of her face, let her breath out and said one word. 'Science.'

She had placed a large wooden box on top of Mrs. Grant's desk. It looked really, really old. And it had a lid that was secured by a small, brass padlock. Miss Metcalf took a small key from a pocket of her black dress and used it to remove the padlock. The lid stayed tightly down. 'I'm very good at science. I think you'll be impressed.'

Most of my teachers always acted like science was their least favorite subject. With them, we either read about clouds and then glued cotton balls onto blue construction paper to show we understood, or the teacher poured water onto a pile of dirt and explained that erosion was just like that only more and bigger. Boring! Once in a while a teacher talked about dinosaurs, but we kids always knew more than the teacher, so dinosaur science never took too long. No teacher had ever said they were good at science! You could hear a rustle as my classmates sat a bit straighter in their desks.

Miss Metcalf raised the lid of the box and peered inside. There was silence as she studied whatever was in the box. 'Let's begin with skeletons.' She reached into the box and removed a skeleton mounted on a board like a miniature dinosaur. 'This,' she said, 'is the skeleton of a very large rat. The scientific name for a rat like this is *Rattus Rattus*.' Let me pass it around so you can hold it. Look at its razor-sharp teeth. Rats are… rodents… and their teeth keep growing so they must gnaw all the time to keep them sharp and worn down. If *Rattus Rattus* was unable to chew, his teeth would keep growing until they curved around and pierced his brain. Close your eyes and think about that. Really, really think about that.' Twenty-two pair of eyes closed, and twenty-two fifth-graders really, really thought about long yellow teeth growing so long that they went into twenty-two fifth-grade brains. It was so quiet, you could have heard… a rat scamper across the floor.

'Now, open your eyes'. In turn, each child sat the rat skeleton on their desk and stared deeply into the empty eye sockets and gingerly touched the dark yellow teeth. When it was my turn, I used the tip of my little finger to brush across the smooth yellow teeth. Miss Metcalf was watching me.

Usually, when a teacher passed something around the room, there were problems. Some kid took too long. Some kid dropped something. Somebody started talking to their neighbor instead of just passing whatever it was along. Somebody got bumped in the back of the head. Somebody said, 'Hurry up!' Occasionally, some kid said, 'Shut up!' when a classmate who thought they were taking too long of a turn made a rude comment. With *Rattus Rattus* it was different. Nobody got bumped. Nobody spoke. Nothing got dropped. If a child had already held the skeleton, they seemed lost in thought about white bones, yellow teeth, and whatever color brains were. If a child was waiting to see the skeleton, they sat forward in their desk in silent anticipation. The only sound was the occasional 'tink' when the last bone of the rat's tail would touch the wooden stand if the skeleton got turned just so when it was passed from one student to the next.

'Tink.'

'Click.'

'Tink.'

'Click'

Finally, the rat skeleton had sat on twenty-two desks. Miss Metcalf gently returned it to the safety of the wooden box.

'Now, here is something very special.' Miss Metcalf whispered. She gently lifted two black jars from the box and sat them gently on the desk. Each jar was the size of a grapefruit and had a new cork stopper in the top. Rubbing her hands gently on the corks, Miss Metcalf said, 'Each of these jars holds a special animal. These animals are known by their scientific names as *Pipistrellus Pipistrellus. Pipa...strell...us...Pipa strell...us*. Please say their name with me.' And she slowly and phonetically sounded out the creatures' name again as we students spoke with her. *Pipistrellus Pipistrellus.* The syllables sounded magical and rolled easily out of our mouths and into our memories.

'Nicholas, please close the shades and turn out the light. *Pipistrellus* does not like daylight.' I got up and used the long wooden pole with the brass hook on the end to lower the dusty brown shades over the three windows. Next, I walked over and turned off the lights. 'While you're there, please close the door also. We don't want *Pipistrellus* to leave this classroom, do we?' Although I had no idea why we didn't want a pipistrellus to leave the room, I shook my head 'no', and Miss Metcalf nodded in agreement. ' Miss Metcalf withdrew a grey pewter candleholder from the wooden box, twisted a thick, butter-colored candle into it, and then lit the candle. Looking back, I don't remember if she used a match or a lighter of some kind. As best as I can recall, suddenly the candle was lit. A sharp, orange flame flickered. Shadows pooled and rippled in the corners of the room and under the desks. Faces seemed to tremble in the candle's light.

Miss Metcalf wiggled the large cork from each black bottle.

Gently, and with a narrow smile on her pale lips, Miss Metcalf slid a hand into each bottle and felt around until she had found what she was searching for. From each bottle she withdrew a dark, curled object, not much larger than some of the brown leaves that were still hanging from the oak trees in front of the school. 'Children, meet my friends!' She opened her hands, palms up, with the brown leaves displayed for all to see. For a few seconds, nothing happened. Then the objects began to move and unfolded jagged, black wings, and reveal tiny, sharp-teethed faces.

BATS!

Miss Metcalf was holding two bats!

Chapter Nine

In fifth grade, girls scream and boys shout. It's almost a rule. If you don't believe me, find any fifth-grader and just ask them. They'll tell you. Girls scream when they see a spider, when somebody jumps out from behind a desk, when they get a good grade, and when they get to pass out papers. Boys shout. Boys shout at recess, when another boy says something stupid in class, when another child cuts in lunch line, and when they're acting up in the bathroom and the teacher can't see them.

But not today.

Nobody made a sound.

Silence. Dark, deep silence and the feeble light of a single candle.

By now the two bats had sat up on their funny legs and wings and were slowly looking around the room with tiny black pebble eyes. Without hesitation, Miss Metcalf raised her arms in front of her and cast the two small bats into the air. Just like tiny airplanes taking off from an aircraft carrier, the bats flew around and around the room, dipping and swooping in their silent dance.

Nobody made a sound.

Not one scream. Not one shout. Nobody even tried to cover their head or act afraid. We just sat there, amazed and awed by the incredible display that was taking place in our classroom.

We spent the rest of the afternoon, mesmerized by two small bats that would glide down, almost touching a child, then flap small leathery wings and swoop upward to hang in a dark corner near the ceiling. It seemed that there was never a moment when a bat was not flying. They often took turns, but every so often they would join each other in mad whirls of movement. Once or twice, they dove close to the candle and made the flame join their dance.

By now, children had become unfrozen and there were some sounds. Not screams. Not shouts. Just an occasional, low, 'Wow!' or a sharp intake of breath when one of the tiny creatures swung close to a child's face.

The magic seemed to go on forever. Like my classmates, I was lost in the wonder of the moment and could no more have told the time of day than I could remember multiplication tables or even my middle name.

Chapter Ten

Clap. Clap.

Miss Metcalf emerged into the light of the candle and looked toward the ceiling. She held her arms up in front of her, and the bats who had been alerted by her handclaps glided down and landed in her palms. She lowered each small creature into its black jar, replaced the cork stoppers, and blew out the candle. Smoke rose and dispersed into the air.

For a moment, all was dark and silent and full of possibilities.

'Nicholas, please turn on the lights and raise the shades.'

As light began to replace darkness, Bethany said, 'Look!' and pointed to the clock in front of the room. It was 3:00. Time to go home. We had spent almost three hours under the spell cast by two tiny, brown bats. Three hours with twenty-two silent fifth-graders. That was both magical and disturbing at the same time. 'Children, I hope you have learned things today. It is time to go home now.' Miss Metcalf opened the door, and the students stumbled out into the hallway, blinking in the harsh light.

As I walked past Miss Metcalf, she brushed a hand against my shoulder and said, 'Goodbye, Nicholas. It really was a special day, wasn't it?'

'Yes, Miss Metcalf' and I slipped out into the stream of students.

Chapter Eleven

I was almost to the yellow bus when I remembered that my jacket and book bag were still hanging in the hallway outside the classroom. In the amazement of the afternoon, I had forgotten them. I turned and ran up the two flights of stairs to the classroom. The hallways were silent, and the custodians had already shut off lights. At the end of the hallway, I could see my jacket and book bag where I had hung them before I entered the classroom this morning.

I quit running and paused.

All the other classroom doors were closed. All except my classroom. The door was open.

I walked quietly to where my jacket and bag were hanging, took them quietly off the hook, put my jacket on, and then my book bag. I slid next to the door and peered around into the classroom.

The candle that Miss Metcalf had used was still sitting on the desk, and there was a thin curl of smoke rising into the air as if it had been blown out just the second before I looked in. You know, like a birthday candle when you blow on it and it smokes… but just for a second?

Then I noticed that the middle window was wide open. Its old-fashioned, slide-up frame had been pushed so high that a person could have used it like a door and walked through it. Except that this door would have been on the third floor with no stairs down!

Just a candle whose wax was just now beginning to harden and whose smell still drifted in the air of the fall afternoon.

Just an open window. Open wide enough for a person to walk through it.

Miss Metcalf was nowhere in sight, and I had not seen her as I returned to the building to get my things. Apparently, she had left soon after the children. And she had taken her old wooden box with her.

I slammed the door and ran quickly to my waiting bus.

Chapter Twelve

I rode silently all the way to my bus stop, and my mother was waiting to walk me to our house. 'How was your day, Sweetie?'

I didn't know what to say. The day had been like no other day of my life. Miss Metcalf had been like no teacher I had ever had. I saw and learned things that I had never seen or known about before but that I would never forget. 'Okay,' was all I could think to say. Mom put her had on my head and squeezed. It was a different squeeze than Miss Metcalf had, for sure.

When I got up to my room, I sat on my bed and started to empty my backpack. Teachers often slipped notes to parents in students' book bags, and I had learned it was best to read the notes before your parents. But there was a strange lump in my book bag that I didn't remember. I slowly unzipped the bag and saw a red silk scarf wrapped tightly around something. I unfolded the scarf

Wrapped carefully was the skeleton of the rat. *Rattus Rattus*.

Folded into the ribs of the rat was a note, written on brittle, brown paper. 'Nicholas. It really, really was a special day, wasn't it? I hope you have a memorable Halloween.'

The note was signed with a flowing *M*.

Chapter Thirteen

The next day was Halloween, and in the excitement of trying to find just the right sack in which to collect candy, the memory of Miss Metcalf began to fade. Fade, that is, until each time I glanced over to the desk in the corner of my room. The rat skeleton reminded me that Miss Metcalf could not be forgotten easily.

By seven o'clock that evening the sidewalks were filled with ghosts, hobos, ballerinas, superheroes, werewolves, vampires, and cowboys. Masks helped conceal reality, and the magic of Halloween drifted through the streets like fog. Before long, my brown paper bag was beginning to fill with candy and the occasional apple.

A vampire wearing Timmy's untied sneakers ran up to me. 'Nicholas? Is that you?' I raised my mask so he wouldn't be scared. Timmy's words rushed out. 'Guess who I saw passing out candy in the old house on Fairview Street? Miss Metcalf! I didn't think anybody lived there, but she was handing out candy bars like there was no tomorrow! I got two!'

A breathless Taylor slid to a stop. Even though he was wearing a sheet over his head to make a ghost, we both knew it was him. Taylor was always a ghost at Halloween. And he always cut out a hole for his nose, as well as both eyes. Taylor's freckles were a dead give-away. 'Yeah! Me too! I saw Miss Metcalf. She was standing on the porch, just like Timmy said. She kept the candy in that big, old wooden box she had at school yesterday.'

At the mention of the wooden box, my mind slid to what Miss Metcalf had kept in it. *Rattus Rattus*. I didn't say anything to Timmy or Taylor, but I wasn't sure I wanted to eat candy after it had been stored in a box with a rat skeleton and bats.

'Come on!' said Timmy. 'We'll show you!' A vampire, a ghost, and a cowboy raced toward the old house on Fairview Street. By the time we arrived, however, the house was dark. The black, iron gate at the end of the sidewalk was closed. There were no lights on in the house that we could see. It was clear that Miss Metcalf was no longer passing out candy bars from an old wooden box.

'Bummer!' said Timmy.

'BIG bummer!' said Taylor.

'I've got to get home,' I said. A vampire, a ghost, and a cowboy took one last look at the old house on Fairview Street and began walking toward home.

At the corner of Oak Street and Hawthorne, I left the ghost and vampire and headed toward my own house. Most porch lights were still on, but the frenzy of Halloween was vanishing, and the evening was cool and quiet. The orange, harvest moon was the only visible reminder of what had been.

Wait!

I heard what sounded like footsteps behind me. Perhaps Timmy or Taylor had forgotten to tell me something. I turned, my mask pushed onto my forehead like sunglasses, and my cowboy hat dangling down my back on its string. Nobody was there. The sidewalk was empty all the way to the corner, and the street light confirmed that I was alone.

But not quite!

As I turned around, I had the odd sensation that long, dry

fingers had just touched the back of my neck. Of course, it was just a sensation since nobody was on the sidewalk but me. I shivered at the memory of Miss Metcalf, and I began to jog. I wasn't afraid, mind you, but there was no reason to be outside by myself on Halloween.

In the bright puddle cast by the streetlight, two bats rose into the darkness and disappeared in the direction of the old house on Fairview Street.

The Little Beast

Octavia Cade

'Daddy,' says the little beast. 'Come look at me in the mirror.' And he goes because he has to, because the alternative is worse. He stares for a long count of five, because any less and there'll be tantrums and shattered glass and prising little flecks of it out of baby fingers. 'Don't you love me, Daddy?' she'll say, face wet with tears and an adoration that's well-practised enough to mostly hide the malice.

'Don't you love me?'

Yes, he says. *Of course I do.*

He's gotten very good at lying.

***

I asked him once what he saw when he looked at her. 'In the flesh or in the glass?' he says. She looks different in glass. I don't know why. But the round red cheeks, the curls and puppy-fat and dimples... none of that survives reflection.

'I don't understand,' he says. 'When she was born, she was so normal. Like her sisters. And now she's nothing but a monster.'

The girls were all abed when he said it. We were alone in our chamber, the door shut tight and our voices low but when the mirror broke, snapped across its surface, we saw her face reflected a dozen times over and knew we'd been overheard.

We never knew, before, that her reflection could travel in mirrors.

We never knew if she'd ever overheard anything else.

***

It wasn't even her reflection that was the worst bit. No-one ever wants an ugly child, but parental love can overcome a lot. I've seen babies with hair lips and twisted limbs, with hunched backs and with the marks of pox all over them. They're all loved just the same.

If only she'd had a hair lip, I think. To be sure, you can watch her now and think she's got perfect manners to go with that perfect face, outgrowing tantrums and growing subtler in her manoeuvres. The way she eats her soup with a spoon, doesn't even slurp or spill it down her front, young as she is, but still... I'd give up perfect eating for ugliness and extra laundry any day of the week.

I could have learned to love the reflection, if I'd had to. If I'd had the chance, if it were only skin deep. I could have learned to see it in windows and wine glasses and saucepans scrubbed to a fine polish without flinching.

It wasn't the ugliness that froze us out.

It was the way she learned to cover it up.

***

We saw it in the mirrors first. The new lumpiness, the way her features stretched and moulded. As if the moments of her flesh were bread dough, to be kneaded and pushed and cut into shape.

It didn't happen all at once. She refined as she grew, learned coordination and sculpture, the value of appearances. She'd watch me at my dressing table, watch while I used paint and powder to accentuate what I already had, to hide the flaws – but she didn't watch as her sisters watched. They giggled and poked and pleaded for their own lips to be reddened, for a touch of charcoal on their eyebrows.

The little beast would skulk in the doorway, forehead furrowed with concentration. In the mirror on the dressing table I could see her face blur and reform in lumps, grotesque. Streaks of colour rose along the cheekbones, under the eyebrows – violent, vivid streaks of red and yellow and purple, the colour of bruises and old blood. But the flesh itself was smeared and the colours didn't stay in place.

Not yet. Not so early... but she learned.

***

Perhaps she thought we wouldn't love her if she didn't learn.
We wouldn't have loved her anyway.

***

You're feeling sorry for her, I can tell. Poor hideous child, not her fault, you're thinking. She's just got terrible parents.

It's true, she does. If we were any kind of parents we would have smothered her the day we saw what she was, the day we saw the beast emerge.

We had two other daughters. Normal girls, happy girls. We should have put them first.

There's something of cowardice in parenthood. We like to call it love, or the hope that things will get better. The beast put paid to all that. We should have trusted to what we saw in the glass.

***

'Don't you love me, Daddy?'

She always loved her father best. As much as she could love anything... I was never sure how much her affection extended beyond herself.

I couldn't fault her cunning. That was the way of it: all the power – economic, legal, religious – was vested with the head of household while the women stayed in the home. Modest, subservient, quiet. No wonder she was always so indifferent to her sisters, to me. There was nothing we had that she wanted.

But her father... he was potential. There was nothing she wouldn't do to snare him. I know it seems ridiculous. I know how it makes me sound: a jealous woman, her own looks fading while her daughter comes into her own. I've seen it happen before. It's not happening here.

Of course I can't expect you to believe that. Not yet anyway. I haven't told you all yet.

I spoke of mirrors, of how she travelled through them. I

spoke of things she might have seen, and how little we knew of it. I covered over the bedroom mirror after that, a heavy wool blanket at night, so she'd never hear what her father said about her again. Never see what we did together in our marriage bed.

She would have watched if she had the chance. Oh yes, I've no doubt. I've seen her. Sat prim of an evening, sewing shirts for the poor with her sisters while their father reads aloud. Industrious at her work, but when I've drunk my claret, when the glass is placed on the side table just right, I can see her reflection in it. The reflection has its skirt hiked up, its clawed and furry beast hands moving busily underneath.

She stares at her father while she touches herself. The long teeth gleam in candlelight.

She smiles at him over the shirts, her legs together and following along with the prayers. Like butter wouldn't melt.

'I love you so much Daddy,' she says.

***

Siblings fight. I know this, and with three little girls there's never been any lack of pinching and tattling and tears. Even when they're trying to be nice to each other there are accidents, so the first time the little beast tripped one of her sisters down the stairs, I didn't assume malice. She cried, after all... seemed sorry about what she'd done.

'It was an accident, Mama,' she said, eyes big and wet and hands clasped together, entreating forgiveness. It wasn't until much later I realised that she'd tripped her in the one part of the house without glass, the one part where I couldn't see a reflection. Looking back, I wonder if that reflection would have been smirking, but at the time I didn't think anything of it.

She waited on her sister all the time her leg was healing, until the cast came off. Never impatient, always obliging. She read and sang and played whatever game was wanted, gave up the most favoured of her dolls. 'What a little sweetheart,' said the doctor, on his visits. 'You're such a help!'

'You might be quite the nicest child I've ever seen,' he said, and she glowed with the pleasure of it, held his bag for him, nestled under his arm.

It was certainly a convincing performance.

***

Such cynicism, I hear you say. No wonder the child was happy – she was getting praised for once. Children like that. Positive reinforcement, and so on.

I still say the best reinforcement I ever gave her was a good hard slap across the face the third time one of my girls fell down the stairs, with the little beast following too close behind. 'But it was an accident, Mama!' she wailed, pretty little face screwed up with crocodile tears pouring down.

'You should be ashamed of yourself,' said the doctor, who had already assigned my eldest girl the role of 'the clumsy one'. 'She's only a child, madam.'

A child who hid behind him, shaking with silent giggles he took for tears and with a hand-print too-bright over her cheek.

'Be that as it may,' I said. 'She'll be more careful in future.'

As soon as the door closed behind him, her cheek faded. I could see her face in the hallstand mirror, the rainbow of colours across the bone, but the plump smooth flesh she presented to the world was unstained.

'I *will* be more careful, Mama,' she said.

***

There weren't any more falls. Though not two weeks later, the sister who wasn't laid up with a broken ankle had her hand badly scalded when the little beast overfilled her tea-cup.

'It wasn't my fault!' she cried, burying her face in her father's arms. 'Don't let her hit me again, Daddy!'

'There, there,' her father said, stroking her head with a hand that shook, and the two of us staring at each other in silence. We could see her reflected in the silver teapot, and we had two girls injured now, and one of them still unburned. He could pretend to believe and let the little beast nurse them – keep them safe under the covenant of her care – or he could risk them further by antagonising her.

There was really only one choice.

'Of course it's not your fault, poppet,' he said.

***

I said the worst thing about the little beast was how she learned to change her face. I was wrong. The worst thing was when she grew into what she learned to show.

***

Her sisters were always safe with her once she'd hurt them. The little beast had a passion for nursing – or at least a passion for having the face of a nurse. Patient, kind, a regular panacea. Neighbours began to ask for her when their own children fell injured or ill. 'Such a little love,' they said. 'A real beauty, and not just her face.'

They never saw her true face, of course. By this time it had been pressed into the mould she made for it.

The few little coins she earned from nursing, she always gave to her father. 'I'm sure we're very expensive,' she said, when they pressed money into her hand. 'And Daddy works too hard already. I'd rather he spent more time at home with us.'

'Such a good girl,' they said. 'Such a lovely daughter.'

All other children suffered by comparison. I think they hated her too.

***

It was her father suffered the worst. She was always hanging off him, and he'd allow it because time spent with him meant time she wasn't hurting anyone else. More and more that time was solitary... the two of them together, kept apart while the little beast did everything she could to convince them both that she loved him.

I don't know how he did it. If it were me, I would have buried her in the woods and said that she'd been taken by wolves. But then he always thought ahead more than I did. The little beast was loved, loved dreadfully and without criticism. People would have looked for her body, he said. And if they found it, well... there's no mistaking a branch to the back of the skull for tooth marks on ribs, for thigh bones cracked open for marrow.

He cried at night, silent tears against my chemise. 'I don't know what to do,' he said. 'I'm so afraid.'

We were all afraid.

***

My oldest girl told me once that she let herself be hurt. 'It's the waiting that's the worst,' she said. 'Wondering if it's going to be today when it'll happen.' When she got scalded or stabbed or broken, when her flesh was opened up or she swallowed poison all unknowing. 'It's better just to get it over with,' she said.

'At least once it's happened everything's nice for a bit,' she said. 'At least then I'm safe.'

I should have killed the little beast then, should have buried and pretended and howled in the place of wolves but I didn't. I was too afraid. Not of what they'd do to me: a hanging's a terrible thing, but it's mostly quick and even if I strangled on the edge of rope it'd be a blessed mercy in comparison, and at least I'd have the satisfaction of knowing I'd gone to my grave and taken the little beast with me. But what would be done to my other girls, when I was gone?

What if the village blamed her father too? What if they blamed her sisters? The children wouldn't do it, wouldn't make that mistake for all they'd been nursed with such tender ferocity, but their parents, the elders, the ones with power...

The little beast could always recognise power. She made up to it, emphasising her beauty, her vulnerability, her helpless feminine quality. Not the sort of girl to die quietly, without mourning and questions.

It would have been revenge from beyond the grave. I

couldn't risk it.

'We only have to wait until she's grown up,' said my girl. 'Until all the children are grown up.' Until the adults now were dead, and there was no-one who would care enough to look towards instead of away.

'I'll be alright till then,' she said, and if I didn't know the scars all over her body, the way that she had learned to stop flinching I might have believed her.

***

'Maybe we could marry her off,' said her father. We were pressed close under the covers, his voice a bare warm whisper in my ear. He'd sold the dressing table with the mirror. We had to pay for doctor's bills, and that was a convenient excuse but by then we'd stopped wanting to take chances. There were still windows, and the smallest breeze could shift a curtain.

'Who would have her?' I said, and we both laughed a little, because who wouldn't? She was a real beauty now, even in the glass, but for those moments she forgot and her face reverted in reflection. Not the young men her own age, of course, but there were plenty older who'd be willing enough, and plenty who lived far enough away that they hadn't had to suffer and learn her.

'It would be a cruelty,' he said, despairing. It was true, too... for all the petty annoyances that came from living with other people – a miller who short-changed the grain, a farmer who dragged mud into the house when he came calling, the doctor who even now overlooked the evidence of his profession for the face of a beast – there were none who truly deserved her.

She was our problem, the little beast. He begot and I birthed and there we were, stuck with her until one or other of us found a way out, one that wasn't suicide or murder, one that wasn't bought with blood.

***

When I entered my room one day and found my cosmetics

scattered over the floor, I knew that her mask had been perfected. I'd kept them safe in a box – silly really, without a dressing mirror to make myself up in, I'd taken to wearing them hardly at all.

The point was not to prevent me from wearing them. The point was to show me that she had no need of them now: that even the glimpses of her I got in windows, in water and glasses and the few mirrors we had left, matched her appearance. She was pink and white and perfect, the years of practise and mutilation and her face bubbling up in surfaces all paid off for good.

'I'm sorry, Mama,' said the little beast, her little mouth plumped up with a particularly insincere distress. 'I think the cat must have gotten in and upset everything. I'll help you clean it up.' And off she trotted for a broom, knowing full well as she did that the cat never came inside anymore. Not of its own volition, anyway.

The cat was the especial favourite of my middle daughter. We all conspired to give it a happy life in the barn, lest it come to grief in the house.

It was too terrified to come inside anyway.

The little beast swept up the powder, scrubbed the paint from the floor. She sang as she did so, and her eyes gleamed over her teeth.

***

When the cat went missing I suspected the little beast had a hand in it. We tried calling for it anyway, a useless endeavour but our daughter missed her cat so much that her father looked for it in the woods and I put out saucers of cream to try and lure it back. We both knew that we were doing it for show.

'Takes after you, don't she?' said one of our neighbours, leaning over the fence. 'In some things, at least.' The news of the handprint had gotten around. The little beast owned to others that she deserved it for not being more careful, and that she was thankful to have parents to correct her and the resentment so carefully seeded had spread.

'Who?' I said, milk-handed.

'The little beauty, of course. I seen her out bringing that creature milk all the last week. Loves her little pets, don't she?'

Loved to put rat poison in with the cream, at least. When we found the poor animal, all foamed up at the mouth and its body a rigor of agony, I knew what had happened to it.

All three girls cried. With the first two it was genuine, but the little beast wept so prettily and read a poem she wrote for the funeral. She insisted on a funeral, even if only for a cat, and most of the village came because she invited them, looking so sweet and sad in her black dress. 'It's for my sister really,' she said. 'Please come. It will make her feel better.'

'What a lovely girl you are to your family,' they said, and forgot, nearly all of them, to say anything to the girl whose cat it was to begin with.

'She's getting worse,' said my husband.

***

Everything was getting worse. We were low on money – business was bad and my husband didn't have it in him to concentrate anymore, to trade and bargain on instinct. All our instincts were bent on survival, on retaining the knowledge of what we housed.

If only we'd have been weaker, I thought. If only we'd believe what she wanted us to believe, that she was as good as she looked, then it might all be over. She'd have sovereignty then, and there was enough self-deception mixed in with monster that she might have been a good ruler if only given the chance. But we slept with a shard of broken mirror under our pillows, her father and I, and when it cut our fingers of a night it reminded us of what she was. Of what the little beast had looked like, before she changed her face.

Then news of a ship came in. 'Can we have some new dresses, Daddy?' said our oldest girl and who could blame her, garbed as she was without complaint in old clothes and out of fashion. Clothes wouldn't keep her safe but they were a distraction, and God knows the poor scarred thing needed enough of those.

'Can you bring me a new necklace, Daddy?' said our middle daughter, and it was something safe to ask for, for the little beast was never jealous of clothes or jewellery for she looked better than her sisters even when they wore beautiful things and she did not. Something safe, for a necklace even if damaged was made of only gold, only jewels and she'd never risk asking for a living thing again.

'I just want a rose,' said the little beast, and that was her all over. Not even a rose bush, which could be transported in a sack and kept easily wet. No, a rose bush just wasn't ostentatious enough. Just wasn't modest enough in its ostentation.

'Isn't she sweet?' we heard. 'Isn't she just darling. Not a materialist bone in her body. Not like her sisters...'

'There's nothing wrong with wanting pretty things,' said the little beast, loyally. 'Just because I don't want a nice dress doesn't mean they shouldn't.' She smoothed down the cheap fabric of her skirt. 'I'm good at mending, and this has a lot of wear in it yet.'

Truly, she didn't care for material things. The little beast never wanted to take up space with her belongings. All the space she wanted was internal. She wanted to be kept in mind always, to be thought about every second. To take up so much emotional landscape that no-one had energy for anything else.

'I just want a rose,' she said. 'And for you to come back safe, Daddy. I know when you see the rose it will remind you of just how much I love you.'

***

A rose is the worst of long-distance presents. It's a cut flower, it wilts. He'll have to wrap the stem in wet tissue, to watch it every second so that it doesn't fall off the cart or get run over, so that it isn't bumped and bruised by packages or the careless elbows of passers-by. He'll end up carrying it himself, the whole of the trip home. It's such a *simple* request, that made by his youngest daughter. Such a *modest* desire.

And every night, when he stops at an inn, he'll have to ask for a vase and fresh water and before he gets it he'll have to explain why he wants it. He'll have to tell about his daughter, about her rose. And they'll coo and congratulate him on having such a loving girl, and none of them will stop to think that she's asked for a gift that'll take more time and trouble than her more conventional sisters. No. They'll be too busy making a fuss for that.

(None of the fuss will be about him.)

But cut flowers die, and no matter what he does, no matter the trouble he'll go to, by the time he gets back home the thing's going to be half-dead anyway, all wilted and with the petals falling off.

And the little beast... the little beast will look at her sisters with their expensive, easy requests and her bottom lip will quiver, just minutely, and then she'll smile anyway and thank him for the present and say that his coming back safe was all she really needed. And all this ridiculous sequence of events will have been set up, by her, for his next line, because there's only one thing he'll be able to say at that point, confronted with that brave, martyred little face and that sad little flower.

'You're such a good girl, Beauty.' (So much better than your sisters.)

***

It's enough to make me want to drown her. I lie awake at night, listening to the rain on the roof and even if I could get away with it, I'm afraid of what I'd see in the water.

Of how her face will change in it.

***

It turns out that both our premonitions are for naught. My husband doesn't come home with gifts and platitudes and gritted teeth, the bitter knowledge that he could have run away from the little beast forever but didn't.

Because he loves me. Because he loves our daughters, and he's spent so much of his life putting himself between that he's forgotten how to do anything but sacrifice.

He comes home giftless, my man, because the ship has

sunk and we're ruined, all of us... or at least we might be, but he's come across an investor who might bail us out, and all the brute wants is a daughter in return.

Her father and I might have despaired of a marriage, but anyone who buys a wife deserves what he gets and the investor lives far enough away that we'll not have to see either of them, ever.

It's too good a chance to lose. 'Of course I'd never let her go,' I say loudly. To the village, to everyone. 'Poverty is nothing compared to the loss of a child! And she's a good girl, our Beauty, but this is a sacrifice too far. I'd never ask her to martyr herself in this way. Who knows what kind of man trades in young girls? He'd have to be a beast...'

He'd never guess he was getting one of his own in return.

And the little beast... our vicious, subtle little beast, has never once thought that in changing her features she taught the rest of us what having two faces looked like. She can't refuse to go, not and keep up the saintly appearance she's constructed for so long, remaking her own flesh in service of praise.

I don't know if she does it because her own generation is growing now, growing into power and with that deep-seeded dislike welling over, or if she's truly bought into her own spell. But 'I'm a good girl,' she says. 'Of course I'll go. For you.'

There are tears and prayers and protestations, but she can't keep her own face intact and not move forward.

Her father gives her the rose he stole, and it's bruised and with petals falling off because that's what a rose is: a present of heart-felt emotion. He even cries, as ostentatious in his grief as the little beast ever was in her martyrdom, because the only alternative is laughter and relief as deep as a new well.

'I'll send you a mirror as a wedding present,' I say.

Perhaps when she sees her own face it will remind her of ours.

The Well Wisher

Matthew Pegg

In my dream I was in the study, lying on the polished wooden floor, gazing up at the plaster ceiling. I was in my nightdress. I couldn't move, pinned like a butterfly on a board. I heard slow footsteps. A grey figure moved into sight, veiled and clothed in cobweb and smoke. It peered down at me. I couldn't make out any features though I strained to see clearly. Dust drifted down from its rags and burned my throat as I breathed in.

The figure held something in its hand, a familiar object, a black glass inkwell. It tipped it slowly until black fluid trickled out, spattering my face and filling my mouth, tasting of iron and something sweet. I choked and coughed up ink; it flowed over my chin, soaked my collar and pooled at the base of my throat. My eyes filled with liquid, light was blotted out. Ink filled my lungs and my chest heaved as I tried desperately to take in air. The room was flooded and I was drowning in a sea of blackness. I awoke with the sheets soaked in my perspiration and the first rays of daylight bleeding through the curtains. I told myself that it was just a dream, that it was all over. And I almost believed it.

It had begun on a bright spring morning. The sun shone through the tall windows of the schoolroom, dust danced in its beams like motes of gold. I studied my charges: Edward, industrious, scribbling, head bowed over his Latin, Rupert distracted by something he had seen through the window, mouth agape and Emily chewing the end of her pencil thoughtfully as she considered some knotty problem in her textbook.

'As it is such a fine day,' I said, 'I propose that we take

our paints into the gardens.' This suggestion was met with general approval. We consigned Virgil to the cupboard, collected watercolour boxes, pencils and paper, left the Hall and decamped to the grounds, to sketch the lake and the faux Temple of Apollo set among beech trees on the hill.

Simon Montague found us there an hour later. 'Miss Andrews!' he cried as he trotted down to where we sat, 'I've been sent to fetch you.'

Simon Montague was half-brother to my charges, the sole issue of Lord Montague's first marriage. Recently returned from a scientific expedition to the South Seas, he was tall, very brown and as ugly as any man I have ever seen. His face was long, his nose too prominent, his hair an indeterminate colour and his mouth too wide. I had met him for the first time on his return five days previously and found myself staring at him whenever we met, in wonderment that such disparate features could sit together on one face.

The two boys dropped their brushes and pencils and ran to meet Simon who horsed around with them good naturedly, pretending to be winded as they tried to wrestle him to the turf.

'Come and see our pictures!' said Rupert. Simon looked at their efforts and praised them both. 'Is that a shark in the lake,' he asked Rupert.

'Yes it is. It's just eaten Edward.'

'No it hasn't!' said Edward.

'Yes it has. It's my picture and if I want a shark to have eaten you in it then I shall have it.'

'Then I shall have elephants trampling you to death on the lawn.'

All the while Emily had been absorbed in her own painting. Leaving the boys to chase each other, Simon looked over her shoulder.

'That's wonderful Em,' he said.

'It's not quite right yet,' she said, chewing the end of her brush.

'I think you've really captured something,' he said.

I was pleased. My own watercolour skills were indifferent. The boy's paintings were what you might expect: Edward's competent but overly careful and blocky, Rupert's careless and full of detail inferred but not actually seen, and of course sharks. But Emily had real promise. Her painting of the lake transformed it into a mysterious landscape of lambent water, reflecting spiny trees and turbulent clouds.

'When you have finished may I have it?' Simon said, 'I will put it on the wall in my room.'

Emily glowed with pleasure and nodded her assent. 'I should like to be a painter when I'm grown up.' she said to him confidingly.

'Girls can't be painters!' shouted Rupert as he raced past.

'Miss Andrews says that girls should do whatever they wish.' Emily shouted back.

I blushed at that. I am firmly convinced that our sex is unreasonably subordinate to the male of the species in many instances, but my own life since Mother died has not been distinguished. Seamstress, school teacher, governess, governess, is the less than illustrious trajectory of my career. Father is infirm and reliant on what little I can send home, so I have had to set aside my own aspirations. But I see no reason why Emily should do the same.

'Miss Andrews is extremely wise,' Simon said to Emily, 'And you would be well advised to pay attention to her advice.'

Emily smiled at him and I was infuriated to find that the wretched, ugly fellow had induced me to blush even more.

'But I forget myself,' Simon continued, 'Miss Andrews, my father wishes to speak with you.'

I worried that I had committed some indiscretion. It had happened in my last employment, where I was outspoken when I should have been silent and silent where I should have spoken out. Suddenly I felt that the bright summer sun and the honeyed breeze that blew across the lake were mocking me. I would be dismissed and banished from this place too and I suddenly realised how much I liked it. I told the children to return their paints to the schoolroom after which they might have the rest of the morning for their own devices.

'Am I in trouble?' I asked Simon as we entered the hall.

Simon looked surprised, 'Father simply said that he wants your advice. About the children I would imagine.'

I relaxed a little. Simon left me at the door to Lord

Montague's study. I took a deep breath and knocked.

'Come.'

Lord Montague was at his desk and rose when I entered. He ushered me to a chair in front of the fireplace and sat facing me. He paused, clasping his hands together, pensive.

'The boys… how would you say they are?' he asked.

'They are well, sir.' I replied.

'They do not seem preoccupied? Sombre?'

I nearly laughed aloud. This was so far from the characters of Edward and Rupert that their father might have been describing another species. But I merely said, 'They are as boisterous and as full of high spirits as any boys I have known. I detect no signs of unhappiness.'

He pursed his lips and gazed into the dead ashes in the fireplace.

'Has something happened, sir?'

'Yes I'm afraid it has.'

Lord Montague arose, unlocked his desk and returned with a piece of folded notepaper which he handed to me. I nearly dropped it. A sharp pain shot up my arm, as if I had been stung by a wasp. The world about me went grey and cold for a moment as if I had been plunged into murky water. I heard a thin inhalation of breath close to my ear, smelled something rank like rotting pond weed, and felt a wave of emotions, not my own, a suffocating impression of frustration, sadness and anger.

A second later it was over. I gave a gasp of shock.

'Are you unwell Miss Andrews?' asked Lord Montague.

I took a deep breath. Nobody in the household was aware of my peculiar sensitivities and I was determined to keep it that way. I did not want to be dubbed irrational or dismissed as a hysterical young woman.

'A moment's dizziness that is all.'

I looked at the folded note. I could see nothing odd about it, nothing that might induce the episode I had just experienced. The paper was thin and cheap, of a kind available everywhere. The note within was written in black ink. At the edges of the letters, where the ink had bled into the paper, there was a slight mauve cast.

I read:

"Sir,

The curate Bastable has a hidden secret. Do you know it? His taste is for young boys. He wants to take them on his knee to kiss and fondle and more! He is a sinner and a hypocrite. He will burn in hell for ever and good riddance!

Do you look after your boys Sir? Do you? Do you know they are innocent still? Look to their safety Sir and act!

Signed Yrs

A Well Wisher"

'This is vile stuff,' I said.

'It is indeed,' said his Lordship quietly, 'But that does not preclude it also being true!'

I felt breathless. I had a limited notion of what took place in private between men and women, married or not. But this was something different and appalling. Did people do such things? Could it be true? Had I neglected Edward and Rupert? Not noticed something terrible happening under my nose? I took a deep breath and attempted to gather my thoughts in a rational fashion.

'The boys receive religious instruction from the curate,' I said, 'But on those occasions all three of the children are present and so am I. Mr Bastable would have to find a way to get one of them alone and I do not believe that he has ever had such an opportunity. If the boys were together he could do nothing. They may squabble but they are loyal to each other and I don't believe that either would allow harm to come to the other.'

'Lord Montague gave a thin smile at that. 'I believe you are correct.' he said.

I thought of tall, stooping, humourless Mr Bastable, his long hands, his fingers like white sausages.

'He would then have to ensure their silence, either through threats or bribes or both. Even if that were possible I am sure their demeanour would be affected. There would be some sign of distress or unhappiness, some alteration in their behaviour. And there has been none. Considering that, I do not believe that anything can have happened to your sons.'

Lord Montague gave a heavy sigh of relief.

I felt compelled to add, 'But I might have missed something vital. I am wholly ignorant of… this kind of thing. So I may not be the best judge.'

He stared at me for a long moment. I realised I was clasping my hands so hard that my knuckles were white.

'If you wish it I will talk to the boys.' I added. The idea put me in a panic, but it was my responsibility after all.

He gave me a wry smile. 'Thank you, but I don't think that will be necessary at present.'

He looked at the paper again.

'This may be simply an attempt to smear the reputation of a good man, motivated by jealousy or spite.'

'Or it may be true and sent to you because you are in a position of authority.'

He nodded. 'I do not wish to ruin anyone's reputation on the dubious evidence of a poison pen letter, but neither can I ignore it. I hope I can trust you to say nothing to anyone else.'

'Of course.'

'Then I wonder if I might prevail upon you further? It's difficult for me to make discrete enquiries but you may talk to Reverend Fletcher. Ask if he has heard any rumours. Find out if these accusations have any truth to them.'

Very reluctantly I agreed to do my best and took my leave.

So that the afternoon found me calling at the vicarage, in a state of some anxiety, unsure of how to broach this subject. I was shown into the Reverend Fletcher's office. The vicar was a rotund man with half moon glasses and a halo of white hair. He was seated behind his desk, examining three pieces of paper. No sooner did I begin. 'Mr Bastable…' than the vicar went rather pale.

'Has his Lordship by any chance received a letter?' he stuttered.

'He has,' I replied.

'Anonymous?'

I nodded.

'I was afraid this would go further!' The vicar indicated the three papers. I was careful not to touch them. They were in the same hand and on the same thin notepaper as the one sent to the Hall. The ink displayed the same mauve cast. The letters accused the curate of the same beastly behaviour, this time with members of the choir.

'Have you spoken with him?' I asked.

'Last night,' he said, 'He denies all.'

'Well he would,' I thought and then chastised myself for this uncharitable thought. 'May I talk to him?' I asked.

The vicar conducted me up the stairs and to a door at the rear of the vicarage.

'This terrible business must be rooted out,' he said.

'I agree.'

'We must find the writer of these filthy letters and stop them. It must go no further. People would lose faith in the church, in me as their vicar. It would be a disaster.'

I stared at him. I had thought he meant we must root out the truth of Mr Bastable's conduct but he seemed concerned only with reputation.

'And if it is true? Would that not be a disaster for the children?' I asked, unable to hide the asperity in my tone. The vicar stared at me and his face reddened in anger.

'Young Lady, Mr Bastable gave me his word that it is untrue. The word of a gentleman and a man of God! I do not doubt him and neither should you.' His eyes flickered to the side as he said this. I knew he lied. He doubted and was afraid. I suppose it was wrong to blame him for that.

He knocked on the door. 'Mr Bastable, Miss Andrews is here from the Hall. May we speak with you?'

Silence.

I rapped on the door myself and at my touch it came upon me in a rush, this thing, the *taibhse*, from behind the door and the unexpectedness stole my breath away.

No light no breath no warmth drenched suffocated bone creak drawn thin stretched vertebrae detached and grating hot needles pierce eyes I'm sorry, I'm sorry, I'm sorry I could not help myself and I have tried and tried but still it dances plagues me forbidden thing in me and burns and burns until I go mad red motes in my eyes are laughing faces withered children loving my agony and despair until darkness, cold and blackness fall.

I collapsed against the door. The spike of pain in my head was like a hot poker but I knew it as an old friend and it brought me back to myself. The vicar fluttered his hands at my partial collapse. I wanted to run but I would not be ruled by fear so instead I flung open the door and saw the curate Mr Bastable hanging in mid air, naked but for his nightshirt, chin on chest, face dark.

The vicar sat down heavily on the landing, and had an attack of vapours. So it fell to me to step into the room. I took in every detail as if I was a camera: the wooden chair on its side on the carpet, the bible fallen from pale hands, long, long fingers curled like dead spiders, his belt affixed to a hook in the ceiling, and the envelope on the washstand, which contained the confession.

I read it, there in his bedroom, next to his cold body, before the gardener and his boy came to take him down and before the authorities arrived.

> "I swear these abominable notes are untrue. I have never laid a hand upon a child, never given in to my unclean thoughts, never acted upon the imaginings which plague me. I do not understand why I am tested so, and can bear it no longer. I am cursed to be a sinner in mind if not in body. I have fought this foul thing until I have no more strength. If my secret thoughts are known by all, there can be no place for me. I make an end of it tonight. Pray for my tormented soul.
> James Gideon Bastable."

I gave the letter to the vicar and left that room and afterwards wondered if he had consigned it to the fire in his study for at the inquest the contents of the anonymous notes and Mr

Bastable's final message were never mentioned. Suicide was the verdict. It was a nine days wonder.

***

I went back to my duties tutoring the three children. Edward would go away to school next year and his brother the year after. I was not sure if I would still have a post. Would Lord Montague retain my services for the benefit of Emily? Or would she be regarded as having education enough to make her a good match?

The business of the still letters nagged at me. Who had written those notes to the vicar and Lord Montague? Either someone had made a lucky guess, or they had known the curate's secret. Had Mr Bastable acted on his desires at some point, despite what his letter had said, and had someone found him out? If so, who?

There was something I had failed to see. But however much I worried at it, it would not come.

A week later I was again summoned to Lord Montague's study. Simon was there too, standing in front of the fire, looking awkward.

'The vicar has received another letter,' said his Lordship.

'What does it concern?' I asked, horrified.

'The vicar will show you, if you agree to look into this again.'

'Why on earth ask Miss Andrews to investigate?' said Simon, bluntly, 'I can't believe she is the right person to enquire into such a horrid business.'

'Why not? Because I am female?' I asked angrily. 'Because a woman must be weak and feeble minded?'

'No. Because it could be dangerous! Because this person, whoever they are, might be violent if discovered!' he snapped, 'It's a business for the police not for a governess.'

I tried to suppress my fury. Simon might be right, though it annoyed me to admit it, even to myself. I had considered the letters as a puzzling conundrum. The possibility of physical danger had not occurred to me.

'I would prefer to keep this discrete if at all possible.' said His Lordship. 'Last year Miss Andrews was instrumental in preventing me from losing a good deal of money and making a considerable fool of myself. I have confidence in her ability to root out the truth of things. We shall inform the police in due course.'

I had almost forgotten the incident he referred to but evidently Lord Montague had not and it had impressed him, probably more than it should have done. I was surprised that he thought so well of me.

'I will speak to the vicar,' I said, before I could think better of it.

'Thank you,' said Lord Montague.

'You have a point,' he added to Simon, 'I had not considered that I might be placing anyone in danger. Will you accompany Miss Andrews and see what you may find out together?' Simon assented and Lord Montague dismissed us both.

We walked to the stables to find the dog cart.

'We shall be Holmes and Watson then,' said Simon, with a grin.

'Which of us will be Holmes?' I asked. I was still unreasonably angry with him, though grateful to not have to visit the vicar alone.

'Why you of course,' he said, 'I shall be your dogged companion. I promise to be amazed at all your brilliant deductions.'

I stalked off ahead, irritated by this mockery and his facetious manner. We were silent until the dog cart had been made ready. With Simon taking the reins we turned out of the stables and along the road to the village. I sat in the rear, though it made me slightly travel sick to face backwards and I would have been more comfortable next to him on the driver's seat. It was an overcast day. Troubled clouds drifted across a sky the colour of dirty linen.

'Are you always this angry?' he asked after a while.

'Yes,' I said, perversely.

He laughed and I smiled too though he could not see. My irritation began to dissipate.

'What was the incident father referred to?' asked Simon. 'You saved him from losing money and making a fool of himself?'

'It was nothing.'

'He doesn't seem to think so.'

'You must never tell anyone,' I said.

'I give you my word.'

'When his second wife, Margaret, died two years ago, your father was distraught. In London, he fell in with a Mr Hilary Devon, a spiritualist medium, who promised to summon the spirit of his wife.'

'Did my father pay him for this?'

'I believe there were some expensive gifts. But what he really sought was your father's recommendation to other members of society. Devon began to visit the Hall to hold private séances for your father. And the spirit of his wife would duly appear, even letting your father embrace her. It was leading up to a big séance at the Hall with many of your father's friends invited.'

'And Devon was a fake?'

'These mediums are all fakes and scoundrels, don't you think?'

'When I was younger I would have agreed. But some of the things I saw in the South Seas…' He fell silent. I craned round in my seat to look at him. He seemed momentarily lost in reverie but then smiled at me. 'And you exposed Mr Devon?'

'I tried to tell your father what I suspected but he did not want to believe me. So during a private session at the Hall I simply came into the room, opened the curtains and revealed the ghost to be rather more substantial than Mr Devon claimed: a music hall performer called Tilly Martin, draped in luminous muslin and very little else.'

Simon laughed ruefully.

'I also contrived to trip over some concealed strings attached to a glowing tambourine and open the draped booth in which Mr Devon was supposedly secured to a chair, revealing him to be free from his bonds and producing the 'music of the spirits' on a battered violin.'

'So my father's reputation and my inheritance were saved. Did he thank you?'

'He didn't dismiss me. That was something.'

'I think you impressed him.'

It hadn't felt that way at the time. I recalled Lord Montague's anger when I first told him I suspected Mr Devon. I had retreated. It was not my place to speak out after all, and if the séances were making his grief more bearable, did I have any right to intervene?

The truth was that I could not discern anything truly strange about the unpleasant Mr Devon, who embraced any of the female staff who crossed his path and who smelled of lavender water and cheap cigars. He attempted to kiss me on the stair one night and his touch produced no uncanny side effects: no pain, no jagged visions. That led me to conclude that his spiritual powers were probably non-existent. Evidence of falsehood was easy to discover. And I acted. But still I wondered if I had done the right thing.

For the rest of the journey we chatted companionably and Simon regaled me with stories of his adventures and mishaps in the South Seas, which filled me with a desire to see more of the world. I had never been further afield than a beach in Norfolk when I was seven.

Arriving at the vicarage, Reverend Fletcher ushered us inside and showed us the new letter.

"Sir

You hid the curate's confession because you feared it would reflect badly on you.

You drove him to his death by shewing him the letters that exposed what was in his heart.

For shame.

A Well Wisher."

The paper and the ink were the same. But something about this new note was different.

'Do you have the other letters?' I asked. I was convinced he would have destroyed them but he produced a large envelope and took out the three letters as well as Mr Bastable's suicide note.

I did not want to touch them for fear of the effect they might have on me, so I asked the vicar to spread them out on the desk and I examined them closely.

'Look,' I said to Simon, 'The handwriting in this new letter is different.'

'It looks similar to me.' he said, peering over my shoulder.

'See the way the t's are crossed? How the odd shape of the y is not the same here? And this new writing slants to the right, in the other letters it is more upright.'

'You think we have two letter writers?'

'I appears so.'

'How could this be?' said the vicar, 'Two anonymous letter writers in a small village? Who are they? What is all this about!' Simon helped him to a chair in the corner while I stared at the notes: two different hands, but the same ink, the same paper. Were they written by a couple? Or members of the same family, working together to spread malicious rumours?

I decided that Simon had been right. This should be handed over to the police. Not because I was in danger but simply because they would be able to investigate properly, interview people, peer into every inkwell in the village.

At that moment my glance fell on the suicide letter and I saw what had lain in front of me all this time. The handwriting in the first letters and in the suicide note was exactly the same. The formation of the letters, the individual quirks, coincided precisely. The same individual had written both. Either, someone else had penned the suicide note, which suggested the curate's death was not suicide after all, or Mr Bastable had for some reason written anonymous notes accusing himself of vile crimes. Both of these possibilities seemed highly improbable, but one or the other must be true.

I excused myself and went upstairs. The curate's room had been tidied and most of his personal effects packed away. In my last visit I had noticed a small escritoire against one wall. I opened it. The front pulled down to form a writing surface and the interior held an array of drawers, cubby holes and small cupboards. I noticed some cheap writing paper, similar to that used in the letters. I pulled out every drawer, discovering pens and a blotter. In a little central cupboard I found an inkwell, half full of black ink. It was unremarkable, small and square, made of pitted and aged black glass, with a lid of plain silver metal. If the ink was the same as that in the anonymous letters then it would lend weight to the theory that Mr Bastable had written them. I took a sheet of paper, dipped a pen in the ink and began to write.

I was not intending to write anything in particular, just some lines of a poem, to see if the ink had the same mauve cast as the writing in the letters. As I wrote, a strange, dreamlike fugue state crept over me. I had the oddest sensation that someone was standing behind me. I saw nothing, but felt an almost imperceptible breath on the back of my neck, where the hairs stood on end. The pen moved and my hand felt cold, as if someone had reached round to clasp it. I could almost imagine chilly fingers resting on my warm skin. I shook my head to dispel the strange sensation.

I finished my writing, wiped the pen carefully and replaced the lid of the inkwell. I blotted my writing and held the paper up to the light. At the edges of the letters blackness bled to purple. It was the same ink.

Then I looked at what I had written.

My intention had been to jot down some familiar verses of Blake; the first thing that occurred to me:

O Rose thou art sick.
The invisible worm,
That flies in the night
In the howling storm:

Has found out thy bed
Of crimson joy:
And his dark secret love
Does thy life destroy.

On first glance that was indeed what I had written. I saw the words, as clearly as can be. But it was as if there was other writing beneath the poem. My fingers tingled where they touched the paper, which suddenly felt damp, like a love letter lost in the rain. I stared at the writing, squinting, for once willing my off kilter senses to see what was under the surface. And suddenly the Blake poem melted, the ink coiling on the surface of the paper to form a completely different message.

> "Sir.
> Do you know what Miss Andrews fears? She is scared she will be dismissed if anyone sees her true self for she suffers from a weakness of the brain and madness lies just around the corner! Ask her about the things she sees that are not really there. Where will it all end? Will she hurt the children in her madness? You entrust them to a woman who should be in Bedlam.
> Yrs
> A Well Wisher"

As I read, the room became dark. By the time I'd finished the letter I was gasping for breath, dizzy, faint. Dull red motes floated in my vision. The windows were shuttered, where a moment before they had been open. A wan light seeped round the edges but scarcely penetrated the gloom. Dust misted the air.

On the floor in the corner a grey thing shifted. When I moved my head it became a pattern of shadows, an abandoned comforter thrown to the floor, a patch of damp on the wall. A moment later it was there again. Stick arms clasped sharp knees, a halo of skirts on the floorboards. Slowly, it raised its indistinct head, all black hollows and a hint of pallid skin or perhaps pale bone.

I was in a dream, caught in a treacle sea, unable to move. The creature raised its fleshless arms towards me, wrapped in lace, caked grey with dust.

'Miss Andrews?' It was Simon's voice from downstairs.

I gasped and the room righted itself. The shutters and the grey figure were gone. Sun shone through the windows again. With a shaking hand I picked up the inkwell, wrapped it in my handkerchief and stowed it in my reticule followed by the letter. I closed the writing desk and tried to compose myself before leaving the room to meet Simon. But I noted two things. The first was that the letter was written in my own familiar hand. The other was that when I stowed the inkwell in my bag it had been ice cold, crazed with frost.

Back at the Hall I was unsure what to do next. Taking the inkwell had been an impulse. I didn't want to leave the thing where anyone else might suffer its malign influence. But now I had it in my possession I didn't know what to do with it. I felt I should repeat the experiment of writing with it, but couldn't bring myself to do so. On the other hand I didn't feel I could just dispose of it. It wasn't mine. I had stolen it. In the end I hid it in the little cabinet beside my bed.

I began to be plagued by dreams in which the dusty figure I had seen in the vicarage, poured ink down my throat, or I was the size of a mayfly drowning in the inkwell, a vast black ocean stretching to a glass horizon, until the silver lid slowly closed and I sank into perpetual blackness.

The unpleasantness was not confined to my sleep. Walking along a corridor I would catch a furtive movement in a doorway, though when I looked directly at it there was nothing there. Shadows seemed to gather in corners of the school room or creep along the skirting towards me. I became distracted and would move around the room to avoid the grey crawling thing I could almost see out of the corner of my eye. Sometimes I was convinced that four people were seated at desks in the school room, though when I looked up there were only my three charges. The boys reacted to my nervousness by becoming overly boisterous and I had to reprimand them more than once. Emily became anxious and distracted.

It seemed that in bringing the inkwell into the Hall, I had unwittingly also brought a passenger.

One morning I awoke to find myself sitting at the little desk in my room where I prepared my lessons. The inkwell was open in front of me. I was clutching a pen and a blank piece of paper lay before me. While I sat, frozen in shock, a drop of purple black ink fell from the pen, staining my nightdress. I had the sensation that I was being watched. I whipped round. There was nobody behind me but the room felt as if someone had just left. I bundled the inkwell back into its hiding place and returned to my bed, but could not sleep.

At least this experience gave me some understanding of what had happened to the curate. If the inkwell could make someone write in their sleep, then Mr Bastable could have accused himself without even knowing of it. And the second note, accusing the vicar, could he have written it himself? It seemed likely.

'What do you want?' I whispered aloud when shadows clotted in my room. But no answer came.

Then circumstances forced me to act.

Lord Montague had mourned long enough for his second wife, Margaret, the mother of Edward, Rupert and Emily. A Mrs Neville had been a guest at the hall several times in the last few months. She was a respectable widow, with property in Lincoln and London. In her vivacious company Lord Montague began to emerge from his gloom, to smile and laugh once more. During her latest visit, we were gathered in the dining room after a splendid dinner. Simon was there, as was his Lordship and Mrs Neville. The children of course, ate separately in the old nursery. It had been a pleasant evening and I felt relaxed for the first time in weeks, which may have been due to the good claret, but also to Simon's comical stories of ship-board life and a rambunctious game of consequences initiated by Mrs Neville.

'The Reverend Fletcher.' announced the butler, interrupting our laughter. The vicar strutted into the room, a portentous expression on his red face.

'I am sorry to interrupt,' he said, looking not in the least sorry, 'But I have received another anonymous letter!' He waved a piece of paper in the air. An expression of irritation crossed Lord Montague's face.

'Could this not wait?' he asked.

'It concerns one of your household!' said the vicar and proceeded to read the letter out loud.

"Sir,
Miss Andrews is a sneak thief. She purloined an antique inkwell from the vicarage. Look to your treasures. What else might she steal? She should be in jail with others of her ilk, not living alongside people of quality.
Yrs
A Well Wisher"

The vicar placed the note on the table with an air of triumph. I gazed at it. The handwriting was my own. I had awoken once, just before the inkwell made me write something. But I had not considered the possibility that I had written other things at other times and not awoken.

'Miss Andrews would not do such a thing,' said Simon.

'The inkwell is gone', snapped the vicar, 'It belonged to my wife. It was very old.'

'Was it valuable?' asked Mrs Neville.

'No, but it had great sentimental value,' said the vicar.

'This is baseless accusation,' said Lord Montague, 'I'm sure Miss Andrews did nothing of the sort.'

I took a deep breath.

'On the contrary,' I said. 'It is perfectly true.'

I could see no other path. The moment I had dreaded had come to pass. I could be dismissed and probably arrested. Any explanation would see me branded as a lunatic. But there was one slim chance to get out of this fix, if I could be bolder than I felt.

The vicar spluttered. He had expected denial and was taken aback by my calm statement. Mrs Neville looked at each of us in turn, a bewildered smile on her lips.

'I should not have removed the inkwell from the vicarage and I apologise.' I said. 'I did so because his lordship asked me to look into this spate of anonymous letters.'

The vicar stared at His Lordship in outrage. Lord Montague merely nodded, acknowledging the truth of what I had said.

'I discovered that the inkwell is... connected to the letters.' I continued.

'Preposterous,' snapped the vicar, 'Are you suggesting someone in the vicarage wrote those things?'

'I propose we conduct a little experiment,' I said. 'If satisfactory, it will demonstrate what I suspect is happening.'

'Very well,' said Lord Montague. The vicar was red faced and looked like a bantam cock. He wanted me dragged off to jail, but in his own household Lord Montague took precedence.

I left the room and scurried up the stairs. I took a moment to try to still my panicked breathing. I retrieved the inkwell from its hiding place in my bedroom, took paper and pens from my desk and returned to the dining room. The vicar, now seated between Mrs Neville and Lord Montague, was being placated with a large glass of port. I placed the inkwell in the middle of the table and sat down.

'Proceed, Miss Andrews,' said His Lordship. 'We are in your hands.'

I picked up the most recent letter.

'You will observe that the ink has an unusual purple tinge,' I said. 'The other letters were the same.' The note was passed around the table so that everyone could see the truth of this.

I gave a piece of blank paper to each of them. My hand trembled though I tried not to let it show. If this experiment didn't work then I would have to explain what I suspected with no proof and I very much doubted I would be believed.

'I want everyone to write something using the inkwell.' I said.

'What sort of thing shall we write,' asked Mrs Neville, treating the whole thing as if it were a parlour game.

'It doesn't really matter: a poem, a shopping list, a quotation; perhaps what you dreamed last night.'

They all dipped pens in the inkwell and began to write. For a long moment there was silence and despite my tension I almost had the urge to giggle because it felt as if they were suddenly a class of studious children and I their teacher.

One by one they completed what they were writing. The vicar finished last, frowning in concentration.

'The ink has a purple cast,' remarked Simon looking at his paper.

'Could someone read out what they have written?' I said. I crossed my fingers. This was the moment of truth.

'What is the point of all this?' asked the vicar irritably.

'I'll read mine,' said Mrs Neville, and began.

> "I dreamed last night I was at Montague Hall again. There were hundreds of children running and laughing in the gardens and herds of zebras galloping up and down. Then you came and took my hand and we flew up in the air and all the children followed us and we flew above it all like a host of larks."

She smiled coquettishly at Lord Montague.

'Very well, I shall read mine,' said the vicar and read his piece, a section of Corinthian's which he apparently knew by heart. Simon read a list of the places he'd visited on his last voyage and Lord Montague read out a speech from Shakespeare's 'A Winter's Tale'.

'Now,' I said, 'Please pass your paper to the person on your right.'

They all did so. Lord Montague looked at what he had received and his jaw dropped. The confused and startled expressions on all their faces told me my experiment had succeeded. Simon had handed me what he believed to be a travel itinerary. I glanced at what he had actually written and was so surprised and shocked that for a moment I could not go on. I found myself blushing furiously. What on earth was wrong with me? I gathered my wits with some difficulty and said to the vicar.

'Please read out loud what Mrs Neville just handed you.'

'I am not sure I should.' He looked embarrassed.

'For God's sake man read it!' snapped his Lordship.

The vicar began.

"Sir.
Mrs Neville loves money more than she can love any man. She hungers to be a proper lady and will say and do anything to be one. Ask her what she done when she lived in Gants Alley, in London. Behind her doting ways lies only greed.
A Well Wisher."

Lord Montague went grey. Mrs Neville, pushed back her chair wildly and rose to her feet, close to tears. I had thought to demonstrate the trick of the inkwell but not considered what might be written. I had to think quickly.

'Please sit Mrs Neville. I will explain I promise. All will be well.' She looked upset but returned to her seat.

'Lord Montague, will you read what the vicar wrote?'

Hesitantly he began.

"Mr Fletcher drove his wife to madness..."

Suddenly it became colder, as if a door opened into winter. The light became ashen. Shadows gathered in corners.

"She became a passionate socialist. She wrote for journals and spoke at radical gatherings. In his small mindedness and fear her husband came to hate her for this."

A grey figure drifted out of darkness behind the vicar. With each step she became more solid, more present, but there was no colour to her. When she was directly behind him she raised her veil and I saw the face that had been hidden in shadows for so long, and I could not bear it and found myself shivering, and I closed my eyes and hoped it would be gone when I opened them.

> "He mewed her up in her room and took away her pen. When she protested the doctors pronounced her mad, gagged and restrained her. She was imprisoned in misery for three years until she died by her own hand. He is no man of God.
> A Well Wisher."

Lord Montague put the letter down. I dared to open my eyes. For a moment I saw her burning eye fixed on her husband. Then she dissolved, became shadow and was gone.

'It is not true!' said the vicar, white faced now. 'My wife was sick in her mind. I got her the best doctors. The best care…'

I looked at their shocked faces, Mrs Neville, tearful, suddenly looking old, Lord Montague hunched, the vicar babbling excuses, almost in tears. What I chose to say now would determine everything.

'The inkwell's influence is malign,' I began carefully. 'We believe we are writing one thing but it compels us to denounce ourselves. Mr Bastable wrote the first letters, accusing himself. The vicar wrote the next and I this last, none of us knowing what we did.'

'How does it do this?' asked Simon.

I shrugged. 'Perhaps it houses some malevolent entity.'

'And does it tell the truth, this entity?' said Lord Montague.

I looked at him. I remembered how I had exposed Mr Devon but in so doing taken away the comfort he had found in the spurious séances. If I answered yes, his relationship with Mrs Neville would be at an end. That might be for the best but was that for me to decide?

I took a deep breath. 'No.' I said. 'It seeks to cause harm that is all.' Guiltily my eyes strayed to the corner of the room but nothing stirred in response to my words.

The next day, Simon drove me and the children along the London Road and down to the river in the governess cart. We disembarked and walked to the centre of the fine new stone bridge. While the children dropped sticks into the water I took the inkwell out of my bag. First I poured out the ink and the wind whipped it away in a grey mist before it could touch the river. Then I dropped the empty inkwell and watched it sink like a stone, leaving nothing but a faint, purple stain that dispersed and was gone in a moment. Nothing untoward occurred and I was not surprised. I'd seen the vicar's wife's unveiled face in those last seconds and it burned with sorrow and pain, but not anger. She desired the truth to be heard and then she was gone. But just in case I was wrong, better the inkwell should rest on the riverbed.

'The inkwell made my father write of his loneliness last night.' said Simon as we watched the children tear up and down on the riverbank. "He fears dying alone."

'Will he still marry Mrs Neville?'

'They were rather wary of each other this morning. The whole thing was quite a shock, perhaps a salutary one. We'll see.' He paused and gazed at the water, 'You never told me what I wrote.'

'No,' I said, 'I didn't.'

'Was it truly awful?'

'It was a letter. To me.' He looked so aghast that I nearly laughed. I produced the paper and held it out to him. He took it and began to read.

I had lied to them about the power of the inkwell. In reality it made us write nothing but the truth as we saw it: our terrors and our hopes, what we hated and what we desired. All its shade had sought was freedom to speak truth. But truth is not of itself good or bad. Sometimes truth is destructive and should be rationed. And sometimes we should conquer our fears and speak up.

So I stood on the bridge in the spring sunshine next to Simon, while he read the letter which he had unwittingly written to me, containing what lay in his heart. I looked at his blushing face, to which I was accustomed and no longer thought ugly, and I waited calmly to see what he would say to me when he had finished reading his own thoughts, fears and most fervent desires.

Where Daemons Don't Tread

Suzanne J. Willis

Lake Forgone was deserted at the end of autumn, its deep water too cold for swimming and its shores shadowed by the surrounding hills. On clear days the gum trees and granite boulders were reflected in the lake in a watery opposite of the real world. Cicadas sang the last of summer memory and black cockatoos skimmed the sky. Underneath everything was a particular silence; this is an ancient land.

That afternoon, though, I hardly noticed any of it as I trailed behind Kat and her boyfriend Kevin. We walked away from the banks and up to the old railway tunnels that are almost hidden in the scrub. The closer we got to the tunnels, the more nervous I was. I deliberately slowed down as they pushed through the scraggly branches and clambered over scattered bricks, following the tracks inside.

Darkness spilled out from the entrance, staining the day. Kevin was right, then. I poked my tongue out at the back of his head. The tunnel openings had been bricked up decades before. Earlier, Kevin had told us that the huge storm last week had made the bricks collapse. Then he said that he was going to go right through the tunnel and out the other side.

It felt wrong to be going somewhere that had been left alone for so long. But I got bad feelings about almost everything and I told myself that, at thirteen, I was too old to be scared of so much. I pushed the feelings aside and ran in to catch up with Kat and Kevin.

Our footsteps crunched on the gravel as we walked through the tunnel, the torchlight bouncing ahead of us. We were halfway in when I first heard the others that were in there.

Under the scuttling of insects and the water sliming its

way down the walls, was the sound of something unknown creeping and spreading over the brickwork. Like a mass of light, fleet-footed creatures padding their way briskly over wet sand. *Phut, phut, phut* – an army advancing on us.

The torch didn't light up the ceilings and the walls. It didn't light up the things making noises all around us.

'Celie?'

I jumped as Kat touched my shoulder.

'Take deep breaths, Celie, we're nearly at the other end, now,' she said. 'Stop laughing, Kevin, she's just a kid.'

I wasn't game to ask if they heard it, too, but from the way they carried on, I knew they couldn't. In the darkness, Kat slapped Kevin. I didn't care about him laughing at me. Hearing her smother her giggles as well, though, made me feel a bit sick. Kat and I had been best friends forever, even though she was three years older than me. But ever since Kevin had come along – with his perfect hair and that stupid scorpion tattoo on his wrist – she had spent less and less time with me. And I was so stuck on her, I wanted to be like her. To be brave and to not care what anyone else thought. To be noticed.

I owed Kat everything. Six years ago I'd fallen into one of the waterholes that surround Lake Forgone. A sudden sand slip and the world was airless, choking. I remember the dark green of the water and the light shafting off the scales of a tiny fish that flickered into the shadows. Then the screaming of the other kids when I briefly broke the surface. I went under again, with heavy, useless limbs and began to sink to the bottom. Suddenly, Kat was there, too, her arms under mine, her strong legs kicking us upward toward the sunlight.

Even though the difference in our ages meant that, lately, it sometimes felt she lived in a different world to me, that kind of bond can't be broken. Except by a rakish boyfriend, perhaps. But that day was different.

'Let her come along,' Kevin had said, when Kat had said she'd go with him and I begged to be taken along, too. 'It'll be awesome – and Celie'll have a story to tell her little friends at school on Monday.'

I was too excited to even get angry with him for that. But once I heard those awful sounds, I thought that maybe he suspected all along how frightening this place was and that this would stop me from bugging them ever again.

'I'm not scared,' I said loudly. 'It's just that I can't see anything in here, and— '

A soft gust of air from the wings of some unseen creature whooshed alongside me and I squealed. Kat sighed and grabbed the torch from Kevin, then shone it on the wall to my left. As the light hit it, the noises abruptly stopped.

The old brickwork was hardly visible under the mushrooms and the green sludge beneath them. It was easy to believe that the walls had disappeared altogether and that the whole tunnel was now just growth and sludge, closing in on itself. The mushrooms were pale and as delicate as veins on an upturned wrist. I walked over to the walls, reached up to touch one, then moved my hand away quickly as it recoiled – for the brief moment I touched it, it felt like raw meat.

'C'mon, Celie, they're just bloody mushrooms.' Kevin was getting impatient. In the darkness on the tunnel floor, just beyond the circle of torchlight, the noises began again – *phut, phut, phut* – over a high-pitched squeal. Kat swung the light towards it. The noises stopped and a rat wriggled out from under the mushrooms and staggered into the shadows, still squealing and with blood oozing from a wound in its side.

Kat screwed up her face, but I turned away and walked quickly toward the far end of the tunnel with its pinpoint of daylight. *Don't cry, don't cry*, I told myself. Poor little Celie, always the cry baby, always the one to drag down everyone's fun. Kat and Kevin walked behind me, giggling, their torchlight giving me just enough light to hurry towards the exit.

I ran the last few steps into the sunlit paddock beyond. Rusted train tracks ran across the ground, disappearing into the distant undergrowth and bush surrounding us. A cool breeze shifted the grass closest to the tracks. That's the wind stirred up from a ghost train, I thought, then shook my head.

Turning around, I watched Kat and Kevin walk out of the tunnel. He wandered off in the other direction behind the trees, to pee, I thought. Maybe he was a bit scared, too – I hoped so. Kat walked over and gave me a little hug, which made up for her laughing at me earlier.

'See, Celie? There's nothing to be scared of. And look over

there – what do you think of that?'

On the other side of the clearing, just before the eucalypts and the undergrowth, were old brick chimneys – at least a dozen of them – poking up from mounds of earth. They looked as though they were growing out of the ground atop the roofs of houses buried underneath. I followed her as she walked towards them.

'What do you think they are, Kat?'

She shrugged her shoulders and smiled at me. For a moment it was just the two of us again, walking together under the autumn sun.

As we got closer, we sidestepped the mushrooms blooming at the base of the chimneys. Some of the fungi were lilac-capped and flecked with dark spots, others spongy and red. The smell of eucalypt oil from the bush around us couldn't disguise the faint smell of rotting that whiffed past us. It became a stench as we passed mushroom patches that were shrivelled and dying.

'Ghosts live down there,' Kevin whispered in my ear. 'And you're going in first.'

'Don't! I'm *not* going down there,' I shouted, smacking out at him. I hadn't even heard him creep up.

Kat raised her eyebrows cheekily at Kevin. 'Smartarse – you're such a tough guy, prove it. You go down there.'

He winked back at her then, pulling his torch from his pocket, swaggered over to the nearest chimney. Mushrooms like beads of blood rested against the crumbling bricks. Shining the torch down, he looked down inside it, leaning on the chimney. Kat was watching him, as usual, so she didn't notice anything was wrong. But I should have said something as I saw the bricks begin to give way, or shouted at him to move away as his shoes sunk into the storm-softened earth. I didn't say anything, though, and it was like watching a slow-motion video as the bricks crumbled and the ground seemed to open up and swallow him.

'Kev!' Kat yelled.

Then, a few seconds later, 'I'm ok... I can climb up over these bricks...' his voice faded to a mutter and we could hear him scrabbling about for a few moments. Then everything was quiet.

Whipbirds called through the bush to one another. Clouds covered the sun and made us shiver in their shadows. Then they moved on and the day was bright again, but still Kevin didn't call out to us or emerge from underground. I knew Kat didn't want to seem nervy, but she began to tap her fingers and finally walked towards the spot he had last stood.

'Kev?' she called out. In the answering silence, the afternoon seemed so unusually vivid. It would have been the perfect moment to stop time: it was the last *before* moment.

'Kev? This isn't funny, Kevin, is everything ok?'

That's when the screaming began, from deep underground. It trailed long and thin and horribly musically from all the chimneys. Kat scrambled towards me and we huddled together, our hands over our ears, but it seemed that the screaming had gotten inside us and nothing could shut it out. Like poison, it made us weak. It made us tremble.

The screaming stopped and was replaced by those terrible sounds of growing, the same that I had heard in the tunnel. *Phut, phut, phut.* Quiet at first, it became a crescendo, filling our ears as it piped through the chimneys. I remembered the bleeding rat in the tunnel and knew what we were hearing. It was the sound of meaty fungus growing, multiplying, consuming flesh to strengthen itself.

As it faded, puffs of something between smoke and white wisps of seeds – *before* I might have said it was like a spiderweb studded with tiny stars – drifted from the chimneys and into the bush. It was so unnatural and I covered my mouth, just as Kat did, terrified of the possibility of breathing of it in.

'Kat?' I looked over at her as she stood and walked toward the chimneys again. I was terrified that she would try to go after him and leave me there alone. 'Kat, we need to leave. It's getting dark. We have to go and we have to tell someone about this.'

The sky was a purple bruise as she turned around and we headed back toward the old rail-tunnel. We were shaky and held onto one another tightly as we walked. Trying to find our way in the gloom was frightening and I began to panic. I looked down, concentrating on every step as Kat determinedly pulled me along. I wished I could be as brave. *You can choose to be scared or not to be, Celie*, she was always telling me. I hated myself for always needing Kat to be the one to solve things and now for needing her, after everything else, to find a way back home.

'Oh, god, Celie.'

The defeat in her voice made me look up. As the moon rose over the trees, ghosting the clearing, I nearly cried. The pale mushrooms that grew inside the tunnel had burst out of the entrance; inside must have been stuffed full of them. They were packed tight and gleamed viscerally in the light of the rising moon. They blocked the entrance. And with the mountains too steep and rocky to even attempt climbing around or over, there was no way out.

Kat reached out to touch the growth.

'Don't!' I said. 'Just don't, Kat, please,' I begged.

'What is this place?' Kat slumped to the ground.

There are places where even daemons don't tread.

I tried to brush away that strange thought, not entirely my own.

'We'll have to leave through the bush, then, and head for the lake.' I sounded a lot surer than I felt. But as I looked over at the trees, any hope that I had disappeared.

Smoky, glittering webs swung gently between the trees, snagged on the trunks and anchored to the undergrowth. We had seen it puff out from the chimneys earlier and now we were trapped by it. Unless we walked out through it.

Kat was huddled over, staring at the tunnel, and wouldn't look at me. I couldn't just sit there and watch her, so helpless. That was worse than getting close to the webs. If I could at least show her that there was a way out, then she could figure out the rest. Just as she always did.

'I'll be right back,' I said.

I tiptoed along the tracks towards the thickest of the webs, although I wasn't sure what or who I was being careful of. I glanced up at the darkened sky, pinned by the first evening stars. They looked farther away than usual, as though they, too, knew well enough to stay away from this place. Ahead of me, the starry web swayed and danced. There was no breeze now: it moved to its own music. Like it had its own mind. Like it was remembering Kevin screaming from the dark.

When I was just an arm's-length away, I bent down and

picked one of the long-stemmed, purple-flowered weeds that studded the long grass. Holding the end, I stretched forward and stabbed the flower into the web. The silvery mass – not quite smoke, not quite solid – rippled and closed around the flower for an instant, then let it go again. The stem quivered and it felt as though a thousand ants were creeping from it under my skin. Then the same strange voice inside me whispered again. *There are places where even daemons don't tread.*

The purple petals crumpled and faded, bled out their colour and composted into a pulpy mass in seconds. I threw the stem down, in no doubt that the same fate awaited Kat and me if we tried to break through these filmy traps.

Walking back towards Kat, I felt the fight leave me, just as it had all those years ago when I went under the water. But this time, both of us were sinking like stones with no-one to pull us free.

She put her arms around me as I sat beside her and, after a long while under the strangest of skies, we cried ourselves to sleep.

***

There are places where even daemons don't tread. Hollow places made by strange tides, and the long-ago voices of dying stars. These are the places where living is shed. What is written in stardust and the winds across time cannot be undone. Sacrifice spored from sacrifice is beginning and end.

There are places where even daemons don't tread. And where daemons can't go, they send you instead.

***

When I awoke the night was still heavy and thick, and the webs still danced in the trees. Those words and their secret song shivered through me. It whispered of the slow and crumbling death that awaited us in the clearing to which we were now bound; singing to me the boundlessness and the forever-renewing atrocity that lived in the tunnel, that fed underground, that bred in the trees.

But there was something else, too. A secret-within-a-secret. I looked down at Kat, sleeping in the grass, and knew that the dream did not run through her, too. But I was the lucky one, this time. I couldn't choose whether to be scared or not. I could choose to be brave, though, to do what I had to even when I was scared through. It frightened me less than the thought of rotting away here, screaming like Kevin had as the fungus grew over us and ate us whole.

The mushrooms that had grown around the chimneys this afternoon were gone, leaving behind a withered mess from which new mushrooms bloomed. I crept over to the closest patch and watched it for a moment, so shiny and pretty and alive. So different from before, in the darkness of the tunnel. As I reached out to touch them, I saw that they were the exact colour of my skin. Under my hand, they were living flesh, soft and warm. The dream shivered through me again, trying to reach that otherworld tissue shining under the earthly moon. *This was written in stardust and cannot be undone.*

I plucked one after another, all plump flesh and kissy gills. When I bit into the first one, it was salt and sour and fallow. It emptied me of myself. I craved more. I filled my mouth with them, chewing furiously and crawling between the chimneys to find the rest. For the more I ate, the hungrier I became. As I chewed I bit the inside of my cheeks, the taste of my blood mixing with the mushrooms.

There was a whimpering behind me and as I turned, Kat ran towards me, grabbing my shoulders and shaking me. 'Spit them out! Celie, *spit them out, please!*' She opened my mouth and tried to stick her fingers down my throat but I pushed her away. I needed to make her understand.

As I opened my mouth a puff of starry web came out instead of words, floating through the darkness to the trees beyond. I breathed out and more came, in twists of smoky gossamer. Kat shook me and yelled, but I couldn't hear what she was saying. I wanted to make her understand, but my voice had left me. I felt myself beginning to sway, then I couldn't feel my body anymore as it crumpled to the earth. As a snake sheds its skin, my body sloughed itself from me. It was the most natural thing there was. Then the rot set in – the skin that was once mine mottled and died remarkably fast. The hands, feet, face, all lost the pink flush of life as the fungus ate its fill from the inside out. Shrivelling, shrinking, composting into loam, the body decayed swiftly, as Kat stood and watched, an expression of disbelief on her face. Then there was nothing of it left.

My body was gone, but I was still *there*, a whisper in the dark or the wind slipping across a faded sky. They couldn't touch me anymore and you can't die twice. I could save poor Kat. *Written in stardust, carried by the winds across time.* Kat wouldn't be the one to sacrifice, this time. She dived into the water all those years ago to save me, true, but it was more than just a debt I owed her. Here, I was the special one. The sounds in the tunnel spoke to me, the dream chose me. This place chose me.

You were right, Kat, I wanted to say. *It's easy to choose if the way has already been laid out for you.*

As I moved over to the trees, Kat rose and began to circle around the clearing, looking for a way out. She looked over at *them*, growing from the chimneys, then turned and walked towards the trees.

Kat picked up a small, fallen branch and gave a couple of practice swings, as though wielding an axe. I still admired her, thinking that she could best them, even after all she had seen. She sensed me, I'm sure she did, but she would have thought I was just as helpless as I'd been before. The webs of spores – I knew, then, what they were – strung among the trees shone as she raised the branch. Before she could swing it, I slunk between them, wrapping the spores around me, feeling their shock at being touched. At being manipulated rather than trapping prey. It renewed them, reformed them, as I let them sing their silent song through me.

From the nothingness that I was, I made a girl-shaped, ghostly Celie for Kat to follow. The clearing had been cleaved from the rest of the world. Everything was so still in that glade, but through the bush and beyond the wind blew bitter. The world beyond was alive and they wanted me to carry the beginning of the hollow spaces out there with me.

Kat stared at me for a moment and reached out uncertainly, as though to touch me. I felt the spores moving toward her, wanting to embrace her, to feed on her.

No! I am the one they chose. A few infinitesimal strands of web unravelled from me and glimmered in her hair, turning the strands the same delicate silver. I held the rest of them tightly to me, feeling how much they wanted Kat's fresh flesh. *Let me,* I whispered through them, moving towards her. She turned and ran through the bush, towards the lake. I followed behind her as she stumbled and caught on branches, tripped on the undergrowth.

The spores clung to me and showed me what the world would be as the hollow places spread out. In the place of the bush, there was barren earth, scarred in places by patches of fungus that moved like beating hearts. Everything else was still and dark. I saw what it would become when the spores separated and scattered. It was a wretched beauty, silent as space.

The trees thinned and the moonlight, earthly once more, shone down on the lake and the sandy shore. It shone on Kat as she ran along the shore, back toward the town without looking back. I watched her from the water's edge, even though their hunger urged me to keep following her, to hold her close and let her nourish us.

The hunger was exquisite. It ran through me and I imagined Kat being turned to pulp then dust, then being ours forever. But I resisted. I had saved her and now this was mine alone. They tried to unravel themselves from me and spoke to me in their old, old voices, to let them go. *What is written can be undone if you know the right way.* They had weaved themselves into me well, but not well enough to make me forget that the hollowness is a special place, that it shouldn't be spread around the whole world. It needs to be kept secret, in the darkness of old tunnels and quiet clearings where people are afraid to go.

I kept the web close around me, danced into the deeper water and let the slow currents of Lake Forgone rise up around me and pull me away. I thought they would fight more, but they are infinitely patient.

There will always be more, they whispered to me. *We can wait for the next ones.*

The voices stopped as the frail net disintegrated, its light drowning in the muddy depths. In the waters of the lake, I was washed back to the sheaf of a once-girl and for a moment I was the last of the moonlight glittering on the surface. Then dawn greyed the world.

Full Tote Gods

D. C. White

One bleak morning in the spring of 1923 a young man stood in the doorway of a shop in Jackson Street, Carringbush, a suburb of the city of Melbourne, in the state of Victoria. The shop was single-fronted and above its narrow door was the sign CTHULHU'S TEA SHOP.

The man was of short, solid build, neatly dressed in a dark-grey suit. His face was clean shaven. He wore a celluloid collar and a dark tie. With his left hand he was spinning a coin. It was a shiny golden coin, a sovereign. Standing on the footpath facing him from a few feet away was a tall policeman in uniform, whose small, unintelligent eyes followed the flight of the coin as it spun up a few feet and fell into the young man's hand, only to spin upwards again and again.

The policeman said, 'This shop is on my beat. I have had complaints that you are conducting an illegal totalisator here.'

The young man paused. The sovereign slapped into his hand, creating a silence where the singing of its spin was expected. He looked down the empty street then back to the policeman. The policeman took a step backward.

'Sod it,' said the young man, and opened his mouth. His mouth opened wide, then wider, distending and pulling the young man's face as though it were a clay pot forming on a potter's wheel. Within his mouth there was a blackness so final it was infinite.

The policeman could not look away. As he gazed into this unexpected abyss his body became limp, arcing over as it was drawn into the black pit, drawing out, thinning, as though it were made of plasticine. His elongated head disappeared first followed by his serge-clad torso and his legs until all that could be seen of him was his size-12 boots sliding through the young man's hideously-distended jaws. The young man hitched then, his body convulsing as his lips, hideous and wide, closed over their prey, and he looked for all the world like a bird, or a reptile, finishing its meal. As soon as his mouth was closed his head began to return to its normal size. He belched, smiled, pocketed the sovereign and checked that the street was still empty. Seeing that it was he smiled, crossed his arms and leaned against the doorway.

A tall but portly figure in an apron came bustling up behind him, peering over his shoulder into the street. 'Who was at the door, Nyarlathotep?'

The young man turned to face the newcomer. "A policeman, Sothy."

'At this hour?' The man in the apron put his hands on his hips. His face was the very picture of fussiness and displeasure. 'We haven't even opened yet. And I've told you before not to call me Sothy. It's Yog-Sothoth.'

'Told me? You asked me.'

'Well?'

'I'm thinking about it.'

Yog-Sothoth managed to look even more displeased. 'What did he want?'

'Who?'

'The policeman.'

'Mustard.'

Yog-Sothoth threw his hands up in the air. 'Please tell me you didn't? Not out in the street.'

Nyarlathotep pushed past Yog-Sothoth and walked back into the shop, past the many tea-chests that littered the front room to the doorway, covered in fly-strips, which led out the back. 'O'course I did,' he replied, 'I ain't eaten anyone since that gangster what came in last week. Look at me, I'm bloody skin and bone I am. Wasting away is what I'm doing. Wasting away playing nursemaid to you.'

Yog-Sothoth turned the sign on the door to "Open" then turned to Nyarlathotep, his hands on his hips. 'As I recall you asked to come down here with me.'

'Someone had to, didn't they?' Nyarlathotep snorted. 'If the boss'd put you down here by yourself you'd have been in the Yarra with a couple of bricks in your pockets long ago.'

Yog-Sothoth walked behind the counter and started fussing with the till. 'I must admit, you have come in handy. You know I'm not good in physical matters.'

'You're a ponce you mean.'

'And I will allow when I hatched his scheme I hadn't been aware of how much underworld activity was centred on horse racing.' Yog-Sothoth glared at Nyarlathotep. 'There, are you happy?'

Nyarlathotep looked away. ''spose,' he replied. 'But I'm still not eating properly. I mean look at me.'

'I can't look at you,' Yog-Sothoth replied, 'You know I can't see your glamour. To these people you and I may look human but to me you still look like an amorphous cloud floating in the middle of the room.'

'Excuse me,' Nyarlathotep retorted, 'What about my beard?'

'Sorry, yes, you are an amorphous cloud which has somehow got a goatee beard stuck on. I don't understand how you even managed it.'

'It makes me look more evil. You're not the only one who reads about humans, you know.'

Yog-Sothoth decided it was too early in the morning to argue further. 'Could you at least try not to eat anyone else today? There's too much to do.' He walked to the front door and propped it open. 'It's the Cup this afternoon, after all. This place should be jam-packed all morning.'

Before Nyarlathotep could reply the first customer of the day could be seen crossing the street and coming towards them. 'Quick!' Yog-Sothoth said, 'It's started!'

The little man, in shirtsleeves and a bowler hat, paused at the door of the Tea Shop, looked around, then walked inside. There he found Yog-Sothoth, now wearing a fez as well as his shirt, tie and apron, sitting behind the shop's small counter. Nyarlathotep was nowhere to be seen. 'Ah,' said the man, 'there you are, Mr...'

'Sothoth, *effendi*,' replied Yog-Sothoth in a poor attempt at an accent.

It didn't seem to matter. 'Right-o,' said the man, 'Mr Sothoth. Funny names you Egyptian blokes have. I met a few of youse back in the war.'

Yog-Sothoth salaamed. 'Just as you say, effendi. Has sir come for some... tea?'

The little man looked around again, then leaned in close. 'Are you taking bets on the Cup?'

'Indeed *effendi*, that is so.'

The little man seemed agitated. 'What odds are youse giving on Rivoli?'

Yog-Sothoth smiled, and his eyes twinkled. 'Very generous. Fifty to one.'

The little man drew his breath. 'Everywhere else is giving three-to one.'

'If he comes home you shall be a rich man.'

'Beauty!' The little man pulled out his bill-fold and drew out a five-pound note.

Before he could hand it over, Yog-Sothoth stopped him. 'Are you certain Rivoli will win?'

'Couldn't be certainer.' The little man leaned close again. 'I had a dream last night. Bloody clear as day it was. The nag romped home half a length ahead.'

'In that case, *effendi*, perhaps you would prefer to bet something more... substantial?'

The little man seemed torn. 'Ah,' he said, rubbing the back of his neck, "It's the missus. If she knows I'm here she'll go spare.'

Yog-Sothoth smiled. 'But surely, if Rivoli is, how you say, a "dead cert", this will not matter?'

The little man looked at his billfold, in which the majority of his wages for the week sat.

'No, *effendi*,' said Yog-Sothoth, 'I do not refer to money.'

There was something in his voice which made the little man shiver, as though the room had grown cold and dark. He looked up at Yog-Sothoth, who was grinning, his eyes dancing with an inner fire. 'What... what did you have in mind?'

'Your soul.'

The little man started. 'Me what?'

'A harmless old Egyptian custom. If you bet five pounds for Rivoli to win I will give you odds of fifty to one. However, if you can give me the Trifecta, in the order in which they are to finish, and you bet me five pounds and your soul, I will give you odds of one thousand to one.'

The little man looked as though the heavens had just opened up to him. He slapped the bank note on the counter.

'My dream!' he replied, 'I can see the finishing card like it was here in front of me.'

Yog-Sothoth drew out a slip of paper from beneath the counter. 'Put the horses down here,' he directed, 'In order. Five pounds and your soul.'

The little man did so and left the shop with a spring in his step. 'Strange customs these bloody Gyppoes have,' he muttered as he put his slip into his pocket, 'Still, I suppose they know what they're doing.'

'Just as you say, *effendi*,' whispered a smiling Yog-Sothoth to the little man's departing back, 'Just as you say.'

The scene was repeated many times that morning. People would drift into the shop in ones and twos, go to put a bet on then discover they had dreamed the full race card for the Cup that day. Working men, housewives, even a few toffs who didn't want to be seen betting at the track came in, put down a pound, or two, or five, plus their souls, on Rivoli. At 1:30 Yog-Sothoth served the last customer and called for Nyarlathotep to put up the "Closed" sign and lock the door. He looked smug as he rubbed his hands together. 'I think Cthulhu will be quite pleased with us,' he said. 'Between you and me, I think it might be promotion time.'

'Well,' said Nyarlathotep, 'I just might have a little surprise for you.'

'What? What?'

'While you were taking care of business, I put a call through.' He slapped Yog-Sothoth on the back. 'You know, Sothy, I have to admit when you brought this idea up at last month's staff meeting I thought it sounded like the usual bullshit.'

'I say, steady on.'

'I mean, remember when you said we should start that florist shop back in 16th century Venice, because you said all those poets were falling over themselves to pledge their souls for their beloved?'

'That was just a timing issue. How was I supposed to know the plague would run through?'

'It was a load of crap. But now that I've seen what you're doing, I've got to say you're onto a winner.'

Yog-Sothoth beamed. This was high praise indeed from the

Elder God who had once judged Yog-Sothoth's flower arranging as being 'all over the place like a mad woman's knitting'.

'And,' continued Nyarlathotep, 'I'm not the only one who thinks so.'

'You mean...?'

'Yep. While youse were busy out here I been on the blower. Cthulhu is bloody pleased. In fact, he told me he was gonna come past and inspect all the souls as they come through.'

'Oh my goodness.' Yog-Sothoth could see Cthulhu now, all smiles, as Yog-Sothoth's star rose a little higher in sunken R'yleh.

'So,' asked Nyarlathotep, as he looked over Yog-Sothoth's shoulder at the pile of betting slips, 'How many we got?'

His head still spinning from his vision, Yog-Sothoth returned to the real world, and the betting slips. 'Counting yesterday and Sunday, one thousand seven hundred and forty two. And they're all....' He frowned.

'What?'

'Ssh!' Yog-Sothoth closed his eyes. His lips moved. He jumped as though he'd been scalded, his eyes open wide. He grabbed Nyarlathotep by the shoulders. 'You did send them the right dream, didn't you?'

'Of course I did. Rivoli to win, Bitalli second, Accarak in third.'

Yog-Sothoth looked at the slips. 'And that's what they've put down.'

'Then what's the problem?'

'I just had a quick scry. It's changed.'

Nyarlathotep snorted. 'How the bloody hell can it change? It's the future. Fixed points in time and all that crap.'

'I don't know, but have a look.'

Nyarlathotep closed his eyes and began waving a few fingers in the air in a complicated way. 'Oh,' he said, 'why the hell am I seeing Rivoli bringing it home, Bitalli miles away in second and Accarak third?'

Yog-Sothoth shook his head. 'What the hell are we going to do? Bitalli was supposed to win, buggering everyone up and leaving us with seventeen-hundred odd souls. Now someone has...' He turned to look at Nyarlathotep.

'What?'

'When you sent them the dream, what spell did you use?'

'Shoggoth's Old Peculier, of course. Best thing for sending someone a dream.'

'But I told you to use Hastur's Liturgy.'

Nyarlathotep shook his head. 'You know that's unspeakable,' he said. 'Shoggoth's is heaps better.'

'Yes,' explained Yog-Sothoth, 'but Shoggoth's doesn't take into account the effect of a bunch of people having the same dream.'

'That don't matter, it's only for whole countries or whatever,' Nyarlathotep replied. 'A couple of thousand people in the local area couldn't possibly have changed reality.'

'You tell me then. Too many people dream the same thing, and what happens?'

'Yeah, but... ah, hell.'

'Quite.'

'It leaks from the dreamlands and into the world.' Nyarlathotep went a bit pale/roiled a bit more cloudily. I still don't see how it could have happened. Bloody hell.'

'Well,' said Yog-Sothoth, 'This is another fine mess you've got me into.'

'Don't start with the anachronisms. Those two aren't going to be around for a few years yet.'

Yog-Sothoth began to pace around the small room. In frustration he kicked an innocent tea-chest. 'What can we do?' He glanced at the clock. 'The race starts in just over an hour.'

Nyarlathotep clicked his fingers and looked hopeful. 'What about a bomb threat?'

'They don't have terrorists yet.'

The two elder gods thought a bit more. 'I know!' cried Nyarlathotep, 'We're going to have to nobble Rivoli.'

Yog-Sothoth looked at him. 'How? If he's scratched, the bets are off. That's the law.'

'This is an illegal betting shop.'

'Not their petty legislation,' Yog-Sothoth said, casually waving away several hundred years of western civilisation, 'The Law of All Things.'

'Oh. Oooh.'

'I can't make them do something that would seem wrong

in their hearts. Cheating isn't allowed. I have to win their souls fair and square.'

'Yeah right. A bit of a stumper, that.'

The two Elder Gods sat and thought for a bit. After a while Nyarlathotep looked up. 'What if we went down there and had a word with Rivoli?'

'Why?'

'Convince him it would be in his best interests not to win.'

Yog-Sothoth screwed up his face. 'Us? Talk to a horse?'

'Why not? If we offer him a bit of inducement he might be up for it.'

'What sort of inducement do you give a horse?'

'A bag of carrots?' Nyarlathotep mused. 'Not getting his knackers belted with a hammer or something like that?'

This was one of the least-thought-out plans Yog-Sothoth had ever heard, yet he glanced at the clock and knew that it was the best they were likely to get. 'Fine,' he said, hoping that something else would occur to him on the drive down, 'Get your motorbike. We're going to Flemington.'

***

The 1922 Waratah motorcycle was a utilitarian machine suited to a single rider. The addition of a sidecar did little for its handling or performance, and the addition of two Elder Gods did little again. The problem with glamour was that, while the external appearance may change, the fundamental physical aspects, mainly mass, remains the same. In Nyarlathotep's case this did not matter too much, but as now, with Yog-Sothoth's mass of tentacles stuffed into the sidecar, the little Villiers two-stroke engine was screaming for its life and using every bit of its 2.25 horsepower as they threaded down Racecourse Road towards the track. The roads leading to Flemington were thronged with people, cars and tramcars, but a few waves of the hand from Yog-Sothoth meant there always seemed to be a space for the struggling motorcycle to squeeze through. Dodging pedestrians and motorists the motorcycle finally wheezed, banged and farted its way through to the car park. At first it did not seem as though there would be a space available for them, but later that day one of the Melbourne Jockey Club officials would develop a splitting headache as he tried to explain to himself and his wife that while he didn't actually remember parking his Ford several streets away before, he did now.

'Right,' said Nyarlathotep, switching off the engine and looking up at the big stand, 'where to now?'

'The stables, I suppose.'

They headed through the main gate, the Porters seeming to choose just the right moment to look away, or sneeze, or swat at a fly for just long enough to allow them to slip through unseen. They ambled towards the general area of the stables. Yog-Sothoth marvelled at the crowds and the course itself. 'Humans,' he chuckled.

'What?'

'What makes them build all this? It's bigger than most of their temples.'

Nyarlathotep snorted. 'It is a temple,' he said, 'Most of them haven't figured it out, and the ones that have are only too happy to help them worship.'

Yog-Sothoth looked over at his companion. 'You're not growing a conscience, are you?'

'Not bloody likely. We take their souls, fair and square. The god of this place, he takes everything they've got. The way I see it we're doing the poor sods a favour.'

They had rounded the stands and were approaching a building that, given the overpowering smell of horse, could only be the stables. 'Wait.' Yog-Sothoth reached out an arm/tentacle and barred Nyarlathotep's path, 'We can't just walk in.'

'You're right.' Nyarlathotep grew very still, then brightened up again. 'Should be alright now.'

'What have you done?'

'Every single jockey, trainer and owner just suddenly decided to go to the toilet at the same time. The dunnies'll be chaos. I'd say we've got at least ten minutes up our sleeves.'

They quickly walked over to the stables and around to the side door. However, they found the door barred by a very large man in an ill-fitting suit and a dark fedora.

'Sorry cobbers,' he said, reaching out a hand and showing

Yog-Sothoth back a pace. 'Business in here is strictly limited.'

Yog-Sothoth pulled Nyarlathotep back. 'I thought you said everyone was taken care of?' he whispered.

'Look at him.'

'I can see him, he's right there.'

'No,' Nyarlathotep hissed, 'Really look.'

Yog-Sothoth stopped using his first sight and switched over to second sight. The man's aura was well into the purple. 'He's protected!'

'Not from this,' said Nyarlathotep in a low voice. He stretched out his arm and a bolt of flame shot from it. It struck the large man in the chest and washed over him. For a moment there was a battle, for those who could see it, as the yellow of Nyarlathotep's fire fought with the purple of the man's aura. Yog-Sothoth could feel the power draining out of Nyarlathotep and into the flames. The large man writhed in silent agony as his protection failed and his body was reduced to a fine, grey ash. Nyarlathotep was sweating heavily, and beneath his glamour his beard had fallen off. He slumped to his knees. 'Whoever protected him, they're powerful,' he gasped.

'Are you alright?'

'I need to eat someone. Fast.'

'There's no time. Come on.' Yog-Sothoth helped him to his feet and led him through the door. Beyond it was dark, and silent. Yog-Sothoth wasn't sure what he was expecting inside the stable, but light and the neighing of horses was quite high up on his list. He put his hand out in front of him and felt for the cord that turned on the light. After a few fumbles he found it, and the room lit up.

In front of him stood a smallish, dark-haired man. He was expensively dressed in a grey, double-breasted suit. On his head was a grey derby, and clamped between his teeth was the largest cigar Yog-Sothoth had ever seen. Surrounding the man were several more suited thugs, and behind him Yog-Sothoth could see a small man with a green celluloid visor. In his hands he held a large syringe. On the other side of him was a tall, thin Asian man, with his hair in a ponytail and two small mustachios which fell down past either side of his chin. He wore a scarlet robe, into the sleeves of which his hands were tucked.

'So nice of you to join us,' the dark-haired man said with a wide smile. 'My name is John West. This,' he indicated the small man in the visor, 'is my cousin Herbert.' He gestured towards the Asian man. 'My associate let me know you were coming.'

'But how did he...' Yog-Sothoth turned to Nyarlathotep, still pale, who nodded.

'The good doctor came to me this morning and told me someone had been meddling with my Melbourne Cup result.' West stopped smiling. 'I don't like it when people meddle in my results. I paid good money for them, and so I have to take steps.' He nodded at the tall man. 'Fortunately, all my associates are very capable. Do get on with it, Herbert. Don't let my talking to these gentlemen stop you.' He smiled again. 'Damn good idea, having everyone nip out like that. Saved us a bother.'

Behind West Yog-Sothoth could see Herbert walking towards the stall marked "Rivoli". He didn't know what was in the syringe but he could take a guess. 'No!' he cried.

'Just a little something my brother concocted. It gives a horse... something. His heart will, of course explode shortly after the end of the race, but until then he'll be quite unbeatable. Unfortunately for you, so am I.'

Yog-Sothoth knew there was nothing he could do. He watched as the little man in the visor jabbed the syringe into the thoroughbred's fetlock and slowly pushed the plunger in.

The tall, robed man began to laugh, a high-pitched, reedy giggle that, had Yog-Sothoth physically had skin instead of generally being covered in suckers and mucous membrane, would have gotten right under it. As he watched the horse's aura deepened, it's healthy, athletic green shifting to an ultra deep, almost neon emerald. The Elder God could feel the power radiating off it.

Yog-Sothoth tore his eyes away from the horse to find that West and his thugs had moved much closer, almost ringing them in. He and Nyarlathotep stepped back until he felt the rough stone of the stable wall behind him.

'Doctor,' said West, 'may I leave these... gentlemen with you?' He lit his cigar and headed for the door at the other end of the stables. 'Herbert and I will be watching the race from my box.' He left.

The doctor's eyes gleamed. 'Long have I waited to meet your kind,' he said, 'I have manacles which may hold you, Messenger, and many interesting devices to which an Elder God may be held in eternal thrall.'

'I wouldn't bet on it,' said Nyarlathotep, his voice still shaky.

'How? You have used all your power, Eater of Souls. Mr West's men and I are protected.'

Yog-Sothoth became acutely aware of the cold bricks pressing up against his back. The man's face was, he could see, full of greed. He had heard stories of Elder Gods who had been trapped by mortals. It was rare, but it did happen. It never ended well for anyone.

'Come on,' he whispered to Nyarlathotep, 'there must be something you can do.'

'Nope,' the other Elder God groaned, 'I'm bloody well spent. It's gone, all of it.'

'Then eat someone! Quickly!'

'Who? They're all protected.'

Yog-Sothoth's eyes flicked about the room. He smiled. 'Yes,' he said, nodding at a point over the tall man's shoulder, 'but he isn't.'

The doctor seemed momentarily perplexed, and he glanced away. At that moment Nyarlathotep gave out a mental shrug, pushing them all over. Yog-Sothoth winced as he saw this had used up almost all of the energy Nyarlathotep had left, but then he saw something wonderful.

Rivoli, glowing over with health, seemed to stretch the length of the stable. Nyarlathotep opened his mouth wide, wider than Yog-Sothoth had ever seen him do before. He drank the horse and its power in, lapping up the emerald aura, sucking it into his gaping maw like a snake eating a rat until, with a final gulp, the racehorse's rear hooves disappeared and his jaw snapped shut.

Nyarlathotep turned and faced the doctor, who took a step backwards. He raised his hands and began to intone an arcane liturgy.

He did not get far. With a roar Nyarlathotep seemed to

turn into pure energy. Yog-Sothoth was almost blinded by the power and light that streamed from Nyarlathotep. The purple auras that surrounded the doctor and his thugs were stripped away like dust in a flood and, with a scream, each of them disintegrated.

Nyarlathotep stopped glowing, looked around and slowly toppled to the floor. Yog-Sothoth rushed to his side. 'Did I get them?' he croaked.

'Yes!' cried Yog-Sothoth, 'Yes you did!'

'Then we're all good?'

'Ah.' Yog-Sothoth looked over at Rivoli's empty stall. Outside he could hear the first flushes of the stable hand's toilets. 'Sort of.'

'What do you mean, sort of?'

'Don't worry,' Yog-Sothoth told Nyarlathotep as he pulled him towards the empty stall, 'I've got a brilliant idea.'

***

Excerpt From The Argus, Melbourne Cup 75th Year Special Report, 1936:

Punters agree that the Melbourne Cup of 1923 was a very strange affair. It was the first race in more than 20 years where noted businessman John West appeared quite distressed about the result. The result itself was more than enough to cause comment. Bitalli won but it was a close thing, as Rivoli led the field for most of the race, dropping back to second only over the last few yards. Several in the crowd swore that over the sound of the horses' hooves they could hear the scream of a two-stroke engine going flat out.

The other incident of note was the resignation of the official Flemington photographer, Mr Richard Upton Pickman, and his relocation back to his native Boston surrounded by controversy. Several stewards claimed Mr Pickman had destroyed the plate and photograph of the finish, instead substituting the picture from a race with a similar result from several weeks earlier. An amount of ash was found in Mr Pickman's wastepaper bin, but as the rumour had no impact on the outcome of the Cup the matter quietly faded into obscurity.

Those Who Can't...

Rosalind Mosis

The day had ploughed on; my colleagues had left one by one. It was gone seven and I must've been the last person left in the school. By the time I had come to my senses and finished my last Numeracy book, the lights were on in the car park outside and the only ones left on inside were the ones in my classroom. I could practically feel all the classrooms dark and silent around mine. I was alone, Friday night, music on and still at work. This was a clear sign for me to get the hell out of Dodge… except… Well, I was only in my first year and still hadn't got my balance yet. I still imagined it was healthy to get it all done in a night rather than stagger it. I was clearly an idiot, but at that moment, I was an idiot who had beaten Year 1s Numeracy Hill and was all set to conquer Topic Mountain. Which, incidentally, I hadn't even touched since we started term *over a month ago.*

'Oi! Miss Hiller?'

The voice made me jump a mile high and pull out an ear bud.

'S'cuse me,' the Site Manager had knocked on my door, 'everyone's gone home.'

I turned to face him, a customary older gentleman with a mild East End accent, in paint-caked trousers and sweatshirt carrying a ring of keys. I had trouble recalling his name.

'Oh… sorry, you kicking me out?' I asked, my pride a little wounded considering how much work I had got done.

'Well, you *can* stay till after half seven, but then you've gotta scarper 'cos that's when I have to turn the alarm system on.'

I sighed and pinched the bridge of my nose 'Yeah… I'll have to stay later. I just need to pack up and grab something in the Staff Room. For my planning.'

'Look…' he said, taking a deep breath 'I know you're keen

to get finished, but… it's not worth it. Trust me. Go home.'

'I will, promise, and I won't keep you any longer than you need to-'

'It's not me I'm worried about love,' he mumbled.

'I'm sorry?'

'Oh… nothing, don' worry.'

I closed the book in front of me and dropped it on the pile. 'I need to go to the Staff Room. You don't even need to turn the lights on okay?'

'You sure?' He frowned 'It's pretty dark there without the lights. Gives me the heebie-jeebies.'

'I won't be there long.'

He rolled his eyes 'A'right, but be quick. If you could hop the fence when you're done, to the car park I mean, cause I'm locking the front.'

I nodded, thanked him and he walked off, keys jingling into the dark corridors. I stood up, replacing my ear buds and changing the track on my phone to something suitably cheerful, whilst working out the kinks in my shoulders, back and legs. I'd stupidly chosen to sit on one of my kids' seats at their tables, since there was sod all room for an actual desk in my classroom. I had a narrow, wobbly table, which the kids pawed at *constantly*. I learned very quickly to actually use the locks on my drawers, after one of the little bastards (was I already so cynical? I'd only been qualified about two years…) had stolen my nice post-it notes and used them to doodle on. Little git. He wouldn't write in his bloody books, but would happily scribble all over my expensive Korean stationery.

Serves me right really, what did I expect? They're children, they have no impulse control.

Then again, I could talk… I'm still here; when it's dark outside, the car park's deserted (except my lonely little hatchback, under one of the floodlights like something out the Exorcist), when most of the *sane* adults had gone home.

I stood up, grabbing my ID to unlock the Staff Room door, taking my insulated mug, pausing to rub the sore spot between my shoulders, then setting off. One more coffee for the road, check my Pigeon Hole and save my Phonics and Literacy planning to a memory stick to finish at home. I'd be done. And it would really only take fifteen minutes. No.

Really.

I stepped out of my classroom, into a dark, empty corridor. None of the lights were on in the other classrooms, except for the moonlight (now *that's* a bad sign) that poured in through the windows and funnelled out in front of me. It's always eerie when a place so normally full of noise, human noise- shouts, chatter, crying, screaming, singing- then it's suddenly completely, utterly quiet. It seems as though all the life has gone, making you feel abandoned. Not to mention the displays along the walls, normally so bright and colourful during the day, suddenly seeming muted, caved in and flat, as if they had been left to rot. The smiles in the drawings on display became oddly empty, and uncomfortable to look at, the glassy-eyed stares of the papier-mâché creations around the library (a snake, a giraffe and a monkey) all looking... leery. Unbearably creepy. The moonlight casting everything in a white glow against the darkness and caught the lumps and bumps in the paint and made it look, to my sleep deprived mind, like skin. Not animal... human, fleshy, with all its pockmarks and crevices. I walked faster, but the silence swallowed all sounds, save my footsteps and a slight clink of my necklace. It only made the echoes louder, bouncing off the polished floors and glossed white walls, emphasising I was really and truly the only person here. Everything seemed taller, wider, nagging at me, creating a feeling of void and hopelessness and slowing me to a stop. I pulled my cardigan around my shoulders against a cold that ate its way into my skin, finding its way into my bones. Did I just not notice before? I could've sworn I was fine just a minute ago. I put it down to ending the day, given how highly strung and busy I was from about seven am till now, a full twelve hours. The stillness was getting to me, but only because I was simply acclimatising to an absence of noise that I had been subjected to all day.

Though, now that I thought about it, I would have probably welcomed it again. Anything was better than this... feeling so utterly isolated here.

It even seemed to even filter through the music I was playing, making it drain away to a distant, tinny squeak before dropping out completely. I sighed and checked my phone and to my confusion, the battery had gone all together, which was odd, since I could've sworn I had had it on charge all day. I tried turning it back on, determined not to traverse the sinister empty hall with no music, but nothing. I sighed, gave up and put it back in my dress pocket, yanking out my ear buds and braving the empty passageway in silence. When I finally arrived at the Staff Room, I whipped off my lanyard and buzzed myself in via my ID card, I had to flick the lights on, promising myself I would remember to turn them off.

Just have a coffee, go back, pack up and find the Site Manager.

Then get the hell out.

I picked up the kettle, turned the tap and filled it, the running water also seeming so bloody loud. I had earned myself one more coffee, I needed it… I just needed the energy to leave. Why did I feel as though I was sneaking everywhere? Trying not to make so much noise? I should be making more noise, try to get out of my own head and not be scared of the dark! I'm a teacher! I'm meant to be the one to reassure others. Whilst the kettle wheezed into life, I wondered over to my Pigeon Hole, trying to whistle or strike up a few chords of a song. Songs I teach my kids, since they are the ones that get stuck in my head. I'll be reciting 'Days of the Week' when I'm senile I reckon. Ha ha ha.

See? I'm alright.

I am the responsible adult. I work here five days a week. I've stayed late (okay, not this late but still) and I've not felt like this before. I'm fine.

'Ah, ah, apple,' I tried, my voice quavering against the empty room, 'I can sound out the letter A…'

I opened my drawer, flicking through the papers for anything I needed for my planning- change to the weeks we were using, anything that needed adapting for my new bi-lingual boy coming in next week, what about Linda's birthday on the twenty eighth etc. etc.

The kettle clicked and made me jump, just as I was reaching the letter C, and I practically threw my badge across the room in shock.

Bloody hell I need to go home. Why am I even here right now?

I walked over to fetch it, then strode back with a confidence I really did not feel (a neat trick if you can do it, especially in front of children who really have your number) reaching the sideboard to spoon in coffee and sugar. It was a familiar dance, I can do it in my sleep- spoon, coffee, sugar, water.

'Christ I could go for a fag right now.'

I stopped, my whole body poised in rigid terror. Had I just heard that voice? It was faint, barely more than a trace, but I swear I had heard someone- I replaced the kettle and breathed in the smell of… burning. Not coffee. It was right in front of me, but I couldn't smell it. Yeah, it definitely smelled of burning. I checked the kettle, but it seemed fine, then I checked my clothes… I don't smoke. Why would I smell of…? No, as I reared my head and sniffed the air around me like a frightened animal, I began to recognise it.

It was *cigarette* smoke.

Was it me? No, it couldn't be, I didn't smoke. No one smoked in here-

'Make us a tea, there's a good girl.'

I shook my head and rubbed my ears. It felt as though it was coming from just inside my field of hearing, distant, as if I were listening through water. I blinked, bent to open the fridge, concluding I was tired and hearing things. And smelling things. Bloody hell.

I had one hand on the counter as the other reached in for milk, maintaining my balance.

'Duh, duh, dog,' I sang as I grabbed the carton, 'I can sound out the letter D.'

As I stood up, I felt some strange weight on my hand, which registered slowly in my desperately distracted brain.

Something on my hand.

The pressure was cold, clammy at first, like someone's

palm. I must've blanked, must've frozen as my mind caught up to what was happening because I didn't react at first.

'You deaf or something? Daft little bird isn't she?'

I moved my arm in a jerk, finally reacting when I realised, and knocking over my mug, spilling hot coffee onto my bare arm. I cursed loudly, the room swallowing it as it swallowed the thunk of my mug hitting the lino-flooring and the splash of coffee on the sideboard. I thrust my arm under the tap and poured cold water on the spot where my skin began to flare and scold. I took the chance, amongst the pain, and the shock, to try and look around for the source of the voice.

I had heard it, it wasn't familiar either- it was educated, male, well spoken, but conflicted with the Cockney-isms it tried to use.

There was no one here, I found myself thinking, there's a voice, but there's no one here. You can't be hearing it.

But I must be. The alternative was too crazy to think about.

There was no trace of the grip on my arm, it was as if it had never been there. The pain was lulled a little by the water, but I would have to go. I could leave with the burn long enough till I got home and put an ice pack on it. I wanted to leave, sod everything else. I'll clean up in the morning. As I shut off the tap, I caught it again; the smell of fags. Old too, clinging to clothes, a fug that would hang around someone who chugged ciggies like a steam engine, but now it was mingled with a sour, sickly boozy smell that threatened to make me gag. It was close, I could feel it like a fine mist on my face.

Then there was the voice, only now it travelled about the room, as if it were seeping out of the walls, closing in, disorientating and slithering in and out of my field of hearing.

'Silly tart.'

'Too soft on them.'

'No wonder they walk all over you.'

'Stick to the kitchen.

You're not cut out for this job.'

It was like a bad joke, a strange distilling of a stereotype that surrounded me with words more spat than spoken. As the voices moved about, the lights began to flicker, going out one by one like snuffed candles.

That's it. I was leaving. I had my ID card, clutching it like a security blanket and tried to turn for the door, when I heard laughter- cruel, bullying, rippling- a chorus of different voices, mostly men, one or two lone women, closing in on me.

'She's a little slapper really.'

'You hear that little gypo in 5A? Who's he think he is?'

'Could you just leave me alone?'

'Yeah, course I would!'

'Look, I'm tired just get off-'

'I'll speak to the Union on the second-'

'Call it affirmative action don't they?'

'Cocky little cow.'

'Show's what happens when you give 'em an inch don' it?'

I found myself trying to speak, but before I could, something heavy landed into my stomach, knocking me, breathless and doubled up, against the cupboards. I had been punched, but

I saw no one, no one there, so who just hit me? I felt tears cut down my cheeks and a sob escape, barely, as I tried to look around.

How had this even happened? How had I got here?

'You'll die here you little whore.'

I forced myself up, my fist clenching around the little card, and falling against the door.

'Stupid little bitch!'

I did not look back, just grabbed for the handle and swiped my card against the lock, the little *beep* sounding and the door swinging outwards. I had left everything there and staggered out, my mind on fire, my breath caught in my lungs and my legs barely working. I turned and began walking, running when I could finally compel my limbs and not stopping until I-

'Shirl? You seen Marcus? He seemed in a bad way.'

I turned back. I stood, confused and trying to gather my wits. I blinked, as if I had stepped out into a bright sunny day after being in the dark for so long. Everything stung and throbbed-my arm especially.

'Shirl? You alright love?'

I tried to look around, but everything was too… bright… which didn't make any sense, it was the middle of the night-no, gone seven. The evening. Certainly not the middle of the day.

'Um,' I began, my jaw feeling loose and useless, but I couldn't work out why.

'I'm… a bit off today. Need to get back.'

I said that.

Except I didn't.

'You go on home love, let Cynth cover you, it's only Music, they can just sing for an hour can't they?'

'No no, I'm alright, can't-'

Wait… Who's Cynth?

My name isn't Shirl either.

'Going somewhere?'

Home. I'm getting my car keys, getting out via the back, car, keys, home. I reached out to the wall to gain my balance, my fingers touched the wall- but instead of a colourful display about the Aztecs, I touched rough brick, the surface scratching my fingertips. I breathed in the floor polish, the cleaning fluid, the pens, the paper, the… chalk.

When was the last time we used chalk? We don't even use pens anymore, most of us have the Interactive Whiteboards-

But that was my rational brain, refusing to accept this. Refusing to believe what I had seen, what I had heard, what I could clearly smell. Now I could hear a bell, a low loud ring nearby and the rush of noise that I recognised; children. They were laughing, screaming, chattering as if they had not a care in their little lives. The voices got closer then farther away, rushing past me and around me, making me a rock in the middle of a stream.

'Did you hear what Rhonda said in Third Period?'

'They said there's a Paki joining our class.'

'What's the score? You find out last night?'

'I'll swap for a coupla fags-'

'She's such a queer, you know it, we all do. Shouldn't be allowed to teach.'

I looked about and the whole place looked blurred and strange, but there were outlines of places I did not recognise as my school- there were wooden desks that opened like a treasure box, clouds of chalk dust, ink wells, the click and fizzle of an OHP (did they still have them when I was at school?). I coughed, retched and moved back, my eyes screwed shut against the pain. I felt burned, confused, still reeling at how fast it had all happened.

'Did you tell 'em? Did you grass me up?'

'What?' I managed, gasping like a landed fish, my voice lost in a wheeze as I groped out in front of me with my other hand. This voice was new, younger, rougher, but nearby and accompanied by running feet.

'Oi! No running!'

'What's going... what-' my own voice seemed only connected to my throat by accident.

'I need the toilet sir! Please let me go-'

That voice was female, sounded barely above fourteen. My outstretched hand found something nearby, intangible, I felt something... cold. Like somehow touching cold air that was forming into something solid, like feeling it take shape. This last voice was a young man to, cracking from desperation, trying to assert himself, but you could hear how he was covering for his sobbing.

'Who'd you think you are?!'

'Don't... know,' I responded, stupidly, forcing my eyes open 'don't... know anything.'

'Well you know what they say eh? Those who don't know...'

She sounded like a colleague- friendly, kind, understanding. She got it. She knew the joke of it all.

'Teach, ha ha ha,' I laughed, finishing the adage, against any rational sense, as the world swam into focus, against a rising tide of-

SMOKE.

I looked around me, the heat and flames enveloping and strangling, catching the children's coats, the paper notices, the wooden desks cracking under the heat and something glass snapping and exploding nearby. The corridor was ablaze, the fire pouring out of the doors, the smoke rising above us and turning everything to ash in its path. I took in a lungful and coughed until my eyes began to water. I could smell petrol to, under the smoke. Footsteps sounded over the cacophony, drawing closer to me.

'I'll take this whole place with me.'

I tried to scream, I did, but nothing came out except something strangled and weak. I tried to walk, but nothing worked, tried to turn away to leave. I want to go home.

I need to get home. I have...

Something so cold, so cold against the heat that rose around me, that clung my clothes to my skin in sweat, clung to my shoulder and pulled me back, spinning me round. I almost pirouetted, everything feeling weightless and strangely distant. I felt something hit my face, hard, right on the cheek and then along my body, the cold of the polished floor flashing along my side. The pain blossoming in slow motion until my eyes adjusted, my head coming into contact with the world around me. I managed to get up, wobbling like a newborn deer, nausea creeping up my throat and my arm now useless, I could feel the bruises- I might have even sprained my ankle, why had I even been running in the first place?

I could feel a great, unyielding pressure against my throat, my arms too weak to move it as it choked me. I must've begun to black out, maybe, because it was as if everything began to fade away, piece by piece, swallowed up by darkness the clouded my eyes and made me feel like I was falling backwards through the floor. My lungs filled with smoke and my breathing grew weaker and weaker. This felt like a descent, like I was being pulled down, slowly, but relentlessly. I opened my mouth to cry out but… what's the point? There's no one else here.

I just need a rest, just need to close my eyes a minute… I'll be better

…when I wake up.

'Morning love, you seem better today!'

'Just think, holidays in three weeks! Cheer up!'

The Site Manager's in a lot of trouble for letting me stay late, but he's too devastated to care. Haven't seen him around the place much since then. They talk about me in assembly, they all gather and try and explain to the gathered throng of children just how a young, healthy teacher died at school, late at night. Strangely enough, they leave that detail out- that I was here. I don't blame them honestly, the children don't need to be scared. So many of them are upset, didn't realise they liked me so much. Despite the attempt at shielding them, however, kids have a way of finding these things out. They know they should be scared, but they are still curious. They talk about me in the playground, especially the older ones.

'I heard she died in the toilets.'

'Did she have a heart attack?'

'She was scared to death, Mum said so.'

'Did she kill herself?'

They whisper about it in the cloakroom and in the toilets, some have heard the rumour about how Miss Hiller died at school. The parents gossip as they wait for their kids.

'She was only young, bless her.'

'Her mum was devastated.'

'We ought to have a whip round.'

'Has someone sent a card?'

The Staff Room is quiet mostly, my friends just sit or stand helplessly nursing their teas and coffees until they have to go and put on another front for the children. I like to sit with them sometimes, waiting for the atmosphere to pick up again, waiting for them to start *talking* to each other.

'Least this time it was an accident,' I overhear a couple of hushed conversations from the Lunchtime staff as they pick up a quick cuppa before going home. The first speaker is Carla, I liked her. A bit insensitive, but nice.

'Yeah. I remember him, Mr Winters. Posh bloke. My three eldest used to go here when he was a teacher, back when it was Lee Hill Secondary. He was nuts, you could see it in him.' I can't remember this lady's name, but I think it's Dot. She's grandmother to half the school by either blood or marriage.

'Though no one thought he'd burn the place down,' Gill is speaking now.

'I did, or do something else mental,' Dot laughed.

'That poor girl though, she hadn't been here long,' Carla remarked, sadly 'I think Callum's mum is doing a collection for her parents.'

'If she is put me down,' Dot sipped her tea, 'least we could do.'

I even made the local paper. There's going to be an enquiry and everything. None of the other teachers stay any later than four now, no matter how much work they have. I think it's probably sensible.

Not that I don't like it where I am. It's actually quite pleasant. During the day at any rate. I stay in my end of the school, I don't go near the Staff Room after dark. I stay in my classroom, amongst the work my children made. They're getting so big, they'll be moving up soon. I notice that the little sods have stopped taking stuff from their new teacher's table. She's nice, the new one I mean. She's always enthusiastic, kind and patient. I'm glad she's here. She's sensitive though, that *could* be her downfall. She's been pushing herself too much.

The thing is… *He's* still there. The one who killed me. He still tries to claim someone else every now and again, but I'm here now too. In time, someone else will be misguided and foolish enough to stay, just a few more minutes, one more cup of coffee, one more book.

I'll be here to tell them to leave whilst they still can. Don't end up like me, I whisper, just go home.

Because those who can't.

Teach.

The Astartic Arcanum

Carol Borden

Josiah Olds Brandt was utterly insane by the time he first gazed into the pool of blood, but he didn't feel mad. He felt completely in harmony with the true nature of reality. He could see lives in the pool. He could see the dreams of the whole world. And more, within the incarnadine depths, he saw fragments of the incomprehensible dreams of eldritch gods and their inconceivably ancient worlds.

Brandt gave himself over to them these visions. He had sacrificed his own father, the brilliant engineer Ephraim Brandt, to see more of the shrieking mindless horror he now knew reality to be. Brandt exsanguinated the old fool, a man who had thought to conquer the world through machinery and his own false god, greed. The vanity of the man still enraged Brandt. He had laughed as his father's blood spurted rhythmically into the bone cistern, the first blood to sanctify the pool. And when his mother, the notorious Abolitionist and Suffragist, Lucinda Olds Brandt, dared call him, 'Beast!' Josiah Brandt slit her open, too, though she was unworthy of sacrifice. He left his mother's blood, useless, meaningless, seeping into Brandt House's great hickory verandah. He sacrificed others to serve his purpose, to see more. No one would miss them. They were forgotten men who sought a better life on the lines of Brandt Motors and found a damnation that served Brandt's destiny.

Josiah Brandt's dreams had led him to a cracked rock behind the woods of Brandt House. In the bowels of the earth, he found a chamber made from the remains of a creature alien to earth's natural order. And in the center of the room was a bone cistern set into the floor and waiting to be filled. Its edges were inscribed with runes old when humankind's ancestors first rose and walked. Before Brandt had been anointed with the mark of his destiny, even looking at the runes had left him dizzy and nauseated. Trying to make sense of them, he vomited.

Brandt saw so much now. He gazed into his scrying pool and saw terrible and incomprehensible things. Now among the sluggish rippling and dark clots, he saw the world as it always should have been. He saw fragments of other dimensions and the incomprehensible dreams of ancient, alien gods. He could bring the world its its apotheosis. Such was his faith. The Great War had changed Brandt much more than it had changed most men. He had willingly taken all the horror within himself—the mud, the gas, the rotting men, the screaming horses crushed beneath the new power of the world. And he transmuted it all into a new and terrible faith. The Great Old Ones found him then and Brandt welcomed their coming. They lodged within his mind and ached within him, like shrapnel that could never be removed, burrowing ever deeper till he could swear he felt his very soul bleed. The alien gods germinated inside him and grew inside his dreams. They curled round and round themselves within his mind until there was no more room. Their tendrils pierced through him, blindly groping towards our world.

The desire to see more, to know more and to share his knowledge buzzed within Josiah Brandt. The world had long been bound by lies and willful blindness. Soon all of humanity would see what he saw. They would rage and froth at their utter insignificance, falling on each other until humanity finally destroyed itself. Then Brandt would take his place among his Gods, shaping and reshaping the world at his whim. He was the genius, not his father, that old pretender. He, Josiah Brandt, was the true creator. The blood stirred and burbled before him, seeming to laugh with him. In its depths, Shub-Niggurath grinned at him, a goat with impossibly human eyes and a voice like an infant's burbling. He saw Cthulhu dreaming in the abyss. He saw the iridescent, almost viral spheres of Yog-Sothoth. He saw the ineffable chaos of Azathoth. Finally, he saw a woman dreaming. He saw her gaze back at him. Brandt had carefully planned the ritual that would open the world to his gods. He would lure the perfect sacrifice to him with dreams. Hers would be the first woman's blood to stain the ancient cistern. It was better if Miss Nita

Sloan knew. Someone should know of his impending glory. And sighing as the images ceased appearing in the blood, Brandt was almost content.

***

The conductor steadied Nita Sloan as she stepped onto the platform at Detroit's Michigan Central Station. Josiah Brandt, the automotive millionaire, had personally invited her to come and to read from her translation of *The Astartic Arcanum* for the benefit of his gentleman's club the following morning. In his letter, he noted that she was the first woman ever so honored. There was to be a reception this evening at his home outside the city in Grosse Pointe Shores. Brandt assured her that it was an informal gathering of friends and, he ventured to hope, soon-to-be friends. Brandt suggested an overnight stay, writing that a driver would return her to the Book-Cadillac Hotel after her reading. Nita had agreed—and had agreed to her fiancé's request not to shock the bourgeois gentlemen of the O.T.A. Club no matter how tempted—and no matter how much she believed they wanted to be shocked. But in truth, she had agreed so that she could investigate a series of strange dreams that had been afflicting the more sensitive minds among her friends. And Nita herself had been dreaming strange dreams for weeks now.

Nita's calling had been poetry. She wrote slim volumes and published in radical, but rarely read magazines with a small but committed base of subscribers. She had stuck close to home, making a small career of reading her own work and occasionally touring with artists, writers primarily. Modern all, with hardly a rhyme between them. Most recently, she had begun translations of ancient texts, poems, hymns, myths and more esoteric works, earning a position in the Department of Archaeology and Occult Research at Butler College, the sister school of Miskatonic University. She had spent the last five years exploring ruins and translating ancient tablets, culminating in her most recent work, a translation of *The Astartic Arcanum*, a collection of hymns and rituals dedicated to Mesopotamian goddesses.

She hadn't wanted to worry her editor at Miskatonic University Press, but she believed she had translated *The Astartic Arcanum* while in a trance. She recalled only sitting down to work and then awoke seemingly a moment later with an entire manuscript and her hands cramped and shaking. *The Astartic Arcanum* had done remarkably well, even garnering a reference by *The New Yorker*'s Constant Reader. Her editor was ecstatic, but Nita quit her translations. In truth, she had quit writing entirely, though she told no one. She occupied her writing hours with crossword puzzles and doggerel. She became a master of the limerick and the double dactyl, starting far too many conversations with waiters, colleagues and even her fiancé with that telling sign of the double dactyl, ' Higgledy-piggledy' and finishing the same conversations with a raunchy flourish. Even then, she was haunted by visions of hideous, gibbering things and clotting blood. Her dreams lately felt unwholesome and very little felt unwholesome to Nita Sloan.

Nita waved off a porter, carrying her two suitcases herself, and followed the crowd down a flight of stairs, up a marble ramp and through wrought-iron gates to a cavernous marble waiting room filled with crowds of travelers. According to the station clock, her train had arrived a half an hour early. She threaded through the crowds and massive Corinthian columns and found a quiet lounge to await the driver Brandt had arranged. She wished she had the Hudson roadster her fiancé, Richard, had given her as an engagement gift. She was very fond of it. Driving herself was so much more convenient, but it was impractical to embark on cross-country journey by automobile when time was of the essence. No matter the speed of her car, the roads were unreliable.

Nita draped her coat over a chair, removed her brown leather gloves and ordered café au lait from a passing waiter. Then she took a notebook from her handbag. She hadn't wanted to worry Richard, but her dreams were very similar to those of her friends recorded in these pages. She had the strangest feeling that Brandt was at the center of all this. The night before she left Manhattan, Nita had dreamed she stood before a tree growing from a cleft rock. Then she saw men in gray robes surrounding a black goat in a cavern carved from the bone of a chthonic monstrosity. Their leader, a man with a hooked steel blade looked at Nita then and she knew that he saw her, too. The men stripped off their robes. They were all ages and sizes, some more athletically built than others, but they were all white men and all were over fifty. The men chanted louder in a language she did not recognize, one that seemed both inhuman and impossibly familiar. The men began to shake. Some fell to the ground convulsing in seizures, but the chant never ceased. It grew more frenzied. Nita covered her ears as the men tore at the goat with their hands and teeth. The men smeared blood on themselves, shrieking. As the goat died, its screams became like an infant's cries. The dead animal looked at Nita and from inside its wrecked body, it said something, something she did not remember afterwards.

She had awoken in her apartment overlooking the Miskatonic River. Richard's hand was on her arm over the satin comforter. 'The dream again?'

'Yes. The men. That poor goat.'

'You said something.'

Nita did not want to know, but she had to. 'What did I say?'

'Names, peculiar names, 'Azathoth' was one. ' Shub-Niggurath' was another.'

'Oh, God, that was part of the chant.: ' Iä, Shub-Niggurath! The Black Goat of the Woods with a Thousand Young!' '

Richard held her closer and kissed her head. 'Can you imagine a thousand young?'

'I can't imagine one.'

Richard squeezed her arm. 'You look positively ghastly. We need scotch.' Richard rose and mixed drinks at the small silver and cherry wood bar kept in the bedroom for what he called, 'medicinal purposes.'

'If the doctor thinks it's best.'

'He does. And he's prescribing a double for both of us.'

'Far be it from me to argue with a man of science.'

Nita glanced at Richard as he handed her the drink. 'You're that worried?'

Richard sat down on the edge of the bed. 'I am, but I

think with the right fortification, we can lick this thing yet.'

'Not an apocalypse.'

'It's always something with you, dear.'

'To Shub-Niggurath!' She toasted with a cheer she tried to feel.

He raised his glass, 'To Shub-Niggurath!'

'I think tomorrow, before I go to Mr. Brandt's wingding, I'll do some reading at the university.'

'Don't tell me you're getting educated.'

'Just you wait. I'm a modern woman. Soon I'll even be voting.'

Nita slid back under the covers. Richard turned out his lamp and slipped back into bed with her. 'Don't worry. You're too ornery to beat, darling.'

Nita lay awake for a while as Richard stroked her arm and back. When she finally slept, she didn't dream.

The waiter had set her coffee on the table without Nita noticing. A little alarmed that she had so thoroughly lost track of her surroundings, Nita took a sip and turned to her notes. A young man with brown eyes and curls escaping his snap-brimmed cap, interrupted her, introduced himself as her driver, Geoffrey. He waited politely as she put her notebook away and left money on the table. He helped her on with her coat and offered to carry her luggage. She declined. They set off through the station's cavernous western entrance and down to the underground parking. Geoffrey led her to a gleaming, scarlet Duesenberg.

'Zowie, that Brandt character isn't fooling around!' Nita set down her suitcases and walked around the car, admiring it from all angles.

'No, ma'am. That Brandt character doesn't do anything by half.' Geoffrey swept up her suitcases and stowed them in the enormous car's trunk. 'This is a Duesenberg SJ.'

'Shouldn't Mr. Brandt send a Brandtmobile Teetotaller or whatever they're making now?'

'Mr. Brandt is not exactly fond of the late, lamented Ephraim Brandt, self-professed perfecter of the automobile.'

Geoffrey gestured Nita toward the passenger side door.

Nita shook her head and held out her hand for the keys. 'Let me know where to let you off, Geoffrey.'

He crossed his arm and stood his ground. 'Ma'am, I was told to take you wherever you wanted to go.'

'I'll have you know I have been taking myself where I wanted to go since you were in short pants and long curls.'

'You're not that old, ma'am. You can't be older than thirty-five.'

'And here I was certain my wizened features gave you youngsters a fright.' Nita took a step closer, her hand still outstretched. 'Give me the keys.'

Geoffrey shook his head. 'Ma'am, Mr. Brandt told me to make sure you didn't get lost. You don't know your way around.'

'I've a Baedeker. It has a map of the city and all Pointes Grosse.'

'Detroit is changing.'

'You are obstinate.'

'And you're stubborn, ma'am.'

They scowled at each other a moment. Nita sighed. 'Well, there are a lot of Grosse Pointes to keep track of—Grosse Pointe Shores, Grosse Pointe Woods, Grosse Pointe...'

Geoffrey looked relieved.

'Oh, alright, but I'm driving,' Nita said. Geoffrey opened the driver's side door for Nita and handed her the keys in one smooth movement. 'And make sure they pay you. I won't stand for a man not being paid for the work he's been contracted not to do.'

'Yes, ma'am,' said as he closed the door.

'Geoffrey, I can see you'll be a comfort to a woman in her twilight years.'

Geoffrey didn't bother to hide his laugh.

'It's a shame that I won't see any of the city,' Nita said as she watched the trees flashing by in the fading light. Just outside the city, they had stopped for coffee and sandwiches at a roadside dinette. She had let Geoffrey take a turn at the wheel. Nita was less persuaded by his argument that he would look bad arriving in the passenger's seat and more by

Geoffrey's argument that it was unfair that she should have all the fun driving the Duesenberg. 'Not that I don't appreciate Mr. Brandt's kind invitation. I'd just like to see that Rivera fellow's murals. And I'd rather go dancing.'

'I wouldn't mind a dance myself, ma'am,' Geoffrey said without looking away from the road.

'If we survive the reception, Geoffrey, I'll teach you to rumba.'

***

Brandt House was not nearly as old as it pretended to be. Ephraim Brandt had built the house as a testament to his family name, which, until recently, had been associated with gamblers and horse-racing aficionados. It was a composite of imposing mansions: a hodge-podge of Beaux Arts, Gothic, Tudor, Arte Moderne and Neo-Classical Revival. Portions of a castle had been shipped in from the Orkney Islands and architects from four competing firms had designed additions, making the house a monument not only to terrible taste but to outraged good taste.

Nita gaped out of her window. 'You're lucky you're seeing the house at night when it is merely unsightly. It's unspeakably hideous by daylight.' Geoffrey helped Nita out of the car. 'Let's see if we can find you a perfectly banal guest room.'

Nita saw something move in the trees, something hard to comprehend, half-lit by an enormous, rusty moon. Turning back towards the verandah, Nita said, 'Banal sounds about right.'

The overly wrought oak door was covered in grape leaves and mermaids. There was a large brass knocker, a minotaur with a large ring piercing through his nose. Geoffrey, however, took a key from his pocket, unlocked the door and gestured Nita inside. No one greeted them at the door, but Nita could hear voices from somewhere deeper inside the house. She followed Geoffrey up a curving flight of heavily veined marble stairs with a balustrade wrapped with cloisonné lilies. Geoffrey led her to the end of a dark-paneled hall and to a room with a bay window that overlooked the driveway. She felt better seeing the Duesenberg. 'My getaway will be grand at least,' she thought.

The room was indeed perfectly banal, completely nondescript with no wrong angles or tributes to ego or poor taste. Just a bed, a chair and a small dressing table with a mirror. Geoffrey left Nita to change, telling her to come down to the banquet room when she was ready. Nita brushed out her bob and dressed in a sleeveless peach silk gown under a gold lace tunic with elder signs and pentagrams worked into the tatting. She had designed it herself. 'Safety first,' Nita said as she examined herself in the mirror. She went downstairs and followed the sound of voices to a large room filled with fifteen or twenty white men in black tie. They all turned to watch her. She was the only skirt in the room, and their intent stares felt more like scientific curiosity than sex appeal. 'Oh, what have you got yourself into, Nita,' she thought

They were men of consequence and indistinguishably graying. One was a former Mayor of Detroit; another a Senator from a nearby state. Each avowed himself a tremendous admirer of her work. The hors d'oeuvres were bad. To drink, there was only a bowl of non-alcoholic and far too sweet punch.

'Mr. Brandt does not approve of alcoholic beverages,' a man drinking cupfuls of the punch informed her. He was a thin and gray with very round glasses.

'Yes, he prefers a healthful punch,' another added.

Deciding against the punch, Nita instead perused Brandt's collection of alchemical works arrayed in a glass case with a lock it wouldn't take her a moment to pick: Daniel Stolz von Stolzenberg's *Viridarium Chymicum*; Kirchweger's *Aurea Catena Homeri*; a gorgeous copy of Salomon Trismosin's *Splendor Solis*; Flamel's *Chymische Werke*; Balfour's *Cultes des Goules*; *The Book Of The Holy Trinity*; Junzt's *Unaussprechliche Kulten*; an abridged copy of the *Corpus Hermeticum*; and, of course, an English translation of Abdel Alhazred's *Necronomicon*, published by Miskatonic University Press. 'Ritual magicians are such bores,' Nita snorted.

'Gesundheit!' She turned to find the thin gray man with very round glasses at her elbow. He offered her a yellowed handkerchief. Nita smiled blandly. 'No, thank you.'

'These old books can be quite dusty, even when locked safely away,' the man said, smiling benevolently.

'There are quite a lot of dusty books in the world,' Nita said, thinking of the *Necronomicon*.

He moved closer and she could smell his peculiarly fishy aftershave. 'I thought I should tell you, Miss Sloan, that Conrad Aiken's warning to his readers about the 'tentacular quiverings' of your verse was quite unfair. I am certain I would find your quiverings most provocative in only the best sense of the word.'

Somehow, she remembered her promise to her fiancé not to tease the millionaires. Nita smiled her blandest smile.

'One has, of course, heard that your lifestyle is quite unique, quite modern, perhaps even Bohemian, shall we say,' the man peered at her over his cheaters.

'We had best not, Mister...?'

'Dodge. Call me, 'Edward.' I am a cousin of Mr. Ephraim Brandt.' Mr. Edward Dodge peered over his glasses at Nita again, 'You are the first woman to be invited to a meeting of our Club, you know.'

'So I've been told.' Nita saw Geoffrey in black tie and tuxedo discreetly drinking from a flask near a titanic sundew in a pot decorated with blue and yellow glazed tiles. 'Mr. Brandt does not approve of alcoholic beverages,' Dodge told her pointedly when he saw her glance. Geoffrey snatched a an empty punch cup and walked over to join them. Dodge scowled and claiming an interest in 'healthful punch,' retreated.

'You drink, Miss Sloan.' Geoffrey pouring her whisky from his flask.

'In a glass and everything.'

'Keeping up appearances.'

'You clean up well.'

'Thank you. Maybe you could put in a good word with the old man.'

'Which one?'

'We do have a surfeit of graybeards at this to-do. But there is only one old man in my life at the moment.'

'A healthy, red-blooded young man like you should be leading three or four around on a string.'

'I am that most awful of things, a cliché. I am the wayward, layabout son of one Josiah Olds Brandt, though he would never admit it. I never knew my mother. A maid, I am told, of 'impure blood.' Whatever he means by that, I am sure I do not want to know. I do know it enraged my grandmother before her accident.'

'Accident.'

'In a great irony, Ephraim and Lucinda Brandt kicked the bucket in a particularly gory automobile accident. My father used his extensive connections to cover up their deaths in the press. Not good for business, you know, when an automobile inventor dies in a car of his very own design. After the accident, I was raised by those very same extensive connections. I'm Josiah Brandt's only mistake, to hear him tell it.'

'Oh, Geoffrey, that's awful. I wish you'd told me.'

'Sometimes it's nice to be someone else.'

Just then, the assembled gray men fell back as Brandt, distinguished and dark-haired in his fifties, entered the parlor. Brandt approached Nita. Brandt stared at her in a most unnerving way. His was the ghastly white face she remembered from her dreams.

'Welcome to Brandt House, Miss Sloan,' Brandt said taking her elbow. 'I was quite taken with *The Astartic Arcanum*. One rarely meets a translator of your talent and sophistication. And I didn't expect a professor—let alone a spinster in her thirties—to be quite so beautiful.'

Brandt's smile never reached his eyes. 'You have of course seen my small public library,' he said. But perhaps you should see something of equal beauty to your own. I saw you admire my *Drosera pyrtlensis* earlier, for you certainly could not be admiring young Geoffrey. There is among my botanical specimens one great wonder, an *Amorphophallus titanum* and in a very remarkable coincidence, its bloom reached their peak this very evening for the first time in years.'

Nita smelled a rank scent as Brandt led Nita down a hall toward a small green room built into the mansion. 'Mine is the first *Amorphophallus* specimen to successfully flower outside of Sumatra since the species was discovered. In English it is called the corpse flower.' The flower dominated the small room both aromatically and physically. It was over ten feet in height, wrapped with a dark green and deep red, almost black sheath containing a titanic, waxy white column. The scent of decay was overpowering. 'Exquisite is it not? The perfect expression of the transformation of death.'

'Oh, phooey, Mr. Brandt. That's not death. That's sex. The odor is the flower's unpleasant way of pitching woo.' Nita's refutation was a little more nasal than she would have liked. She had resorted to pinching her nose shut with her fingers because of the flower's relentless woo.

'It is as Kirchweger wrote,' Brandt responded. " Decay is a wonderful smith.' From the illusion of death we see a transmutation into new life.' Brandt looked past Nita and for the first time, Nita noticed the doorway had filled with the men silently staring at her.

Brandt turned to the men and raised his arms as if to forestall any protests. 'We've enjoyed ourselves and now, my friends, it is time to retire. I must attend to preparations for the great event and I'm sure Miss Sloan is tired from her journey.' He turned back to Nita, 'Sweet dreams is so trite, wouldn't you agree, Miss Sloan? I shall wish you instead interesting dreams.' As he spoke, Nita imagined she saw a writhing mass of inchoate shapes where Brandt stood.

Geoffrey shouldered his way through the silent men. 'Miss Sloan, you look a little pale. I'll show you upstairs.' Geoffrey glared pointedly at his father as he continued, 'I'll be next door, if you should need anything.'

Nita nodded at the elder Brandt and took Geoffrey's arm. She wished she had never agreed to come to Brandt House. She hardly knew why she had, except for the dreams. The dreams that inevitably led to corpses arrayed on a cavern floor. She just couldn't allow that to happen if she could stop it.

'Buck up, Sloan. You'll get through this,' she told her reflection in the dressing table mirror. That night, Nita's dreams were more intense than ever. Thick bloody tentacles pulled her toward inconceivable darkness. She thought she heard Geoffrey screaming in agony. But when she struggled awake, sweating and shaking, the house was silent. Listening as still as she could be, Nita felt an almost irresistible compulsion to go into the woods behind Brandt House. She rose and fumbled for the silver flask in her suitcase. Nita took a swig of bourbon, grimaced, then took a second. 'Well, I guess it's time to get this over with then,' she said sadly to her flask.

Nita dressed quickly in the dark. She wore a plain white shirt, tan slacks tucked into knee high, lace-up brown leather boots and an aviator's jacket. She was slipping a canvas satchel over her shoulder when she heard a quiet knock. She opened the door. It was Geoffrey stood fully dressed in the doorway. 'You weren't going alone, were you, Nita?'

'He's your father, Geoff.'

Geoffrey said nothing. She wished she could see his face. Geoffrey walked into her room and sat at the small stool in front of the dressing table. He waited until Nita had closed the door again to speak. 'I think he killed my mother and my grandparents. I thought my dreams were only dreams, but it was all real, wasn't it?'

Nita sat on the end of the bed and sighed. 'He wants to bring madness to the world. He's summoning... something very unpleasant. I have to stop him.'

'I'm coming with you.'

Nita put her hand on his shoulder. 'Good man.'

Nita and Geoffrey had no trouble slipping out of the house unseen. It seemed almost completely empty, aside from the loud snoring of one of the maids. It had rained recently and there were hoof prints pressed into the mud on the path leading into the woods.

'Deer?' Nita asked.

'Let's hope so.' Geoffrey gave a brave laugh. They stood looking at the hoof prints. 'I don't suppose you left your book in your room, did you? My father is obsessed with it. I have the strangest feeling he'd destroy it if he could.'

'Geoffrey, I am surprised at you.' Nita pulled a small, square book from her bag. It was bound in goatskin with the hair still attached. 'The Astartic Arcanum, the original pocket edition borrowed from the Maude Gonne Occult and Rare Manuscript Library at Butler College.'

'Is that goat hair?'

'Why yes, do you like it?'

'It's macabre.'

'It gives the book an artistic touch.'

A deer bounded from the tree line, then stopped abruptly before them, stamping her hoof. Two more deer leaped out of the woods, spooking the first. Nita almost touched them as they sprang past. The whole clearing smelled musky, and the warm scent comforted Nita a little. Then she felt *The Astartic Arcanum* in her hand, eerily cold, and she shivered.

'I'm not asleep,' she said.

'Neither of us is,' Geoffrey answered. 'Unfortunately.'

Watching the deer disappear across the clearing, Nita wanted to run, too, but instead she moved toward the trees. 'Okay. Here we go. I'm doing this for all of humankind,' Nita said. 'And deer. I'm doing this for all of deer-kind. And bunny rabbits. And I suppose even for stupid old pigeons, because right now I admire their moxie and their visceral disrespect for captains of industry.'

'I'm doing this for dear old Geoffrey. He's a fine fellow. He could grow up to be a captain of industry, if he plays his cards right and the world doesn't end.' Geoffrey's smile was strained.

'The terrible thing is that the world will never end if we fail. It will just be blood and madness and goats screaming like babies forever and ever, Amen. Oh, Geoffrey, you don't know how the sound of babies crying gives me the heebie-jeebies.'

They followed the path into the woods. They walked in silence and after a while they saw a light ahead of them. Something was burning, but there was no smoke or heat. Geoffrey and Nita felt themselves pulled, half-consciously, towards the fire. They came to a clearing. Across from them stood a tree growing in the cleft of a massive rock, as in their dreams. Nita was surprised that she didn't shudder with horror at seeing an apparition from a nightmare. It seemed so naturally unnatural that she felt almost nothing, not even fear. The tree's branches and the trunk were already ash, but they still stood. Red cracks glowed in the gray limbs and bark. Even this close, only a few feet from the tree, they felt no heat or smoke from the fire. The rock itself was strangely phosphorescent in the darkness. The light comprised ever-shifting, never-imagined colors. It was much taller than either Nita or Geoffrey. At its base, the cleft was wide enough for a person to enter. Above the crevice, there was a twisted goat skull that appeared no longer truly animal. It was pierced through by a iron spike driven deeply into the stone. Bits of blackened flesh adhered to reddish bone.

'Poor little goat,' muttered Nita.

Chiseled beside the entrance were marks that Nita recognized from her researches at the Maude Gonne Library as the Sigil of the Gateway and the letters, 'O.T.A.' Geoffrey gestured towards the letters. 'My father's club, ' Ordo Templi Azathothonis.' You met most of them earlier.'

'I can see why you never joined.'

'Father pushed me to attend meetings. I thought it was some kind of hootenanny—wealthy fossils chanting and wearing robes.' Geoffrey stopped and looked up at the tree ignited from contact with the eerily glowing white stone. 'I never realized...'

'How could you?' The stood for a moment and the only sound was the eerie crackling of the burning tree.

'We're stalling,' Geoffrey finally said.

'Yes, we are. Stalling is the better part of valor.'

'Did you bring a revolver, Nita?'

'No, it seemed a gun would do as much good as sending a certain unspeakable horror a strongly worded letter.'

'I brought mine. Well, my father's pistol from the War.' Geoffrey pulled a revolver from his pocket. 'The way I figure it, unspeakable horrors might entertain some human callers.'

'And it makes you feel better.'

'And it makes me feel better.'

Nita was glad she had worn her leather gloves. She put her hand against the wall to keep her balance as they started to descend a flight of stairs cut into the earth. Even through her leather gloves, the wall felt gelid and unspeakably foul. The wall gave beneath her hand, more like bone than stone. She slipped a small flashlight from her bag to take a closer look and revealed runes covering every inch of the wall, ceiling and stairs. They looked familiar, but when she tried to decipher them, her vision swam and she became queasy.

Their descent could not have been more than a few minutes, but Nita felt as if they were somewhere beyond time. And she felt watched. She began to whistle, 'I've Got 'It,' But It Don't Do Me No Good.'

Geoffrey touched her shoulder, 'They'll hear us coming, Nita.'

'I'd rather that than think of him watching and listening to us in that ghastly pool.' Geoffrey started to sing with her but stopped as they approached a sickly light at the bottom at the stairs. As they walked into the light, they entered a columned chamber made of the same material as the stairs and walls. Nita was still pretending to herself that it was only bone-colored stone.

'Allow me.' Geoffrey slipped ahead between the columns with his revolver in hand. 'Oh,' he said.

Standing in concentric circles were the men from Brandt's reception. Their faces were terrified, eyes fixed on something beyond the terrestrial world. Looking in the the face of the closest man, Edward Dodge, Nita almost became fixated herself, seeing a glimpse of something incomprehensibly vile. She shook her head. Poor, terrible little man, she thought. The cultists appeared uninjured, but the floor was sticky with gore. As Nita moved further into the chamber, the gathered men took off their robes. Each in turn took a hooked steel knife and very precisely cut himself in strange patterns before passing the knife to the next man. The cultist would stand, so marked, for a moment, and then collapse. Blood began to flow down the gently sloping floor to channeled grooves and then into a pool in the center of the room. The last four men collapsed, naked and bloodless as Nita and Geoffrey watched. They died in utter silence.

The charnel smell was terrible, but it was the awful squelching as they stepped around the bodies that sickened Nita. The corpses gradually spiraled down to the pool—the same pool of blood from Nita's dreams. And beside the pool, amid his once friends, stood Josiah Brandt, in a robe with a yoke made from tanned human skin. A woman's face stretched across his chest .

'Good, you are here,' Brandt said. 'My disappointing spawn and his Scarlet Woman.'

'Father, what have you done? These men...' Geoffrey stopped, reeling before a terrible realization. 'My God, what are you wearing? You murdered her!' Geoffrey sagged against Nita.

Brandt reached down and took the hooked knife from the hand of his ritual's last victim. 'I had thought to teach you strength, ungrateful child, the strength to remake the world. But you are worthless, less than worthless. I give you everything and you cry about your mother. The woman gave me you and you suck me dry, a parasite. But I, your loving father give you one more thing—a marriage, a sacred marriage, to this beautiful woman. You'll make an honest woman of Miss Sloan. And, together, you will open the gate to eternity and hold it open, forever.' He smiled at them with bloody teeth and red eyes. ' Make your father proud, son.'

'Mr. Brandt, I must protest. I have a fiancé and I'll have you know he is quite old-fashioned. I don't think he'll overlook me marrying someone else,' interrupted Nita as she fumbled in her bag for *The Astartic Arcanum*.

Brandt ignored Nita as he stepped towards his son.

'Don't think I haven't seen how you look at her, Geoffrey. The marriage will be very short-lived and decidedly painful, but this is your chance to make something of your life. You will be the source of the transmutation of our base world into what it always should have been instead of merely wasted seed.'

Geoffrey had gotten his legs under him again. His fists were clenched with rage. Nita found the book and pulled it open to the page she had marked in the Gonne library that very morning. 'The ritual will certainly be of interest to the Department of Unspeakable Reproduction Studies back at ol' Butler U.' She began backing away from Brandt. It wouldn't do for him to interrupt her once she began her own incantation.

Nita's movement attracted Brandt's attention. 'Decay is a wonderful smith,, It makes such changes without respite until heaven and earth melt together. Do you see now, Miss

Sloan? You mocked me. Called this all phooey, but I am magnanimous even when you deserve nothing but death, your blood and skin never glorified. You will be free, Miss Sloan. No longer condemned to this gruesome, mortal body. You and my son will both fall into the Black Sun of Azathoth. He is the unifier of inner and outer so many philosophers have sought. Azathoth's fire will free me from this intolerable abyss. He has promised me the purity of his nuclear furnace. We will consume everything and wipe this sickly world from existence. I will know eternity and I alone will shape the new world! And you, though you do not deserve this honor, you will be the first to enter the world to come by means of my grace.'

Brandt plunged the dagger into the blood-filled cistern and then pointed it toward Nita and Geoff. 'Your blood is my blood, thankless child. Return it to me.'

Geoffrey raised his gun as Brandt raised his dagger and began chanting in a terrible language Nita did not know, but seemed familiar. Geoffrey froze, his body rigid, held by some unseen force. The gun fell from his hand and slid into the cistern. The pool roiled as sticky red ropes of blood formed and struggled toward Nita and Geoffrey. *The Astartic Arcanum* grew so cold it almost burned Nita's hand. But the pain kept her from succumbing to whatever trance had overtaken Brandt and Geoffrey, or so she thought. She gave a Geoffrey a hard punch in the arm, but he didn't respond. 'I guess we'll have to do this the educated way,' Nita said.

She began to read from a hymn that she had not allowed to be printed in the final publication, the summoning of the Great Goddess Erishkigal. 'Ninnanah, Ištartu, Erishkigal, Kilili, Asu-Shu-Namir, hear me! Hear me and close the Seven Gates! Deny the Great Old Ones passage! Destroy this abomination that would blight the earth and all the houses of the Gods!'

At the sound of Nita's voice, Geoffrey convulsed and fell to the floor.. The older man did not break his chant. The voice that came from his throat was not longer his and his words were no longer words. It sounded like thin flutes and scratchings in hidden places. It sounded like the buzzing of Jerusalem crickets and terrible nameless insects. As

Nita named the most powerful of the seven hundred names of Erishkigal, Geoffrey's convulsions ceased. He charged his father grabbing for the knife. Brandt slashed and Geoffrey's blood spilled on the floor. The pool's tentacles reached for Geoffrey's blood and lapped at it almost delicately. The men wrestled dangerously close to the edge.

The cold from the book ran through Nita now and she felt as if she were no longer alone in her own mind. As she continued the invocation, her voice began to change and she felt the dark Goddess within her.

'If you refuse my entry, I will smash the lock,
I will crack the door-posts. I will force the doors.
I will call the dead to eat your heart.
I bring you love, the love that embraces. The love that destroys.
I am the Lady of the Great Place, the Lady of Kilili and Attalu and you shall not deny me.
You shall not usurp me in my house.
As the Lady of Owls, my talons rake you in the night.
As the Lady of Lions, my teeth will tear your throat.
I hunt you now, usurper.
I send you Namtar.
I send you Death.'

Nita began the nameless chant that bound Brandt, words that none should pronounce or hear. And as she finished, she returned to herself just as Geoffrey tore the dagger from his father's grasp. Brandt's eyes were blank and his lips still moved, but a thin foam dribbled from his mouth. Buzzing noises came from within his throat. His limbs seemed wrong somehow, as if they were broken or as if he had extra joints. Brandt twisted to hurl Geoffrey into the bloody pool's depths. The pool overflowed eagerly towards the men and began to spread across the floor. It oozed between the cracks of the mortar. It reached the older man first. And at its touch he went pale. Brandt stumbled and lost his grip. Geoffrey reflexively caught hold of the old man's robe.

Nita shouted, 'Geoff, let go!' Geoffrey did. Brandt gibbered mindlessly as his body, occupied by some alien thing, struggled to save itself. Brandt had almost righted himself when Nita kicked him in his stomach, knocking him into the wildly thrashing entity congealing in the bone cistern. 'That's for calling Geoff ' worthless,' you old goat!' Brandt went gray as bloody tentacles attached to him, drawing his own blood into its mass. There was a terrible pressure in the room as Brandt's body dissolved into the creature. For a moment, Nita could see the hideous visage of Azathoth. And then the cavern echoed with maddening shrieks as what was left of Brandt collapsed bonelessly into the cistern. The pool slowly filled the room, still reaching for them and whispering to them foul things. 'All the blood in the world,' Nita thought. 'Pumped through a terrible heart.'

Nita felt the brush of wings and smelled a warm musky scent. Erishkigal had come to claim what was hers. As she watched the blood began to blacken and harden in the cistern and gradually along its cilia. Nita shouted, 'Run!', as she hurtled up the smooth bone stairs leading to the clearing above. Geoffrey ran, the flood close behind. Dark red cilia touched him briefly. Skin tore away from his foot and calf, but Geoff kept struggling after Nita, dragging his leg as he tried to escape. The blood lapped at the bottom step. The stairs cracked under Nita's feet. She grabbed Geoffrey's arm and pulled him forward, urging him to move faster. The foundation cracked and the masonry crumbled as she reached the entrance back into the world. Nita tugged at Geoffrey as he dragged his leg behind him and, again, urged him to hurry. 'If you ever want to rumba again, Geoff, we must get farther away from this rock.'

The earth around the entrance was an enormous wet wound, red with blood and rotten with dark mold. The trees at the edge of the clearing turned to gray ash and crumbled as they passed. The ground itself blackened and they felt a terrible heat coming off it. And then the tree on the cleft rock collapsed and they could feel whatever corruption pursued them retreat. Nita and Geoffrey collapsed on green grass, panting at the edge of the clearing. The rubber soles of Nita's boots were melted. They stared at the perfect circle of death surrounding the entrance to Brandt's underworld. Nita turned to the east, hoping for sunrise, but it was still dark.

'Geoffrey, once your foot is better, let's go dancing.'

'That sounds pretty good to me, ma'am.'

'Geoffrey, we've been through too much together for you to call me, ' Ma'am.' Call me, Nita.'

'Whatever you say, ma'am.'

K. A. Laity is the award-winning author of *How to Be Dull, White Rabbit, Dream Book, A Cut-Throat Business, Lush Situation, Owl Stretching, Unquiet Dreams, À la Mort Subite, The Claddagh Icon, Chastity Flame*, and *Pelzmantel*, as well as editor of *Respectable Horror, Weird Noir, Noir Carnival* and *Drag Noir*. She also writes historical fiction as Kit Marlowe and crime as Graham Wynd. Her bibliography is chock full of short stories, humour, plays and essays, both scholarly and popular. As a 2011-2012 Fulbright Fellow in Galway, Ireland she worked in digital humanities at NUIG. Dr. Laity teaches medieval literature, film, gender studies, digital humanities and popular culture at the College of Saint Rose, where she is also the director of the Digital Humanities Initiative. She divides her time between Hudson, New York and Dundee, Scotland.

Jack of several trades, master of none, **Ian Burdon** started writing fiction in his fifties. When not occupied by his day job, Ian spends his time at his desk in the shed, exploring the subconscious he has so far kept hidden from his unsuspecting family, often to the accompaniment of wildly unfashionable music. He lives in Edinburgh. You can find him at www.cosmicsurfer.co.uk or on Twitter @Cosmic_Serf

Anjana Basu is a lady of sensibility based in Calcutta, India who has penned 7 novels to date, umpteen poems and left her mark on various magazines, including Vogue India. She can be reached on twitter AnjanaBasu@AnjanaBasu

Maura McHugh lives in the Irish countryside, in a house watched over by rooks, and visited by hares. Her short fiction and essays have appeared in publications in America and

Europe, as well as two collections - *Twisted Fairy Tales* and *Twisted Myths* - published in the USA. She's written several comic book series, including co-writing *Witchfinder* for Dark Horse Comics. She's also a screenwriter, playwright, a critic, and has served on the juries of international literary, comic book, and film awards. Her web site is http://splinister.com and she tweets as @splinister.

HV Chao

See www.EdwardGauvin.com

Coddled within the coterie of Contessa Cadenza Crimpildi's College for Cultured Young Ladies in the temperate cheese forests of a forgotten Swiss canton, **C. A. Yates**, as she is currently known within certain hallowed circles, perversely cultivated a curiosity for all things respectably macabre during her early teenage years. Although frequently cited for insubordination and flagrant contempt, she eventually excelled in all her studies, most notably in Comportment, Gracious Conduct, and Finger Boxing (Heavyweight). By the end of her education, even the Contessa herself, had she not, some years previously, become ill-advisedly dead at the hand of her erstwhile Bavarian paramour, Colonel Dandy Von Nichols, would have been proud of how very respectable Ms Yates had become. Should you wish to follow her continued pursuit of excellence and, of course, respectability, you may visit her most courteous web presence at www.chloeyates.com or follow her, @shloobee, on the tawdry garden path that is Twitter.

Alan C. Moore is a writer, blogger, digital strategist, husband, and father from Virginia. He has been a writer for most of his adult life through academic, professional, and personal sources.

Catherine Lundoff is a Minneapolis-based award-winning writer and editor. Her stories and articles have appeared in such venues as *The Mammoth Book of the Adventures of Professor Moriarty*, *The Mammoth Book of Jack the Ripper Stories*, *The Cainite Conspiracies*, *Callisto*, *Tales of the Unanticipated*, *Nightmare Magazine: Queers Destroy Horror* and *SF Signal*. Her books include *Silver Moon* and *Out of This World: Queer Speculative Fiction*.

Website: www.catherinelundoff.com

Jonathan Oliver is the Editor-in-Chief at Rebellion Publishing, overseeing Solaris, Abaddon and Ravenstone books. He is the author of two novels and a forthcoming short story collection, *The Language of Beasts*. He twice won the British Fantasy Award for Best Anthology, for *Magic and End of the Road*. He lives in Abingdon, Oxfordshire with his wife, two daughters and their faithful cat.

Richard Farren Barber was born in Nottingham in July 1970. After studying in London he returned to the East Midlands. He lives with his wife and son and works as a Registry Manager for a local university.

He has written over 200 short stories and has had short stories published in *Alt-Dead*, *Alt-Zombie*, *ePocalypse – Tales from the End*, *Horror D'Oeuvres*, *Murky Depths*, *Midnight Echo*, *Midnight Street*, *Morpheus Tales*, *Night Terrors II*, *Siblings*, *The House of Horror*, *Spectral Press's 13 Ghosts of Christmas*, *Trembles*, *When Red Snow Melts*, and broadcast on *BBC Radio Derby*, *Pseudopod*, and *The Wicked Library*.

Richard's first novella, "The Power of Nothing" was published by Damnation Books and his second, "The Sleeping Dead" was published by DarkFuse. His next novella "Odette" is due out early in 2016.

His website can be found here www.richardfarrenbarber.co.uk

Su Haddrell is a British writer in a picturesque and peaceful area of Worcester that's been cleverly disguised as a noisy council estate. She has had stories published by Fox Spirit and Phrenic Press and enjoys editing and beta reading for other authors. In addition to writing, she also paints, sews and organises the UK's only *Judge Dredd* convention. She loves rum, her cat, her boyfriend and movies where things explode within the first 14 seconds.

Ivan Kershner

Growing up "poor and on horseback" as part of a cattle ranching family on the Lakota Sioux Pine Ridge Reservation in South Dakota, USA, provided Ivan with opportunities and perspectives rare in today's world. Uniquely, Ivan was a minority in a Native culture not far removed from its roots in the open Western plains. His family's hired man, Paul Bear Saves Life, had been a baby at the Massacre at Wounded Knee and Ivan's best friend was Chucky Looking Elk.

The roots of *Miss Metcalf*...as a Halloween story...likely began with Ivan's ranching family's remote and rural lifestyle. On Halloween, Ivan and his brother and sister would put on their costumes, exit the back door, go around to the front door, and knock. Their father would answer the door and hand out treats. The children would then reverse their trek, entering the back door, and surprise their parents with the treats they had received. ikershner@netscape.net

Octavia Cade is a New Zealand writer. Her short stories have appeared in Asimov's, Strange Horizons, and Apex Magazine, amongst others. She recently won a Sir Julius Vogel award for a ghost story about Ernest Rutherford splitting the atom, and her latest novella, "The Convergence of Fairy Tales" is a horror mash-up of fairy tale retellings. Her website is https://ojcade.com/, or you can find her @OJCade on Twitter.

Matthew Pegg is a writer based in Leicestershire.

Most of his early writing was for theatre and his plays include work for puppet companies, youth theatres, community casts and a script designed to be performed during a medieval banquet. His most recent theatre work was Escaping Alice, a love story with chains and handcuffs, for York Theatre Royal. Most recently he's written a community audio drama based on the life of Wordsworth and has been commissioned to create a puppet play which will tour to care homes for people suffering from dementia.

In 2012 he completed an MA in Creative Writing, and since then he has been working on a novel, and placing short fiction with a variety of publishers. His fiction is influenced by youthful encounters with M.R. James and Carnacki the Ghostfinder.

His website can be found at www.mpegg.co.uk

Suzanne J. Willis is a Melbourne, Australia-based writer, a graduate of Clarion South and an Aurealis Awards finalist. Her stories have appeared or are forthcoming in anthologies by PS Publishing, Prime Books, Fablecroft Publishing and Falstaff Books, and in Fantasy Scroll Magazine, SQ Mag, Mythic Delirium, and Lackington's. Suzanne's tales are inspired by fairytales, ghost stories and all things strange, and she can be found online at suzannejwillis.webs.com

D. C. White lives in Blackwood, South Australia with his possum Cheeky. D. C.'s work has been published in Australia, the UK and the US. He is currently wondering what to have for tea.

Rosalind Mosis is an arts graduate and classroom assistant by day, hunched gargoyle/slash writing creature by night. She is typically found at her desk, somewhere in deep dark Essex, drinking tea next to a storage heater because she spends about 80% of her time too cold and antisocial to function. Her main obsessions include Japanese horror, ghosts, urban legends, the paranormal and folklore. If it involves screaming relentless spirits with long black hair and twisted faces, she'll probably be interested. Outside of horror, her favourite writing genres are fantasy, sci-fi and comedy.

Her main horror/weird writing influences are Clive Barker, H.P Lovecraft, James Herbert, Neil Gaiman, Banana Yoshimoto and Haruki Murakami. Her writing hero is Terry Pratchett. She also mainlines horror survival games like Ikenie no Yoru, Calling, White Day, Yomawari as well as the Silent Hill and Fatal Frame games.

And a lot of graphic novels.

Somehow Rosalind managed to acquire a husband and daughter, who worry about what awful deeds she commits after dark and quietly appease her with biscuits.

Her first novel is THE RITES OF LEMURIA, available on Inkitt.

Under some strange, irresistible compulsion **Carol Borden** was drawn to the manor library. She found the forbidden tome already opened, as if some has had left it for her ready to read. And she did read the book, though she knew she should not. Some had gone mad merely from glimpsing the subtitle. No, Carol Borden counted herself lucky to retain her sanity after what she learned. Decades later she still fell into trances of automatic writing, in which she produced dozens of short stories, including one published in this very book.

91552242R00150

Made in the USA
Columbia, SC
19 March 2018